Kailie's Song

K. J. Olson

PublishAmerica
Baltimore

ISBN: 1-4241-0377-0
PUBLISHED BY PUBLISHAMERICA, LLLP
www.publishamerica.com
Baltimore

Printed in the United States of America

For my grandchildren, my golden ones

Also by K. J. Olson
The Path Between

HÆNOLIR

Sinnich Isle

Lorn Isle

Strait of Tears

Cliffs of Sorrows

Landsend

Dark Land

Thanion Woods

Shiptown

Bethron Isle

The Diarmids

Ferry Landing

Kilton Hills

3 Rivers

High Ghilana Plain

Skara River

Guardians' Fort

Fort Gate

Wall of Rhade

River Gate

Gampeon Marsh

Trayonian Sea

North Fork

Skara River

Riversend

Balagorn Sea

South Fork

Horn of Valare

Valare Bay

Lake Country

Lowlands

Fairtown

Uranor Hills

The Legend

When mists of time shrouded the halls of Ancient Ones and the realm of Faerie, two sons were born to the king of Kaenolir, a rich and peaceful kingdom set between two seas. The elder son, Alpean the Steward, grew fair and strong, and he cared deeply for the land of his birth and its people. As Alpean grew older, his father prepared him for the day when he would rule.

The second son grew equally strong but was dark in coloring and in nature. This son, Maelorn, hungered for power and was jealous of his brother. He vowed that the crown of Kaenolir would one day be his, that he, not Alpean, would be king.

So it happened that the old king died, and Alpean the Steward came to claim the crown, as was his right. The people of Kaenolir gathered to see their prince crowned, and they celebrated with music and dancing.

"The king is dead. Long live the king!"

When the glistening crown was placed upon Alpean's head, a great cheer rose. His heart swelled with love and pride as he listened to the outpouring of joy. He raised his arms for quiet and tried to greet his subjects, but the cheering continued. Then Maelorn stepped forward, and sullen clouds began to block the sun as the Darkling Prince came to stand before Alpean. People fell silent, shouts and cheers dying in their throats. Maelorn demanded the crown, claiming he had as much right as Alpean to be king. Alpean smiled indulgently and asked Maelorn to pledge his allegiance and friendship to king and country. He drew Maelorn into his arms in a brotherly embrace, but instead of returning the gesture of affection, Maelorn struck the king a slashing blow on the cheek. As blood welled in the wound, Maelorn swore that the crown of Kaenolir would soon be his. Alpean touched his fingers to his cheek, then smeared the blood of their common ancestors across

9

Maelorn's forehead. There would be a fight for Kaenolir's crown, and it would be a fight to the death.

"So be it," Alpean whispered, his heart heavy. "So be it."

~

Maelorn withdrew to The Dlarmids, brooding mountains in northern Kaenolir, and began to gather an army. It was whispered that he made a pact with the Dark One, for not all the soldiers he commanded were human. Large, ugly creatures, called Spriggans, came when Maelorn called, and mercilessly dispatched their prey with slashing claws and dagger sharp teeth. Ghillies, larger of stature and equally hideous, slaughtered men and animals in an insatiable thirst for blood. Spriggans and Ghillies, shadowy creatures that skulked in the darkness, killed at every opportunity.

Alpean gathered his army of stalwart, loyal Kaenolirians—farmers from the southern lowlands, fishermen from the eastern and western coasts, merchants, shipbuilders, rivermen. Half-savage highlanders, who from the beginning of Kaenolir's history had been warriors, came to follow Alpean's banner. Golden Ones, handsome men and women endowed by the Faerie with magical songs and sent to the people of Kaenolir in appreciation for a kindness given long past, came, too. And great silver wolves, fantastic beasts of the Faerie world, answered Alpean's call.

~

In the halls of the Ancient Ones, gods watched the brothers prepare their armies for battle and began to wager on the outcome. It amused them to see the fair Alpean, the good and rightful king, pit himself and his people against the forces of the dark Maelorn and his creature army. For sport, those who favored Alpean began to aid him, while those who favored Maelorn helped him. And so it came about that while the gods laughed and toyed with mortal lives, many men died in the War of the Brothers.

Battles raged over the fair land of Kaenolir, but neither brother was able to subdue the other until, finally, the gods grew tired of their game. Those who were partial to Alpean imprisoned Maelorn in a stone tomb in a mountain of fire on Sinnich Isle off the northern coast of Kaenolir. Without his leadership, his forces retreated in confusion, pursued by highland warriors. When the beasts reached the Dark Land beyond The Dlarmids, they were able to hold Alpean's forces at bay for a short time. Just when it appeared the beastly army would be overrun and destroyed, the gods meddled one last time. Alpean was taken and imprisoned in the fiery mountain, there to lie helpless and powerless beside his brother.

Although they were without a king, the highlanders hounded the remnants of Maelorn's army deeper into the Dark Land until at last the inhuman forces scattered, disappearing into the fog that came rolling off the Strait of Tears. The valiant warriors marched back across the mountains, and when they reached their homeland on the High Ghilana Plain, they vowed to keep Kaenolir safe from the forces of the Darkling Prince for all time. The rest of Alpean's army disbanded, and men went home to their farms, their shops, their fishing, their ships. The great silver wolves slipped away to roam the shadowy realm of the Faerie once more. The Golden Ones took their places among the people to protect and aid them. From Lorn Isle, Golden Ones called Warrior Singers guarded the mountain prison with a magical song that promised to keep Maelorn in his fiery tomb and, one day, to set Alpean free.

True to their vow to watch and guard, the highlanders built a wall at the edge of the high plain between the mountains and the Skara River, seventy miles long, twenty feet high, and eight feet thick, that stretched the width of Kaenolir. Guard towers were set at every mile. If the Dark forces ever came across the mountains again, they would find their way blocked by a formidable wall of stone and rubble and guarded by fierce warriors.

Peace settled upon the land. People were content, knowing that the Golden Ones and the Guardians, as the highland warriors came to be called, would keep them safe. They had no king to guide them, but wise mages, once advisers to Kaenolirian rulers, gave counsel and arbitrated disputes.

And so it was for centuries, until the dark brother began to stir in his tomb of stone.

11

Chapter One

Andrew Goldenhorn awakened, drenched with sweat and gasping for breath. He had been chained to living stone in a small, dark chamber where flames spouted from vents within the rock and roiling, pungent gases made it painful to breathe. When he tried to move, shackles at wrists and ankles held him upright. Exhausted but unable to rest, he sagged against his bonds; his head pounded with pain, his eyes burned with fatigue. Occasionally he forced himself to stand upright, tried to sing his Song, but no sound came from his raw throat. A cruel leather strap circled his neck, giving him only enough freedom to take in shallow breaths of the searing air.

Stone. . .fire. . .chained. . .a prisoner. . .unable to sing. . .agony. . .

"Sing for me, Goldenhorn. Sing for me."

An apparition came to stand before him, dark, hulking, obscene, a monster incarnate. When Goldenhorn struggled against his chains, the creature threw back his head and laughed. And the savage, triumphant laughter echoed and reechoed as Goldenhorn fought to leave the nightmare behind.

~

"What is it, Andrew?"

"Nothing, Katrine. I just need some air. Go back to sleep, love."

He rose from the bed and pulled on his trousers and boots. "I'll be back in a few minutes." He leaned down to kiss his sleepy wife and quietly left their bedchamber, taking his tunic from the hook by the door on his way out.

The night air was cool, almost cold against his heated skin, and he pulled the tunic over his head, absently rubbing his hands against his arms for warmth. It was nearly spring, but while the days grew warmer, the nights still held their winter chill.

He began to walk, and of their own volition, his feet carried him along the path that led up out of the valley to the steep granite ridge that fell away to the sea. The path was worn deep into the rocky soil by the feet of his kind over countless years, companions all gone now, leaving only him, Andrew Goldenhorn.

The last Warrior Singer, gifted by his Faerie ancestors with powers beyond those of mortal men, he was tall and strongly built, able to wield sword and lance with deadly skill. By look and manner he was marked as Faerie. Golden hair fell to his wide shoulders in a rich cascade; his large eyes glowed amber. An aura of power cloaked his elegant, graceful form.

Soon after the Brothers' War, the Warrior Singers were sent to live on the small island of Lorn, situated in the wild waters of the Strait of Tears between Sinnich Isle and the mainland of Kaenolir. Each morning they lifted their voices, sending their magical Song across the waters to Mt. Sinnarock where two brothers, Alpean the Steward and Maelorn the Darkling, lay imprisoned by a whim of the gods. Not only was the Song sung to keep the Darkling, a prince who aligned himself with the powers of darkness, forever in his tomb of stone, but it was also to promise Alpean that one day he would be set free.

Time passed. Years stretched into centuries, and the number of Warrior Singers slowly dwindled. Some died and others quietly sailed away from Lorn Isle never to be seen again. Perhaps the Faerie magic that touched them, the Faerie blood that flowed in their veins, called them back to the mythical land from which they came. Perhaps their powers were no longer needed by the people they had been sent to protect. Whatever the reason, only the Goldenhorn remained to sing the magical Song and send its message across the Strait of Tears to Sinnich Isle.

The path brought Goldenhorn to the promontory, a prodigious mound of gray-black granite that thrust its glistening mass into the crashing waves. From its lofty height he sang his Warrior Song each morning, just as the sun lifted above the water. A Song of infinite beauty, it was at once command and promise, charge and summons, mystical, powerful, enthralling.

Goldenhorn climbed to the top of the promontory and stood silently staring out across the dark, restless sea toward Sinnich Isle, shrouded day and night by fog and smoke. In the darkness he could define the mass of Mt. Sinnarock, which lifted up from the center of the island, by the lightning that flickered almost continuously through the surrounding clouds.

The Singer knew what lay in Mt. Sinnarock; he had been taught long ago the reason for his Song. His days on the Horn of Kalora, spent learning the intricacies of his Warrior Song and training his magnificent voice to sing it, were days in the dim past. He thought back to his time with Rhianna Lanee, the mage who trained all the Singers. She was a relentless taskmaster, content only with perfection. He spent hours with her, singing the Warrior Song over and over.

"Once more, Goldenhorn." The liquid tones of her voice came to him as clearly as they had all those years before. "Let the power you possess flow with the music. You are a warrior; sing your Song like a warrior. The one who hears you must never doubt your strength."

Goldenhorn sighed deeply as the memories of Rhianna drifted away. He seldom thought of her or his fellow Singers, but tonight he missed them all, missed their companionship, their knowledge, their strength. He needed someone with whom to share his nightmares, someone to tell him what they meant. Deep within his heart, he feared that the dreams were a portent of what was to come.

He shivered with cold and thought of his warm bed and his Katrine. He could still see her as he had that first time. With dark, auburn hair coiled becomingly on top of her head, melting brown eyes, a slender form that seemed to invite his caress, a mouth that asked for his kiss, she had touched him with desire as no mortal woman had ever done. Love had come swiftly on the wings of his desire, and love had touched Katrine, too, with her first look into the amber eyes of Andrew Goldenhorn.

The eldest daughter of a rich lowland merchant, Katrine and her brothers and sisters had been born and raised in Fairtown, a seaport on the southwestern coast of Kaenolir. Their town sat close to the low Hranor Hills that marked the border between Kaenolir and Timis, a small, mountainous country to the south, and was a hub for the exchange of goods that flowed between the two countries.

Her father's warehouse was a busy, bustling place, a rather exciting place to the young Katrine's eyes; and she was firm in her resolve to be a part of the activity, not stuck at home with her mother and younger sisters. She appeared on the doorstep of her father's store early one morning and announced she was ready to work, and not at sweeping floors or dusting shelves. She had a mind, bright and well schooled, and wanted to use it. A bit harassed and much too busy to argue with his determined daughter, her father put her to work arranging new merchandise. When that task was finished, to his grudging satisfaction, he found another for her and then another, and so it went for many months until he wondered how he had ever got on in his business without her.

Katrine's life could well have continued in the same pattern. Eventually she might have married the son of an acceptable, well-placed merchant family, if she had listened to her mother's harping. However, all of the "might have's" became moot on the day Andrew Goldenhorn came into her father's store in search of a specific kind of rope sold only in Fairtown.

Many customers passed through the doors of the Seton Mercantile Exchange every day. Katrine rarely acknowledged them except on those occasions when her father asked her to assist a client of some importance. She was far too busy with the accounting books and order sheets to deal with the daily flow of customers. But on that warm summer's day when the tall, golden man looked into her eyes, nothing seemed of any consequence except that he look upon her and find her to his liking.

Goldenhorn's lips twitched in a fleeting smile as he recalled how he had told her of his life, tried to make her understand that he was somehow different, that his life was unlike hers in every way. Lorn Isle where he lived was far away. It was lonely there. She was hardly more than a girl. If he were to ask her to come with him, did she realize how much she might miss her old life, her family, her friends? Katrine had smiled at him and said she would be content, because they would be together.

And so they had come to live in the isolation that was Lorn Isle. She was companion, lover and friend, as he was hers, and she was content. There had been three Warrior Singers then, which made it possible for Katrine and Andrew to leave the island for an occasional visit to her family on the mainland. He knew she grew lonely sometimes, but she never complained. Their love grew deeper with the passage of time, and when their daughter, Kailie, was born, the threads of their lives were woven even more tightly together.

At last Goldenhorn could bear the cold no longer and turned to climb down from the headland. It would be dawn in a few hours, and he would need to sing his Song. He made his way off the promontory and followed the path back to the cottage.

~

Dawn came softly, spreading its shimmering light across the seething waters of the Strait, and touched the Goldenhorn where he stood once more on the granite cliff. He lifted his head and the Warrior Song poured out. The lightning that always flickered intermittently over Mt. Sinnarock suddenly flared, and jagged spears of light pierced the gloom surrounding the volcano. As the music built to a powerful crescendo, dawn brightened to day, and the lightning quieted to sporadic pulses.

The notes of the Song drifted away on the morning breeze, but for just a moment the Singer thought he heard an answering tone that hung briefly on the air. He shook his head in puzzlement.

"It must be the wind," he murmured to himself, "just an echo." He looked toward Sinnich one last time, then turned away. As he followed the path down into the valley, the cottage came into sight. The comfort of weathered stone reached out to him as it always did, and he quickened his step, knowing that Katrine and Kailie waited for him.

Katrine looked up from preparing the morning meal as he entered the door. "Your breakfast is ready," she said, noting with concern the shadows in his eyes. "Kailie isn't back from her ride yet, but she should be soon. Eat while it's hot."

Even as she spoke, the sound of laughter, high and bright, floated to them on the spring-laced air, and Kailie entered the house with a rush and an apology. She was just at that awkward stage, not quite woman but more than child.

"Sorry I'm late." Her blue eyes sparkled with humor and energy. She took the mug of tea her mother handed her. "The eagles are back," she smiled at her mother, knowing that such an event was excuse enough for her tardiness. "May I go see them after breakfast?"

"Finish your chores first," her mother replied. "And do something about the tangle of your hair. Goodness, Kailie, how do you manage to get it in such a mess?"

Kailie grimaced and sat down across the table from her father while her mother served the morning meal of hot oatcakes and applesauce. Her father looked at her and winked before giving his attention to his breakfast.

She was such a lovely little thing, he thought, all arms and legs and hair. He wondered, not for the first time, what would become of her. Soon they would have to send her back to the mainland. It was not fair to keep her isolated here, away from people, away from her family, away from life. He and Katrine must discuss it soon, he decided, but thinking of letting her go

17

brought a lump to his throat. He rose, taking his empty plate and cup to the counter under the window.

"Did the eagles return to the old nest site? The last winter storm nearly toppled it from its perch." Goldenhorn turned to his daughter.

"Yes, they did. I don't know if they'll stay, but they were at the aerie when I saw them. After breakfast, I want to climb up to the nest." At her mother's little sniff, she hastened to add, "After I've finished my chores, of course."

"Of course," her father laughed and ruffled her hair as he passed her chair, tangling the golden mass of curls even more. "I'm going to work in the garden," he called on the way out the door.

Kailie watched him go and chewed her bottom lip for a moment before turning to her mother.

"Is something bothering father?" she asked.

Katrine poured a cup of tea and took a seat next to her daughter. "Why do you ask?" She lifted her teacup with both hands, her elbows resting on either side of her plate. Taking a quick sip, she set the cup back on the table and sighed.

"Mother?"

"He hasn't been sleeping very well lately. Last night he woke in the middle of the night and went for a walk. He's been having nightmares, but he won't tell me what they're about." Katrine, a slight frown furrowing her brow, rose, her tea forgotten, and began gathering the remains of breakfast. Kailie jumped up to help put the kitchen in order.

"I'm sure it's nothing to worry about," Katrine smiled at her daughter. "He's just restless, that's all. The winter storms have kept him cooped up for too long; he's anxious for spring."

Kailie nodded and wiped the dishes her mother washed. When the kitchen tasks were done, she excused herself to tend to her bedchamber and to the tangles of her hair.

~

Kailie climbed steadily, her hands and feet sure on the stone, to the top of an outcropping of jumbled rock. A storm-blasted tree that served as the eagles' nesting place rose starkly against the sky. From the flattened top of the crag she could look back down the valley to their cottage. Almost directly below, the sea crashed against the rocky promontory from which her father sang each morning. To the north lay fog-covered Sinnich Isle. She gave it only a cursory glance, for her interest this morning lay in what the eagles were doing.

The male eagle came gliding in with a branch, and Kailie watched as it was placed just so in the rapidly expanding nest. The majestic pair would soon finish their repairs and set about the business of housekeeping. Kailie liked the time best when the eggs were laid and the pair shared the task of keeping them warm. It was then that she was allowed to come close to them. After the eggs hatched the eagles were much too busy feeding their young to pay her any attention. Kailie was content then merely to observe the comings and goings of the adults and watch the progress of the chicks, for the eagles did not drive her away as they would have any other intruder who came so close to their young. They sensed a kindred spirit, one who would do them no harm.

Once more the eagles lifted into the sky on powerful wings. Kailie squinted against the glare of the sun and followed their flight until she could no longer see them. She hunkered down to await their return, resting her back comfortably against sun-warmed stone. She stretched her long legs out before her, and lifting her face to the gentle breeze, she began to sing a slow, haunting melody. It was a quiet, lazy morning, full of the promise of spring, and she soon grew sleepy. The eagles took turns bringing sticks to weave into the fabric of the nest, murmuring to each other as they worked. Small songbirds flitted through the air, calling to potential mates and flashing their mating plumage. The sun rose higher and Kailie ceased her singing. With a deep sigh, she closed her eyes, rested her head against the stone, and dozed.

The breeze stilled. Something prickled the hairs on Kailie's arms, and she opened her eyes. It seemed the day held its breath. Birds ceased their chirping, and with a whir of startled wings they all took flight. The eagles lifted off from their nest and climbed rapidly into the nearly colorless sky. Puzzled by the sudden silence, Kailie sat quietly, waiting. The air about her grew stifling and she shifted uneasily, breathing deeply to take in the heated air.

Just as it became even more difficult for Kailie to breathe, as if all the air had been sucked away, a sudden muffled explosion tore through the silence, and a huge pillar of flame set fire to the clouds surrounding Sinnich Isle. Kailie jumped to her feet with a jerk, her heart pounding loudly in her ears, her breath coming in quick, hard gasps. While the gray clouds concealing the island turned black before Kailie's frightened eyes, an unearthly shriek that made the hair on the back of her neck stand on end came rolling across the water, accompanied by another explosion and tongues of fierce red flame.

The air about her, warm and bright but moments before, grew chill and suffocating; the sky darkened and black clouds scudded across the sun. Trembling, with unsteady steps, she moved to the edge of the rocky crag. Her blood pounded as her heart beat fast and hard against her ribs, but an intense sense of urgency mixed with her fear.

Sing! Sing the Warriors' Song. Now!

She lifted her head, and the rich, vibrant music of her father's Warrior Song poured from her throat, gaining strength and power as she sang.

~

Time stood still.

And then it came rushing at him, chattering and shrieking, filling him with dread. The force of the volcanic eruption shook him to the core of his being. Andrew Goldenhorn dropped the spade he was using to till the garden and raced up the path toward the promontory.

"No, oh no," he cried.

"What is it?" Katrine called as she hurried out of the cottage toward him. "Where's Kailie?"

"Mt. Sinnarock is erupting," he shouted as he dashed past her.

"Kailie, where's Kailie?" Her frantic cries followed him, but there was no time to answer her. Fear thudded through Goldenhorn as he ran up out of the valley, and the fear was not only for Kailie. When he rounded a bend and could see the neighboring isle, his breath caught in his throat. Billowing clouds of black smoke and ash interlaced with shooting flames writhed about the island like something alive. Already the water that separated the islands heaved in violent agitation. He dared not go out on the promontory, for the crashing waves would sweep him away. Moving as close as he could to the edge of the rocky shore, he lifted his head to send the Warrior Song out over the plunging sea. As he did so, he heard the clear, powerful notes of his Song sung by a female voice, every nuance, every note in perfect pitch and sequence.

"Who...?" He turned toward the sound and looked up to see his daughter standing atop the eagles' crag.

"Kailie," he breathed. He stood in stunned silence, listening to her. She was blood of his blood, and the magic of the Faerie coursed through her veins and touched her soul. But there was danger for her in the magic. He knew and understood that danger, but she did not. The Song she sang marked her as a Golden One, even a Warrior Singer, and the Warrior Singers had been anathema to the Darkling Prince for five centuries.

"No," he groaned. "No, Kailie."

For a moment he hung his head, his hands clenched in tight fists at his side. With a deep, quaking breath he calmed himself and turned back toward Sinnich. He listened for a moment longer to Kailie's singing, then lifted his own voice to join hers. Their combined voices sent a potent command out over the water. A furious howl of frustrated rage mingled for a time with the music. But as the force of the Song grew, the howls diminished, and the fire and smoke of the eruption subsided. The sea settled and calmed; the clouds parted, and the sun shone as brightly as it had earlier.

Goldenhorn and Kailie sang the Song one more time. As the last note still vibrated on the air, he turned away from the water's edge and climbed to the top of the eagles' crag. He found Kailie slumped in weariness against the rocks. Drawing her trembling form into his arms, he held her, rocking her gently.

"Hush, little one, hush," he crooned. "It's all right. Hush, sweeting, you're safe now." He wondered how true his words were as he looked out across the water, and clasped his daughter's slender form more closely.

"Father," Kailie whispered. "What happened? What was that terrible howling?" She pushed herself away so she might look into his face. "What is on that island? How did our singing stop the eruption? Our singing did stop the eruption, didn't it?"

Goldenhorn sighed and set his daughter away from him. Her face was streaked with tears, and curls escaped the golden braid.

"It's an ancient story, Kailie, one I hoped never to have to tell you. But for now, let it suffice that the Song I sing each morning is touched with a power that is older than time. It is sung to keep an evil force that means only harm to Kaenolir and her people imprisoned on Sinnich Isle." He wiped away the last of her tears with his fingertips and sighed. "Now I have a question for you. How did you know to sing when you did?" His amber eyes looked intently into her blue ones. "And how did you know what to sing?"

""I don't know how I knew. I just knew. Something deep inside told me to sing the Warrior Song." Her brow furrowed in thought as she tried to recall those first few moments after hearing the explosion of Mt. Sinnarock. "It was almost as if someone actually said *Sing the Warrior Song.*" She shook her head in disbelief at her own words. "And I've known your Song since I was little. I've heard you sing it every day of my life." Uncomfortable under his scrutiny, she shrugged her shoulders and looked away.

Another thought brought her troubled eyes back to his. "Was it wrong? Shouldn't I have sung the Song? I'm sorry, Father, I…"

He laid a finger against her lips to stop the rush of words. "No, Kailie, it wasn't wrong." He sighed deeply. "I had hoped to spare you the need for singing it, that's all." Goldenhorn smiled and rubbed his thumb across her cheek.

"Father, I don't understand. I don't understand at all."

He rose and pulled her to her feet. "I know you don't. Later I'll tell you what's on Sinnich and why I sing, but for now, come, we must find your mother. She'll be terribly worried." He took her slender hand in his, and together they walked across the top of the crag and climbed down.

~

That night, when at last Kailie slept, Goldenhorn and Katrine sat before the fireplace and watched the crackling flames. The old house creaked as the night wind whispered under the eaves. Goldenhorn stared morosely into the fire, gently rubbing his finger up and down on the handle of the mug of tea he held while thinking of the disturbing events of the day.

"Andrew," Katrine spoke into the silence. She reached out to touch his hand and gain his full attention. "What happened today?" Her worried expression and softly voiced question demanded an answer of him in a way no loud threat could have.

He set the cup aside, laced his fingers with hers and looked at their entwined hands. Before speaking, he carried her fingers to his mouth and kissed them, one by one. At last he looked into her eyes.

"I'm not sure. Perhaps nothing. Perhaps the start of something…." Her fingers tightened on his and he caressed them with his thumb. "Do you remember the legend of the two brothers?" At her answering nod, he continued. "Do you also remember that I told you the Faerie had touched the Golden Ones and given the Warrior Singers magical powers embodied in our Song?"

"Of course, Andrew, I remember all that you told me. You wanted to be sure I knew what I was getting into before I married you." She smiled at him, but when the full import of the questions he asked became clear, the smile faded, and she drew her hand from his and rose to stand before the fireplace, staring into the flames. "Do you think that the eruption today has something to do with the two brothers?" She turned to face him. "Andrew, they lived centuries ago! Surely they have long since turned to stone within the mountain."

"Perhaps. But the mountain has never erupted so violently, at least, never in my lifetime. The terrible howling that Kailie and I heard today...." He turned away from the fear beginning to grow in Katrine's eyes and rose to stand beside her, his hand resting on the mantle. "I've never heard it before," he said quietly.

"Couldn't it have been a trick of the wind across the water?" she asked. "Andrew, that's it. It must have been the wind." She gripped his arm tightly while her eyes begged him to say yes.

He reached out to gather her close. "I can only guess what it was, my love. But I do know this: I want you and Kailie to leave Lorn Isle as soon as you can be ready."

Katrine drew away from his protecting arms, shaking her head. "I'll not leave you, not ever. We can send Kailie to my family if there are any more disturbances from Sinnich, but I will not leave you. I know you're not telling me everything because you want to protect us." Her voice trembled on the last words, but she remained firm in her resolve. "I will not leave you." She accented each word with a light thump of her fist against his chest.

"All right, love, all right." He drew her back into his arms. "We'll speak no more of it tonight." He held her tightly for a long time until she quieted. When she sighed, he set her away. "Come, it's been a long day. Let's go to bed." He stooped to tend the fire while she gathered the tea mugs. When her steps sounded in the hall leading to their sleeping chamber, he moved to join her. The uneasiness he had felt for weeks had not abated. He sensed something was happening, something he could not explain, but real enough nevertheless. His Faerie blood quickened. Something stirred on Sinnich Isle, something powerful and monstrous and dangerous.

Chapter Two

Alexander Lamond read the report again. If it hadn't come from a competent sergeant of the Guardians and one of the few men he called friend, he would have dismissed it as the ravings of a lunatic. An additional report written by the frightened mayor of Shiptown gave weight to facts that made his stomach lurch.

A fishing vessel had come ashore near the docks of the once-bustling shipbuilding company that gave Shiptown its name. One of the crew employed to patrol the buildings and docks had gone down to check out the derelict vessel. What he found onboard was something too horrifying to be believed.

Alexander rose to his feet and walked to the open doorway of the small room that served as the office for the Captain of the Guardians. A tall man with the powerful shoulders of a swordsman, he moved with an easy, silent tread. He was dressed in a dark blue uniform, the gold crossed swords pinned to the collar of his tunic the only insignia of his rank as commander of the Guardians. Blond hair cropped close to his head curled slightly near his ears and down his neck. Dark green eyes viewed his world with growing concern, and lines of worry etched the corners of his wide mouth and creased his brow. He brushed away the sweat beading on his forehead.

"Simon," he called. "When did this report from Shiptown come in?"

A young man wearing a blue uniform similar to that of his captain came to the door of Alexander's office. "Just this morning. Early, shortly after dawn."

"Where is the Guardian who brought it?"

"In the barracks. He was pretty tired. He'd ridden his horse nearly to death, the poor beast," Simon replied, shaking his head over the animal's condition.

Simon Stewart was a highlander, as were all the Guardians. Their fierce love for and pride in the swift horses they rode was second only to the deep love they held for their country. To have ridden a horse so hard indicated the importance of the papers the Guardian carried.

"Find him and bring him to me. I need more information from him if I'm to make sense of this report." Alexander turned away to reenter his office. Simon's voice stopped him.

"What's in that report anyway? He looked scared half out of his wits."

Alexander paused a long moment. "I'm not sure. That's why I want to talk to him." He turned away again. "Now, Simon." There was an edge of command to his deep voice, and Simon left the room to find the courier.

Captain Lamond walked across the room to the open window. He leaned against the frame, arms crossed over his chest, and gazed out upon the Guardians' permanent fortification. His ancestors built the fort to protect the massive gates that allowed a flow of traffic through the Wall of Rhade. Three long buildings constructed of stone and heavy timbers and covered with slate roofs and two small buildings with thatched roofs comprised the fort. A low wall of stone surrounded the buildings on three sides. A heavy wooden gate in the middle of the outer wall stood open, as did the ancient, deteriorating gate set in the high wall at the Fort's back. The gates in the Wall of Rhade had not been closed in nearly five centuries, and Alexander doubted that rusted mechanisms and decaying timbers still functioned. The fact gnawed at him. He knew that whatever was afoot in Kaenolir posed a grave and growing danger to his people.

His eyes swept over the Fort, seeking out the strengths and weaknesses of the old structures. Two small buildings, one on the east side of the outer gate and the other on the opposite wall near the Wall gates, were used to store non-perishable foodstuffs and equipment. Two of the long buildings, set along the west Fort wall, housed the Guardians. Across the dusty square from the barracks, another long building with wide stout doors sheltered the sturdy but fleet horses bred on the High Ghilana Plain. The great wall of stone mixed with rubble that formed the fourth wall of the Fort rose up as a stark reminder of its ancient purpose, but not many of the soldiers remembered or cared why the wall marched seventy miles across the width of Kaenolir. Hands and backs of men long dead had built it twenty feet high and eight feet thick to

25

keep out an enemy thought long dead as well. Guard towers had been placed at every mile marker, and once Guardians had watched over Kaenolir from every one. Time had dimmed the purpose of the decaying, crumbling wall, and now only the dusty little fort that sat with its back to the Wall of Rhade held Guardians.

Alexander chewed on his bottom lip as he finished his survey. Gates that would not close, a low wall that offered little resistance to an opposing force, Guardians who had never seen a battle. He swore softly.

There was another worry, too, that gave him little confidence in his ability to protect the people of Kaenolir. The Skara River passed through the adjoining section of the Wall on its way to the sea. Once the mighty river had rushed headlong between massive pillars placed in the Wall as supports for iron gates that closed to block traffic on the river. The volume of water in the river had been drastically reduced by drought, but it still touched each of the pillars as it flowed sluggishly under the Wall. The iron gates had been constructed in such a way that they slid into the interior of the Wall when opened. But because no enemy had threatened since the end of the Brothers' War, the gates had never been closed. Not in five hundred years. Rust and corrosion effectively locked them in the open position.

Alexander absently swatted at a persistent fly as he watched the sun create shimmering heat waves. He almost wished for some winter winds to replace the inexorable heat; it was hotter this summer than any he could remember. His muttered curse encompassed heat, the thick dust, and irritating flies.

As far back as history recorded, the seasons had come and gone with gentle regularity in the land of Kaenolir. The spring sun shone to warm the earth and begin anew the cycle of birth and growth. Rains triggered blossoming meadows in the northern highlands and rolling pastures of the southern lowlands. Cries of the newborn heralded a time of renewed vigor for man and beast after the confinement of winter.

Vibrant days of spring blended into hot, drowsy days of summer. Fields burgeoned with growing crops. Animals grew contentedly fat on rich grasses of pastures drenched by rains that rolled across the verdant countryside with accompanying crashes of thunder and flashes of lightning. Fishermen went far out to sea to find vast schools of fish; loggers sweated in the still, hot air of the forest while miners labored in the iron mines in The Dlarmids.

Fall heralded a time of hectic activity when men and animals worked long, hard hours to complete the harvest in the fertile fields of Kaenolir, in its rivers and forests, and in the seas that surrounded it. The fiery hues of autumn were everywhere as trees and bushes dressed for one final burst of glory before fading to the dullness of winter.

In the north, snow covered the starkness of the mountains in a mantle of living white. The Thanian Woods to the west shivered in cold winds blowing in from the sea. Along both the eastern and western seashores ice covered boats, and nets slept under leaden skies while fishermen sought snug cottages to keep them safe and warm from winter gales. The High Ghilana Plain was swept by winds laden with snow. Highland ponies, sturdy sheep, and hardy people settled in to await the spring that was sure to come. In the south, beyond the Skara River, each day of winter brought gray skies and dreary rains.

So the cycle of spring blending to summer mellowing to fall settling to winter had continued unchanged for generations of Kaenolirians. Time had always passed in this moderate pattern. The lives people lived, methods of commerce and industry, all were dictated by changing seasons. To change the seasons disrupted the pattern, disrupted the way of life in Kaenolir.

And the seasons were changing. Gradually, slowly, during the past seven cycles the pattern had somehow been disturbed. Winter storms howled down from the north spreading cold and snow and ice even into the far southern reaches where snow rarely fell. The Hranor Hills were as white as The Dlarmids. Ice imprisoned the deep blue lakes of the Lake Country, unheard of in times past. The Trayonian and Balagorn Seas that had for ages brought a limitless bounty of fish raged on either side of the land and crashed against it with such fury that few men dared venture to the shores, let alone set sail. The Skara River and its tributaries lay in icy bondage. Animals unable to find shelter froze to death. People huddled in houses and cottages, never truly warmed by the fires kept burning night and day.

When spring came at last, it was a season so short it might never have been. Grudgingly, winds abated and snows melted. Ice in the rivers broke up, and the floes drifted with the current to jam against docks and bridges until finally they broke free, often carrying away the structures that had impeded their progress. As the sun rapidly warmed the land, rivers filled with water from melting snow and ice, and devastating floods engulfed the land. The very oldest among the people could not remember, nor did the written histories record, a time when the rivers inundated the fields and plains of Kaenolir.

Summer, with burning sun and blistering heat, brought only a short growing season, and crops that had flourished in Kaenolir became a part of the past. Herds that had once thrived on succulent grasses diminished along with the pastures; the animals that survived were lean and stunted. Fishermen found fewer and fewer schools of fish for their nets. Loggers worked less and less at their trade because the shipwrights no longer built the wooden vessels which had proudly sailed the seas around Kaenolir. All too soon cold winds announced the coming of winter, and meager harvests were quickly garnered, while people tried to prepare for the onslaught of frigid temperatures and wondered how the forces of nature could change so drastically.

A shout from somewhere near the gate brought Alexander's troubled reverie back to the report from Shiptown. A fishing boat had drifted ashore, guided only by tide and wind, carrying a meager cargo of rotting fish.

And the butchered bodies of eight fishermen.

The sergeant writing the report indicated he could think of no word more appropriate to describe the way in which the men had died. Their throats were torn away, their bodies ripped open and entrails dumped on the deck. When the sergeant searched the boat, the smell of death and putrefaction was so strong he was hard pressed to complete his investigation. There was something else—a black slime covered many of the bodies, the likes of which he had never seen. If he had not gone himself to investigate, he would not have believed the horror found on the boat. The fishermen had died violent, gruesome deaths. Why? Who or what had killed them?

The letter from Shiptown's mayor that accompanied the official report corroborated the facts, but went on to tell of other inexplicable occurrences in the Thanian Woods and in the Dark Lands. The mayor spoke of beastly shapes seen in the dark, of the sound of howling that sometimes came on the night wind. He demanded, somewhat hysterically, that the Captain of the Guardians come to Shiptown and put an end to whatever was stalking the good people of his community.

What was going on in the north? Alexander chewed his bottom lip as he stared out the window. This latest report, telling of horrors never seen by anyone before, was only one of many that piled up on his desk. What was happening to Kaenolir? Endless, frigid winters, droughts, floods, short growing seasons with meager harvests, polluted rivers, dying animals, men who mysteriously disappeared or were brutally murdered, stillborn babies— all of this occurring over a span of about seven years. He had gone meticulously through all the reports for the past ten years and traced the beginning of the changes to a reported eruption of Mt. Sinnarock that had occurred seven years earlier.

Alexander morosely shook his head and stepped away from the window to take a seat behind the narrow table that served as his desk. What did all this mean? How could he stop what he couldn't understand? How could he battle fear and shadows?

"Captain." Simon stood in the doorway. Behind him was a disheveled and bleary-eyed Guardian.

"Captain, this is Douglas McClain. He brought the report from Shiptown." Simon stepped aside to let the other soldier enter the room, and then closed the door behind him.

"McClain." Alexander nodded and pointed to a chair for the man to take. His long fingers tapped the report that lay on top of a pile of papers in the middle of the table. "What do you know about this?"

McClain shifted uncomfortably on the hard chair and looked everywhere but at his captain. "What I know for sure or what I've heard?" he asked at last.

"Both." Alexander's gaze never left the soldier. "Look at me," he commanded.

Wide, glittering eyes lifted to Alexander's. In them he found the fear that he saw in the eyes of so many.

"I was not with the patrol that went to check the boat that drifted in, but one of my friends was there. He said he'd never seen anything so horrible. The men had been murdered, Captain, their bodies mutilated, and from what he could see, no human hand killed them."

"What do you mean, no human hand killed them?" Alexander sat forward in his chair, pushed the pile of papers aside and clasped his hands loosely together on the tabletop.

"My friend described the wounds on their bodies as the wounds that claws make. Some of the wounds looked like something had bitten the fishermen, especially the wounds on their throats. He said he'd seen the body of a man once that had been killed by a bear and that the marks of teeth and claws were like those on the bodies of the fishermen." McClain looked down at his hands as he clasped and unclasped them in agitation.

Quietly Alexander spoke to the young Guardian. "Go on. What else did your friend see?"

"Not so much see, Captain, as smell. The boat had probably been drifting for a few days and it's hot, so the bodies of the men and the fish were bound to be putrid. But, Robert, that's my friend, Robert said there was a stench like hell about the boat. There was a black slime that oozed over some of the bodies, and the smell seemed to come from that. He's not been the same since he went down to check that boat, Captain. He has bad dreams and wakes up screaming. I heard others on that patrol do the same." McClain swallowed convulsively and looked away from Alexander's intent gaze.

"Can you tell me anything more? Anything at all? Rumor, fact, I want to know all you've heard or know."

"There's other things going on, Captain Lamond. Some loggers disappeared out of the Thanian Woods and nobody's seen them again. Their saws were dropped and just left behind, and you know no woodsman leaves his saw in the woods. I've heard stories about people seeing things at night, things that aren't human."

"What kind of things?" Alexander interrupted.

"I don't know. Beasts, maybe, but creatures that walk on two legs, not four."

"Have you seen anything like that while you were on patrol?" Alexander asked.

"No, sir. But something's out there, Captain, something from the Dark Land."

Alexander sighed. "All right, McClain. That's all for now. Get some rest. Tomorrow you'll accompany me back to Shiptown." Alexander rose from his chair in dismissal.

McClain gave a nod and got up from his chair. "Captain, we need help to stop whatever is out there." His voice trembled.

Alexander gave him a quizzical look. "Help?" he asked.

"Yes, like from olden times. My grandmother used to tell me stories about the Ancient Ones and wizards and magic, Faeries and such. That's the kind of help we need."

Alexander snorted in disdain. "Do you really think those things ever existed, McClain?"

"I don't know, sir, but my grandmother did, and she was a very wise old woman."

"With all due respect to your wise old grandmother, I don't think we'll get any help but what we can provide ourselves. That's all, McClain."

The young Guardian turned away.

"Leave the door open," Alexander called after McClain as he left. "Faeries and gods," he grumbled as he went in search of Simon. "Beasts and the smell of hell. Has the world gone mad?"

~

Dawn was just a promise when the six-man patrol and their captain left for Shiptown. Once the sun came up, the unrelenting heat would be upon them; thus Alexander set a rapid pace. They crossed the bridge over the Skara River and followed the road through the Kiltan Hills toward the coast and Shiptown.

The creak of saddle leather, an occasional cough, the thud of horses' hooves on the hard-packed road announced their passing. No other sound intruded on the early morning air.

As it grew lighter, Alexander viewed the countryside they passed through. Once the hills had been covered in lush green grasses; trees had grown thickly; birds and small animals had abounded. Now the trees lifted near-leafless, skeletal limbs to the sky; no hint of green remained anywhere. Whatever tried to grow was immediately sucked dry of moisture by the sun and turned a sickly yellow before being burned to a withered brown. The birds and small animals had either died out or gone in search of more hospitable surroundings. Dust rose up in stifling clouds as the horses passed, and man and beast grew more uncomfortable and irritable as the hours passed.

A small fishing village lay to the left of the road, and Alexander brought the patrol to a halt. They should be able to find water for themselves and their horses at the village well.

"We'll stop here for a short time. Rest and water your horses and do the same for yourselves. There used to be an inn here. If it's still open, we'll get something to eat there." Alexander turned to Douglas McClain. "You know this area better than we do. Perhaps you could tell us where to stop."

McClain was shaking his head before Alexander finished speaking. "Not much here now, Captain. There's no fish anymore, and the people moved elsewhere. There's still a well where we can get fresh water, but the inn is closed."

"Lead us to the well then, McClain, and find us a bit of shade," Alexander nodded for the young Guardian to lead the way.

The deserted village was eerily silent as the riders made their way toward the well that stood in the middle of what had been a bustling community of neat stuccoed cottages with thickly thatched roofs. There was little evidence to show the pride and care that had once been taken in homes and gardens. Now the gates to the house yards sagged open; scraggly weeds choked the gardens; shuttered windows and barred doors spoke of abandonment.

The horses plodded wearily through the dust of the single street to the well. The men dismounted and began taking turns bringing up buckets of tepid water for themselves and their mounts.

Somewhere the wind banged a loose shutter in a rhythmic clatter that reminded Alexander of a death knell. A dust devil whirled down the street before disintegrating in the hot, dry air. After caring for their horses, Alexander and his men lounged about in whatever sparse shade they could find, silently eating rations or drinking the musty-tasting water from the well. The sudden screech of a hawk brought Alexander's head up, and he watched the bird wheel in slow, stately circles. He was not a man given to premonitions, but as he watched the bird and listened to its cry, he felt a clear and intense sense of impending death. He shuddered under its impact and rose hurriedly to his feet, anxious to put this forsaken place behind him.

"Let's get out of here." He dumped the last of the water from his cup and made his way to his horse.

The Guardians rose quickly to follow their captain, and no one grumbled about having to move on before they'd had a chance to rest. If they'd been asked, all would have admitted to feeling uneasy with their surroundings.

As Simon tightened the cinch of his saddle, he looked around at the abandoned cottages. "This place makes my skin crawl," he muttered to no one in particular. The hairs on the back of his neck prickled, giving him the unpleasant sensation that someone, or something, watched them.

The seven men mounted and rode back to the main road. No one looked back at the deserted village left baking under a scorching, uncaring sun. If one of them had, he might well have seen an indistinct shape skulking in the shadows of a lean-to. As the patrol rounded a curve in the track and moved out of sight, the form stepped away from its hiding place. It was very large. Long arms with claw-like hands dangled past its bent knees; scraggly hair covered its head, parts of its misshapen face, and much of its body; tiny, beady eyes peered out from under lowering brows. No human took such shape, but no beast moved on two legs as this thing did. A snuffling grunt emanated from the open, drooling mouth before it turned and trotted back through the village and down to the shore. It ran along the beach for some time before climbing a steep cliff to take shelter in a cave dug back into the stony ribs of the earth by the action of tide and waves. It was hungry and the puny men and their horses offered a tasty meal, but the sun was still high in the sky. When night came, then it would hunt. For now, it would rest and hide itself from the light and wait for darkness to come.

~

Alexander pushed his patrol along at a grinding, mile-eating pace. The sun beat down mercilessly, but they only slowed their pace from time to time to give the horses a respite. Twilight found them on the outskirts of Shiptown, tired, hot and dirty. As they made their way through the streets of the town, the smell of suppers cooking reminded them they hadn't eaten since the meager lunch in the fishing village. Lamplight glowed from open windows and doors. At first glance the squares of light seemed cheerful, but Alexander noted that only a few windows glowed. The streets were quiet: no laughing, shouting children, no barking dogs, no neighbors calling to one another in friendly greeting. Those few still on the streets hurried along with only a surreptitious glance at the soldiers. The noise the riders made in passing came back to them in a muffled echo.

Fear walked here. Alexander could smell it with every breath he took. He saw his men cast furtive, wary glances at the shadows near darkened buildings and cottages as they passed.

The letter from Shiptown's mayor had spoken of reported sightings of beasts that prowled the night bringing death and terror. No one could say exactly what these creatures looked like; only vague, indistinct shapes had been seen. Some of the people who reported seeing 'something' may have suffered from overly stimulated imaginations, but, nevertheless, men had been brutally killed. Perhaps only they, at the very end, could have named their attackers.

It was a relief to every man of the patrol when the small cluster of buildings sheltering the Guardian detachment came into view. One low building made of stone and covered with a thatched roof housed the men, while behind the barracks another building of much the same construction was used to stable the garrison horses. The flag of Kaenolir hung limply from a pole in the center of the dusty yard. Anticipation of a bath, a meal, a pint or two of ale, and a chance to catch up on the news momentarily pushed aside the reality of the miserable, hot journey and the disturbing uneasiness that had followed them all the way from the fishing village. A Guardian came out to greet them as they dismounted.

"Welcome to Shiptown, Captain." He gave his commander a casual salute and nodded to Douglas McClain.

Alexander returned the salute and looked about him. The garrison had been placed in this area long ago when the docks and waterfront were the focal point of the town's expansion and bustling commerce. Ships from all over the world had docked here, and seamen celebrated their shore leave as sailors had been doing since men first put wood and sail on water and searched for adventure, profits, and new lands. The Guardians served to keep the celebrations in tolerable bounds and offered protection to villagers, merchants, and seafarers alike.

But the docks were quiet now. No ships came to Shiptown anymore.

"Please see that my men are fed and housed and our horses stabled," Alexander commanded the soldier.

"Of course, sir. You'll want to see Sergeant Cameron, too, I'm sure. He's in the dining hall."

Alexander handed the reins of his horse to Simon and mounted the steps to a wooden porch that ran the length of the barracks. The dining hall was at the end of the building, and he walked toward it. He pulled the wide brimmed hat from his head and sighed with relief at the bit of momentary coolness. Rivulets of sweat marked the dust on his face, and he longed for a soothing soak in a tub and a glass of the heady ale brewed in the southern lowlands. His shoulders slumped in weariness, and he wondered when he had ever been this tired. If he were honest with himself, he knew that the fatigue of the ride here was not all that he was feeling. Something evil—yes, he decided, evil—was afoot in Kaenolir, and the frustration of not knowing what it was or how to keep it at bay weighed heavily. He and the Guardians who served under his command had pledged themselves to protect the people of Kaenolir, but how could they do that if there was no recognizable, tangible enemy?

"Alexander," Sergeant Ian Cameron called to him as he entered the dining hall. He stood near a table toward the back of the long room to catch Alexander's attention. A tall man, he nearly equaled his captain's height, but carried more weight on a bigger frame. Bushy, sandy-colored hair accentuated his round, open face. He came forward, his large hand extended in greeting. "I thought you would come," he said. Weary eyes looked into the equally weary eyes of his commander and friend. Lines of worry and concern creased his face on either side of his mouth and across his brow and were matched on Alexander's face. "Unpleasant journey?"

Alexander grunted in answer. "Until I've had a drop of ale to wash the dust of the trail from my throat, I'd just as soon dispense with pleasantries, if you don't mind," he remarked sourly.

Ian's snort of laughter grated on Alexander's ears. It was a dry sound, lacking in Ian's usual jovial warmth.

"Come, sit down and have some food and something to drink. When you've had a chance to eat and get cleaned up, I'll tell you what's been happening in Shiptown and the surrounding area."

Ian turned to lead the way to the table where he sat with two other Guardians. They nodded and gave Alexander the casual salute that labeled them as comrades, then returned to their conversation and meal. When Alexander took a seat on the wooden bench across from them, Ian pushed a pint of ale toward him and signaled for food to be brought. The strong brew hit Alexander's empty stomach, and he welcomed the warmth that spread through his aching muscles. A steaming plate of food was set before him, and he began to eat. After satisfying the basic needs of hunger and thirst, his sense of despair lifted somewhat. He glanced up to see his men come in. Douglas McClain led them to a table where some of his friends were seated and began introducing them around. They were soon all eating and talking, and for the moment the camaraderie of fellow Guardians overcame their tiredness.

"I've asked that water be heated for you in the bath house. For your men, too. It should be hot soon." Ian broke the silence that had prevailed during Alexander's meal.

"Thanks." Alexander leaned back to stretch tightened shoulder muscles. "I find it hard to remember riding through Kaenolir when the dust didn't cover everything. And everyone." He hunched forward and rested his arms on the table, his hands wrapped around another pint of ale. "Any problem with water shortages here yet?"

"No, not yet. The wells are all at low levels, but we've fewer people in the town to use the water. So far, none of the wells have been fouled, but that may change at any time."

Alexander gave Ian a considering look. "I've had no reports of fouled wells."

Ian shrugged. "First the land, Alexander, then the water." He took a sip of his ale. "Look at what's happening in Kaenolir. I've not been in the lowlands for some time, but I've heard how things are there. Drought, less than half the normal harvest. In the highlands it's no better. And here in Shiptown, it's as if the Trayonian is trying to destroy us—merciless gales, few fish, flood tides." He shook his head and sighed. "If the land is dying, what's to stop the rivers and streams from being next? The wells tap underground rivers, so it would seem logical that the water we get from the wells would be affected, too."

Alexander sighed wearily and ran his thumb and forefinger along the bridge of his nose. Ian's conjecture that the waters of Kaenolir would soon die was all too valid. Preliminary reports from the Ghilana Plain indicated the headwaters of the Skara River were being polluted by run-off from the mines in The Dlarmids. Within a short time the other rivers flowing down out of the mountains would also carry pollution. As far as he was able to ascertain, the mines and the rivers had always existed in harmony. Until now. However, he said nothing of this to Ian. Ian had enough to worry about here in Shiptown.

"I'm going to take a bath. Then if there's a cool, quiet spot in this camp, let's find it. I want to know everything about what you found on that fishing boat."

Alexander rose, taking his cup of ale with him.

"I may be able to find a quiet spot, but forget the cool part. At least until winter comes," Ian said with a grimace, then turned to lead the way from the mess.

~

After bathing, Alexander went in search of Ian and found him slumped in a chair in his quarters. The windows and door of the narrow, sparsely furnished room stood open to catch whatever night breeze there might be. Even so, the room was stuffy and uncomfortably warm. A single lamp, turned low, sat on a rough-hewn table and kept most of the room in shadows. Its tiny flame did little but add more heat to the heavy air.

Ian handed Alexander a goblet of wine. Alexander took it, one eyebrow arched in surprise. "Where did you find this? Surely, it's not Kaenolirian wine." He sat in the only other chair the room offered.

"No. I've been hoarding it. It's from one of the last shipments to come in from overseas. This seems an appropriate time to get drunk." Ian lifted his goblet in a mocking salute and drank.

"What do you want to know about the fishing boat? I covered nearly everything in my report, but it was difficult to put into words what I saw." Ian stared into the depths of his wine, a haunted expression on his face. At last he lifted troubled eyes to Alexander.

"Baskers, Alex, you can't imagine what it was like on that boat." He drank deeply and turned his head to look at the flickering flame of the lamp. "I've never seen men killed in such a brutal way. There were eight of them; at least only eight bodies were onboard. Two of them were boys. That size boat usually carries a crew of twelve, but I don't know what happened to the other four. As I told you in my report, someone or something had torn out their throats and disemboweled them. From what I could tell, three of the bodies looked as if whatever killed them decided to have a feast."

"What?" Alexander whispered incredulously.

"Three of the bodies had been partially eaten."

Alexander stood and walked to the window. He looked out into the night as he swallowed the gorge that rose in his throat. "You didn't mention that in your report," he said finally.

"No. If you hadn't come here, I planned to go to the Fort to see you. There's more, Alex."

Alexander swore softly. He turned from the window and moved to the table. Wordlessly he refilled Ian's goblet and then his own before resuming his seat. "Go on."

"Their legs and arms had been torn from the sockets, not cut away or hacked off with a cutting edge, literally torn from the bodies. Whatever killed those men must have been incredibly strong. Bones were scattered about the deck of the ship, picked clean of flesh. With the way in which those men died, you might think there would have been a great deal of blood, puddles of it, in fact, dried on the deck. There was none, Alex, not one drop." Again Ian drank deeply of the red wine. He rose to pace restlessly, passing in and out of the shadows cast by the lamp.

"The other five bodies were lying apparently where they fell. A black slime oozed over them. When we went on board to investigate, the first thing I noticed was the awful smell. The smell of decaying flesh was to be expected, but the slime also gave off a stench like..."

"Like the stench of hell."

"Yes. If such a place exists, it must smell like that. Three men went with me when we got word of the boat drifting ashore. None of us sleeps much anymore. When we close our eyes, the whole unbelievable scene is there to see again. It's in our nightmares, waking and sleeping. We drink too much but find food somehow distasteful after seeing what had been eaten aboard that boat." Ian stopped his prowling to take his seat again. He hunched forward, elbows resting on his knees, his head in his hands. "Alex, it will drive me mad," he whispered, his eyes welling with tears. "I knew most of the men on that boat."

Alexander stared at his friend and comrade-in-arms. They had known each other since childhood, Alexander being the older by a few years. When Ian's father was badly injured in a fall from a horse, Alexander took the younger boy under his tutelage. He taught him to ride, taught him how to use a sword, and when the time came, sponsored him when he joined the ranks of the Guardians. For the first time since they had grown to manhood, Alexander listened to Ian weep deep, wrenching sobs that came from his soul. The tears were for the men who had died on the fishing boat, but Alexander knew the tears were also for Kaenolir.

Neither man had fought a battle. The last war on Kaenolirian soil had been the War of the Brothers, centuries before. In effect, the Guardians were policemen who jailed the occasional rowdy sailor or petty thief, helped to settle disputes, and patrolled the coasts and the border with Timis, as well as the countryside. What faced them now was beyond what any of them, officer or regular soldier, could comprehend or know how to deal with, and perhaps it did border on madness.

At last the raw, distressing sobs subsided, and Ian noisily blew his nose. He found it difficult to meet Alexander's eyes. He couldn't bear it if he saw pity there. He rose from his chair and went to stand in the doorway. "What is to become of us, Alex? Where can we go to find help?" His voice was harsh in the quiet of the room.

Alexander sighed ruefully and drank from his near-empty goblet. "Your man, McClain, suggested we enlist the aid of the Ancient Ones and the Faeries. Maybe he wasn't too far off the mark. The only problem is, I haven't the vaguest notion how to find any of them."

"Talanor would know."

"Talanor? Are you sure he ever really existed? I used to think he was merely the stuff of old legends and tales.

"He lived five years ago. On Cathorn Isle. A ship stopped there once a year to leave supplies for him. But since the Trayonian has gotten so rough and the ships don't come to Shiptown, he may no longer be alive."

Alexander got up to get more wine. Ian's suggestion about getting drunk was becoming decidedly more pleasant. "Even if he does live, can we get to his island? I know a few fishermen still brave the high seas, but they are very few. Would you know where to find Talanor on Cathorn if we were able to get there somehow?"

Ian shrugged. "The isle is not so large and he is an old man. Surely we could find one old—"

A high-pitched scream filled the night air to be cut abruptly short with a gasping, gurgling sound. The hair on the back of Alexander's neck stood on end.

"Baskers, what was that?"

Both men set down their wine and ran outside. A Guardian came running toward them. As he came up to them, Alexander saw the fear in his eyes, felt his terror.

Ian took the young man by the shoulder and shook him slightly. "What is it?"

The frightened soldier could only gesture toward the darkness. Ian shook him harder. "What happened?" he shouted.

"It's Robert, Sergeant, Robert Campbell," he croaked. "I think he's been killed."

Ian swore. "Where is he? Take me to him."

The Guardian could only shake his head in a negative motion. "Not out there," he whispered. "It might still be out there."

Alexander grabbed Ian by the arm. "Get a light. We need to find out what's down there." He turned back to the trembling soldier. "Was he on guard duty?"

"Yes, sir. He was patrolling the docks. Down there," he gestured again toward the darkness of the waterfront.

Ian returned with a lighted lantern, and he and Alexander ran in the direction the Guardian indicated.

They'd not gone far before a shadowy shape rose up over a form lying on the rough planks of the dock. It gave a menacing growl and came fully erect. Ian held the lantern higher, and for a moment the thing stared back as the two men slowly and cautiously approached it. Both Alexander and Ian came to a stop as the creature swayed from side to side as if trying to decide what to do. Ian drew his short sword from its scabbard, but Alexander had not donned his weapons after bathing and had nothing with which to protect himself but his own strength and wits. Neither man took his eyes from the creature.

The look of the thing would forever be imprinted on their minds. It stood at least seven feet tall, a head or more taller than the two men it faced. Long arms dangled nearly to its knees, and rough, shaggy hair covered its head and body. The light was not bright enough to see clearly, but the size and shape of the creature was discernible. It was huge and grotesquely ugly. The stench that rose from it was almost overpowering, and Alexander gagged as his abdomen muscles spasmed.

The creature seemed to decide that the two man-things offered little threat, and it took a step toward them, hesitating only when Ian began swinging the lantern to and fro. It threw up a protecting arm to shield its eyes from the light. A guttural growl came from deep in its throat, and it paused. The urgency of its hunger, however, overcame its primary distaste for the light, and once again it moved toward the two men. Ian handed the lantern to Alexander in order to have his hands free to use his sword.

Alexander noted the way the beast's beady eyes followed the path of the light. He waited until it was only a few steps away; then with accuracy born of desperation he heaved the lantern at the approaching menace and hit it squarely in the chest. The fuel from the lantern soaked the shaggy hair, and fire spread rapidly over the front of the creature's body. A howl of pain and fear cracked the heavy night air, and the beast tried unsuccessfully to beat out the flames. That was the opening Ian needed and with a quick, practiced stroke he thrust his sword deeply into the neck of the creature. It gave a hideous scream and slowly sank to its knees, black gore flowing from the wound, its claw-like hands clutching and grasping at its throat. More flames shot up to engulf the creature as the gore ran into its hair, and it slumped to the dock in the final throes of agony and death.

Alexander and Ian stood staring at the thing, their breathing ragged and shallow, blood pounding in their veins. Ian swore, savagely, in the aftermath of terror, and it took a moment before the sounds of running feet and voices drew his attention away from the creature. Alexander called out and six Guardians led by the soldier who had reported Robert Campbell's death came rushing up to them. They all stopped when they saw what lay burning on the dock.

"May the gods protect us," someone half-whispered.

Alexander stepped forward. "Bring a light and let's have a look at Campbell." One of the Guardians carrying a lantern brought it forward, and the group clustered around the fallen soldier. Alexander knelt and slowly turned the body over onto its back. Robert Campbell's mouth opened on a silent scream; his eyes were wide and unseeing. Where his throat had been was a gaping, bloody wound. One of the soldiers standing next to Ian gagged and turned away. Alexander clenched and unclenched his left hand and cursed as rage boiled up inside him. How many more, he wondered, would die like this?

He rose from his kneeling position beside the dead Guardian. "Someone get a stretcher and carry Robert back to the barracks. Get a bucket or something to dump some water on that." He jerked his head toward the still smoldering carcass that lay a few feet away. Two of the soldiers hurried away to do his bidding.

"Captain," someone spoke into the gathering silence. "What is that thing?"

"A creature from hell," Alexander said flatly

Chapter Three

The sun had barely climbed above the horizon when the Guardians buried Robert Campbell, quickly and quietly. Appropriate words were spoken, his few earthly possessions gathered together and placed in a box, a letter written to his family telling of his untimely death while on patrol, and an honor guard sent on its way to the Campbell family.

Ian Cameron sat behind his desk, morosely staring into a mug of rapidly cooling tea. He felt empty, raw, weary. He couldn't help thinking about the young Guardian they had buried this morning. Robert had come to Shiptown as a recruit, eager to test his manhood and his new skills. No matter what the task, he set about it with rare good humor. His laughing eyes and caustic wit made him popular not only with his comrades but also with the young women of Shiptown. He was eager, dependable, and a good soldier. Robert had been with him when they found the rotting cargo on the fishing boat.

And now Robert Campbell was dead at the hands of a creature Ian could not name. There was little comfort in the fact that the creature was dead, too, little comfort in the fact that it was his sword that had killed it.

Ian looked up as Alexander came into the room. Slouching back in his chair, Ian watched his friend walk to a small table that stood beneath the window. A big man who moved with silent grace, Alexander's broad shoulders carried the weight of command easily. The youngest captain to lead the Guardians, he was highly regarded and respected by soldier and civilian alike, but few men felt they truly knew him. He was not a man who made friends easily, but when he did that man was his friend for life. Ian felt honored to call Alexander his friend and be called friend in return.

Alexander poured a mug of tea from the ceramic jug and dropped into a chair. Leaning forward, he rested his forearms on his knees, his long brown fingers wrapped around the warmth of the mug. He sipped the hot liquid for several minutes before speaking to Ian.

"How do we go about finding a fisherman willing to take us to Cathorn Isle?" he finally asked.

Ian gazed at Alexander a long time before answering. "I can get the word out along the docks immediately. However, we may not be able to find anyone willing to take us."

"I realize that." Alexander sat upright in his chair and looked at Ian. "How long has it been since you've done any sailing?" His mouth quirked in a smile that didn't reach his eyes.

"I'm not much of a sailor under the best of conditions. I can ride any horse that lives, but I'm no good in a boat. With the way the Trayonian has been running I couldn't possibly get us to Cathorn without drowning us in the attempt."

"Well, then," Alexander drained the last of the tea from his mug. "Let's hope you can find someone with enough skill to get us to Cathorn but not enough sense to realize the danger we'll be in." He rose to place his mug on the table and turned to leave.

"You know that even if we do reach Cathorn, we may not find Talanor, or he may not want to be found."

"Yes, I know." Alexander sighed heavily and placed a hand on the doorframe. "We've not many options at this point, Ian. Maybe Talanor can help us, maybe not." He turned away once more to leave.

"What have you decided to do with that thing we killed last night?" Ian's quiet question stopped Alexander at the door.

"I made a rough sketch of it after it was light enough to see. Then I had my men bury it." Alexander gazed out over the dusty yard and watched the flag of Kaenolir billow briefly before collapsing against its pole. He looked back over his shoulder at Ian. "It seems fitting that it died in flames. I hope we sent it back to the place that spawned it." His mouth set in a mirthless smile. "I'm going to get some sleep. Let me know as soon as you find a fisherman to take us to Cathorn."

He walked out the door and into the sunshine. Although the hour was still early, the day was already hot. There would be no relief from the heat today either. He swore softly, cursing the forces that had set the events in motion that were destroying Kaenolir and its people while he stood by helplessly, unable to keep the promise he had made to protect his country.

~

Like a boiling cauldron, the Trayonian Sea heaved and foamed, seemingly intent upon dislodging from its surface the irritating little boat that dared to wallow its way toward Cathorn Isle. Although both Alexander and Ian had spent some time sailing, neither had ever been out when the waves raged as high as the mast of the vessel they were in. The boat was carried on top of a wave for a moment or two, then sent headlong into the trough created by the action of the water, only to be lifted high once more.

"Good thing I've a strong stomach," Ian muttered through clenched teeth. "If I ever get my feet on solid ground again, I'll never set foot in a boat for as long as I live."

"How will you get back to Kaenolir from Cathorn?" Alexander drawled. "Swim?"

Ian threw a withering glance at Alexander's sprawled form. He rocked easily with the turbulent motion of the boat and grinned at Ian's discomfiture. But his grin turned quickly to a grimace when a particularly violent wave sent them crashing into a cavernous alley of water. When they raced toward the top of the next wave, the old fisherman who had agreed to take them to Cathorn Isle, a man named Hugh, shouted something they could not hear. When he pointed to the sky, they quickly understood what he was trying to tell them. Black, roiling clouds were scudding across the heat-whitened sky, and they were sailing directly into them. Alexander came to his feet, and grasping the gunwale of the bucking boat made his way toward the fisherman.

"What now?" he shouted to be heard above wind and water. "Can we outrun the storm?"

"Not likely," the fisherman replied. "We'll just have to ride 'er out."

Alexander uttered some particularly profane words. "What do you want us to do?" he shouted back at the stoic helmsman.

"Get yourselves situated so you've got something solid to hang on to. If you know any prayers, I'd say 'em if I was you."

Alexander made his way back to Ian. Already they could feel increased agitation in the wave motion and intensified pressure in the wind.

"What did the old man say?" Ian shouted.

"He said to hang on and say your prayers."

Ian's mouth moved but Alexander could not hear what he said. Jagged spears of lightning split the sky, and a crack of thunder heralded the arrival of the squall. Rain poured out of the black clouds, the wind driving it in sheets that blurred clouds, sky and sea together. The little boat heaved and rocked like a creature struggling to escape a trap. The old fisherman, his face and hands as weathered as the wood of his boat, set the little vessel into the teeth of the wind and said his own prayers. He held her steady until he ached with the strain. His eyes squinted to keep out the rain and spray while the two Guardians clung to the ropes of the mast. They were all fools to be out on these seas, but the Sergeant had said it was a matter of life and death. And besides, he paid very well. Hugh hoped he lived long enough to spend the gold in his pouch.

They battled the storm for hours, long after they should have made Cathorn. Just as the fisherman made up his mind they would never reach their destination, the boat broke through the edge of the storm and sailed into the calm waters of a sheltered cove that protected the landing dock at Cathorn Isle.

"Have the gods dropped us off the end of the world?" Ian turned incredulous eyes to Alexander. To be at the mercy of a fierce storm one minute and in placid shallows with the sun shining down brightly the next gave a man reason to doubt his sanity. Even Hugh's face registered disbelief.

The boat bumped softly against the weather-beaten dock and Alexander jumped out to tie it fast. He looked about him with wondering eyes. There was no drought here; everything was green and lush, cooled by breezes that blew from the bay.

Ian joined Alexander on the dock. "Now I know the gods sent us into another world," he said. "Look at this place. I haven't seen this much green in years."

Alexander turned to Hugh. "Do you know where we can find the recluse who lives here?" he asked him.

The old man scratched his chin in thought. "I used to bring him fish once in awhile back before the bad times, but he always met me here. He's not the friendly sort, so I never got invited to his house." He shook his head. "Cranky, too. Had a big wolf for a pet that always came with him to the dock. Wolf growled all while I unloaded. I'd watch out for the wolf, if I was you."

Alexander looked back toward the beach. There was a path of sorts, leading into the thick forest; perhaps it would take them to Talanor.

"Let's get our gear and get going," he said to Ian. "We may have a long trek ahead of us." The two men moved to take the heavy packs the fisherman handed up to them.

"I have no way of knowing how long it will take us to find Talanor," Alexander said to the old man. "It may be several days before we can get back here." He hefted one of the packs into place on his back. "Don't leave without us," he admonished.

"I'm not likely to leave this spot," Hugh gestured around him. "Green trees, cool breeze, warm sun. Not likely I'll leave this place until I have to." He saluted the two Guardians as they settled their packs more comfortably on their backs before walking down the dock.

~

"Yes, I know, Jagar, three men have come to Cathorn."

A huge silver-gray wolf prowled restlessly, sniffing the air periodically and growling deep in his throat. He did not sense danger, only that men came.

"It's all right," the man said, placing his hand gently on the massive head when the animal stopped its pacing and came to stand beside him. "I've been expecting them for some time now. They mean no harm." Content with his master's assurance, the wolf lay down in front of the low burning fire in the hearth and closed his eyes. He appeared to sleep, but the occasional twitch of his upright ears indicated he was still alert. The man smiled and went on with his work.

There were many pots and small jars on the table before him. Several wooden trays held dried leaves and flowers, bark, stem, and roots. He carefully crushed, broke or twisted together the various items on the trays in patterns that only he knew. The resulting materials were placed in containers and meticulously labeled before being set away on shelves that lined one wall of the room. There would be need for all he prepared, a great need, and soon.

He had hoped this time would never come, that Kaenolir would be spared the dreadful confrontation between what he knew to be good and what he had learned was evil, but the signs he had observed did not lie. He knew the moment Maelorn had awakened, knew the moment he had somehow freed himself from his imprisonment. The huge explosion of Mt. Sinnarock had shaken the foundations of the small island on which Talanor lived. Soon after the eruption he sensed the changes that began to take place on the mainland

and in the seas. And it became harder to keep his own island inviolate and sheltered from the evil growing ever stronger on Sinnich Isle. Though Maelorn was not yet powerful enough to leave his mountain stronghold, Talanor felt certain it would not be long before he would come to take what he felt was his—Kaenolir.

Talanor could only guess at the powers Maelorn now possessed. He knew that dark forces were ever present in life and that at times those forces took a recognizable form in an effort to gain control over all that existed. From the beginning of time, good had struggled to defeat evil. And sometimes, as during the past five hundred years in Kaenolir, good had reigned.

Kaenolirians had come to take their good lives for granted, had been lulled into a sense of false security while the Dark One groomed and strengthened an eager Maelorn. The intangible became tangible, evil became personified in the form of a man, a man who craved power and lusted after wealth enough to give up his spirit to the source of evil.

So it was time again for the forces of good to fight against the forces of evil, but Talanor feared that mankind might not win the coming battle, that inherent goodness would not be strong enough to defeat Maelorn and the creatures he commanded.

Talanor was the last of his kind; and while once his ancestors had possessed great powers and commanded the realms of magic, he did not. He could still the waves and keep evil at bay around his island; he knew how to cure the sick and heal the wounded; but he feared he could not stop the growing canker in Sinnarock.

He sighed and paused in his work to look out the large window to the mountains that ringed his valley. Men were coming to him for help. If they had not come to him, he would soon have gone to the mainland. He did not know how much help he could give, but he knew he must use all his resources, all the powers he still possessed to try to help Kaenolir. He still needed time, however, before he would be ready to go.

Jagar lifted his head and growled low.

"Yes, Jagar," he murmured and paused a moment to wipe the sweat from his brow. "They're nearly here. Go greet them and lead them up the trail. I still have work to do."

The huge wolf rose and silently left the cottage.

~

Alexander and Ian had been hiking since first light, gradually working their way out of the mountains and down into the valley. Although the sun was nearly at its zenith, the air remained cool. Alexander wondered, not for the first time, if Ian's observation about the gods dropping them in another world might be true.

But how could this island remain untouched by the ravages of the weather patterns that affected the mainland? It was only a few nautical miles from the shore of Kaenolir; thus it would seem logical that Cathorn would suffer the same fate.

Lost in his thoughts, Alexander was not aware that the path was blocked until a low growl warned him of danger. He stopped so suddenly that Ian nearly plowed into him from behind.

"Baskers, Alex, what the ...?" Ian's explosive profanity was cut short by another louder, more menacing growl. He quickly drew his sword and stepped to Alexander's side.

The two men faced an animal like no other they had seen. It stood, huge feet firmly planted, in the path the men were following. Its massive chest supported an equally massive head from which keen eyes surveyed them. Its coat glistened silver. It was shaped like a wolf but more than double in size.

"Baskers," Ian swore again. "What is that?"

"It's a wolf. I think. But not like any wolf I've ever seen." Alexander continued to stare at the animal, and slowly drew his sword, alert for any sign of attack. None came. In utter amazement, he watched as the dark plume of tail began to wag. The wolf opened its mouth, and for a moment it appeared to laugh at them, its tongue lolling in wry amusement. Then it turned and moved down the trail. It stopped, turned to look back at the men, then moved on. A bit further it paused again, again looking back at them.

"I think he wants us to follow him." Alexander looked at Ian, a flash of humor in his eyes.

"Our welcoming party?" Ian asked.

"I guess so. Remember old Hugh said to watch out for a wolf. I'd say we found a wolf, all right."

Both men sheathed their swords and set off after the wolf. Someone knew of their presence on the island; perhaps they were even expected.

~

The two Guardians followed the wolf down out of the mountains. The trail was easy and meandered along a gurgling stream. There was no evidence here of the pollution that fouled the upper reaches of the rivers traversing the highlands. This stream was crystal clear, its water sweet and very cold.

The wolf waited for the men to catch up. When they were but a few steps away, he turned away from the stream and led them through an apple orchard. Gnarled but carefully pruned limbs attesting to trees of great age, heavy now with ripening globes of fruit, evidenced the great care with which they were tended. They passed a vegetable garden; its neat rows of crisp, green foliage promised abundant produce.

The wolf came to a gate in a low stone wall, looked at the men once, and stepped aside. The two men paused and looked at each other. Ian shrugged and Alexander strode through the gate. A small wooden building stood to their right, and as they rounded it a cottage came into view.

Smoke curled lazily from a large chimney set to one end of the slate roof. Built of logs and stone, the cottage looked substantial enough to withstand the ravages of endless time. A large window looked upon a magnificent view of mountains that rose up stark above the valley. A carefully laid path of washed gravel curved through a riot of fragrant blossoms and led to the cottage's front door.

A very large front door, Alexander noted.

The reason for the size of the door quickly became apparent as a man, taller by a head than the two men who faced him, filled the doorway. His imposing frame was accented by a shock of curling snow-white hair that fell past broad shoulders and by a full beard that flowed down his chest. Startling, intense blue eyes pierced whatever they looked upon. His skin was tanned and his face, deeply lined and creased, had the look of aged leather. Hands with slender, almost elegant fingers rolled down the sleeves of the long brown robe he wore. He stepped from the doorway into the sunlight, a figure from another time, another life.

Power radiating from the man whose penetrating gaze examined them made the hair on Alexander's neck and arms prickle. And in passing, Alexander was sure those eyes saw the smallest secret in the darkest recesses of his soul. Rarely had Alexander encountered men physically larger than he and never had he felt awed by the sheer size and presence of another man. But this man, who stood larger than life in a garden of wildly blooming flowers, made Alexander quickly decide that if they ever drew swords, he'd want this man standing beside him, not facing him. One glance at Ian's astonished face indicated he was feeling much the same way.

"So," the voice boomed, resonant and deep and rather gruff. "You've come at last, Alexander Lamond and Ian Cameron. I'm Talanor Rowan and I've been expecting you."

~

The three men talked long into the night, Alexander and Ian taking turns telling Talanor what was happening in Kaenolir and answering the many questions he asked. He was already aware of the changes in the weather patterns, but he could not hide his dismay when Alexander spoke of the ravages to the once fertile land and gently flowing rivers. His shock at Ian's recounting of the deaths of the fishermen was obvious. He rose to pace the confines of the room, lighted now by a flickering fire and a lamp left burning on the table where they had eaten a simple evening meal.

"I did not know. All of them dead?" he whispered.

"Yes," Ian answered.

Talanor shook his white head. "What they must have suffered before they died," he murmured.

Alexander told of the reports he had received from the Ghilana Plain, from the outlying reaches of the highlands and other areas in the north of men murdered, of people who just disappeared, and of many stillborn babies.

"My poor Kaenolir," Talanor murmured and shook his head again. He sighed as he resumed his seat. "It has happened far more quickly than I anticipated."

Alexander and Ian exchanged glances of puzzlement.

"What do you mean, Talanor?" Alexander asked.

Talanor did not answer him and for a long moment he seemed lost in his thoughts. At last he roused himself. "Is there anything more?"

"Yes." Alexander rose from his chair near the fireplace to rummage in his pack. Jagar lifted his head to follow the movements of the man, and Alexander paused to give the wolf an absent pat as he resumed his seat across from Talanor. He handed the mage a rolled parchment. "What is this?" he asked the old man.

Talanor unrolled the parchment and stared at the rough sketch of the creature that had killed Robert Campbell. "How did you come by this?" He raised troubled eyes to Alexander.

"I sketched it after Ian and I killed it."

"Where?" Talanor asked sharply.

"On the dock at Shiptown. It had just killed one of Ian's men." Alexander ran a hand impatiently through his hair. "What is it? Where does it come from?"

Talanor looked again at the sketch of the creature. "It is something I thought killed off long ago." He carefully rolled the parchment before handing it back to Alexander. "It's called a Spriggan, and it was conceived in the pit of hell."

Alexander cursed softly "Do you think others like it are responsible for the deaths of the fishermen? And perhaps the other murders throughout the north as well?"

Talanor nodded. "I would say it is a very good possibility."

"How can we stop them?" Ian asked. "It was only a stroke of luck that Alex and I saw this one and were able to kill it."

"They are stupid creatures, easily manipulated and controlled. A whole army of them once nearly destroyed Kaenolir but only because their master was very clever." Talanor stared into the dying embers. "As you know they can be killed, but in the killing many men die."

The room fell silent as each man pondered his own distressing thoughts. At last Talanor rose. "It is very late and you must be weary. We will talk more of this tomorrow before we begin preparations for our return to Kaenolir."

"Our return?" Alexander asked. "You will come with us then?"

"Of course I will come," he snapped. "Kaenolir has need of my help. I am an old man and I fear I will not be strong enough to give her all the help she needs, but perhaps I can show you the way to save her." He picked up the lamp, offering no explanation of his strange statement.

"Come," he said abruptly. "Follow me. I'll show you where you may sleep."

~

Although Alexander was exhausted, he found it impossible to sleep. His mind whirled with many thoughts, and Ian's snoring chorus made it difficult to settle. He heard Talanor's voice several times during the night. As he mulled over what they had discussed, he realized Talanor had raised more questions than he had answered. He hoped there would be some answers tomorrow. At last, as the first faint blushes of dawn touched the eastern skies above the mountains, he slept.

While Ian and Alexander rested, Talanor spent the rest of the hours of darkness working at his long table, filling and labeling more jars and pots. He rested for only a brief time just before dawn, before rising to prepare the morning meal. He rose from the hearth with a kettle of hot porridge and a jug of steaming tea as Alexander and Ian came into the room. Hot cakes already sat on the table along with honey and apple butter.

Talanor motioned the men to the table. "Sit, eat, he instructed them. "We have much to do today," he said cryptically.

~

"Do you still feel we've dropped into another world?" Alexander asked Ian as they each carried a large bundle to the cart Talanor had brought around to the front of the cottage.

"Baskers, yes." Ian was breathing heavily from his exertions. He hefted his bundle onto the cart and pushed it up against the others they'd already put there. "He sometimes makes me think he knows exactly what I'm thinking. How could he know who we were before we had a chance to tell him?" Ian shook his head. "This is beyond my understanding, Alex." He turned troubled eyes to his friend. "I don't understand what's happening in Kaenolir either."

"I know." Alexander grunted as he lifted his bundle into place. "Perhaps Talanor will give us some answers today."

The men went back to the cottage for more of the large bundles Talanor was packing. The long table and the shelves that yesterday were filled stood empty. When Ian asked what was in the many pots and jars, Talanor told him only that they contained supplies Kaenolir would need.

"How do you know what Kaenolir needs?" Ian asked.

His only answer was an irritated snort as Talanor turned his back and went back to packing. Ian sighed and took another of the carefully packaged bundles out to the cart. Alexander met him at the door.

"I feel like a schoolboy who's just been reprimanded for talking during lessons," he groused.

"Why?" Alexander asked with a chuckle.

"I guess I asked a question out of turn." Ian stepped past Alexander.

"Captain." Talanor's imperious tones demanded Alexander's attention.

Alexander watched Ian heft the pack onto the cart, and then turned to join Talanor in his workroom. "You called me?" he asked.

"Yes," Talanor said, glancing at him. "This is the last to be packed here. There are other items stored in one of the buildings out back, which I'll show you and Ian in a moment. They are for Kaenolir, too. How much cargo do you think the fisherman's boat can carry?"

"Certainly all that's in the cart now. Perhaps a bit more. With the Trayonian running so high, I'm sure Hugh won't want to overload his boat."

"The Trayonian will be quite calm on the return trip."

"How do you know that?" Alexander asked in surprise. "There's never a calm day anymore."

"Questions, always questions. Ian, too," Talanor muttered irritably.

"Yes, and I'd damn well like some answers, Talanor Rowan." Alexander drew himself up to his full height and stared into Talanor's angry features. They faced each other for some time, two strong men, neither of whom was willing to back down. At last Talanor shrugged and gave Alexander a lopsided smile, more grimace than smile.

"I suppose you are entitled to some," he grudgingly agreed. "But later, after all this is packed and moved down to the landing."

"Your word, Talanor?" Alexander asked.

"Yes, yes, of course, my word," Talanor snapped. "Here take this out to the cart. That's the last from my workroom. Then come round to the back of the house, and I'll show you what else must go."

~

The three men rested in the shade of a large oak tree with mugs of cool, crisp ale that tasted faintly of apples, some crusty brown bread, and creamy yellow cheese. The sun stood high in a cloudless sky, but the day was pleasantly warm. Two large oxen stood patiently, yoked to the fully loaded cart, ready for the trek down to the bay and Hugh's boat.

"I'll go with you and help load the boat." Talanor spoke into the silence. "Sergeant, I'd like you to accompany the fisherman back to Shiptown and see to the proper storing of all that I'm sending. I've written instructions for you to follow." He took a small roll of parchment from the folds of his robe and handed it to Ian. "See that everything is done just as I instruct," he ordered before turning to Alexander. "Captain Lamond, I'd like you to come with me to Lorn Isle."

"To Lorn Isle? Why?" Alexander asked in surprise.

"More questions," Talanor muttered disgustedly.

"Sorry. I usually give the orders not take them," Alexander said, his tone laced with sarcasm. "I also like to know why I'm doing something before I do it."

The two men stared at each other. "All right, all right," Talanor said at last. "It seems the Guardians chose very well when they elected you their captain."

"I like to think so," Alexander said with a wry grin.

"Hmph. A bit of conceit is necessary, I suppose, for one in your position." Talanor drank the last of his ale and wiped his mouth with the back of his hand. "If you've finished eating, let's get going. I'll explain on the trail."

The men rose and walked to the cart. Talanor stored their mugs in a pack at the back of the cart before moving to the oxen. He spoke a quiet word of command and the beasts pulled against the yoke. The cart squeaked and groaned in protest as it began to roll down the rutted track. Jagar silently took his place beside his master. Leading the way, Talanor stepped out at a swift pace, the two Guardians following the cart.

The track led them through a part of the valley they had not traveled on their way to find Talanor. The path they followed when they came was steep and at times treacherous as it snaked through the snowcapped mountains. The rutted track they were on now traversed the valley in a more direct route and climbed gradually to a pass through the mountains before descending to the sheltered bay. A red sun sat low in the sky when they reached the shore.

They found Hugh perched on the weathered dock with his back resting against a piling, a fishing pole in his hands. His surprise at seeing Talanor and the wolf registered only momentarily before his face settled back into its stoic lines.

"Welcome back," he nodded to Alexander. A tug on his line called his attention, and he lifted the pole to bring in a large fish. It joined three others on a stringer hanging in the water. The glistening silver fish would serve as a tasty evening meal.

Putting his pole aside he stood and looked up at Talanor. "M'lord," he said respectfully in greeting. "It's been a long time since I brought you fish."

Talanor held out his hand to the fisherman and smiled. "Yes. Instead of fish you brought me these two," he jerked his head toward Alexander and Ian. "But, you did well. I have need of them, and I thank you for bringing them to me." He turned to include the two Guardians. "It will soon be dark. Let's try to get as much of this loaded tonight as we can." Turning back to the fisherman, he gestured to the boat. "Show us how best to stow the cargo."

The old fisherman looked at the heavily loaded cart and shook his head. "My boat can't take all that through those seas out there."

"Yes, it can," Talanor said patiently. "The trip back to Shiptown will be in calmer waters, I assure you."

Skeptical, to say the least, Hugh glanced at Alexander, who merely shrugged at the unasked question. "All right," he said at last. "I got the Captain and his man here; I suppose I can get them back again."

"Good." Talanor moved briskly to the back of the cart. "Let's get to work."

~

They finished loading the boat by lantern light. As the three men stored the last of the bundles, they smelled cooking fish. Hugh grilled his catch slowly over a smoky fire. Fruit, bread and ale from the pack Talanor had brought with him made for a tasty repast, and they ate and drank hungrily. When the last morsel of food was eaten, Talanor refilled his mug and then passed the jug around. Hugh declined and smothered a yawn behind his hand.

"It's been a long day," he said. "I'm going to find my bunk." With a nod that encompassed the men around the fire, he rose and left them.

When the old man was gone, Alexander took a swallow of ale and looked at Talanor. "It's time, Talanor," he said quietly. "You've put us off long enough."

Talanor looked up from his contemplation of the slowly dying fire. "You are persistent, aren't you," he said mildly.

Alexander saw the blue eyes flash with irritation for a moment.

"Yes. I need some answers. That's why we came to find you. I pledged my life to protect Kaenolir, but I find that I don't know how. We're confronted by something none of us understands. Some of the shadows may now have names, but that doesn't help to understand what's happening to this land."

Alexander leaned forward earnestly. "Give me some answers, Talanor Rowan. What am I fighting?"

Talanor looked at the younger man for a long, disturbing moment. "You are fighting, Alexander, evil forces come from hell to conquer Kaenolir. Whether or not you will be victorious in your fight is another matter."

Ian swore softly.

Alexander sighed. "Who are you?" He asked the question gravely. "How did you know our names before we even spoke them?"

Talanor took another sip of ale. Smiling slyly, he looked at the two men across the fire. "I am Talanor Rowan, mage of the people of Kaenolir. And I have known you both since you were born," he said, his tone matter-of-fact and direct.

Alexander and Ian looked at each other in amazement. "How could you possibly know us?" Ian asked incredulously. He ran a hand in jerky nervousness through his shock of red hair. "How?" he repeated softly as if to himself.

Talanor looked at Alexander and laughed, his laughter a deep booming sound on the soft night air.

The old bastard, Alexander thought in disgust. *He's enjoying himself.*

"I'm sorry," Talanor said at last. "It's been such a long time since I've had an audience." He had the good grace to look sheepish at Alexander's snort of exasperation. "All right," he settled himself more comfortably, the jug of ale close at hand. "In order to explain, I must tell you a story that begins five centuries ago with the War of the Brothers."

The fire burned down to glowing coals while Talanor talked, his voice taking on a dramatic tone as he told the story of Alpean pitted against his brother Maelorn. He told how the war was waged with the men of Kaenolir fighting creatures like the one Alexander and Ian killed on Shiptown's dock. He told how the Warrior Singers, men with magical gifts from the Faerie, came to the aid of Alpean, how the huge silver wolves, of which Jagar was a descendant, fought along side the men of Kaenolir. At the sound of his name, the wolf, dozing beside his master, lifted his head and looked at the mage. Talanor reached down and lovingly scratched the great beast's neck. Content, Jagar once again laid his head on his paws and closed his eyes.

"Mages," Talanor continued, "men and women who knew the ancient arts and mysteries, gave advice and tried to turn aside the power of evil that Maelorn had enlisted." Although both Alexander and Ian had heard the old stories, they listened intently to the tale Talanor wove for them. He told them how the gods laughed and played out their games while people fought and died, how the gods finally imprisoned the two brothers, side by side, in tombs of stone deep within a volcanic mountain on the island of Sinnich, and brought an end to the hostilities.

"For nearly five hundred years the land of Kaenolir flourished, its people prospering in peace and contentment. The Guardians, as you know, promised to protect and preserve the way of life established here, and your ancestors built the Wall of Rhade to keep out the remnants of Maelorn's army and to insure that no attack could come from the north without a line of defense to hinder it.

"Mighty Warrior Singers lived on the isle of Lorn and sang to keep the evil brother forever entombed. Other Singers were dispatched throughout Kaenolir, and they sang to keep the land and its people thriving. They helped with crops, with animals, with the waters of the sea, the lakes, and the rivers. And the mages continued to advise the people, helped them learn to govern themselves without a king.

"Time passed, quite quickly and easily, as time is sometimes wont to do. People forgot the legend of the brothers, forgot the hardship of war, forgot the source of evil. There no longer seemed to be a need for magic Songs, and the Singers began leaving Kaenolir, either in death or to return to the land of Faerie, until only one remains." Talanor paused and looked up into the night sky. "At least I think he still lives," he said quietly. He looked at Alexander and then Ian before continuing. "His name is Andrew Goldenhorn, and he is the last of the Warrior Singers to inhabit Lorn Isle.

"As the years passed in peace, the need for mages lessened as well. The ancient gods who caused so much sorrow were forgotten, except by a very few, their powers diminished. I am the last of my line, the last to keep the old ways, to know the old laws of man and nature, to practice the ancient arts. The last of the Singer mages still lives on the Horn of Kalora, and if you find it surprising that anyone lives there, it is her doing. Rhianna Lanee finds little to interest her in the doings of men and has always kept herself apart from them. The Golden Ones, as the Singers were called, were sent to Rhianna to learn their Songs and perfect their skills. She is very beautiful . . ."

Talanor sighed, took a deep drink of ale and refilled his mug before continuing. Neither Alexander nor Ian spoke, their minds filled with what Talanor told them.

"About seven years ago something happened to change the patterns of life in Kaenolir. Mt. Sinnarock erupted. Alexander, you were right in pinpointing that as the exact time when life as Kaenolirians knew it began to change. With that eruption, I believe Maelorn broke the fetters of stone that imprisoned him in the mountain. All the tragic events occurring in Kaenolir point to the fact that he is free, and it appears he grows stronger each day. He will continue to strengthen himself and build his army until he feels he can conquer Kaenolir and rule it as he desired to do centuries ago."

Alexander could not believe what Talanor told them. No man, no mortal man, encased in stone could break free and continue his pursuit of a crown five hundred years later.

Unless … unless …

Alexander rose to pace out into the darkness and back again. As Ian added more wood to the fire, he crouched beside Talanor. "If what you say about the War of the Brothers is truth rather than legend—"

"'Tis truth," Talanor said quietly.

"If Alpean and all his combined forces of men and Singers and wolves could not stop Maelorn, how can we expect to?" he cried.

Jagar opened his eyes at the sound of Alexander's harsh words, but Talanor laid his hand on the wolf's head and began to pet him.

"You say Maelorn grows stronger every day. One lone Singer, if he still lives, stands between us and the forces of hell. You, Talanor, and one other mage, who doesn't give a damn about Kaenolir, are all that's left to aid us." He jumped up to pace again, his green eyes bleak and filled with pain. Jagar's eyes followed the agitated man.

"How, Talanor?" he asked from the shadows at the edge of the firelight. "In the name of all the gods, how?"

"I'm not sure." Talanor pushed himself to his feet and Jagar rose to stand beside his master. "That's why I'm sending Ian back to Shiptown, and you and I are going to Lorn Isle. We must try to find Goldenhorn. He will know how strong Maelorn has grown and how much time we might have to prepare our defenses."

Alexander swore. "It's hopeless." He clenched his hands into fists and turned away to pace again. "Completely hopeless. No war has been fought in Kaenolir for five hundred years. The only weapons in the land belong to the Guardians. How can we prepare ourselves when we have nothing with which to prepare?" he raged.

"Must you ask so many questions?" Talanor shouted. "I don't have all the answers right now, but together we will find the answers. We just can't sit back and let Maelorn destroy this country."

Alexander came to stand before the old mage. He wanted desperately to hit something, to shout, to swear until the rage and fear that grew inside him were released. Talanor grasped Alexander by the shoulders and gave him a gentle shake. Blue eyes bore into green, and Alexander knew Talanor saw and understood the frustration, the fear, the sense of helplessness that filled his mind. He closed his eyes and wearily bowed his head, absently rubbing the bridge of his nose with thumb and forefinger.

He looked up at last, forcing himself to speak more calmly. "Do you read minds, too?"

"Only sometimes," Talanor smiled. He released Alexander and turned to include Ian.

"It has been a long day, as the fisherman said. There is much to do tomorrow. Let's try to get some sleep. There are blankets and your packs in the cart. Ian, may I ask you to get them for us?"

Ian looked to Alexander and at his captain's reassuring nod, he moved away into the darkness.

Talanor shifted his glance to rest again on Alexander. "The days that lie ahead will be filled with danger and death. That much I know. But that is all I can tell you. Sometimes I can see into the future. I knew you and Ian were coming to find me; I know that Ian and the fisherman will reach Shiptown safely. You and I will reach Lorn Isle, but I don't know what we'll find there. Don't ask me how I know; I can't tell you, even if I wished to. You'll have to take on faith the fact that I can 'see' things no one else can.

"I am old and have lived a long life. I suppose I am selfish, but I wish to live for a while longer. I will try to help you all I can; sometimes you will not understand what I do, nor will you always know where I go. But know this: before I die I will see Kaenolir set free of Maelorn's evil control."

Chapter Four

When the last notes of his Song drifted away on the fog-ladened air, Andrew Goldenhorn turned from the rocky tip of the promontory. The only sound now was the thunder of waves crashing against the granite projection, sending up plumes of icy spray that wet him through as he sang. He shivered as he made his way wearily down the valley toward the cottage, each step an effort, his aloneness pressing down on him. Only empty yearnings would greet him when he opened the door, for weeks earlier he had at last convinced Katrine that she and Kailie would be safer with Katrine's family in Fairtown, and he'd sent them to the mainland.

His sense of impending danger increased each time he sang the Warrior Song, but he'd stayed behind to keep the ancient promise. Every day and often at night he sent his Song ringing over the roiling waters. He prayed the music would impede the dark power, that somehow his lone voice could contain it within Mt. Sinnarock. Goldenhorn thought of his departed brothers and longed for the companionship and solace their presence had given, longed for their combined strength. For he was certain that Kaenolir had desperate need of the Singers' magical strength.

The Warrior Singers had truly been a brotherhood. While other Singers were dispersed singly or in pairs throughout Kaenolir, one hundred Warrior Singers had lived together on Lorn Isle. Each morning their combined voices had risen to hold the Darkling within the stone of Mt. Sinnarock. Tall, golden men, born of Faerie, fierce warriors as well as superb musicians, trained to sing only one Song for a lifetime, they had carried out their duties until the urge to return to their Faerie world had become too strong to resist.

Goldenhorn knew that he, too, would have followed his brothers were it not for Katrine. It was not possible to take a mortal into the mystical kingdom from which he had come, and he could not bear to leave her behind. So he had stayed on Lorn, loving her and their daughter, suppressing the need and the longing to be with his own kind.

His steps dragged as he came to the cottage. His wet clothes clung to him like a second skin, making him aware of fatigue in every muscle and bone of his body. He opened the door and stepped inside. Before finding dry clothing, he crossed the dimly lighted room to the fireplace. Kneeling, he pushed together the few coals that glowed and slowly added slivers of wood until flames licked at the kindling. When the wood began popping and snapping, he added larger pieces and swung a kettle of water over the heat. For a moment he held his cold hands out to the radiating warmth. With a sigh, he placed his palms on his thighs and pushed himself erect.

It was then that the shadows in the corner of the room near the fireplace took shape. Surprise froze Goldenhorn in place for a moment. Fatigue and cold must have dulled his perception, and he cursed himself for not sensing the lurking danger. His hand reached swiftly for the hilt of his sword, and the threatening flash of the blade momentarily stopped the advancing shadow. Goldenhorn needed no other opening. A swift step forward and his sword bit deeply into the chest of the thing that had been waiting for him. A hideous scream of pain became a whimpering gurgle of death as it fell.

A movement off to his left brought Goldenhorn around, his sword poised, dripping with the black gore of the creature he'd just killed. The room seemed suddenly to be full of dark shadows; their overpowering stench rose to fill his nostrils and he gagged. Why hadn't he detected that when he entered the cottage?

Slowly they came toward him, grunting in anticipation, four huge, shaggy creatures with clawed hands ready to slash, teeth bared to rip and tear. From tales and legends he'd studied as a young boy on the Horn of Kalora, he knew the creature he'd just killed was a Ghillie. The four that advanced on him now were Spriggans. All were creatures his ancestors fought in the War of the Brothers; all had been thought destroyed centuries ago. If he needed any more proof that Maelorn was free and readying an army to attack Kaenolir, it stood before him.

Goldenhorn moved his sword in a slow, mesmerizing circle. He lifted his head and the Warrior Song burst from his throat into the confined space. The startled creatures howled in shock and surprise and clawed at their ears to block out the powerful music. They retreated toward the door but before they could reach it, Goldenhorn moved. In a deadly dance he used his sword. A grim smile spread across Goldenhorn's face as he felt steel plunge into flesh and bone and nearly sever an ugly head from its short neck. As the creature crumpled to the floor, he whirled to dispense another. All the while he sang. He stalked the third thing and it cried in fear as it tried to flee, but it was too slow.

Only one remained, eying the Singer in hatred. No man-thing had ever attacked like this one did. With more cleverness than its fellows it slowly circled the room, effectively moving Goldenhorn away from the door. When it neared the hearth, it stooped and picked up a stout log from the wood basket. Holding the log like a club the Spriggan stepped toward Goldenhorn.

Watching and waiting for an opportunity to strike, Goldenhorn changed the pitch of his Song, and the creature cringed in agony but did not drop the log. The sword flicked out with the speed of a striking snake and opened a deep gash on the creature's arm, another across its chest, and yet another slash down its cheek and along its jaw. Squeals of pain mingled with the Song, and Goldenhorn moved in swiftly for the kill. Before the creature could lift the log in defense, it felt a fiery pain rip through its thigh. Unable to support itself on the severed muscles and tendons, it crashed to the floor, thrashing and whimpering. Goldenhorn kicked the log out of the limp hands of the beast, and as it lifted its clawed hands to ward off the blow, he plunged his sword into its heart. It jerked and spasmed and then lay still while black gore slowly pooled around it.

The Song drifted away to silence. Goldenhorn stood gasping, his body shuddering with the aftermath of battle. He wiped the back of his free hand across his forehead. Unable to bear the stench in the room, he stumbled from the cottage. Damp air cooled his heated skin and made him aware once again of his wet clothes. His chest still heaving from exertion, he leaned against the solid wall of the cottage and closed his eyes. His breathing gradually slowed, and he shivered with cold. Deep within his weary mind some sixth sense suddenly gave a warning, and his eyes flew open. A huge form loomed before him, but before he could lift his voice in Song or defend himself with his sword, the world exploded, then went black.

~

He awakened to intense pain. Every part of his body was suffused in fiery torment. His arms and legs, stretched wide, ached unbearably, but he was unable to move them to find relief. Bands of metal chained him against a hard, rough surface that cut into his flesh. His parched throat was swollen and raw, but a stricture around his neck prevented him from swallowing. Pain like a dozen resonating drums throbbed in his head and blurred his vision; shafts of it shot through his body at the slightest movement. And when his mind and body could bear no more agony, he gratefully sank into unconsciousness.

The pain was still there when he woke again, but this time there was no escape. His sight cleared and he viewed his prison. He was chained to a solid, unyielding surface of stone; its jagged edges and sharp points cut deeply into his back and shoulders. Gashes covered his arms and legs, and pain seared his lungs whenever he breathed in the hot, sulfurous air. Flickers of light danced on the edge of his vision, but it took him some time to realize that he was bound in an upright position in a small cavern. Suffocating heat unlike any summer sun or winter hearth surrounded him and seemed to invade every part of his battered body. It sapped whatever strength he might have called upon and made it impossible to think.

Where am I?

His sluggish, scattered thoughts began to coalesce, and he remembered the fight in the cottage. He'd killed four, no five, ugly brutes, but his mind refused to move beyond that point. He could not remember being brought here, could not remember being chained.

The vapors he breathed made his eyes water and his nose and throat burn. His naked body, glistening with sweat, shuddered with pain and dripped blood from many wounds. Slowly, deliberately, he forced himself to think, to block out the pain.

My Song. I must sing my Song.

But no sound came from his dry, lacerated throat when he opened his mouth. The band around his neck was too tight to allow the music to flow.

A Warrior Singer with no Song.

And as if to taunt him in his misery, his sword lay across the chamber from where he stood in chains. Its bright blade was covered with gore from the creatures Maelorn had sent to Lorn. But the blade might still have been on the isle, for he could not use it to free himself.

A warrior unable to use his sword.

The desperateness of his predicament slowly registered, and he knew where he was: He was chained in the bowels of Mt. Sinnarock, Maelorn's prisoner. His nightmare had become a reality.

With the realization that Maelorn had grown powerful enough to free himself and to begin an assault on Kaenolir came anguish and despair.

Katrine, my beloved Katrine. And my precious Kailie. What will become of you?

Tears slipped down his cheeks as he imagined the horror that would befall the people of Kaenolir. The pressure of wracking sobs grew in his chest but could not be released. The agony of his physical and mental suffering was profound; and he wept for Katrine, for Kailie, for Kaenolir, and, finally, for himself.

"So, Singer, why don't you sing?"

Andrew Goldenhorn slowly lifted his eyes. The flames that danced and flickered on the walls of his prison leaped high at the sound of the mocking voice. A dark form stepped forward into the chamber, filling his field of vision. Goldenhorn's eyes widened with the sight of what stood before him.

Maelorn the Darkling had been dark in coloring as a man. As a creature, formed by evil and hatred over long centuries, he was black, not the deep richness of ebony, but a dull, flat black.

Death, Andrew thought. *He is the color of the ashes of death.*

Everything about Maelorn was oversized. Goldenhorn was tall but Maelorn stood more than two heads taller than he. His powerful neck and shoulders supported a large head, crowned with a beaten circlet of gold set with gleaming rubies. Bulging biceps and thick thighs radiated strength. Black, red-rimmed eyes viewed Goldenhorn with malevolent cruelty. A frightful maw that had once been a mouth parted to show glistening, razor sharp predator's teeth. Goldenhorn involuntarily shuddered as Maelorn tapped his chin with long, pointed fingernails of a dusky gray hue. The only clothing he wore was a short, black leather, skirt-like garment slung low on his hips. He stood before Goldenhorn with powerful legs spread wide, clawed feet firmly planted on the hot stone floor.

"Sing me a song," the hollow voice jeered. "No? Is the band about your neck too tight? Pity." His red maw opened and laughter, harsh and loud, filled the small chamber.

"You sang so magnificently for so long, you and your brothers," he mocked. "But I grew weary of your singing." He lovingly drew his hand down his body. "As you can see." He moved closer to stand directly in front of Goldenhorn. "Look upon me, Singer, and see what I have become. In spite of your paltry Song." His power and strength seemed tangible entities as he stood there, defiance and hatred written in every line of his monstrous, once human body.

"Nothing can hinder me now that I have the last Singer imprisoned in my mountain. Nothing and no one. You will sing no more unless you sing for me. It has taken me longer to gain my strength because of you. You kept me in that tomb of stone, kept me from my destiny far too long." He ran a long, pointed nail down Goldenhorn's chest, leaving a thin trail of blood. The muscles under the nail contracted, but Goldenhorn uttered no sound.

"How does it feel to be chained to the stone, Singer? How does it feel to know you cannot speak or cry out your agony? Hmm?" His laughter again filled the chamber. With a vicious swipe, he drew the pointed nail low over Goldenhorn's belly. Turning his hand he used the nail like a spoon and followed the path of the welling wound, filling the curve of the nail with blood. With a sadistic leer at his prisoner, he licked the blood from the nail.

"Delicious." He watched with delight as the skin of Goldenhorn's abdomen quivered in reaction. Again the pointed nails came near Goldenhorn's belly but stopped short of touching him.

"Ah, Golden One, I shall find much enjoyment in your flesh before you die," he whispered hoarsely. "It pleases me to think of you chained here in this place. The stone that holds you fast once held me prisoner. Can you feel my hate still permeating it? My brother sleeps beside you, just there where the fire burns brightly in a circle." A grimace that passed for a smile creased his face. "The good brother imprisoned with the good Singer. Ah, yes, how that pleases me."

He turned to go. At the entrance of the chamber he paused and looked back. "Tell me, Singer, what do you think will become of this considerable benevolence?" He gestured to include the chained man and the stone tomb. Throwing back his head he laughed, a triumphant roar that bounced off the walls of the cavern until it filled the space with unearthly sound. When the echoes died, Maelorn left the chamber, and the circle of fire around Alpean's tomb leaped high for a moment before flickering to a low flame.

Goldenhorn cried out in silent agony and thought he heard Maelorn's maleficent laughter from deep within the mountain. Echoing screams of terror and pain followed the laughter and continued for a long time. He was not the only one imprisoned in Sinnarock and tortured for Maelorn's pleasure. Goldenhorn struggled against his chains and felt them bite into his tormented flesh.

It was useless. There was no escape.

The screams stopped at last and the silence that followed was a relief, though somehow more terrible. It was some time before another sound began to penetrate Goldenhorn's anguish. He became aware of a soft, crooning whisper that came from somewhere within the small chamber. It reached out to him offering comfort and solace. Thoughts of Katrine began to sift through his exhausted, beaten mind, and he relaxed, allowing sleep to take him to forgetfulness. Or perhaps to madness. He cared not which overcame him.

~

Panic and disorientation gripped Goldenhorn. Claws reached toward him, and he shrank back against the restraining chains. He steeled himself to feel more pain, but the creature only loosened the band about his throat. A cup of tepid, rancid gruel was pushed against his lips, and he was forced to drink. The cup was removed, and he swallowed convulsively. Another cup was brought to his lips, and this time he drank gratefully of the water it contained. He gulped greedily, but the cup was taken away all too soon.

Food and water. Maelorn must want him to live for a while longer.

The creature grunted as it fastened the band again about Goldenhorn's neck, and then it shuffled out of the chamber.

How much longer? Goldenhorn wondered. *How many more days will I be allowed to live? And why? What does Maelorn want of me?*

The soft sound he had heard before he slept came again. This time he listened carefully, trying to pinpoint the origin of the crooning. Fires sizzled about the chamber and made it difficult to hear, but the sound seemed to come from close beside him.

From the tomb?

"Alpean," he whispered. "Do you live?"

The intensity of the sound level built as if in answer to his question. Without thinking he gathered himself and mentally sang his Warrior Song. He felt its power course through his veins, felt strength returning to aching, cramped, blood spattered limbs, felt an answering pulse of power from somewhere within the chamber.

Alpean lives!

A roar of rage split the heated air, and Maelorn strode rapidly into the chamber to stand before Goldenhorn.

"You dare to sing your Song within my mountain? I shall teach you a lesson, Singer, a lesson in silence," he shrieked.

Maelorn raised his hands and the pointed nails were brought down with brute force to stab and slash at Goldenhorn's naked body. Again and again Maelorn ripped and tore at his helpless victim until his rage was spent and Goldenhorn slumped against his chains. Massive chest heaving and glistening with sweat from his exertion, Maelorn growled as he stepped back. He heard a low hiss of derision come from the tomb, and his fury boiled anew. He moved to stand at the foot of the stone bier.

"Be still, brother," he shouted. "I will have only silence from you."

He was answered by soft, mocking laughter. Maelorn uttered a terrible curse and shook his clenched fists impotently in the air. Then, unable to vent his temper in any other way, he swept aside the brief leather covering on his loins and relieved himself on Alpean's tomb. Satisfied with the degrading insult, Maelorn threw back his head and laughed. Steam rose where the urine pooled.

"How did you like your first drink in five hundred years, brother? Was it to your liking? Drink deep of it, Alpean. 'Tis all you shall ever taste."

Hitching his garment back into place, Maelorn turned and strode from the chamber. When he was gone, the fire at the foot of the tomb burned bright and hot, boiling away the mark of contempt Maelorn had left. As the flames flickered low once more, laughter came softly from the tomb before silence descended upon the chamber. Goldenhorn swam at the edge of tormented consciousness.

Help me, Alpean, he silently entreated. *I cannot endure much longer.*

Despair overwhelmed him. There was no Warrior Singer to bring the magic of the Song's power to bear on Maelorn. No one to free Alpean.

When he remembered the day he and Kailie had sung to stop the eruption of Mt. Sinnarock, his desperation knew no bounds.

Kailie could sing the Song. Faerie blood flowed in her veins. If Maelorn learned that she could sing the Warrior Song, he would find her and kill her.

Somehow she must be warned. But how? Chained in a cave deep within Mt. Sinnarock, the Warrior Song effectively stilled by the tight band around his neck, Goldenhorn knew he dared not think of Kailie nor attempt to reach her with his thoughts. Maelorn might sense what he was doing and learn of her existence. The hopelessness of his imprisonment nearly crushed him when he realized that he could do nothing, nothing to save Kailie, nothing to save Kaenolir. Nothing to save himself.

He prayed then for death. It was preferable to the pain in which he wallowed. The crooning that had come before whispered soothingly through the chamber. Goldenhorn heard it and welcomed the comfort it brought him.

After a time he slept.

Chapter Five

Dawn was only a pale promise as Alexander helped Talanor stow the last of the gear in a small sloop they were readying to sail to Lorn Isle. No one sailed the Strait of Tears anymore; the seas in the narrow strait were too wild, the current too strong. Yet Talanor calmly finished the last of his preparations, seeming no more perturbed than if they were about to embark on a pleasant morning's sail. They had worked for two days and most of two nights, closing Talanor's cottage, taking his animals to pasture in the hills, packing food and several odd shaped bundles.

Alexander heaved a roll of blankets into the boat and looked out over the quiet cove. He could hear the pounding surf, but it was too dark to see the white-capped waves. He thought of Ian and the fisherman, Hugh, and wondered how they fared. Talanor said they would find calm waters for their journey back to Shiptown.

"I just hope he knows what he's talking about," Alexander muttered under his breath.

His thoughts were interrupted by a low hum, but he paid little attention to the sound as he lashed the last of the gear snugly into place. The humming persisted and became an intricately phrased incantation. Turning his head he found Talanor, standing knee-deep in the water, head uplifted to the sky, eyes closed, arms extended out over the water. Alexander watched in amazement as dark skies brightened, and the waters beyond the cove settled into a calmer rhythm.

The impetration ended and Talanor turned to find Alexander staring at him. When Alexander opened his mouth to speak, Talanor raised a silencing finger, strode from the water and made for the boat. Alexander's mouth snapped shut, his question unasked and unanswered. Talanor's words echoed in his mind.

"Sometimes you will not understand what I do."

What an understatement, Alexander thought, a wry half-smile shaping his mouth for a fleeting moment.

Jagar rose from the rough planks of the dock, where he had watched the men load the boat, to greet his master. Talanor leaned over the magnificent head, roughly rubbing the thick fur of Jagar's neck.

"Ah, old friend, I must leave you behind for awhile." The silver-coated wolf nuzzled Talanor's arm and whined.

"Yes," Talanor murmured. "I will call you when I need you. Stay now and protect the island." With a final pat, Talanor turned away and stepped into the boat.

Alexander untied the line securing the craft before stepping into the bobbing vessel. When he glanced back over his shoulder, Jagar stood at the end of the dock, watching them go with bright eyes and wagging tail. Turning his back on Talanor and the wolf, Alexander settled himself against the packs. He refused to think about the treacherous seas and winds that lay ahead. He hadn't slept more than four hours in the last two days and he was exhausted.

"Let him sail the damn boat wherever he wants," he muttered to himself. Perversely, he closed his eyes and sank immediately into a deep sleep.

~

"Alexander." Talanor's booming voice brought the Guardian captain to his feet with a jerk. His hand automatically reached for his sword, and he spun around to face a surprised Talanor.

"Do you always wake up ready to do battle?" Talanor grumbled.

"Sorry," Alexander murmured as he sheathed his sword. He ran his hand through his hair and looked around him. "Where are we?"

Talanor grunted, then gestured ahead to a bank of fog lying low over the water. "That's Lorn Isle. Two nautical marks beyond it lies Sinnich."

"I do know my geography," Alexander snapped, grouchy from the rude awakening and groggy with sleep.

Talanor snorted impatiently at Alexander's remark, but he did not speak as he carefully steered the boat through the fog. Once or twice Alexander thought he heard the low strains of the chant Talanor had sung earlier, but he did not look back at the man at the tiller.

Fog reached out with wet, clammy tendrils to ensnare them. Now and again Alexander heard crashing waves and the whine of the wind somewhere off in the distance. He felt the roll of the boat beneath him and wondered at the powers Talanor possessed, powers that evoked obedience from sea and wind.

"There," Talanor called to Alexander. "We're coming up on the west side of the island. There's a small dock that the Singers used farther to the south— at least there used to be. We'll make for that."

They felt their way silently through the gray shroud. "Bring down the sail," Talanor called to Alexander. "We're nearing the dock."

Alexander swiftly did as Talanor commanded, but he wondered how the man knew where they were. Within a few moments the boat nudged shadowy pilings of an old dock. He jumped out to secure the line Talanor tossed to him. Uneasy with his surroundings, he waited for Talanor to join him.

"What now?" he asked the big man quietly. For the first time he noticed that Talanor carried a long staff, worn smooth by his hands. Talanor gestured with his free hand for Alexander to follow and turned to lead the way.

"How can you see in this stuff?" Alexander asked as he stumbled over a loose board at the end of the dock. The mage gave him a sharp-eyed glance that spoke of impatience, but he did not slow his pace. The Guardian sighed, irritated with himself for asking yet another question. Since meeting Talanor he often felt like a small boy who viewed the world through childish eyes and understood only a little of what he saw.

The two men trudged along the shore for some time until they came to a jumble of rocks. Massive boulders, many with sharp, blackened edges, lay scattered about on the sand, some singly, others in piles. It looked, Alexander thought, like someone, like some giant of legend, had picked up the stones from one spot and, in a fit of temper, tossed them down in another. Shaking his head at the fanciful way of his thoughts, he turned to find Talanor staring at the barrier in utter silence. His piercing eyes seemed to bore into the stones, demanding what, Alexander could only guess. Finally Talanor shook himself and looked at Alexander. He saw the unspoken question mirrored in the Guardian's eyes.

"This was the promontory from which the Singers sang their Song. We are on the northern point of the island with Sinnich just over there." He gestured straight ahead with his staff.

"Was?"

"Yes. It jutted out into the sea for some distance."

Alexander stared at the rocks, then looked off into the distance toward the island that lay so near and shook his head in disbelief at the path his thoughts took. At last he looked at Talanor.

"Baskers," he whispered. "Is he strong enough to do that?"

"Yes," the mage responded and then turned abruptly away. "Come, we must go to the valley where Goldenhorn lived. He has not been here for several days." Leading the way again, he strode with sure steps down a worn path into the valley.

The fog lifted somewhat as they moved farther from the sea, and trees and shrubs that grew along the path began to take on distinct shapes and a little color. Alexander heard the splash of a stream close by as it meandered on its way. Once the screech of an eagle, high and far away, intruded on their otherwise silent trek. They walked for some time before a cluster of stone buildings came in sight, and Talanor slowed his steps and waited for Alexander to come abreast. Both men stopped simultaneously, each with different perceptions of the scene they viewed.

Talanor breathed deeply, his eyes closed. He smelled the stench of death and discerned the remnants of great power. He knew they would not find Andrew Goldenhorn in the cottage, nor was he anywhere on this island. He opened his eyes and looked again at the deserted buildings. The Singers had always kept horses, sheep and goats, but there was no evidence of any animals. The doors to the sheds stood open; the gate to a fenced enclosure hung drunkenly on one hinge.

Alexander, too, sensed that death walked here. His breathing came raggedly as he relived the scene on the dock at Shiptown. The same feeling of horror and impending doom that had filled him then coursed through his veins now. His soldier's eyes quickly took in the smokeless chimney of the cottage, the silent, empty buildings. What had been a well-kept vegetable garden near a side door of the cottage was trampled, plants and clumps of earth pulled up and tossed about. A wall built to keep out small foraging animals was pushed over in several places. The shattered front door and broken windows of the cottage spoke of violence and anger. A torn yellow curtain hung partially out a broken pane and fluttered now and then in a passing breeze. It made Alexander think of a bird with a broken wing, flopping about helplessly. He knew they would find nothing alive in the cottage.

"Come," Talanor said. "I must see what's inside."

Alexander walked silently beside the mage, sword drawn, alert for any danger. Wind suddenly kicked up dust in the yard and somewhere a shutter or door banged loudly. He jerked toward the sound before realizing what it was. Swearing softly he continued on toward the cottage.

Both men stopped as they reached the doorway. The heavy oak panel lay smashed and broken, like so much kindling, off to the side of the path among a patch of wilted, crushed flowers. Talanor reached out with sensitive fingers and touched the wall near the doorway. Dried blood colored the stone and his heart cried out when his spirit touched that of the Goldenhorn's.

"What is it?" Alexander asked as he perceived Talanor's distress. He looked to see what the mage touched and saw the blood.

"Is it Goldenhorn's?"

"Yes," Talanor whispered. He closed his eyes and muttered something Alexander did not catch. "But he is not dead. I can still feel his life force beating."

"Is he somewhere on the island?"

"No," Talanor shook his head. "We'll not find him on Lorn Isle." He stepped into the dim and shadowy great room of the cottage and viewed the carnage. A broken chair lay in the way, and Alexander stooped to move it aside and saw a puddle of the black gore he recognized as the blood of the creatures Talanor called Spriggans. His eyes adjusted to the dim light, and he saw and, at the same instant, smelled the pungent odor of several dead, scraggly-haired creatures lying on the floor amongst the broken furniture and shards of glass.

Goldenhorn had fought an astounding battle here, but Talanor had found his blood outside the cottage. He must have been taken as he stepped through the door. The stench of putrefaction was overpowering, and Alexander's stomach rolled in protest as he viewed the grisly scene. Forcing himself to move into the room, he found a lamp near an overturned table. He lit it and lifting it before him he felt a prickle of horror slide down his spine as he saw clearly what lay in the room.

One dead thing lay crumpled in the corner near the fireplace. Alexander guessed it had fallen first. Two others, similar in appearance but smaller than the first, lay close together. He recognized them as Spriggans. Goldenhorn must have dispatched them quickly before the other two had a chance to attack. One body lay close to the doorway where they'd just missed tripping over it when they entered the cottage. The last body lay at the hearth, a club-like piece of firewood not far from its outstretched claws. Had it tried to use the log as a weapon? Against a swordsman like the Goldenhorn, the creature hadn't had a chance.

Five. One man killed five creatures. Talanor said the Singers were excellent swordsmen. Alexander wished he had a whole army of Golden Ones. As sure as night became day, he knew Kaenolir would have need of such an army. Alexander walked past the brute near the hearth and moved down the hall that led to the kitchen and bedchambers of the snug cottage. He checked the kitchen first and found cupboard doors gaping open, the contents of shelves dumped on the floor. The table was overturned and several chairs lay broken. Whatever food might have been stored here had been taken or fouled.

Down the hall the two sleeping room doors stood open, but both rooms were untouched by Goldenhorn's attackers, with shutters still tightly closed, beds neatly made. In the room Goldenhorn shared with his wife, no sign of her remained. The light from the lamp Alexander carried showed no pretty bottles, no brushes, no sewing basket she might have used. When Alexander opened the door of the large cupboard that stood against one wall, he found only Goldenhorn's clothing.

In the next chamber, there was only furniture. A small cupboard stood empty, a book stuffed back in a corner as if put there but forgotten by its reader. The neat blue quilt covering the bed gave no indication that a female lived in this room, but Alexander sensed that this was the room of a young woman. He turned as Talanor entered.

"Did the Goldenhorn have a child?" he asked.

"Yes. A daughter. She would be about nineteen or twenty now, I think. Pretty little thing, last time I saw her."

Talanor stopped talking and gave Alexander a quizzical look. "Why do you ask?"

Alexander shrugged. "Two bedrooms, the larger one probably Goldenhorn and his wife's, the other smaller one perhaps for a child. However, only the Goldenhorn's belongings are here. I don't think either woman has been here in some time."

Talanor looked about him with curious eyes. "Andrew must have taken them to the mainland. Perhaps he took them to Landsend for safety." He walked about the room, gently touching the quilt on the bed, the book Alexander had found in the cupboard. He stepped to the window and stood before the locked shutters, his head cocked to one side as if listening to a voice only he could hear. He murmured something too softly for Alexander to understand. At last he turned away from the window. "We've seen enough here. It will soon be dark and I don't want to spend the night in this cottage. The boat, I think, will be safer."

Alexander followed the mage out of the bedchamber and back to the great room. At the front door, he paused a moment to look back over his shoulder before blowing out the lamp and setting it on the floor. With long strides, both men walked rapidly away from the death-filled cottage. They skirted the blasted stone of the promontory and were well on their way down the beach before darkness overtook them. Dense fog made the going treacherous, but Talanor did not slow down until they reached the sloop.

"We'll eat. Then we should try to get some rest. At first light we'll set sail for Landsend. If Goldenhorn sent his family to the mainland, they would logically have stopped there. Perhaps someone will remember seeing them." Talanor rummaged in the bag of food to find bread and cheese, some dried fish and apples, and a jug of ale.

Both men ate in silence, each alone with his thoughts. Night settled heavily around them, the mists sometimes obscuring one man from the other though they sat side by side.

Alexander finished his ale while Talanor placed the remainder of the food back in the pack. He took two heavy wool blankets from another bundle and handed one to Alexander.

"Sleep for awhile. We can't sail until it begins to get light," the mage said quietly.

"No, you sleep. I slept on the way here. One of us should be on guard while the other sleeps. Besides," he said reaching for the blanket and placing it around his shoulders, "after what I saw today, I couldn't sleep anyway."

"All right," Talanor replied. "But wake me after a few hours so you can get some rest, too." With that he covered himself with one of the blankets and lay back, using a pack for a pillow. His even breathing soon indicated he slept.

Making himself as comfortable as possible, Alexander listened to the sounds of the night. His ears strained to hear anything that might warn of approaching danger, but he heard only the gentle slapping of water against the sloop and the pilings of the dock. Once Talanor muttered in his sleep and turned over.

The scenes in the cottage slipped through Alexander's restless mind and nagged at him. Not the Spriggans and the Ghillie sprawled in death, but the destruction, both in the cottage and outside, bothered him. Had Goldenhorn surprised the creatures when he returned from the promontory, or had they been waiting for him? Who or what had ransacked the kitchen and trampled the garden, knocked down the fences? More of the beasts? There were no animals in any of the sheds or pens. He supposed they could have been frightened enough by the intruders to run away. Why then did he feel that the whole island could be searched, but no animals would be found?

Talanor said the Goldenhorn was not on the island but that he still lived. Had he been taken captive? For what purpose was he being held? Where?

The answer crept slowly into Alexander's consciousness though he tried to push it away: The Singer had been taken to Sinnich. He was sure of it.

He swore softly. If Sinnich was no longer Maelorn's prison but his stronghold, could the Goldenhorn be rescued? Could his Song still keep Maelorn on the island, or had the Darkling grown too strong for even Faerie magic?

How had the promontory been destroyed? An earthquake perhaps? If that were the cause, why was only the promontory affected? Had some force purposely shattered it? Why? The destruction of the rocky point, like the destruction of Goldenhorn's home, seemed to have been done in an outburst of rage. Was that possible?

Alexander scrubbed his face with his hands. The questions whirled around in his head, and the answers that were beginning to form brought little comfort.

Maelorn.

Had Maelorn destroyed the rib of stone in a fit of pique? Had he come to the island himself to see to the capture of the Goldenhorn, to the silencing of his Song? Were the Song and the Singer such thorns in Maelorn's side that the Golden One must be silenced, even if it meant that Maelorn had to leave his island stronghold?

And what of the Warrior Song? Was it powerful enough to stop Maelorn? If the Goldenhorn could be freed and brought to the mainland, would his Song be enough to save the people of Kaenolir? Alexander thought not. He feared that Maelorn was now able to shrug off the Song's magical power. But there was something about the Song or about the Singer that nagged at Alexander, something he did not see or did not understand.

He rose noiselessly to prowl the confined space of the deck of the sloop. Other questions flooded his mind. Why did Talanor want to go to Landsend? To learn if anyone knew of the whereabouts of Goldenhorn's wife and daughter, he said. Why did he want to see them? They could not know where

Goldenhorn had been taken or by whom; it was obvious they had not lived in the cottage for some time. What might they know that would be helpful to Talanor?

Alexander turned this new idea over in his mind. By the gods, why hadn't he thought of it before? Not how might they be helpful, but how might she be helpful. The daughter, Goldenhorn's daughter was part Faerie! Did she know the Song? Could she sing it with the same efficacy and force her father had?

Stunned by this observation, Alexander came to a halt near the feet of the sleeping mage.

That's why we're going to Landsend, he thought, *to find the daughter.*

On the heels of this observation came a sense of near panic. If Maelorn knew about the daughter, she would be in terrible danger. They must find her before Maelorn did, find her and protect her.

Alexander stared so intently at Talanor, so lost in his disturbing thoughts, that he did not realize the mage was awake and watching him with knowing eyes. After a long moment, the big man spoke softly.

"So, my young friend, you have figured it out without having to ask me any of your infernal questions." He rolled over to come to his feet. He stepped to face Alexander and placing his hands on the Guardian's shoulders, he gave him a slight shake.

Alexander stared into Talanor's eyes. "She's in harm's way, isn't she?" he asked at last. "Goldenhorn's daughter. She's the reason we're going to Landsend."

"Yes."

"Yes, she's in danger or yes, she's the reason we're going to Landsend?"

"Yes to both," Talanor said quietly.

Alexander sighed wearily, and, in a motion that had long been habit, lifted his hand to rub the bridge of his nose with thumb and forefinger. "May the gods protect her," he whispered. "May the gods protect all of us."

"I think you should try to get some sleep now," Talanor said. "It will be light soon." He nudged the shoulder he still held. "Go. Sleep."

Alexander's shoulders slumped as the mage's hands fell away, and he nodded his head. "Sleep," he murmured. "Will I ever truly sleep again?" he wondered aloud, his face a mask of pain and distress. Without another word he moved to trade places with Talanor and lay against the bundles, pulling the pack Talanor had used for a pillow into a more comfortable position. He sighed gustily, closed his eyes, and within minutes lay in uneasy sleep, his thoughts still in turmoil, his mind filled with the horrors he had seen and would in all likelihood see again, over and over until Kaenolir lay in ashes.

~

Talanor's hand on his shoulder awakened Alexander a short while later. "It's getting light," the mage said softly. "Help me get under way."

Alexander sat up, breathing deeply of the damp air to clear the cobwebs of sleep. He came to his feet and moved quickly to untie the line securing the boat to the dock. The fog was very thick, a lighter gray now as the sun rose, but claustrophobic and cloying.

"I hate this stuff," he muttered. "Can't see anything, don't know where you're going. Don't know where you are. Hate it."

"Just be glad for the protection it offers us," Talanor said quietly. "If we can't see, it also means we can't be seen."

Alexander shook his head. "I still prefer the light."

Talanor smiled briefly as he maneuvered the sloop away from Lorn's dock. "Get ready to raise the sail when I tell you."

As they slipped noiselessly through the waters of the small cove and headed for the open sea, a brisk wind filled the sail and sent the boat swiftly toward Landsend. Again and again, Alexander heard Talanor's voice, singing the slow, strange chant while the Strait of Tears rose and fell in heaving waves. Somewhere above them the wind howled, but its force did not touch them, only filled the sail and sent them through the fog. Its eerie grayness rode the running waves and obscured the sky, making it seem to Alexander that they did not move, only stayed in one gray place, suspended in time, adrift in a small boat and lost to the rest of the world.

Alexander lost track of time as Talanor's steady hand guided their craft along a route only he knew. Lulled by the hypnotizing movement of the boat, he dozed from time to time. After what seemed like hours, a gull's sharp cry alerted him to approaching land.

"Are we near Landsend?" he called to Talanor.

"Yes, not much farther now."

Inexplicably, they broke into a patch of warm sunlight for a moment. Directly in front of them lay another bank of fog, marking the coast of Kaenolir but hiding the seaport of Landsend from their view. Alexander strained to see and hear anything that would indicate they were close to the docks of the town.

They were soon back in the mists, making their way more cautiously now. The sail flapped once and then hung limply, the wind dying as if strangled.

"Take it down." Talanor nodded toward the useless canvas. "We've no need for it now."

Alexander moved to the ropes, uneasy with their situation. He looked at Talanor, but the mage seemed unconcerned, his hand steady on the helm as the tide carried them. However, close by within easy reach lay his heavy staff. Alexander turned his attention back to the sail and quickly brought it down.

They drifted for several minutes through the pressing silence. Alexander moved to take up a position beside Talanor, his hand ready on the hilt of his sword. Suddenly out of the grayness loomed a large, dark shape, and Talanor swung the helm hard to the right to avoid it. Both men were breathing heavily by the time they realized that the shape was a ship at anchor in the harbor of Landsend.

Alexander swore harshly. "Baskers, what's that doing there? No lights, no horn, nothing."

"Perhaps they weren't expecting visitors." Talanor's dry comments brought another spate of profanity from Alexander.

They drifted on, both men alert now for any other ships that might be anchored in their path.

"We should be close to shore," Alexander murmured.

"Yes. Look there." Talanor pointed a long finger.

Alexander peered intently in the direction Talanor indicated until he could make out the wharf and some buildings, the buildings rising phantom-like out of the fog. As the current carried them still closer to shore, they saw lights gleaming dully here and there, a boat or two bobbing on the tide. They heard voices call and then fall silent. A gull flew by, its raucous cry piercing the gloom.

Talanor brought them alongside a pier, and Alexander jumped out to tie the sloop to a piling. He offered Talanor a hand as he stepped out, carrying his staff.

"I suggest we head for the Guardians' garrison. Sergeant Graham is in command here, and he knows almost everything that goes on in Landsend and the surrounding area."

Alexander's suggestion was met by Talanor's nod. "Lead on," he said simply.

Alexander had not been in Landsend for several months, but even the fog could not hid the deterioration, the sense of desertion and decay, that greeted them as they made their way along the wharf—empty buildings, nearly empty mooring spaces, no people working the docks. The scene was all too reminiscent of Shiptown. Both had been busy seaports, but now they rotted where they stood, their businesses dead or dying, many of their people gone. Wisps of fog parted as Alexander led Talanor toward the welcoming warmth of a large building constructed of heavy timbers, its windows glowing with light. They mounted the steps and crossed the porch. Alexander paused only momentarily before pushing open a stout door and entering a brightly lighted room. A startled soldier jumped up, his mouth agape as he recognized his commander.

"Captain." He threw Alexander a stiff, jerky salute, and then came forward around the table at which he'd been working.

"We weren't expecting you." His eyes slid over Alexander and rested on Talanor. Both men watched the surprise register on the young man's face as his eyes lifted to Talanor's imposing height; his Adam's apple bobbed as he swallowed noisily.

"McNeil, isn't it?" Alexander asked.

"Yes, sir, James McNeil."

"Well, McNeil, would you see if you could find us something to eat? But first, tell Sergeant Graham that we're here and that I want to see him."

"Yes, sir. If you'll follow me, I'll take you to Sergeant Graham. He's still in his office." The young soldier turned briskly to lead Alexander and Talanor down the hall. He paused at the first door and knocked twice before entering.

Henry Graham looked up at the interruption; his eyes passed beyond McNeil to take in Alexander and the big man who accompanied him. Captain Lamond was a frequent visitor to the Landsend garrison, but the tall, white-haired man with the long beard and piercing eyes that seemed to bore right through him was a stranger.

"Captain Lamond," Sergeant Graham rose to grasp Alexander's extended hand. "I just finished a report for you and was preparing to send it by courier. I guess I won't need the courier now." He smiled briefly and motioned the two men to chairs before returning to his. "That will be all, McNeil," he nodded as the soldier saluted and left the room, closing the door behind him.

"Captain, what brings you to Landsend?" he asked. "And whom have you brought with you?" He turned his gaze to Talanor and wondered what time period the man had stepped from. He had never seen him before, but he looked as if he could take care of himself, big as he was. That staff he carried could crack a few skulls. He would have need of it if he stayed long in Landsend.

"We need some information, Graham," Alexander began. "And this is Talanor Rowan." He gestured toward his companion. "We've just come from Lorn Isle and—"

Before Alexander could finish speaking, Graham leaned forward in his chair, an incredulous expression on his face. "You've just come from where? How did you get there? Baskers, how did you get here? No one has sailed the Strait in months. How—"

Alexander held up his hand to silence the questions. "I'll explain everything shortly, but right now I need some information. Tell me, have you seen or heard from Andrew Goldenhorn within the last few days?"

"Goldenhorn? The Singer who lives on Lorn?" Graham looked from Alexander to Talanor. "No. Why do you—"

Talanor moved impatiently in his chair and Graham halted mid-question. He cleared his throat. "No," he said again. "I've neither seen him nor heard from him in several months. The last time I saw him was about six or eight months ago, I believe, when he brought his wife and daughter to Landsend."

Talanor leaned forward. "He brought his wife and daughter here? Are they still here?" his deep voice rumbled.

"No sir. They stayed only until a patrol went to Three Rivers. My men put them on a riverboat that took them down the Skara. They were going overland to Fairtown."

"To Fairtown, you say?" Talanor asked.

Graham nodded. "That's where the family of Goldenhorn's wife lives. He felt it would be safer there. Katrine, the Singer's wife, didn't want to go, but he finally convinced her that he couldn't protect them on Lorn. Kailie didn't want to leave her father either." Something about the way Sergeant Graham's voice softened made Alexander look at him sharply. Graham's gaze was fixed on something beyond Alexander's head, but when he realized his captain was staring at him, he brought himself swiftly back to the matter at hand.

"Sorry, sir," he apologized. He glanced at Talanor and shrugged.

Talanor grunted. "As far as you know, Katrine and Kailie reached Fairtown safely. Is that so?"

"Yes, sir." Something about the big man's piercing blue eyes made him feel very uncomfortable.

"And Goldenhorn returned to Lorn when his family left with your patrol?"

"Yes. He brought them here, to the garrison, and asked me to see to their welfare and left soon after saying goodbye to them. He told me he would hold me personally responsible if they did not reach Fairtown safely." Again, Sergeant Graham shrugged. He looked at his captain. "I took him at his word. It looked as if he knew how to use the sword he wore," he said quietly.

Alexander smiled grimly, remembering what they had found in Goldenhorn's cottage. "You did well to follow his directive, Sergeant." He rose from his chair. "I asked McNeil to see to food for us. After we've eaten I'll fill you in on some details, and then I want your report." He turned to leave the room.

"Sir," Graham's voice stopped him at the door. "You may want to read the report before you eat." At Alexander's arched eyebrow he continued. "It's very important. And very … disturbing," he said quietly. "I sent two patrols into The Dlarmids last week. Only one of them came back. What my men saw is …" He shook his head and sighed deeply, "… unbelievable."

Talanor rose from his chair, his staff firmly gripped in both hands. "What did they see, Sergeant?"

"An army, sir, but not an army of men."

Talanor turned to Alexander. "So," he said gravely. "It begins."

Chapter Six

Alexander read Sergeant Graham's report while he ate, but the meal grew cold and forgotten long before he finished the account of what the patrol saw in The Dlarmids.

The Guardians had proceeded cautiously into the mountains. Clouds concealed the snow-topped peaks, and the cold and snow at the lower elevations they traveled made their trek uncomfortable and treacherous. As the fourth day of the patrol neared its end, two scouts were sent ahead to find a suitable campsite. They stumbled onto an army encamped in a hidden canyon. One of the soldiers stayed to observe the activities below him while the other Guardian hurried back to alert the rest of the patrol.

What they saw was unreal. The light was poor and the men were hidden high in the cliffs surrounding the canyon, but they were able to determine that the army consisted of large, shaggy creatures with long arms and heavy bodies. Some of the creatures were larger than others, but all exhibited tremendous strength as they went about setting up what seemed to be a permanent encampment.

The Guardians observed the horde until nightfall. They made themselves as comfortable as possible in their cold and icy hiding place and chewed on dry jerky while continuing their dangerous vigil.

The next day saw more creatures gather in the steep-walled canyon. Wagonloads of supplies and armaments were brought to the camp, and some of the creatures were seen practicing with war axes and spears. The report noted that the creatures were clumsy and unused to handling weapons; and dark men, clothed all in black robes, who appeared to be training them, used whips and clubs to force the beasts to do as they commanded.

Fearing they might be discovered if they stayed where they were much longer, the patrol moved out early in the afternoon. They did not stop to rest or eat until they reached the garrison and reported to Sergeant Graham.

When Alexander finished reading the grim report, he wordlessly handed it to Talanor. "You said you sent two patrols, Graham." At the other's nod, Alexander continued. "Did the second find any signs of the first?"

"No. Nothing."

"How long has it been since anyone has been able to reach the iron mines?"

Sergeant Graham thought a moment. "I'd have to check back through my reports to give you an exact time period, but offhand I'd say at least ten months. Perhaps a year. Do you want me to check for certain?"

"No, I don't think that's necessary. The amount of ore brought out has been steadily decreasing for the last few years. Whatever stockpile there may be will be minimal, I would guess. Am I correct in that assumption?"

"I'm afraid so, sir. Very little steel has been produced here in the last three years." He gave Alexander and then Talanor a long, intense look. "The steel has been used for farm implements, tools, things like that." He paused. "No weapons were made that I'm aware of."

"And what of the miners and their families?" Alexander asked quietly

"No word, Captain, and no sign of them. It's as if the earth opened up and swallowed them all." Graham wearily shook his head.

Alexander sighed and pushed to his feet. He moved to a window of the room that served as a lounging area for Guardians not on duty. A fireplace, in which a fire burned cheerfully, filled one wall, and two large rather threadbare easy chairs had been arranged before it. A full to overflowing bookcase and a table completed the furnishings. It was a simple but pleasant room, but he took little comfort from it.

He stood motionless for a long time, staring unseeingly into the dark night, the images of the room reflected in the pane of glass, and contemplated what few choices he had. At last he turned back to the two silent men.

"Sergeant, I want two men from that second patrol to take me into The Dlarmids so I can assess for myself what's happening there. I want you to get the townspeople packed up as quickly as you can—tell them they can take only bare essentials and all the food they have—and move them to Riversend or Fairtown. Every able-bodied man is to report to the Guardians' Fort as soon as he settles his family. Your men will accompany the people as far down the Skara as the Fort. Take all the weapons and supplies you can carry.

We'll need everything you have. You'll join the Fort garrison under my command.

"Send couriers to Riversend and Fairtown alerting the garrisons and the people of those towns that the Landsend evacuees are coming. I'll send orders that the garrisons are to go on full alert and be prepared to move out to the Fort whenever needed. In the meantime, they are responsible for helping the Landsend people get settled. Any questions?"

"No, sir. I'll get my men working on evacuating Landsend immediately. There aren't many people left, so it should go quickly. There's still a river ferry that travels the Skara River. It will take perhaps a day or so to reach it, but then we can load everyone onboard and take the ferry down river." Graham rose from his chair and left to carry out Alexander's orders.

"Talanor?" Alexander turned to the mage.

"I must go to Fairtown to find Kailie Fairchild, Alexander. She may be able to help us. If I can persuade her to accompany me, I will take her to Rhianna Lanee on the Horn of Kalora."

"Kailie is very young, Talanor. You said the Singers trained for many years before they were ready to sing their Songs. How can one who is hardly more than a child help us?"

Talanor picked up his staff and ran his hands up and down the smooth surface of the worn wood before giving Alexander an answer. "I'm not sure that she can help Kaenolir, Alexander, but Rhianna will be able to determine what powers or talents, if any, Kailie possesses. We haven't many alternatives and time is short. I must try to get Kailie to Rhianna as soon as possible."

"When will you leave for Fairtown?"

"At first light. I'll sail down the coast as far as Riversend and then go overland to Fairtown. If I'm successful in finding Kailie and Rhianna feels she can help, I'll bring her to the Fort."

"All right. May I expect to see you at the Fort in any event?"

"Yes, I will be there to offer any help that I can."

Alexander nodded and looked into the old mage's eyes. "Thank you. I will need your guidance and advice," he said quietly. He held out his hand and grasped the strong brown one offered in return. "Go with the gods, Talanor."

"And you, Alexander Lamond." He murmured something else and then touched the younger man's forehead with his fingertips. He reached into the pouch he wore on the belt at his waist and extracted a small silver knife in a plain leather sheath. He held it out to Alexander. "Take it. You will undoubtedly have need of it."

Alexander looked down at the knife in the palm of Talanor's hand. With a question lurking in his eyes he reached out to take it. It was warm to his touch. He pulled the knife from the sheath and nearly dropped it in surprise when he felt it pulse in his fingers. He stared at it as the light from the fire shimmered and flickered along the silver blade. When he looked up, Talanor smiled. "It will warn you of danger and it will protect you when the time comes. Do not hesitate to use it." Talanor looked at Alexander intently for a moment.

What does he see when he looks at me that way? Alexander wondered.

At last the big man nodded and turned away to walk rapidly from the room.

Alexander caressed the small blade with the thumb of his left hand, sheathed it and tucked it inside his tunic, next to his skin, where it lay in warm comfort. Briefly he wondered if the craftsman who forged it lived in the shadowy mists of a land where mortals did not walk. The thought appealed to him and he smiled as he left the room.

~

Dense fog still shrouded Landsend in the light of a bleak dawn. Four men parted at the gate of the Guardian garrison, three of them moving out on horseback while the fourth made his way along the silent waterfront to a small sloop.

Alexander and two Guardians, Angus and Edward Mackay, brothers and crusty veterans of the service, rode silently through the city, the sound of their passing muffled in the fog, and into the foothills of The Dlarmids. They soon began to feel the heat from the sun, and for a short time it was a relief to have left behind the cold, depressing fog. By late afternoon they reached the snow line and left their horses to fend for themselves while the men hefted packs of blankets and food and made their way into the mountains.

Afternoon of the third day found them near the canyon Angus and Edward had discovered on the earlier patrol. The men moved with extreme caution now, for they did not know how far the dark army's patrols might roam.

"Captain," Angus Mackay called softly. "It's not much further. Do you want to find a place to rest for the night or shall we move on?"

Alexander looked around, his breath coming rapidly in clouds of vapor. They were at the base of a steep incline that rose above them in a jumble of rocks and snow.

"Can we see the canyon from the top of this ridge?"

"Yes, sir. That's where we spotted them the first time," Edward replied. "The canyon is just on the other side of the ridge."

"We've still enough light to see by. Let's get up there and find a spot where we can look down into the canyon."

Angus nodded and turned to lead the way up the steep ridge. They climbed steadily but with care. They had no way of knowing who or what might be just ahead, and a dislodged stone or the sound of a voice could alert a creature on watch to their approach.

When they gained the top of the ridge, they left their packs in a protected lee and moved stealthily among the rocks to a vantage point that gave them a view of the entire canyon. What Alexander saw as he peered down into the wide slash surrounded by mountains was enough to halt the breath in his lungs. He expelled it in whispered profanity.

Below the Guardians, huge fires lit the darkening gorge. The daylight was rapidly fading, but from what Alexander could make out, the entire floor of the canyon was filled with fires and shaggy creatures. He watched for some time, and was struck by the chaotic confusion that seemed to pervade the encampment. The creatures moved about aimlessly, halting now and then by a fire to get warm before moving on. An almost deafening cacophony of grunts and growls carried on the cold night air to the men hiding in the rocks.

Alexander moved back and motioned to Angus. "Are there more of them now than when you were here a week ago?" he whispered.

"Yes. I estimated about five hundred of the beasts were camped here when we found the place. Now I would say there are several thousand."

Alexander nodded. "That's what I would say."

Edward silently joined them. "Noisy bastards, aren't they?" he murmured. "What do you suppose they're waiting for?"

Angus grunted. "Probably the chief bastard. What do you think Captain?"

Alexander chewed on his bottom lip. "For an army, they appear to be pretty disorderly." He nodded to Edward. "I think you're right when you say they're waiting." The fact that he had a good idea for whom they waited made the situation all the more dangerous and frightening.

"I'm going to watch for awhile longer. You two go back and bring our packs up here. Then I want both of you to eat and get some sleep, if you can.

I'll waken one of you to take the next watch. I want two sleeping and one watching during the rest of the night."

The Mackays moved silently into the darkness while Alexander again took up a position among the rocks to observe the camp. Down below fires burned brightly, but he was unable to see little more than shadows moving in and out of the circles of light. The noise abated somewhat as the creatures bedded down. He heard the quiet sounds the Guardians made as they returned with the packs.

"Captain, I thought you might want a blanket and something to eat while you watch." Edward handed the items to Alexander and he took them gratefully. With the darkness had come a deeper cold, and it would be a long night without the warmth of a fire to ward off the chill.

Alexander nodded his thanks and turned back to the scene below him. Several hours passed with little activity in the camp, and when he felt his eyes grow heavy, he moved from his cramped position to awaken one of the Mackays. When Angus immediately answered his light touch, Alexander changed places with him and fell asleep almost before Angus had positioned himself to watch.

Dawn found all three Guardians observing the camp. The sound level rose again, but there was an edge of excitement to the noise. Movement near the narrow open end of the canyon caught the men's attention. About a hundred black-robed men, at least from the Guardians' observation point they appeared to be men, strode forward into the massed Spriggans and Ghillies. Some of the robed figures carried what looked like clubs; others carried coils of rope or whips. They all wore swords. The beasts cowered away from the path the dark men took. When the men reached the center of the camp, a large circle was formed, the perimeter created by shuffling creatures. Two of the robed figures entered the circle, and then two of the shaggy creatures were shoved into the open space.

"Baskers," Angus whispered. "What are they doing?"

The two beasts, probably Ghillies as suggested by their larger size, carried stout clubs and moved cautiously on the advancing men, who brandished swords. Circling and waiting for an opening, the Ghillies tried to slip under the blades. Neither was successful and moved quickly away from the swordsmen. One of the Ghillies, perhaps with more courage than the other, lifted his club to bring it crashing down on a dark man's arm, but the blow was easily parried.

Angus touched Alexander on the shoulder. "When we were here before, we didn't see them doing that." He gestured toward the canyon floor. "The beasties were fighting one another with clubs and axes; a few used spears. The men were showing them how to go about it."

"It appears this is the next step in their training."

Edward swore softly. "Would you look at that." His voice brought Angus' and Alexander's attention to the circle and its deadly business.

One of the Ghillies was down on its back, its club raised to ward off a blow from the swordsman poised above it. Howls of excitement from those watching from the edge of the circle rose into the cold air, and the stamping of many feet echoed off the canyon walls until the din was deafening.

The sword sliced under the raised club and the Ghillie slumped in death. Two shaggy bystanders jumped into the circle to drag away the body, and before the horrified eyes of the men watching from the cliffs, it was torn apart, limb by limb. In a frenzy, those closest to the edge of the circle fought and grabbed for the pieces of flesh and bone. The lucky ones greedily ate while fending off those trying to take the prize away.

Angus swore. "They aren't very fussy about what they eat, are they?"

Alexander's eyes were fastened on the swordsman and the creature still circling one another. The Ghillie suddenly lunged and the robed figure went flying, his sword spinning through the air. Immediately another howl went up, but before the fallen swordsman could be attacked, other men moved in with spears and whips to beat the creatures back. A commanding shriek rent the air and utter silence descended on the milling throng. For a moment everyone froze, and then the dark men began moving. With clubs and whips they restored order. More of the robed figures came to help, and soon there were several circles with swordsmen and club-wielding Spriggans and Ghillies fighting each other. A large number was set to drill over and over again the rudiments of storming a wall that had been built in one section of the canyon. It took the three Guardians only a moment to realize that the practice wall was a replica of the Wall of Rhade. Alexander swore savagely. A battering ram was brought up, and the beasts took turns knocking down portions of the wall.

"We've seen enough," Alexander said quietly. "Let's get out of here."

The three moved from the rocks and quickly picked up their packs. Although they had seen no patrolling guards, they moved with stealth. They were nearly to the base of the steep ridge when Alexander felt the skin of his abdomen begin to burn and pulse. He laid his gloved hand against the woolen tunic and felt the pulsing against his palm. He'd forgotten about the little silver knife Talanor had given him, and it was the knife that lay hotly against his skin.

Alexander hissed a warning and the two Guardians came to a halt beside him, swords in hand. They stood silently, straining to hear above the sound of their own breathing. A snuffling grunt came from the rocks off to the right. At the same time they saw the shaggy-haired Spriggan, it saw them and reared up to its full height.

The little knife sang against Alexander's skin as the beast began a shuffling trot toward them. Swords at the ready the three men stood their ground.

"Baskers," Angus swore. "Over there, off to the left. Two more."

"Spread out and watch your backs," Alexander commanded in a low voice. "Let them come to us."

Three Spriggans moved toward the man-things. They were hungry, and the men would make a good meal. Mouths agape and drooling, they came at their quarry in a rush. Long arms reached out to crush, claws poised to tear, but the Guardians were ready for the attack. Deep wounds were quickly opened on two of the attackers, and their howls of pain and anger rent the air. Angus went down under the onslaught of the third, but Edward moved in quickly to protect his brother. He thrust his sword into the shaggy back; the Spriggan fell forward, its long arm reaching back to assuage the pain. But it slumped over on its side, mortally wounded. With no time to check on Angus' condition, he whirled to aid Alexander who was fending off the other two. Although both Spriggans were wounded, they fought ferociously. Cold, controlled violence made the two men dangerous, but the beasts were not afraid. They had killed men before with ease.

With a terrifying howl, the Spriggans rushed Alexander in a blur of speed. Somewhere in the back of his mind he was amazed that anything that large could move so quickly. Edward moved to Alexander's side, and with swords poised the men met the beasts' attack.

Edward sidestepped the assault of the creature that came at him and slashed deeply into its side as it charged past. With a cry of pain it went down only to bound up again, gore spilling in black clots from the wound. It reached out as Edward moved in for the kill and caught him on the left shoulder with a clawed fist. Edward felt the burning pain but moved under the Spriggan's swinging arms. His sword found vital organs, as it sliced downward, and disemboweled the creature. He did not wait to see it drop, but turned to help Alexander.

He was backed against a large outcropping of stone, his sword held awkwardly in his left hand. Blood saturated the right shoulder of his heavy wool tunic, and his arm hung uselessly at his side. The Spriggan smelled the blood and with a crazed scream moved in for the kill. It did not see the other man-thing move up behind it, did not sense its death until the blade bit deeply into its neck and its life blood gushed from the wound. Black gore spilled to the snow, and it sank slowly to its knees, clutching its neck. It looked at Alexander with hatred before its eyes glazed and it toppled forward to lie at his feet.

The two Guardians stood staring at the thing between them, their breath coming in deep, rasping gasps.

"You're hurt," Edward pointed to Alexander's shoulder.

"Look to Angus first," Alexander replied, wiping the sweat from his brow with his good hand.

Edward stumbled away to his brother's side, and Alexander slowly slid down the rock to sit with his back against it. He rolled his head against the cold stone and swallowed convulsively. The pain was excruciating; his arm and side were sticky with blood. Black spots danced before his eyes when he closed them.

"Captain Lamond."

He heard a voice call his name from a great distance, but when he tried to focus on Edward's face, his head dropped forward, his chin resting on his chest.

"Captain Lamond. We must get out of here. Angus was only knocked unconscious, and he's coming around. There may be other beasts on their way up here. We've got to move."

Alexander felt Edward's hands gently lift the torn tunic away from his shoulder and apply a compress. He bit down on his lip to keep from crying out with the pain.

"I'm sorry, sir," Edward murmured. He lifted Alexander's good arm to rest over his own broad shoulders. "Come on, Captain. Let's get out of these mountains." Edward hoisted Alexander to his feet on the last word. The blackness swimming before his eyes opened to reveal a bottomless chasm, and mercifully, gratefully, Alexander sank into it.

Chapter Seven

Katrine Seton lifted a hand to shield her eyes from the burning sun. A tall man, using a sturdy staff as a walking stick, strode toward her. She recognized him immediately, even though it had been nearly fifteen years since she had seen him last. How could she not? Talanor was taller by a head or more than most men, even her Andrew, and the shock of snow-white hair and flowing beard set him apart.

Why had he come to Fairtown? Did he have word of Andrew? Had something happened to Andrew? Her heart began to pound when he stopped before her and gazed at her with eyes that saw beyond what others were allowed to see.

"Katrine." His greeting came rumbling up from deep within his broad chest.

"Talanor." Katrine's voice was hardly more than a whisper. Her brown eyes could not mask the concern and worry she felt.

"What brings you to Fairtown?" she asked hesitantly. As soon as she asked the question, she sensed that he brought news that she did not want to hear. She reached out to grasp him by the arm. "Andrew." Her fingers dug into his flesh through the fabric of his sleeve. "Is Andrew all right? Talanor, tell me."

He lifted a hand to press against her straining one. "He lives. But I fear he has been taken by Maelorn and imprisoned on Sinnich Isle."

"No." Katrine shook her head in despair, her eyes round with horror. "No." Her eyes filled with tears, and her grip loosened on his sleeve. She turned away and clasped her arms tightly about her waist. "I did not want to leave him. He would not allow us to stay. He feared for our safety but thought nothing of his own."

She buried her face in her hands and quiet sobs shook her shoulders. Talanor listened to her for a moment, and then he laid a comforting hand on her shoulder.

"Come, Katrine. Tears cannot help him now. Kaenolir has need of his talents, and I promise you a way will be found to free him."

He led her to a bench beside the small, neat house. A patch of flowers struggled to grow near the door, and for a moment he remembered the trampled garden on Lorn Isle. Faded blue curtains fluttered now and then in windows left open to catch any errant breeze.

Katrine struggled to control her fear and her tears. At last she lifted her eyes to Talanor. "If Maelorn is free of his prison and strong enough to take Andrew, how can you possibly free him?"

Talanor shook his leonine head. "I do not know yet, but I hope Kailie will be able to help."

"Kailie?" she gasped. Her hand flew to her throat where once again her heart pounded in fear. "What do you mean? She's hardly more than a child, Talanor," Katrine cried in agitation. Unable to sit still, she rose from the bench and paced a few steps away before turning back to the old mage. "If Maelorn has Andrew, I will not give him Kailie, too." Her voice shook, her hands clenching and unclenching with agitation. "Do not ask me to give you Kailie, old man, because I will not do it."

"The decision is not yours to make, Katrine," he said quietly. "The decision is Kailie's."

"No," Katrine cried. "No, I will not allow it!"

"You have no choice, Katrine. She is part Faerie, part Singer. And besides Andrew, she may be the only one left who can help Kaenolir." Talanor rose to stand before Katrine. He leaned wearily on his staff and looked intently into her eyes. Their piercing blue issued a command she could not turn away from. "Look around you. You needn't look very far to see that Kaenolir is dying. I have reason to believe that soon there will be a war fought against a power far stronger than the people fighting alone can withstand. The Goldenhorn and his daughter may be our only hope, Katrine." He reached out a gentle hand to wipe away the tears that slid down her cheeks. She was a lovely woman, warm and caring, and he saw why Andrew loved her though she was not of his kind.

"I'm sorry, Katrine. If there was another way, I would pursue it." He dropped his staff and pulled her against his chest, holding her tightly while the sobs once again tore through her.

At last she quieted and stepped back, wiping away tears with the back of her hand. "I cannot bear to lose them both, Talanor. I cannot," she said sadly.

"I know. I know." He touched the soft brown hair at her temple with his fingertips. "I will use all my power to bring them both back to you," he said quietly. "I give you my word."

Katrine looked at him for a long moment, seeking the truth of his words. With a deep sigh she gestured toward the open door. "Come, I've some ale and bread and cheese. You can rest and eat before Kailie comes home. She spends part of the day helping my father and brothers in the store, though there's little enough to sell and only a few customers who come to Fairtown these days."

She led the way inside, and after the bright sunlight it seemed dim and cool. The little cottage, though sparsely furnished, showed Katrine's care. Talanor leaned his staff beside the door and sat at a table that had been polished until it shone. Flowers in a pale green bowl added a spot of color and fragrance to the room.

She set a mug of ale before him, before bringing him cheese and brown bread still warm from the oven. "I'm sorry I cannot offer you some fruit, but the trees have almost all died in the drought."

"I know, but I thank you for your hospitality." He thought of the ripening apples on Cathorn and sighed. But perhaps, because he was not there, the trees on his beloved island had begun to wither and die. He sighed again and silently beseeched the Ancient Ones to help him.

~

Talanor watched Kailie come swinging up the path. She was tall for a woman, tall and slender, with dark gold hair caught up in a neat, heavy coil at the back of her neck. Unruly curls had slipped the knot, however, and lay against cheek and temple. Her skin glowed not only from the touch of the hot summer sun but also with warmth from within. Brilliant blue eyes sparkled with life, and a mischievous glint lurked in their depths. Her rather wide mouth smiled easily and drew a man's eyes. Her features were finely drawn and marked her Faerie heritage, but she elicited a feeling of earthiness rather than fragility. Long, sensitive fingers reached to brush away a wisp of curling hair and Talanor sighed. Katrine had said Kailie was hardly more than a child.

This was no child who came toward him, but a woman, lovely and bright, a perfect blending of mortal and Faerie.

An image of Alexander Lamond slipped into Talanor's mind, and he grinned to himself, then laughed softly.

Katrine looked up from her sewing at the sound. "Did you say something to me?" she asked the man looking out the window.

"Kailie comes," he said in explanation.

Katrine set her sewing aside and rose. "She will be thirsty and hungry; she always is when she gets home."

"Hello, Mother," Kailie called as she entered the house. Her voice was exactly as Talanor expected it to be, low and pleasing, with a hint of music softening its edges.

"Kailie," he murmured on a sigh.

Kailie turned toward him, and her eyes opened wide in surprise at the sight of the imposing figure who stood before the window. She had been very small when she last saw him, probably about five, but she would never forget Talanor.

"Talanor," she cried in pleasure and moved with a graceful step to stand before him. She looked up into the blazing blue eyes and smiled.

He was dazzled.

Kailie held out her hands to him in greeting, and when he took them he found them warm and soft. "What brings you to Fairtown? How did you find us?" she asked with a laugh.

Talanor looked at the young woman before looking at Katrine. She stood at the table, a plate of bread and cheese in her hands, her bottom lip caught in her teeth as she looked worriedly from one to the other.

"Come, child, your mother has prepared a meal for us. You must be hungry after your day. We'll eat and then we'll talk." He caught Katrine's look of fear before she turned away to finish setting the table. "I've much to tell you and much I want to hear from you." He smiled at the upturned face before him. "You've grown a bit since I last saw you," he teased.

Kailie freed her hands with another smile and moved to help her mother with the meal preparations. Katrine looked wan and tired, she thought, not like her mother at all. She wondered again why Talanor had come.

She took the pitcher of water from her mother's hands. "Sit down," she urged. "I'll do this."

Katrine refused to meet Kailie's eyes as she turned away to take her place at the table.

Something was not quite right here. Kailie knew when her mother was upset by the way she worried her bottom lip between her teeth, as she had been doing all while fixing their simple supper.

"Mother," Kailie said softly. She reached over to touch her mother's shoulder after seating herself at the table. "Are you all right?" She searched her mother's pale features.

Katrine lifted her eyes to Kailie's. "I'm all right," she said. "Eat your supper now." She passed Talanor the platter of bread and cheese. "Were you busy at the store today?"

"No, not particularly. Grandfather had me dust the shelves that I'd just dusted yesterday." She smiled at her mother and received a brief smile in return.

Kailie turned to Talanor. "I detest dusting shelves and Grandfather knows it, but he says if he doesn't keep me busy I'll get into mischief." She laughed, the sound of amusement husky and delighted. "He didn't discover until it was time for me to go that I'd turned the jars around so the labels were all to the wall." She looked at her mother and grinned.

"Oh, Kailie," Katrine sighed. "He'll just make you turn them around tomorrow."

"I know." Kailie's grin did not fade. "But maybe I won't have to dust those shelves again for awhile." She took a sip of water and broke off a piece of bread.

She shrugged a slender shoulder and turned her amused glance to Talanor. "Grandfather has very little patience with females. I sometimes wonder how Mother was able to twist him around her finger the way she did and get him to give her the job of keeping the account books." She gave her mother a glance before turning her attention back to Talanor. "I don't think Grandfather has ever quite forgiven my father for stealing her away. They met in the store, you know."

"Yes, I believe I did know that. Do you like working there?"

Kailie gave him a searching, rather puzzled glance. The question was innocent enough, but she felt a current of tension running between her mother and the mage. She had sensed it the moment she stepped into the house.

"It's something to do. I would much rather be on Lorn Isle, but Fairtown is pleasant enough, I suppose. It has changed since I was young. It used to bustle with lots of people and activity." Kailie looked off into the distance. "Nothing in Kaenolir is as I remember it. We used to visit Grandfather and Grandmother two or three times a year when I was growing up, and I remember everything being so green with lots of animals in the pastures and birds always singing." A sad look crossed her features. After a moment she turned her gaze back to Talanor. "I know something is wrong, Talanor. Father would not tell me and neither will mother." She gave her mother a long, searching look.

Unable to sit still under her daughter's scrutiny, Katrine rose and began clearing away the remains of the meal. "Would you like some tea now, Talanor?" she asked without looking at the man.

"Yes, tea would be fine, Katrine." He, too, rose from the table.

Kailie watched him intently as he moved to the door. He paused in the doorway and turned to meet her gaze. "Walk with me while your mother prepares the tea," he said.

Kailie thought she heard her mother gasp, but when she glanced her way, Katrine was setting out the tea things. Kailie rose, uncertain if she should go to her mother or to the big man who waited at the door. She stood, her hands clasping the back of her chair.

"Kailie," Talanor's low, rumbling voice came again. With a last worried look at her mother, she followed him out the door and into the heat of the lowering sun.

They walked in silence along a dusty path that wound its way eventually to a street of the town. Katrine's cottage sat at the far edge of Fairtown. She had chosen the out-of-the-way place expressly for its quiet, rather rustic setting. After living so long in the isolation of Lorn Isle, she found it hard to live among people.

When the path forked, Kailie took the narrower track that led into a field, bordered on the far side by a line of drought-strickened oak trees. The field lay fallow, but dry grass and a few scattered weeds still tried valiantly to grow.

A fence halted their progress, and Kailie leaned her arms against the rough wood of the top railing, her hands lightly clasped together, and looked over the barren countryside.

"What's happening to Kaenolir, Talanor?" she asked quietly. When her question was greeted by silence, she turned to face the mage. He, too, leaned against the fence, absently chewing on a stalk of dry grass.

Talanor sighed deeply, and then turned his head to look at the young woman beside him. "Kaenolir is dying," he said roughly. "Dying because a dark power has gained enough strength to slowly strangle the land and its people."

"Why?" Kailie thought for a moment. "How?"

Talanor took the stalk from his mouth and tossed it away. He turned to face Kailie as he spoke.

"Once Kaenolir was the loveliest of lands," he began.

~

The tea grew cold and the sky darkened. Katrine looked out the window for the hundredth time. When tears threatened to fall, she resolutely blinked them away and straightened her shoulders. She must be strong; Andrew would want her to be strong for Kailie. She moved away to light a candle. Its soft glow gave her a bit of comfort, but her heart ached.

Her Andrew seemed far away from her, and she yearned so for the touch of his strong arms about her.

Where is he? What is he doing? Is he all right?

Talanor said he feared Andrew had been taken by Maelorn and imprisoned on Sinnich Isle. How could anyone free him from such a place? Who had strength enough, courage enough to challenge Maelorn, if he had, as Talanor intimated, freed himself from Mt. Sinnarock's stone?

Apparently Talanor thought Kailie might possess such strength, such courage.

Kailie. My beautiful Kailie.

How could Talanor think one young woman could dare to defy what the gods had set in motion so long ago?

Katrine's thoughts whirled, mixed with a fear that was steadily growing.

Talanor had come for Kailie. And once Talanor had told her what had happened to Andrew, there would be no way Katrine could keep her daughter in Fairtown. Kailie was her father's child.

Kailie. Oh, my sweet Kailie.

~

Kailie listened in rapt silence to the tale Talanor wove. It was a tale filled with magic and wonder, with power and terror, a tale of an eternal struggle between good and evil. The twilight deepened, the evening star rose in the heavens, and the stars glimmered dimly in the darkening skies. Still the deep, rumbling voice went on.

"When I went to your cottage on Lorn with Captain Lamond, I found evidence that your father had been taken captive."

"I knew something was very wrong," Kailie spoke for the first time since Talanor began his story. Her soft voice touched him in the darkness. "After Mt. Sinnarock erupted, Father forbade me to sing the Warrior Song." She gave Talanor a sidelong glance. "I can sing his Song, you know." She looked up at the brightly shining evening star before continuing. "I think he knew even then that something brutal and powerful was set free within the mountain." She sighed and looked off into the night. "He would not permit Mother and me to stay with him. And I think I knew the exact moment he was taken. I felt him leave Lorn, and not because he wanted to; someone took him away." Tears filled her eyes when she looked again to Talanor. "I thought my heart would break."

"How did you know, Kailie?" he asked quietly.

She shrugged. "Sometimes I sense things others do not. I cannot explain it; it just happens."

Talanor smiled. "Yes."

Kailie looked to Talanor who stood now in deep shadow. "Why did you come to Fairtown?" Her face was touched by starlight, making her Faerie features all the more pronounced.

"I came," he said at last, sadly and simply, "to find you. You are half Singer, and I believe you may be able to help Kaenolir."

Kailie turned away to look out over the dark field. "Will I be able to help my father?"

"I don't know."

"But there is a chance I may be able to help him, isn't there?"

"Yes, there's always a chance as long as we have hope."

An unladylike snort escaped Kailie's elegant nose. She glared at the mage. "Don't patronize me with platitudes, Talanor."

First surprise registered on Talanor's features, and then he laughed. "You sound just like your mother. I'm sure she said similar words to her father when he tried to make her dust the shelves in the store."

Kailie smiled and, as it had the first time he saw it, her smile dazzled him. "Now," she said with determination, what is it you want me to do?"

"I want you to go to the Horn of Kalora with me to find Rhianna Lanee. She is the Singers' mage and can assess your voice and your power."

"And after that?"

"After that …" Talanor looked away from the searching gaze. "If she finds that Faerie magic flows through your veins, if the talent you possess is strong, I will ask you to go with me to the Guardians' Fort. I will ask you to help me save Kaenolir."

She stared at the mage for several moments. She knew now what she had not known as a five-year-old child. Talanor had powers, not like those of her father's, but powers of a different sort. She didn't pretend to understand them, but she knew he spoke truthfully to her. Kaenolir was in terrible danger. A force conceived in the pit of damnation was slowly squeezing the life from the land. But the Kaenolirians would not fall meekly beneath Maelorn's yoke. They would fight, as they had fought before, and in fighting the malevolent forces, they would die. Talanor asked for her help and she must go with him.

"When do we leave?" Kailie asked quietly.

"As soon as possible. Tomorrow morning at dawn."

"All right. I want some time with my mother."

"Of course."

They walked in silence down the meandering track through the field. Crickets chirped in the brown grass, and an occasional breeze rustled dry leaves of once majestic oaks slowly dying in heat and drought. Kailie stumbled and Talanor reached out to steady her.

When they came to the cottage, Talanor did not enter. "I'll see you in the morning." He turned to go.

Kailie's hand on his arm stopped him. "Where are you going? Please come inside."

He shook his head. "'Tis better if you have the time alone with your mother."

"Where will you sleep?"

"Don't worry about me, child. I don't sleep much anymore." He touched a curl by her ear. "Go to your mother, now."

She gave him another searching look, and turned away to enter the cottage.

~

Kailie sat on a stool beside her mother's chair and watched Katrine Seton sleep. It was not a restful sleep, but one filled with uneasy dreams. She murmured Andrew's name and then Kailie's. When she cried out, Kailie reached to take her mother's hands and held them tight.

"Mother," she said softly, "wake up. You're having a bad dream."

Katrine looked at her daughter with the glazed eyes of a sleepwalker, sighed and closed her eyes. When she opened them again, they were clear.

"I was dreaming."

"I know."

"Frightful dreams, Kailie."

"I know, Mother, I know," Kailie soothed.

Katrine rolled her head from side to side against the back of the chair. "I'm frightened, Kailie. Your father is in danger, and now Talanor asks you to share that danger." She freed her hands from Kailie's strong grasp and framed her daughter's face with trembling fingers. "He asked you to go with him, didn't he?" She could not keep the tremor from her voice.

"Yes," Kailie said simply. She reached to cover her mother's hands. "I must go, Mother. I must."

"Yes, I know you do, but that doesn't make your leaving any easier." She rubbed her thumbs over the delicate cheekbones. "When do you leave?"

"At dawn tomorrow."

"So soon?" Katrine whispered. With a ragged cry, she drew her daughter close and held her tightly against her heart. For a long moment the two women embraced, but at last Katrine drew back. She touched the hair at Kailie's temple and gave her a watery smile.

"May your father's magic protect and keep you," she whispered. "Come back to me, my darling daughter. Please come back to me."

Kailie smiled, too, then, and touched her lips to her mother's cheek.

"It's very late, Mother. We must try to rest." Kailie rose and picked up the candle from the table near her mother's chair. Katrine stood and together they made their way down the narrow hallway to their sleeping chambers. Kailie paused to light another candle on a stand just inside her chamber door before handing her mother the candle she carried.

"Good night, Mother."

"Good night, Kailie. Rest well. You've a long journey ahead of you."

Kailie nodded and smiled wistfully at her mother. She turned then and closed the door. She stood quietly for a moment until she heard her mother's door close. Wrapping her arms tightly about her waist, she moved to the window that opened to the field she and Talanor had walked through. Tears filled her eyes and silent sobs shook her shoulders.

"Oh, Father, wherever you are, help me be strong."

After a time, she wiped away the tears and slipped from her clothes. She drew a sleeping gown over her head and freed her hair from its knot. She blew out the candle and sank down upon her narrow bed. A thousand thoughts and images spun through her mind, but one that stood out sharply was the image of her father, chained and beaten, imprisoned in a fiery cavern within the bowels of Mt. Sinnarock.

With dawn only a few hours away, she slept at last.

Chapter Eight

Kailie looked back over her shoulder one last time and blinked rapidly to quell the tears that threatened to wreck her composure. Katrine Seton stood at the end of the path and lifted her hand to wave. To Kailie it seemed such a forlorn little gesture.

She is so alone, she thought. Not for the first time, Kailie murmured, "Forgive me, Mother, but I must go."

"Your mother understands, child," Talanor spoke quietly, his voice a low rumble.

Kailie sighed and hitched the pack on her back into a more comfortable position. The sun was barely up, but already the day promised to be hot. They followed the dusty road that would take them along the edge of the Lake Country and eventually to the Bay of Kalora. Talanor hoped to find someone willing to take them across the bay to the Horn of Kalora; otherwise, they would have to trek the long distance around the bay and lose precious time in doing so.

Talanor set a swift pace. He wanted to be well on the way before they were forced to find some protection from the burning sun. Kailie's long legs managed to keep up with his mile-eating stride, but he knew they would both tire rapidly in the summer heat.

They had been on the road for nearly four hours when they saw a cart coming toward the main road from a track that wound through the central part of the Lake Country. Talanor stopped and turned to Kailie. "Let's hope he's not heading to Fairtown. Perhaps he'll have room to let us ride for awhile."

Kailie nodded. It would be good to rest. She was not used to walking such long distances, and she sighed in longing for the horse she been forced to leave behind when they'd come to the mainland.

"We're in luck," Talanor's voice broke through her reverie. "The man and his wife are going to a small village north of here, and they would be glad for our company."

The couple greeted Kailie, the wife's lined face creasing in a friendly smile.

"We're going to visit our daughter," the woman explained to Kailie. "She's soon to deliver her second child, and we're anxious to see our new grandchild."

Kailie and Talanor settled themselves in the back of the cart. The man slapped the reins against the rump of the skinny white horse, and the cart swayed and squeaked as it began to move. A ragged tarp shaded the occupants, but even though the sides were rolled up to allow air to move through, it grew stifling in the cart as the afternoon wore on. They stopped once to rest and water the horse and took some sustenance themselves, and then moved on again.

Kailie's eyelids grew heavy and she dozed. She had slept neither well nor long during the night, and the day's heat added to her fatigue. Talanor, too, dozed from time to time, waking with a jerk when the cart came to a stop.

"This is as far as we can take you," the man said over his shoulder. "We take this road," he gestured with the reins to the right fork of the rutted track, "to our daughter's village."

Talanor and Kailie retrieved their packs and got down out of the cart. Hard wood and cramped quarters had made both of them stiff, and Kailie grunted as she settled her pack once more on her back.

"We thank you for the ride, good people," Talanor said. With a wave to the couple, he and Kailie watched the cart rumble away before they turned to the west.

The sun was sinking toward the horizon when the travelers heard the sea crashing against the formidable cliffs that formed Kalora Bay.

"We've not much farther to go now, Kailie," Talanor called.

Kailie trudged wearily several paces behind him, and he turned to smile encouragingly at her.

"We'll rest here for a short time before we look for some shelter for the night. There used to be an inn not far from here. We must try to find it before it gets dark. I'd rather not camp out in the open if we don't have to."

With a nod, Kailie dropped her pack and slumped down on the ground, her back against a boulder that was one of many scattered about the desolate cliffs. She closed her eyes and breathed in the familiar scent of salt air.

~

They found the inn at sunset. Built to last through the passage of time and the vagaries of storms from off the sea, it sat atop a cliff, its back to the bay, its foundation the living stone beneath it. Once it had sheltered many people from many lands within its sturdy walls of logs from the Thanion Woods, but it offered no welcome to the weary travelers who stood before it. The wide double doors were bolted and barred, the windows tightly shuttered against intrusion. Cold chimneys lifted starkly into the darkening sky.

As Kailie glanced about, her shoulders drooped in fatigue. It had been a long, hot day, and she had looked forward to a good supper and a soft bed. It appeared she was to have neither.

"Now what?" Kailie said as Talanor checked first the locked door and then one of the windows next to it.

"Hmm," he murmured absently. "There must be one window that we can force open." He moved along the wide veranda that ran the width and down both sides of the inn, and stopped to check the windows and doors he encountered.

"You mean to break in?" Kailie asked in surprise.

Talanor did not answer her as he disappeared around the corner. Too tired to follow, Kailie slipped her pack from her shoulders and plopped down on the rough floor of the veranda, her back against the stout wall of the inn. She absently rubbed a sore spot on her shoulder that the strap of her pack had bruised. Talanor was gone for several minutes before rejoining her.

"Come, I've managed to get a window open into the kitchen."

Kailie rose to follow him to the back of the building. The window was narrow, and it was obvious that Talanor would not be able to enter the inn through this small portal.

"I'll give you a boost up, and when you get inside, find a door you can unlock." Talanor rummaged in his pack until he found the stub of a candle and his flint.

"Here, take these; you'll need them once you're inside."

"I don't know about this, Talanor. Somehow it just doesn't seem right for us to break into someone else's property," she said as she slipped the items into a pocket.

"Come, come, come. My old bones cannot take another night on the hard ground when there are any number of beds to choose from inside. Besides, no one has been here in a long time." He cupped his hands and stooped to give her a boost. "Up you go," he commanded.

She dropped her pack to the ground and with a hand on Talanor's shoulder for balance, stepped into his hands. He lifted her easily, and with more strain than grace she pulled herself through the window.

Her feet thumped on the wood planks as she dropped to the floor. She breathed the musty smell of dust and stale air; odors of cooking still permeated the room even after weeks, perhaps months of disuse. Her eyes adjusted to the darkness, and she saw the outline of a long table immediately in front of her. She set the candle on its gritty surface and struck the flint to set a spark.

"Are you all right, Kailie?" Talanor called.

"Yes, I just lit the candle. I'll see if I can find a door that I can unlock to let you in."

Kailie lifted the candle to carry it before her, shielding the flame with her cupped left hand. The flickering light revealed a door off to her right, and upon closer examination, it did not appear to be nailed shut, only bolted with a heavy iron bolt. Setting the candle again on the long table, she tried the lock. It refused to move, but she persisted and soon the stubborn bolt screeched in rusty protest. Kailie used all her strength to pull it back, and the bolt suddenly shifted. She grunted as she barked her knuckles against the latch, but the bolt slid free and she swung the door open to admit Talanor.

"Good girl," he murmured as he stepped inside. "Let's see what we can find."

~

A small lamp guttered low, creating a myriad of shadows about the common room. Long tables, their benches upended on top of them, served as silent sentinels in the stuffy darkness. Talanor and Kailie sat in comfortable overstuffed chairs before the lifeless fireplace and silently contemplated its blackened maw as if a fire burned there. Kailie felt restless, uneasy with her surroundings. She worried that her feeling of uneasiness came from something other than having broken into the abandoned inn. Talanor, too, from time to time, glanced about him, listening intently to the creaks and groans of the old building as it shifted and settled after the heat of the day. Wind rose and added lonely moans and mournful whistling to the night. Soft rustling in darkened corners indicated small rodents had taken up residence after the human occupants left. A cricket chirped halfheartedly, its song an irritating rasp against Kailie's already heightened senses.

Talanor turned to his quiet companion. "You should get some rest. It's been a long day."

"I am tired, but I don't think I can sleep just yet."

Earlier Talanor had explored the second floor of the inn and brought down two dusty pallets that smelled of old sweat and the four-legged residents of the inn and placed them on the floor near the fireplace. He'd also done a careful check of each shutter and door, testing bolts and bars for security. While Kailie prepared their spartan meal, he'd made sure that the window and door through which they'd entered were once again locked and bolted. He could not explain his own feeling of uneasiness any more than Kailie could explain hers, but he knew that from the time they came in sight of the bay and climbed the steep path to the inn, they had not been alone.

At last Kailie could no longer keep her eyes open. She spread the blanket from her pack on one of the pallets and after murmuring good night to Talanor slipped into a dreamless, but restless sleep. She thought once she heard Talanor's voice murmuring softly in a low singsong rhythm. However, before she came fully awake the song stopped, and she never decided if what she heard was dream or reality.

Some time later another sound disturbed her sleep, this one frightening and strange. When it came again, she jerked upright and looked wildly about her. Talanor was not sleeping beside her, nor was he seated in a chair. The lamp still flickered, but its light offered little comfort.

"Talanor?" she whispered. "Where are you?"

He materialized out of the shadows, startling her, and she choked back a gasp of fear. He lay a quieting finger against his lips and motioned for her to come to him.

"What is it?" she whispered when she stood before him.

A snuffling, grunting snort came from outside, somewhere close by the front door. Kailie's eyes were drawn to the direction of the sound, and when she jerked back to Talanor for an explanation, he moved to retrieve his sword from where it lay on the floor beside his pallet. She trembled when the sound came again, and shivers of fear ran up and down her spine. It was not a sound of any animal she knew; she would not have felt so frightened by a familiar animal. Whatever was on the other side of that door was, indeed, something to fear.

The snuffling stopped. Talanor and Kailie waited, straining to identify the sounds from beyond the door, blood pounding in their ears. When the battering began on the door, Kailie shoved her fist against her mouth to keep from crying out. She had felt such fear only once before—on the day Mt. Sinnarock erupted.

Talanor touched her arm and motioned for her to get behind him. His touch calmed her somewhat, and in that instant she remembered her father's Song. She began to sing the powerful music softly, even though she had promised her father never to sing it again. Some instinct warned her of their danger and urged the Song from her throat.

With the first notes the pounding and scuffling halted. Kailie continued to sing, louder now, more sure of herself. From outside a howl of rage and pain split the night air. Hair on the back of Kailie's neck prickled at the inhuman sound, and she reached out to clutch Talanor's arm. The music of her Song bounced off the walls and filled the large room with power and beauty.

Talanor was entranced. He had never heard the Warrior Song sung with such force and brilliance. Whatever power the Goldenhorn possessed and gave to his Song, in Kailie the potency seemed to have been doubled. He slipped free of her clinging hand and moved to pick up the lamp. Turning its flame higher, he walked toward the door. He pantomimed to Kailie what he intended to do. She joined him and took the lamp from his hand, the Song fading to a low, vibrating hum. Carefully, Talanor lifted the heavy bar from across the door. When he drew his sword from its scabbard, the metallic whisper joined the Warrior Song. He pulled the latch back and opened the door.

A large, shaggy hulk cringed in the light from the lamp, its clawed fists pawing its ears in pain. When it saw two human shapes before it, it screamed. The Song rose again in intensity, and the creature sank to its knees in agony.

Talanor did not hesitate. He raised the sword and with a swift, sure blow thrust the blade deep into the beast's neck. It clutched at the wound and with a grunt toppled forward to lie dead at Talanor's feet. His breath coming in ragged gulps, Talanor stepped back quickly and swung the heavy door shut, set the latch and lifted the bar in place. He leaned against the door for a moment to catch his breath before turning to meet the terrified look in Kailie's eyes. She let the last note of the Song fall into a silence fraught with death and apprehension. With a trembling hand she pressed her fingertips against a throbbing temple. The lamp nearly tipped from her hand and Talanor reached to take it from her.

"What was that thing?" she whispered. "It would have killed us if it could have."

Talanor moved back to the fireplace before he answered Kailie's question. He set the lamp on the mantle and turned to her.

"The thing I just killed is a creature from the legends of the past. It, and others like it, threatened Kaenolir five hundred years ago, and it has returned to do so again."

Kailie sank into one of the large chairs. She pulled her feet up beneath her and wrapped her arms tightly around her waist, trying in vain to blot out the sight that had greeted them when Talanor opened the door.

"Now, my child, do you see why it is imperative that I take you to Rhianna Lanee? You may be the last hope for Kaenolir. If you did not fully understand that before we set out, I think you do now. Yes?"

"Yes, I understand. But, Talanor, I broke my promise to my father. He forbade me to sing his Song. Did I do something terribly wrong by singing it?" A new thought struck fear into her heart once more. She jumped from the chair and frantically clutched the sleeves of Talanor's robe. "What if I endangered his life? What if—"

"Shh, Kailie, hush. 'Tis done. We cannot know if the Darkling is powerful enough to detect the Song so far from Sinnich Isle. I'm sorry I cannot ease your fears, but the Song must be sung. It will be sung, over and over, before our struggle with Maelorn ends." He drew her rigid body against him, seeking to console her. Gently he caressed her golden curls while she trembled but did not cry. Little by little, she relaxed and let his strength surround her.

They stood quietly for some time, until Kailie sighed and pulled away from the comforting arms. She gazed at the lined face above her. He had represented something magical and fanciful to her when she was a child; he still did. He was different because he possessed a kind of power that was not given to common men, a power steeped in legend and in time. She possessed a kind of power, too, she realized. She felt it beating in her blood when she sang her father's Song. And even though fear had filled her mind, she was somehow untouched by it. The force that rested within her was stronger than the fear, its energy dispelling the terror she had felt and leaving the power of the music in its place.

"So," she said quietly, sadly. "If the Warrior Song is to be sung, then I must be the one to sing it."

~

Fires flared deep within Mt. Sinnarock, and Maelorn reared his ugly head, red eyes burning with hatred. He ground his teeth together and grunted as the beat of an unknown power came to him for only a brief moment and then was gone. The Darkling turned his head from side to side, nostrils flaring, ears straining to determine its source, but he detected nothing more.

He watched the flames flicker low again. With another grunt he settled once more and sank quickly into the deep stupor that nourished him and gave him strength.

~

Talanor found the boat early in the morning, moored to the rickety pier that had once served the inn. He awakened Kailie and together they climbed down to the water, following the path that was both steep and treacherous, its surface slippery and strewn with rocks.

Kailie took several deep breaths when she reached the shore and waited for her legs to stop trembling. A scruffy little boat bobbed on the morning tide, and she eyed it skeptically. She had sailed the waters around Lorn Isle all her life, and she felt she could handle almost any kind of sailing craft. However, this small skiff did not engender a sense of confidence.

"I don't know, Talanor. This doesn't look like much of a boat. It was probably left behind by the owners of the inn for a good reason."

Talanor humphed in agreement and stepped into the boat for a closer inspection.

"I'm afraid we don't have any other choice. Here, help me get our packs secured, and we'll be on our way."

Kailie hesitated a moment longer, her brow furrowed with worry, as she gave the craft another perusal.

"Kailie, the packs," Talanor called. "Hurry, child, we haven't time to dawdle."

She turned to do his bidding, and after untying the frayed line she stepped into the boat and helped Talanor push away from the dock.

"I don't like this," she muttered as she worked to raise the tattered sail. Talanor ignored her, his hands busy with getting them under way.

"Get the sail up, Kailie," he snapped irritably.

"I'm trying," she gritted through her clenched teeth. "It's stuck." With a well-placed kick she freed the recalcitrant sail and raised it into position.

The boat sailed sluggishly on the nearly calm waters of Kalora Bay. A fitful breeze filled the sail while Talanor struggled with the tiller. A sudden gust of wind sent the little craft skimming over the water while its occupants worked to keep the bow headed for the opposite shore.

The Horn of Kalora was wrapped in an almost transparent haze that permitted a dim, shadowy view of the shoreline. Talanor beached the craft on a wide strip of sparkling white sand and moved to help Kailie tie down the sail she had just lowered. When the task was complete, he handed Kailie her pack, settled his own comfortably on his back and hefted his stout staff. They stepped over the side of the boat into the cold waters of the bay and splashed the short distance to the sand.

Kailie halted and stared in wonder. Gauzy mists moved and gathered and shifted away, with a life of their own, allowing glimpses of trees that formed what appeared to be an impenetrable green wall. Birds sang somewhere off in the distance, but they sang songs Kailie had not heard before. She listened carefully and mimicked their call in a clear, trilling voice. After a moment's silence her song was answered, and she smiled.

Talanor looked at her with interest. "Are you able to do that with all birds' songs?"

Kailie shrugged her slender shoulders. "I guess so. Every song I've heard I've been able to repeat." She listened again to the birds. "This song is unfamiliar, though. Do you know what kind of bird is singing?"

"Hmm. I might."

Kailie waited a beat. "Well?"

"Well, what?" Talanor turned away and began striding down the beach.

"What kind of bird is it?" Kailie ran a few steps to catch up with Talanor.

"Hm? Oh, I don't remember the name right now. You'll have to ask Rhianna Lanee."

Kailie's wide mouth quirked in irritation. Talanor was several steps ahead of her again, and she had to hurry to keep pace with him.

They walked along the shore of the bay for some distance before Talanor stopped to get his bearings. It had been many years since he had been here, and time had a way of distorting remembered landscapes. The mists parted for a moment, and he saw the pillar of rock he had been looking for.

"This way," he said to Kailie and headed into the green jungle that the mists veiled.

Tendrils of moss reached out to the pair as they followed a path that only Talanor saw. Wisps of gray/green fluff caught at Kailie's hair, and when she reached up to brush it away, it caressed her fingers. It was an unsettling sensation but oddly pleasant, almost soothing. She looked around her with curious eyes and watched sunlight filter through the dense canopy. Mists suddenly swirled about her, and she laughed in delight at the dizzying sensation she experienced. It reminded her of her childhood when, after whirling round and round until too dizzy to stand, she fell to the ground and waited for the world to right itself, spinning sky above and warm grass beneath her.

The dizziness passed and Kailie walked for some time before she realized she was alone, but she felt no fear. Trees no longer crowded close to the path but opened to form a small glen. In its center, a shaded pool glinted with sapphire and green as a beam of sunlight pierced the leafy ceiling to touch the water with ripples of gold. She moved to stand near the pool and laughed with pleasure as she gazed about.

"Who are you to disturb my peace and interrupt my solitude?"

A voice, more tone than words, came from close behind Kailie. She whirled to face a woman of great beauty. *She is Faerie,* was her first thought.

Tall and slender with golden hair shot through with silver, the woman came toward Kailie and stopped a step away. Her amber eyes searched Kailie's face intently before long, elegant fingers reached out to touch her hair.

"Golden One," the melodious voice whispered. She gazed into deep blue eyes that gazed back at her in curiosity. The woman smiled and was answered by an equally dazzling smile.

"So, child, who brought you to the Horn of Kalora?"

"Talanor, my lady."

"Talanor? I might have known that old fool was involved."

Kailie's eyes widened in surprise at the woman's chiding tone.

"Tell me, what is your name and why did you come?"

"I'm Kailie Fairchild, my lady, and Talanor brought me here to see Rhianna Lanee."

"To see Rhianna Lanee? Whatever for, Kailie Fairchild?"

"Mt. Sinnarock erupted and Maelorn broke free of his prison. Once again he threatens the people of Kaenolir, and Talanor feels I may be able to help them. My father is Andrew Goldenhorn." She paused. "Talanor believes Maelorn imprisoned him on Sinnich Isle."

The woman's voice hummed. "Ah, Goldenhorn." Her eyes once more perused the slender form of the golden-haired young woman. "Does he still live?"

"I pray that he does. Talanor thinks so, but Maelorn is growing very powerful."

Rhianna nodded. "You are part Singer," she mused. "No wonder I recognized a kindred spirit when I heard you sing to my birds; now I know why." Again her fingers touched Kailie's hair. "I am Rhianna Lanee and Talanor was wise to bring you to me." She turned her head to look into the trees.

"You can come out now, old man. I know you're here."

A disgruntled harrumph accompanied by a rustling of leaves announced Talanor's presence. He came to stand near the two women, leaning lightly on his staff.

"Well, old woman, it seems your tongue is as sharp as ever. If it were not for this old man, you would not have known this Golden One existed." An irritated snort punctuated the last word. "Bah, Rhianna Lanee, you are as exasperating as ever."

Rhianna laughed. "It has been a long time, Talanor Rowan, a very long time since we matched wits. Welcome to the Horn." She smiled beguilingly at him and then turned to Kailie. "Come, my child, we have much to do and little enough time in which to do it, I think." She took Kailie's hand to lead her away.

After only a few steps Rhianna turned back to Talanor. "Well, aren't you coming?" she asked.

"Am I invited?" Talanor asked sharply.

"Of course. Don't pout. You know I hate it when you pout."

Rhianna squeezed Kailie's hand in silent communication, and Kailie found it necessary to hide a grin behind the back of her free hand.

"Well," Rhianna huffed. "Are you coming or not?" She held her other hand out to Talanor.

After a moment he shifted the staff and moved to take Rhianna's offered hand. He looked long into her beautiful face and then his booming laughter echoed through the forest and sent startled birds flying away. "It's good to see you again, Rhianna. Yes, good to see you again."

Chapter Nine

"Where are we?" Alexander croaked. His head pounded; his right shoulder and arm were stiff with pain; and he was so weak he could barely lift his head.

"We're nearly to the Skara, Captain." Angus Mackay came to a stop and tried to catch his breath and talk at the same time. He slipped leather straps from his shoulders and eased the makeshift sledge carrying Alexander down onto the ground. "Would you like a drink of water?" he asked the wounded man.

"Yes, please."

The water was ice cold, but a soothing balm for Alexander's parched throat.

Angus touched Alexander's forehead with his rough hand. "Fever's gone." He nodded. "I think maybe you'll make it, Captain." He grinned down at Alexander. "For awhile there, Edward and I had our doubts."

Alexander grunted. "How's your head?"

"It's fine. It would take more than a knock on the block by some ugly beastie to get me down."

"And that's for sure," Edward chimed in. "His head is as hard as the stone of The Dlarmids."

Angus snorted in response.

"You were hurt, too, Edward," Alexander said. "Are you all right?"

"'Twas just a scratch, nothing more. I'm fine."

Alexander nodded. "How long have we been traveling?" he asked hoarsely.

"This is our fourth day," Edward answered him. "We managed to put together a sledge of tree branches, some of our blankets, and the leather straps

114

from the packs and our belts. We've taken turns dragging you out of the mountains and into the foothills above the Skara River."

"You've been dragging me around for four days?"

"It wasn't exactly a pleasant trip, I grant you, what with you either shivering with chills or sweating with fever. I think you cursed every god that ever walked the halls of the ancient world," Angus grinned. "I thought I'd heard every profane word known to man, but I learned some new ones from you, Captain. Especially when we'd hit a big rock." He chuckled good-naturedly.

Edward picked up the tale. "Late this morning your fever finally broke." He took a swig from his water bottle, thumped the cork back into it, and looked around at their snowy landscape. "We've got about three more hours of daylight. We better get moving. I'll take the straps now, Angus."

Alexander groaned as the sledge began its jostling movement. He almost wished for the oblivion of unconsciousness that he'd been swimming in. He felt every rock, every bump, and he clenched his teeth against the pain.

A particularly bad bump made him cry out. "Sorry, Captain," Edward called back over his shoulder. "I didn't see that one under the snow."

When they found a protected spot out of the wind some time later, the Mackays decided to stop for the night even though it was light enough to have gone on for another hour. The torturous journey came to a halt and Alexander sighed with relief. It took the two brothers only a short time to set up camp and find enough dry twigs and wood to build a fire, its cracking warmth a welcomed respite from the bitter cold.

Alexander frowned. "Is it safe to light a fire?"

Angus dropped his armload of wood and hunkered down to warm his hands. "We haven't seen a sign of the creatures since we killed those three. Figured it was better to light a fire and keep from freezing to death than to worry about the risk of drawing attention to ourselves. Didn't seem like we had much of a choice."

Alexander thought a moment before nodding in agreement. "You've done well," he said simply. "I owe you my life."

Edward brought the Captain a mug of hot tea. "You'd do the same for us, no doubt. Here, drink this. I've a pine bark soup brewing, but it will be awhile before it's ready. Ran out of jerky yesterday."

The hot tea was soothing, and the three men drank it in silence while the heat from the fire slowly began to warm their aching muscles. Although the Mackays were strong, tough highlanders, pulling and sometimes carrying

Alexander's dead weight through the rough terrain was exhausting labor. They were forced to be vigilant, and both men wondered about their ability to survive should they stumble across the creatures' path again.

"Do you think we'll reach the river tomorrow?" Alexander asked into the lengthening silence.

"Should make it by midday," Angus replied.

"Let's hope we're lucky enough to meet Sergeant Graham and the Landsend ferry when we get to the Skara," Alexander muttered.

Edward checked the pot of bark soup. "If Sergeant Graham got everybody from the garrison and Landsend loaded up and moved out, the ferry made its last run when it took them down river. This is the eighth day since we left Landsend." He shook his grizzled head. "I don't know, Captain, we're cutting it mighty close. For our sake I hope it took the Sergeant longer than he anticipated to get the people out of Landsend."

Angus finished his tea. "That soup ready yet?"

"Yes. Hand me your mug. Yours, too, Captain."

Edward filled the two mugs and handed them back. Alexander hesitantly lifted the cup to his nose. "This smells terrible, Edward." He took an experimental sip and nearly spit it back out."

"It may not be meat stew, but it's about all there is to keep us alive," Edward said in apology. "No rabbits or birds left in the hills, so it doesn't do much good to go hunting."

Alexander took another sip, swallowed and tried not to gag. He knew the bark soup was nutritious and would keep a man alive when there was nothing else to eat.

Baskers, he mused. *If it weren't for Angus and Edward Mackay, I'd be dead now. Better drink my soup so I don't make all their work in lugging me this far for naught.* He gulped down the contents of his mug.

"Want some more, Captain?" Edward grinned.

"No thank you." Alexander's mouth puckered in distaste. "One cup will do me just fine."

Angus laughed and emptied the contents of his mug. "You can bet it will be a long time before I eat bark soup again." He threw more wood on the fire and watched the sparks shoot into the air and die out. "You two get some sleep. I'll take first watch." He drew a blanket snugly around his shoulders and settled back. "Glad you're still with us, Captain. We were a bit worried about you for awhile."

Alexander smiled at the understated comment. His eyelids drooped and just before he slept, he wondered how bad off he'd been.

~

The Guardians reached the Skara River shortly after noon the next day. After a brief rest they followed the river as it wound its way along the edge of the High Ghilana Plain. The bitter cold of the mountains eased somewhat, and the rush and tumble of the river was a pleasant sound after the oppressing silence of The Dlarmids. Still on the alert for danger, the Mackays began to relax, for an attack seemed less likely to happen here in the open. It was late afternoon when Alexander called a halt.

"What do you think, Captain? Should we camp here and wait a bit, or do we push on?" Edward Mackay asked as he hunkered down beside Alexander.

Alexander groaned as he rolled to his left side and pushed himself to a sitting position. Edward reached out to aid him, but Alexander shook his head, determined to overcome the debilitating weakness of his wounds. He sat quietly, breathing deeply of the cold air. Wind whipped the snow into a brief flurry and blurred land and horizon into one. Alexander shivered with cold and the strain of remaining upright.

"Let's camp here for the night. There's not much daylight left anyway. We'll push on again tomorrow. If we're ahead of the ferry, it will catch up to us. It not, we should make the Fort in a couple more days." He cast an anxious eye to the gray-white sky. "I just hope the weather holds," he muttered as he eased himself down flat on the sledge. With a sigh that was half moan, he closed his eyes. "Don't know how much more of Edward's bark soup I can take."

They camped in a small stand of stunted ash trees not far from the riverbank. A few shrived berries still clung stubbornly to withered, twisted branches, perhaps in silent defiance to the power that was attempting to strangle their life force. An ample supply of driftwood insured the Guardians of fuel for a fire to keep them warm during the night.

Edward crouched beside the leaping flames, warming his numbed fingers. Water for tea was just beginning to boil when he raised his head, straining to hear.

"Listen," he said sharply, interrupting the desultory conversation between Angus and Alexander.

117

All three men turned their attention toward the river, senses alert for the repetition of the sound Edward had heard.

Seconds ticked by and then, faintly, far up the river, the sound of a horn floated on the wind. A few more breathless seconds and it came again, slightly louder and closer.

The Guardians looked at each other and grinned.

"We made it, Captain," Angus said. "By the gods, we jolly damn well made it."

~

A shadow moved, his black robe blending with the rocks and dark trunks of trees. He watched men lift another man into a small boat sent ashore while a river ferry waited in midstream, watched the ferry pull away and continue down the river until it disappeared in the distance.

Silence descended once again over the river, and the dark man stepped from his hiding place. Snow began sifting slowly through the branches of the trees. He looked about, his hooded head turning slowly from side to side before fading into the shadows.

His master would want to know about the three dead Spriggans he'd found deep within The Dlarmids at the base of a ridge that overlooked the army's camp and about the three men he'd been following out of the mountains. He must hurry. He'd been away for several days. His master would be pleased with his surveillance and his information.

Snow fell faster and a cold wind whipped it into a white flurry. The dark form moved swiftly, his footprints rapidly obliterated by the accumulating snow.

"I'm coming, Master. I'm coming," he murmured.

~

Gentle hands carefully lifted Alexander into a bunk, and his boots and heavy garments were quickly removed. He soon lay warm and clean under several blankets, his shoulder tended and securely bandaged by a middle-aged woman named Sarah.

She had tut-tuted all during the process, and when Alexander winced at a particularly sharp pain produced by her probing fingers, she pursed her lips and rummaged in the small brown pouch she wore at her waist.

"This will sting some, Captain," she muttered as she smeared a revolting smelling salve on his wound.

Alexander clenched his teeth against sudden, searing pain until he thought his jaws were permanently locked in that position. "I think," he wheezed as the pain began to subside, "that was an understatement, Madame."

Sarah merely went on with her ministering, and soon his shoulder was comfortably bandaged, and his arm in a sling to prevent any unnecessary movement. He sighed wearily as the woman stood up to leave.

"Thank you," he said quietly.

Sarah smiled for the first time since she entered the small cabin. "Those two heavy-handed highlanders did very well, considering. You'll soon have the use of your sword arm, and by the looks of things, we'll have great need of your sword." She tucked the blankets securely about him. "I'll see that some food is brought to you. Then you should get some rest."

At his nod, she gathered her things and left. Soon after, a steward brought him a large bowl of hot stew and a round loaf of dark bread; and propped against a couple of pillows he ate ravenously although he found feeding himself with his left hand awkward. He briefly wondered where the cook had found enough vegetables for the tasty meal, but he was too hungry to think about it for long. Replete at last, he set the bowl aside. With a contented sigh, he closed his eyes and slept.

~

"Captain Lamond."

Someone shook him gently, urging him to wakefulness.

"Go 'way," Alexander muttered groggily. He wanted to burrow back into the warm cocoon of sleep, but the ill-mannered lout who kept insisting he wake up would not go away.

Alexander swore irritably and came fully awake.

A contrite-looking Sergeant Graham sat on a stool beside the bunk.

"I'm really sorry to wake you, Captain." He retrieved a tray from the small table beside him. "Here, I've brought you some breakfast. Sarah thought it was time for you to eat again."

Alexander grunted and pushed himself into a sitting position. He rubbed his face with his left hand to push away the last vestiges of sleep.

"Thanks," he said, accepting the tray from Henry Graham and balancing it on his lap. "Sorry I snapped at you."

A smile flickered briefly over the sergeant's mouth and he shrugged. The Mackays had told him last night that they really hadn't expected their captain to survive the trek out of The Dlarmids. A little ill humor on being awakened from a sound sleep was easily overlooked.

Alexander took a long pull of the hot tea that accompanied the hotcakes on his breakfast tray. His eyes opened wide as the liquid hit his stomach.

"Baskers," he finally wheezed. The tea was heavily laced with the fiery whiskey brewed in the highlands.

Sergeant Graham grinned. "Sarah thought you might be needing a drop or two to get the blood flowing."

Alexander raised the mug in silent tribute to the thoughtful Sarah and drank more judiciously of the potent tea.

He chuckled with satisfaction before tackling the stack of oatcakes. "That Sarah is a mighty good woman."

Alexander ate silently for a few minutes before turning his attention to Graham. "I assume the Mackays gave you a full report?"

"Yes, sir, they did."

Alexander nodded and sipped on his tea. "They saved my life," he said quietly. "See to it than an appropriate commendation is given to them."

"I'll take care of it, Captain."

"Good. Now, how far are we from the Fort?"

"We should be there soon."

"The evacuation of Landsend went smoothly, I take it?"

Graham shrugged. "With a few exceptions. There were some folks who found it difficult to leave so much behind." He hunched forward on the low stool, his elbows resting on his knees, his chin on his clasped hands. "It took one more day than I thought it would to get everybody packed. I guess that was your lucky day, Captain."

Alexander stared into the depths of his mug for a long moment before draining it.

"What was the situation before you were able to get everybody on the ferry? Any more sightings of Spriggans?"

"Yes. Several sightings. Of course, hysterical townspeople reported most of them, so I'm not sure how accurate the number is. My men saw a couple of small groups of the creatures lurking about. We also killed two when they attacked a patrol near the waterfront."

"Any of your men hurt or killed?"

"No. It was strange, though, Captain. The beasts were carrying war axes, but they didn't really know how to use them. That's the first time I've seen them with any weapons."

"Did you retrieve the axes?"

"Yes." Sergeant Graham lowered his clasped hands and sat staring at them. "The axes were made of Kaenolirian steel."

Alexander nodded. "I expected as much. The Mackays and I watched the beasts being trained in the use of weapons. It appears that Maelorn is attempting to make them into a real army." He sighed deeply. "Let's hope he's not successful."

The boat lurched and both men felt it slow.

"Looks like we're close to the Fort, Captain." Sergeant Graham rose to go.

"See if you can find some clothes for me, Sergeant. Oh, and by the way, where is the silver knife I was carrying inside my tunic?"

Graham went down on one knee beside the bunk and reached under the mattress. He extracted the small knife and handed it to Alexander as he rose. The knife pulsed in Alexander's hand when he took it. He smiled slightly at its steady beat. The knife had done what Talanor said it would do—protect him. He would not have known of the Spriggans' presence if the knife had not warned him. He closed his fist tightly around it and nodded to Graham in dismissal.

~

"We'd about given you up for lost, Captain." Simon Stewart helped Alexander into his bed and pulled the blankets up around him. He fussed about the room, making sure there was a fresh pitcher of water close at hand, emptying Alexander's pack and putting things away.

"Simon." Alexander's patience was sorely tried, for the young Guardian had been hovering near him since the river ferry docked. "Leave that. I'll take care of it myself."

"But I don't mind, Captain, and besides, you shouldn't—"

"Baskers, Simon, I'm wounded but I'm not helpless," Alexander exploded. "Now leave that be. We've more important things to be concerned about right now."

"Yes, sir." The young man fidgeted. "Sorry, sir," he shrugged.

Alexander sighed. "First of all, I want you to see to the quartering of the garrison from Landsend. Then arrange to have someone familiarize the new men with the area around the Fort. Form a detail to see to it that the supplies they brought with them are stored. Sergeant Graham will help you." Alexander pushed back one of the blankets Simon had so carefully tucked around him. "That's all for now."

Simon quickly left the room, glad for something constructive to do. When the door closed behind him, Alexander pushed the rest of the covers away. He swung his long legs over the edge of the bed, and with a determined effort he stood. His head spun with the unaccustomed movement, and he reached out to steady himself with a hand on the wall.

"Baskers," he swore. There was so much to be done and so little time in which to do it; he couldn't afford the luxury of lying abed. He moved carefully across the sparsely furnished room to a small square table and eased himself into one of the chairs that stood near it. His pack and gear lay on the floor nearby where Simon had dropped them. He reached for his boots and struggled to put them on. Savage curses singed the air, and sweat beaded on his forehead as he tried to pull on a boot with one hand. By the time he managed to get both boots on, he was panting with weakness. Still swearing, he forced himself to stand and made his way slowly and deliberately to the door.

His office was down a long corridor that had somehow grown longer in his absence. He paused to lean against the wall and gathered what strength remained to him. The temptation to turn around and head back to his bed was great, but the urgency of the work that awaited him proved greater. Resolutely, he pushed away from the wall and, moving with the studied care of a drunken man, continued down the hall.

Chapter Ten

Kailie listened to the lyrical voice, concentrated on its cadence, and absorbed its beauty. Rhianna Lanee held a large book bound in gilt reverently in her hands.

"This is the Quair, Kailie. It contains all the Songs given to the Singers by the Faerie. My ancestors and I have been responsible for teaching the Golden Ones the Songs their voices are best suited for." She stroked the book lovingly. "It has been a long time since I've had the pleasure of teaching a Singer." She smiled sadly at Kailie. "I remember your father very well. He has a magnificent and powerful voice. Talanor tells me you sing at least as well as he does." She opened the book. "We shall see."

The two women sat in a room whose large windows stood open to the gentle breezes. The towering trees that sheltered the Singers' Hall muted the sun's bright light and cast shadows across the gleaming floor.

Kailie reached out to touch the fragile parchment. Her fingertips caressed the page in the same way Rhianna's did. She felt the slightest of vibrations and sensed the innate power of the printed Song.

"This is the Song sung by those who helped Kaenolir's farmers. Farmer Singers have been gone a long time now, but I think this music will be helpful when the time comes for the land to blossom and live again."

Kailie closed her eyes, her fingers still touching the Quair, and sang. The notes of the Song rose and fell, whispering of rain, humming of growth.

"It's a most appealing Song, Rhianna," she said when she finished.

Rhianna gazed for a long time into Kailie's sky-blue eyes. Her interpretation of the Song was both sensitive and sensual, a combination of aesthetic appreciation and earthy knowledge. Rhianna could not remember ever having heard it sung with such feeling. Kailie had sung the Song with a vibrant understanding of its power to restore the land and give it life.

"Yes, it is. Talanor tells me the Darkling has caused much of the land to die and the weather to turn to extremes." Rhianna sighed. "Kaenolir was once a land as lovely as this Song."

Rhianna turned the page and explained the Song of healing. Again Rhianna sensed the power the young woman unknowingly possessed when she sang this Song. As more Songs were explained and sung, the hours passed, but the two women were too engrossed in the Quair to notice. All that was important to them was the music and the magic of the Songs.

As the sun began to set, they came at last to the Warrior Song, but when Kailie would have sung it, Rhianna stopped her. "No. Your father warned you not to sing this for good reason. Maelorn must not know of your presence yet. If he has grown so strong that he can disrupt the seasons and the life of Kaenolir and take your father captive, he must be able to withstand the power the Song imbues."

Rhianna closed the Quair and rose to put it in its special place in the music room. The rays of the setting sun pierced through the trees and filled the room with glowing light.

"Rhianna, you did not show me all the Songs," Kailie said softly.

"What?" Rhianna turned in surprise.

"The pages that are sealed with a gold seal at the back of the Quair. What are those Songs, Rhianna?"

Rhianna placed the Quair on its pedestal, and came to stand before Kailie. She looked at the beautiful young woman, and her heart ached with the realization of what would be asked of Kailie Fairchild. Rhianna reached out to take Kailie's face in her hands. Both women were tall and slender, the power of the Faerie apparent in both.

"You will sing that music as well, Kailie," she whispered. "But I will not be the one to teach you."

"Who will?"

Rhianna shook her head. "You will see soon enough." She touched the curls near Kailie's ear that had slipped free of the confining braid. "Come. You must eat and rest awhile."

~

Rhianna and Talanor walked in the quiet twilight that settled over the Horn of Kalora. Nightingales sang, soft breezes touched them, then slipped away. Soon the moon would rise to cast its silver sheen over the landscape. The Horn was unlike any other place on earth, and Talanor never ceased to marvel at its mysterious beauty and the quiet power it embodied.

It was a most fitting place for the Singers to have lived and trained. Singers' Hall was silent now, had been silent for a long time. Its impressive walls, arched and gilded, had echoed with the music of a time now passed; its massive doors and windows were closed and shuttered. Silently, majestically, a testament to the ageless power of the Faerie, the hall stood waiting for the music of the Golden Ones to ring again.

Talanor looked up into the branches of the trees that grew beside their path and formed a thick, rustling canopy overhead. He could not see where trees ended and sky began. Flowers of every variety, many of which he could not identify, covered the Horn like a carpet . Birdsong filled the air with music. Mists swirled and then glided away, creating a world of shadow and illusion. While Kaenolir withered and died, the Horn remained the same as it always had, untouched except by Faerie.

While he was the last of the line of mages who gave counsel to the people of Kaenolir, Rhianna Lanee was the last mage to have trained the Singers. She was wise, beautiful, ethereal, and seemingly ageless.

Many years had passed since he'd last seen her. She had become more and more a recluse, living here on the Horn alone, seeing no one, wanting nothing to intrude on her tranquility. He had often thought of her and wondered how she fared, wondered why she remained at the Singers' Hall. He had thought it possible that he and Kailie would not find her on the Horn, that she might have followed the path back to the world from which she had come.

"Why have you stayed here?" Talanor put word to thought.

They walked along for some time before Rhianna answered him. "I stayed because Goldenhorn still lived, his Song still needed," she said at last. "And I stayed because I knew that I would some day be needed again." She stopped and turned to him. "I have been waiting." She paused and looked deeply into his eyes, now cast in shadow. "Waiting for Kailie. And I'm glad it was you who brought her to me." She smiled softly at him and then began to walk again.

"She is … unique … and special, Talanor. I spent years training voices, teaching Singers their Songs. Today I went through each Song in the Quair with Kailie. She sang each one perfectly. The first time through. And with a depth of feeling unlike any I've ever heard." She paused before continuing. "She has the talent of all the Singers gathered within her. I know she is only half Singer, but the Faerie have chosen to give her more power than any one Singer has ever possessed, more power than her father, more power than even I." She came to a stop and gazed long at the man who looked at her with troubled eyes. "I fear for her. Talanor. She is just one and yet she will be asked to do so much."

"Is she strong enough to do all that she must in order to protect Kaenolir?" he asked gravely.

Rhianna sighed deeply. "I don't know." She reached out to take Talanor's arm, and they continued to walk, their footsteps cushioned by a mat of leaves, their way illuminated by the moon.

"When she has rested, I'll take her to the tip of the Horn. You will not be able to follow us, nor must you try. I do not know how long we will remain there, but we shall return."

"Why?"

"No, Talanor. Do not ask. It is not for you to know."

Talanor grumbled irritably but did not press Rhianna for answers he knew she could not give him.

Rhianna smiled and squeezed his arm in silent gratitude.

"Look," she pointed ahead. The path had come to a misty bower surrounded by giant oak trees and nodding willows. The grass grew here in a thick carpet, and overhead a nightingale sang as if only for their enjoyment. "Will you stay with me?" Rhianna asked quietly. "It has been such a long time."

Talanor drew her with him into the bower. "Too long," he rumbled low in his throat. "Much too long."

~

"Kailie," the lilting tones roused her. "We must go."

Rhianna stood beside the bed in which Kailie slept. "Hurry, child, we have much to do."

Brushing the sleep from her eyes, Kailie pushed the covers away and rose. She washed quickly and turned to dress.

"No," Rhianna stopped her when she reached for her own simple gown. "I would have you wear this." She held up a white gown shot through with gold.

"Oh," Kailie breathed.

Rhianna slipped the gown over Kailie's tousled curls, adjusted it at the shoulders and waist, and fastened the tiny buttons that ran down the back. The gown molded Kailie's slender form and fell from her shoulders in long flowing lines. The sleeves ended in points on the backs of her hands. Gold threads gleamed here and there as she turned.

"Sit," Rhianna commanded and took a brush to the tangled mass of curls that hung down Kailie's back to her waist. She did not braid the strands as Kailie did, but let them tumble free.

"There," Rhianna laid the brush aside. "Stand up and let me look at you."

Kailie was a vision of white and gold, with the beauty of woman, the mystery of Faerie. Her skin glowed, made golden by the sun and her own inherent serenity. Her eyes sparkled with life and delight. Rhianna felt a sudden sharp pang near her heart, knowing that she was about to set Kailie on a path from which there could be no turning back, a path Rhianna knew to be fraught with danger and death.

"You are lovely," she said.

"Where are you taking me, Rhianna?"

Rhianna took the young woman's hand, in much the same manner as when she led her to the glen. "Come with me," she said simply. "'Tis time to go."

~

The path followed a brook that skipped over rocks and reflected the sunlight in diamond droplets as it rushed on its way to the sea. Willows bent low over the water and rustled in a morning breeze as the two women passed. Here and there, pockets of mist floated above the brook and through the branches of the trees, drifting down to lay moist fingers to hair and cheeks of the passers-by. Birds sang, but though Kailie searched, she could not see them. As they walked on, she hummed the Song of the forest, and Rhianna smiled as she listened to the melody.

Mists swirled closer and more thickly. The birdsong drifted farther and farther away until they walked in near silence. The music of the silver burn still sounded close by, but the stream was visible only when the mists parted.

Although she felt unafraid, Kailie was uneasy with the surroundings and turned to Rhianna.

She was alone.

"Rhianna?" she called. "Rhianna."

She came to a standstill and looked about. Fog, thick and gray, swirled around her and obscured everything. She took a hesitant step and then another, but no solid ground met the force of her step, only the mist. She thought she heard a sound and turned toward it, but there was nothing of substance to be seen.

The mists began to eddy and twist around her, making the long gown she wore twirl about her legs and thighs. Her arms lifted in self-protection; she spread her fingers wide before her but could not see them. Kailie gasped, not so much in fear as in surprise. When she moved again, she felt her body lift. The feeling was like that of floating on the surface of a cool pond on a warm summer's day. She laughed as the floating sensation carried her. Her senses heightened to feel the velvety touch of the mist, to smell the heavy fragrance of flowers she could not see, to hear music that filled her mind and opened her heart.

Kailie.

The music called to her.

"Kailie Fairchild, come to me."

The voice was achingly familiar.

"Father?" Kailie cried. "Father, where are you?"

The mists continued to carry her while she tried desperately to see.

"Father," she cried again, this time more frantically.

"Hush, my child. You have nothing to fear." The voice was close by, she was sure of it. "Here I am."

The floating sensation stopped. Although mists continued to swirl about her, her feet were on firm ground.

"Look at me, Kailie."

She turned her head in the direction of the voice and saw him standing there. The shimmering haze parted to reveal a tall, golden-haired man with amber eyes, but Kailie fretted that she was unable to see his features distinctly. A circlet of gold gleamed upon his head. He held out his hand and she took it.

The golden man smiled. "Walk with me."

They walked for what Kailie believed to be a long time, her hand held firmly in his cool one, until she heard the sound of the sea. She took a deep breath and smelled the tang of salt air. The Golden One stopped and turned her to face him. He looked into her eyes for a long moment, searching for answers.

"You are a true child of the Faerie, Kailie Fairchild, but with the touch of your mother, too." He stepped away and offered his hand to her once more.

They had gone only a few steps when a door appeared before them. It opened and Kailie entered a vast chamber. A vaulted ceiling ascended to the sky while long, narrow windows allowed light to filter in. The air hummed with music so subtly that Kailie felt it more than heard it.

The Golden One led her to the center of the room where a large slab of white stone stood. Upon it rested a book. Kailie had but to glance at it to know it was the Quair. With much the same reverence that Rhianna Lanee had shown, he opened the book, but passed over the Songs that Kailie had sung for Rhianna and turned to the section with the gold seal.

He paused with his hand on the seal. "Come here, Kailie Fairchild."

She moved to stand beside him, and he took her hand and laid it on the seal. The pulse and rhythm of music vibrated in her fingertips.

"Open the seal," he commanded.

She looked into his amber eyes for a moment before doing his bidding. The clasp loosened easily at her touch and fell aside, opening to the last Song in the Quair. When she touched the page, she felt her heart leap, her spirit soar. The power and force of the Song beat against her, and for the first time since leaving the Singers' Hall, she was truly afraid.

Kailie stepped back from the Quair, but gentle hands reached to steady her.

"There is nothing to fear in the Song," the Golden One whispered as he held her. "I am here with you."

She calmed with his soothing words. When her fear at last subsided, she raised her head to look at him.

"What is this Song?" she asked quietly.

"It is a Song that has never been sung by any Singer. It was composed after the War of the Brothers in anticipation of a time when war would rage again, when the forces of good and evil were pitted against each other in a struggle to the death. The Song will be sung only once, and you, my child, are the one destined to sing it."

"How do you know this?"

"Because, Kailie, the seal could only be broken by the one who is capable of singing the Song."

"Why will it be sung only once?"

"It is of such power that the need for its music will be very great, and the Singer who sings it invested with a mission to save Kaenolir and its people from unspeakable evil. But, Kailie, you must know that the Song may well be sung at great cost to the Singer."

"But to save Kaenolir. And my father?"

"Yes."

His arms fell away from her and she stepped away from the white stone, her mind full of questions.

Why was she the one chosen to sing the unsung Song? How could she know when to sing it? What would happen when the Song ended?

She turned back to the Golden One. "It is a gift from the Faerie, like all the other Songs, isn't that so?"

"Yes," he said quietly. "Long ago, the people who inhabited the land that is known as Kaenolir saved a king of the Faerie from death. When he asked what he could do to repay them, they wanted only one thing: They asked that he protect himself from the dark power that sought to kill him and keep himself and his people safe. He was so astounded that they thought only of his safety and well being that he promised he would, in keeping himself and his Faerie kingdom safe, also protect their land and its people.

"He gave them the Golden Ones and their Songs, and for centuries the Songs were all that was needed to help protect Kaenolir. But the time has come when the music of the Quair is not enough. The time has come for a Song of such power that the evil threatening Kaenolir can be overcome. There was no one, however, who possessed enough talent to sing it. Until now. The power to save Kaenolir rests only within you.

"You have been chosen to sing the Unsung Song, the Last Song. Your voice, only your voice, will lift the music from the Quair, just as your hand broke the seal. The Song will demand everything of you, Kailie, perhaps even your life." He shook his head and stood waiting.

Kailie walked back to the Quair and stood staring down at the music of the Last Song.

Tears filled Kailie's eyes and she lifted her head, turning away from the Quair, seeking some solace in the lofty arches of the chamber. Sobs filled her mind, and she sank to her knees before the cold stone.

The enormity of her task seemed too great to comprehend. "How?" she whispered.

The Golden One knelt beside her. He touched her trembling shoulder and, murmuring softly, soothed her fears. At last, when she stilled, he lifted a basket from the stone and held out a small round, white fruit, the size of a large cherry.

"This will give you wisdom to know when and how to use the Faerie music to save Kaenolir and her people."

When she hesitated, he merely waited patiently beside her, offering her the delicate fruit. Taking a deep breath she took the fruit and ate it, savoring the exotic taste. Its flavor was sweet but unfamiliar.

The Golden One touched her lips with a second fruit. This one was slightly larger than the first and blood red in color. Its smooth surface was warm on her lips. Again she ate and found the red fruit's flavor to be very sweet.

"You will need courage, my child, in your endeavors. Sometimes you will need to delve deeply within yourself, but you will never lack the determination and resolve to do what must be done."

He reached once more into the basket and offered Kailie a third and final fruit. Blue in color, it was the sweetest of all, its taste exploding on her tongue.

"This is my gift to you, little one. When all else is done, this will remain. My gift is love. Know that this gift is without price and without end."

When she finished the blue fruit, he gave her a golden goblet filled with wine. She gasped as she looked into the chalice; the wine was the dark, rich color of blood.

"Now," he said, "you must drink this as you ate the fruit. It is bitter, but it too will give you strength when you accept that there will be pain and sorrow before peace and joy."

Kailie drank, and the wine was bitter, so bitter it burned her tongue and throat. But as the taste filled her mouth she felt a surge of power, and she rose from her knees. The Golden One rose with her.

"Take the Quair in your hands, Kailie, and learn the Last Song."

~

Rhianna Lanee sat beside the bed in which Kailie slept. Talanor stood near the open door and watched the almost imperceptible rise and fall of the blanket covering Kailie's still form. He and Rhianna had been in these same positions for some time, with little change in Kailie's condition.

Since Rhianna returned with Kailie, Talanor feared that the young woman would die. She appeared so fragile, her eyes sunken, her skin pale, almost transparent. Wherever Rhianna had taken Kailie, the child had gone a long, long way. He prayed she would be able to find her way back.

The form on the bed stirred. "Father," Kailie murmured.

Rhianna took the slender hand that picked at the blanket between her own warm ones. "Kailie, wake up, child."

Kailie turned her head on the pillow toward the sound of the lilting voice and with a great effort opened her eyes. Talanor stepped to the end of the bed and shook his head in despair. The blue eyes once so filled with life were dull and cloudy. She licked her dry lips and rolled her head back and forth on the pillow.

"Help me lift her, Talanor. We must get her to drink this." Rhianna held a cup in her hand, and as Talanor stepped around to the side of the bed and lifted Kailie's head and shoulders, she placed the cup to Kailie's lips.

"Drink, Kailie, you must drink all of it."

When Kailie finished drinking the contents of the cup, Talanor laid her back against the pillows. She hardly weighed anything, and he worriedly watched her as she closed her eyes once more and slipped back to sleep.

"Will she be all right, Rhianna?"

"Yes. She'll rest comfortably now for some time, and when she wakens, her strength will have returned."

Talanor looked doubtfully at Rhianna. She gave him a tired smile and touched his haggard face. "Trust me. She went far away, but she will come back to us."

Talanor sighed and looked at the sleeping woman. "Where did she go, Rhianna?"

"You must ask her yourself. When she awakens. We'll leave her to sleep now, and you must get some rest, too. You've a hard journey ahead of you, after you leave the Horn."

With a last look at the sleeping figure, his gaze sad and troubled, Talanor turned and followed Rhianna from the room.

~

Time had little meaning on the Horn of Kalora, and Talanor had no way of knowing if he and Kailie had been there for several days, several weeks, or only several hours. He felt a deep sense of urgency, however, and knew that if Kailie did not regain her strength soon, he would be forced to leave without her. He had promised Alexander he would come to the Fort as soon as he could. Kaenolir needed him.

"Talanor."

His thoughts were interrupted by the sound of Kailie's voice. She came to him and when he did not speak, she touched his sleeve and smiled.

It was Kailie who stood before him, but she had changed from the young woman he had found in Fairtown. She was now more beautiful than any woman he had ever seen, even more beautiful than Rhianna. An aura surrounded her that he knew came from inner strength and knowledge. Her blue eyes were once again bright and alive, but now he saw flecks of amber in their depths. Her voice, too, had changed, perhaps only subtly, but changed nonetheless. Its tones were more melodic, shaped and rounded by an enchantment he could not know. She seemed wrapped in a cloak of Faerie magic, and he felt a kindred spirit in the beauty he saw and the strength he knew she had gained.

"Talanor? Are you all right?"

He sighed and cupped her face with his hands, rubbing his thumbs lightly over the fragile bones of her cheeks. "Yes," he rumbled low. "Are you?"

She smiled and placed her hands over his. "Yes, I'm all right now." She lowered their hands but kept his clasped between her cool ones. "It will soon be time to leave the Horn. Kaenolir needs us."

"Yes. As soon as you feel up to it, we will bid Rhianna Lanee farewell and make our way to the Guardians' Fort. I promised Captain Lamond I would come as soon as I could. I also told him I would bring you if Rhianna thought you could help."

"I'm ready to go at once. I have only to say goodbye to Rhianna and then we can leave."

"Good."

Kailie freed Talanor's hands and turned to go.

"Kailie." Talanor's voice stopped her.

"Yes?"

The big man looked into her eyes. She didn't know what he saw there, but his own were deeply troubled. "How far did you travel, child, when you walked with Rhianna? How far do you have yet to go?"

Kailie's smile was tinged with sadness. "A long way, Talanor, a very long way."

He did not know if she answered the first or second question.

Chapter Eleven

Alexander paused in his inspection of the Wall of Rhade to look out over the dry plain. He removed his hat and wiped the sweat from his forehead. It was nearly the end of the day, but he knew there would be no cool breezes when darkness came. The ancient stones radiated heat from beneath his feet, and the lowering sun beat upon everything it touched. He spat and cursed the heat, the dust, and the stench of unrelenting fear.

Wearily replacing his hat, he absently rubbed his right shoulder, still stiff from his wound. It had healed cleanly, but he didn't have time to rest and let the shoulder recover completely. Every day was filled with frantic preparations for the attack that was sure to come from the north. He was needed; there was no time to lie abed. So while Simon groused at him to get more rest and he swore at his weakness, he organized men and supplies and work schedules.

He continued his inspection and despaired at what he found. Even knowing the Wall had long ago begun to deteriorate did not make what he found any more acceptable. It would take more men, supplies, and time than he had to repair the crumbling rampart. All that could be done was fill breaches as quickly as possible, shore up watchtowers, and repair the gates.

"Simon," he called, "as soon as the lumber arrives from Shiptown, set the carpenters to work on the Wall gate."

"Yes, sir."

"I want to talk to the chief ironworker and the head mechanic at the end of the day for a report on their progress in repairing the river gate."

The massive iron gate, forged hundreds of years ago and set in place with the help of ancient magic, was meant to close off the river from any advancing enemy force. But the gate had stood open for so long that the gears and pulleys of the operating mechanism had frozen from disuse and rust. For several days craftsmen had worked around the clock to repair the mechanism that would close the gate and lock it in position.

Simon nodded. "Anything else, Captain?"

"Do the masons have everything they need to patch the breaks in the wall?"

"I'll check."

Alexander nodded. "Let me know what's needed."

Simon saluted briskly and hurried away.

Alexander walked slowly toward the next tower, gazing out over the chest high parapet. The sun was a blood-red sphere caught just above the horizon. The violent color of the sunset seemed to him a portent of what lay ahead.

Red for blood. Blood and death.

When would Maelorn's army come pouring down out of The Dlarmids, he wondered. Would Maelorn wait until the cold of winter set in, or would he attack before the Kaenolirians had a chance to prepare for war?

He hoped he would have an answer soon. Three days ago he had chosen four of his best men, including the Mackay brothers, and sent them into the mountains to judge the size of Maelorn's army, its location, and, if they could, its readiness to move. It was a dangerous mission, but without information Alexander knew he could not improve the vulnerable position of the Guardians.

"May the gods protect them," he said quietly and turned to make his way back to the Fort.

~

"Captain, there's someone here to see you." Alexander looked up from helping one of the masons set a stone in place to face a perspiring Simon.

"I showed them into your office and gave them something to drink."

"Who, Simon?"

"What?"

"Who is here to see me?" Alexander asked patiently.

"I'm not sure."

Alexander lifted an eyebrow.

"What I mean is, I'm not sure, Captain. He's the biggest man I've ever seen and she, well, she—" Simon gulped and stumbled to a halt.

Alexander bit the inside of his bottom lip to keep from snapping irritably at the young soldier. He'd never seen Simon at such a loss for words. What was wrong with him? Had he been out in the heat too long? He looked absolutely dazed.

"She?"

"What?"

"Baskers, Simon, what are you stammering about? I haven't got all—" Alexander stopped abruptly. "Big man, you say?"

"Yes, sir."

"Long white beard and blue eyes that look right through you?"

"That's him."

Alexander wiped his forehead with the heel of his hand. "Talanor," he smiled. No wonder Simon looked a bit dazed.

"What did you say, Captain?"

"I said 'Talanor.' The man is named Talanor Rowan."

"Oh."

"Here, help get these stones cemented in. If you need me, I'll be in my office."

"Sure."

"What?"

"I mean, yes, yes, sir." Simon's face turned a deep shade of red. "Sorry, sir," he mumbled.

As Simon took his place, Alexander picked up a rag from a nearby bench and wiped his hands before tossing it aside and striding away.

~

Talanor turned from perusing the map of Kaenolir that hung on the wall behind Alexander's desk at the sound of hurrying footsteps. When Alexander stepped through the doorway, the big man moved to greet him.

"Alexander," Talanor said with a smile. He touched the younger man's shoulder and the smile faded. "You've been wounded. And badly." Piercing blue eyes scrutinized the face before him. It was paler, more haggard, with dark shadows under tired green eyes. "What happened?"

Alexander returned the mage's smile with a lop-sided one. "I ran into something bigger than I am." He placed both hands on his hips. "And hello to you, too."

136

Talanor huffed impatiently. "A Spriggan or a Ghillie?"

"Spriggan."

"Where?"

"In The Dlarmids."

"When?"

"About a month ago."

"Will you let me look at your shoulder?"

"Later perhaps."

"Huh. We're going to need that shoulder, you know."

"Yes, I know. Perhaps even better than you."

"Well? What did you find in The Dlarmids?"

"It's a rather long story." Alexander motioned Talanor to a chair and moved to his desk. Simon had placed a pitcher of water and three mugs there, and he reached for the pitcher. He continued to speak while he poured.

"Simon said there was a woman with you. Did you find Kailie Fairchild, then?"

"I am here, Captain Lamond."

The voice danced along his nerve endings and set them humming. Alexander hastily set the pitcher down and looked in the direction from which the voice came. Kailie rose from a chair in a shadowed corner of the room. She doffed a wide-brimmed hat and came to stand before him.

The first thing he noted was her height. Her head came just to his shoulder. She had tilted it back slightly now to look into his eyes.

And her eyes...

Even in the filtered light of the office he could tell they were the color of the sky and flecked with gold. She smiled in greeting, and his eyes dropped to her mouth. It was wide and inviting.

Kailie stood quietly under Alexander's intense scrutiny and wondered why he looked at her as he did.

"Captain?" she questioned softly.

Alexander remembered to breathe again and silently chastised himself for his rude behavior. He realized why Simon had tripped over his tongue. Not because of Talanor, but more likely because of Kailie.

Finding his voice at last, he noisily cleared his throat.

"My lady," he said inclining his head. "Welcome to the Fort."

"Thank you, Captain." The voice slid down his spine again, and he wrenched his eyes away.

"Did Simon see to quarters for you both?" His brow furrowed as he turned to Talanor. The big man sat smiling; for once his blue eyes twinkled with something akin to delight.

"Baskers," Alexander muttered to no one in particular and glared at Talanor. *Does he ever miss anything?* "Well?" he demanded.

"No, not yet. He went off to find you."

"We're crowded, but I'm sure we can work something out. You might wind up bunking with me."

"I don't mind," Talanor smiled slightly. "Do you?"

Alexander growled as he sat down in the chair behind his desk.

A chuckle rumbled deep in Talanor's throat. He turned to Kailie and met her quizzical gaze. "Would you like to clean away a little of the road grime and rest for awhile?"

"Yes, I would. I'm sure you have much to talk about with Captain Lamond."

Alexander glanced briefly at her and came to his feet. "I'll show you to my quarters. You should be comfortable enough there until we've made other arrangements for you." He stepped away from his desk and waited for her to precede him.

The long golden braid swayed with each graceful step she took as Alexander followed her out the door. He swore softly to himself when he remembered the small, neat room in the Goldenhorn's cottage and the feeling that he had experienced when stepping into it.

He had sensed then that the woman who lived in the room was beautiful, but 'beautiful' somehow did not adequately describe the Goldenhorn's daughter.

~

"So," Talanor said when Alexander returned a few minutes later. "Tell me, what do you think of Kailie?"

"She's very beautiful," Alexander said flatly.

"Hmm, yes, she is, isn't she?" the old mage gave Alexander a benign smile.

"Will she be able to help?" Alexander asked, ignoring Talanor's attempt at innocence.

Talanor's features took on a serious cast. "Yes," he said, "she will be able to help us." He absently toyed with the edge of his sleeve, remembering what Rhianna Lanee had said of Kailie's talent.

"I told you that if she were willing I would take her to the Horn of Kalora to the Singer's mage, Rhianna Lanee, did I not?"

"Yes. And what did the mage say about Kailie's abilities?"

"She has an extraordinary voice and great power. Rhianna feels that the Faerie gifted Kailie with a magic that no other Singer has ever possessed. Rhianna called her special and unique because she is capable of singing all the Songs of all the Golden Ones." Talanor paused and turned to gaze out the window of the airless office. He debated about sharing his thoughts with Alexander concerning where Kailie had gone with Rhianna and what had occurred.

"Is there something else you should tell me, Talanor?"

"Hmm? Later perhaps. Now I want to hear about the circumstances here at the Fort and what's happening in the north."

Alexander knew it was useless to pursue the topic of Kailie Fairchild any further. Talanor would tell him what he needed to know in his own good time, and no amount of prodding would make the mage divulge more than he wanted.

"I took two men into The Dlarmids to see for myself what Maelorn is building there. A month ago the army numbered several thousand Spriggans and a creature that is uglier and bigger. Ghillies, I believe you called them?" At Talanor's nod, Alexander continued. "We watched at least a hundred robed men train the creatures to fight with weapons."

"Men?" the mage asked. "That's odd. Are you sure they were men?"

"Not absolutely sure, no. They looked and moved like men, but they all wore dark robes and hoods pulled over their heads. We were too far away to see clearly, so I can only assume they were men."

"Hmm. Yes. Go on."

"On our way out of the mountains we were attacked by three Spriggans. We killed them all, but not before two of us were wounded. I was the most seriously hurt, and without the aid of the Mackays I would have died. They carried me for four days before we reached the Skara. The ferry from Landsend was making its last run down the river and, luckily, our timing was such that we caught it." Alexander lifted his mug of water and drank.

"Did you encounter any more Spriggans along the way?"

K. J. OLSON

Alexander shook his head. "No. Oh, by the way. The little knife you gave me? We would have walked right into the Spriggans without knowing they were there if the knife hadn't warned me of their presence." Alexander set the empty mug back on his desk. "Thank you for giving it to me."

"I'm glad it helped."

"I don't suppose you'd tell me how the knife was able to pulse against my skin when I was in danger, would you?"

Talanor smiled and shook his head.

Alexander sighed deeply. "Thought not." He looked for a time into Talanor's eyes. "Some day, old man, I'm going to get you in a position where you'll have to tell me some things I want to know."

Talanor laughed, his booming merriment bouncing off the walls. "Not likely, Alexander," he chortled. "Not likely."

Alexander grunted and moved behind his desk to slump tiredly in his chair.

Talanor's laughter died quickly. "Tell me what you've been doing to prepare for Maelorn's attack."

"I ordered everyone moved out of Landsend and settled in either Fairtown or Riversend. The Guardians from the Landsend garrison are posted here. The people on the plain have been warned to get out, and each day highland families are coming through on the way south. Shiptown is nearly deserted, too. A few loggers remained behind to get a shipment of lumber ready that we'll need for repairing the Wall. That lumber and the loggers should be coming any day now. And the Guardians who are protecting them.

"I've asked every able-bodied man to report to the Fort as soon as his family is situated. Men are coming in every day. I'll soon have to set up a bivouac area on the south side of the Wall.

"The highlanders are bringing what horses they have left, which we are sure to need. And no highlander would be caught without a weapon, so we've added to our arsenal. The blacksmiths' forges are going night and day, turning farm tools into pikes and spearheads. The Guardians are training civilians in the use of the weapons; I've set up shifts so there is training going on at the same time as work on shoring up the Wall." Alexander paused and rubbed the bridge of his nose. "So much to do, but we've no way of knowing how much time we have."

Talanor drummed his long fingers restlessly on his knees. "How bad is the Wall?"

140

"The years of neglect have taken their toll. About all we can do now is patch the worst breaks and hope the structure holds. Ironworkers and mechanics are working on the river gate mechanism. It's very slow going, however; the gate hasn't been closed in centuries." He rubbed his nose again. "When the Mackays and I were in The Dlarmids, we saw Spriggans and Ghillies practicing with battering rams. What they were practicing on was an exact replica of the Wall of Rhade."

Talanor grunted. "Maelorn has gown more clever with the passing of time it seems. When he fought Alpean, his unholy horde used no weapons other than their claws and teeth. It appears this time he will come with a better equipped army."

"I'm not too sure of that. The creatures are not comfortable with the weapons. In fact they appeared very awkward and clumsy. I'm hoping they won't improve with training." Alexander hunched forward to lean his forearms on his desk, his hands clasped loosely together. "When the patrol gets back, we'll be able to assess just how adept the creatures have become. Unfortunately, I'm afraid most of the Kaenolirians will not have time to become proficient with weapons either." Alexander sighed and brought his clasped hands up and rested his chin on them. "When it comes time to fight, I don't know how unseasoned men will react. I'm not really too sure of the Guardians. We've never been asked to fight a war."

Talanor rose to pace the floor, his head bowed, hands clasped behind him. Alexander watched silently as the mage moved back and forth across the small room.

At last Talanor halted. "The supplies Ian Cameron and the old fisherman took to Shiptown, where are they?"

"They're here in one of the storage sheds. Ian sent them with the first load of supplies from Shiptown."

"Good, good. At first light I'll want to get to work. I will require a small space to work in; a lean-to would suffice, just something to keep me out of the sun."

"That can be arranged. Do you need someone to help you?"

"Mmm, yes, but Kailie should be able to assist me."

"Anything you may need, just ask. If it's available, it's yours." Alexander rose stiffly from his chair. He glanced at the darkened window and realized that it had grown late while they talked. "Let's get something to eat, and then I'll have Simon take you to the quarters he's undoubtedly arranged by now." He moved toward the door.

"Alexander," Talanor's voice stopped him. "What is the food situation?"

Alexander hunched his shoulders as if the weight there had grown suddenly heavier. He turned to look at Talanor. "Not good," he said flatly. "The drought has killed practically every crop—fruit, vegetables, grains. If Maelorn mounts any kind of siege, we'll not be able to hold out for long." He gave Talanor a long, considering look. "If you know any magic, have any power the rest of us do not, use it soon, Talanor." Alexander turned then and stepped into the gathering darkness. After a moment Talanor followed him.

Lights glowed from most of the windows of the Fort except for the stables. Here and there clusters of men were gathered, enjoying a quiet visit before going back to work on the Wall or to another training session. Conversations were desultory, voices low. Someone softly stroked the strings of a lute and was soon joined by the haunting, flute-like tones of a pipe.

Alexander stopped before the door of his quarters and knocked twice. Kailie immediately opened the door, light from a flickering candle framing her as she stood in the doorway. Her beauty touched him again, and the thought came, unbidden, that he wished they might have met in a different time and place.

"Would you care to join Talanor and me for the evening meal?" he asked.

"Yes, thank you. I would. Let me blow out the candle." She turned away and the room darkened. Alexander stepped back from the door as she pulled it shut behind her. The scent of wildflowers filled his head.

"Were you able to get some rest?" Talanor asked quietly.

Kailie smiled at the old man. "A little, yes. It's a bit noisy around here." She turned to Alexander as they walked. "I watched some of the Guardians trying to train some men to use a pike. Pikes and pitchforks have some similarities, I suppose, but the men seemed to find very few."

Alexander smiled ruefully at the woman who walked by his side. "It has not been easy for Kaenolirians to make the transition from civilian to soldier. They've much to learn and little enough time to learn it." He stopped outside a brightly lighted doorway. "I'm afraid we can't offer you much besides simple fare. It's hot and nourishing but that's about all."

"No need to apologize, Alexander," Talanor spoke brusquely.

"I know, but we Kaenolirians have always prided ourselves on our hospitality, and old habits and customs die hard. I wish I could offer you more." He shrugged tiredly and motioned for Kailie and Talanor to enter the dining hall.

~

"Captain Lamond."

Alexander sat bolt upright. Someone called his name again and pounded on the door of his office.

Baskers. He'd just closed his eyes. Whoever was on the other side of that door damn well better have a good reason for waking him. Mumbling dire threats to the life and limb of the hapless Guardian who disturbed his rest, he pushed himself up off the pallet he'd thrown on the floor to serve as his bed and staggered to the door.

"Yes, what is it?"

The soldier sent to awaken him duly noted the Captain's ill humor, and the man wisely prefaced his message with an apology.

"Sorry to awaken you, sir, but the patrol just came in from The Dlarmids. You asked to be notified whenever they got back."

Alexander sighed sleepily. "All right." He scrubbed his face with his hands. "All four of them?"

"Yes, sir, all four, no wounded."

"Good. Where are they?"

"They'll be here in just a few minutes, Captain."

Alexander nodded. "Go find Talanor. I think he's somewhere on the Wall and tell him I want to see him right away. Get Ian Cameron and Henry Graham, too."

The Guardian saluted, closed the door, and hurried away.

Fumbling about in the darkness, Alexander found a lamp and lit it, turning the flame low to conserve oil. He picked up his discarded breeches and dragged them on, but it was too hot for a shirt or boots. As he buttoned the last button, there was another knock on his door.

"Come," he called and looked up to see Angus Mackay's grim, dirty face.
"Captain."

Alexander lifted his shoulders and let them fall on a gusty sigh. He nodded to Angus and then looked at the other three as they filed into the room. Their fatigue was obvious, their distress written in furrowed brows and haunted eyes.

Baskers, what had they seen? He was almost afraid to ask.

143

"Sit." He motioned to the couple of chairs and the pallet he had just vacated. With movements slowed by weariness, they did as he ordered while he took the chair behind his desk.

"Edward, in the cupboard behind you you'll find a bottle of whiskey I've been hoarding and some small mugs. Help yourself and pass it around. You all look like you need a drink."

Edward obligingly filled a mug and passed the bottle on until all five men sat with a mug of the smooth, fiery liquor Kaenolir was famous for. Silently, each raised his mug to the others in the stuffy room and drank.

"Thanks, Captain," Angus said as he sat back to ease some of the ache from his limbs.

All looked up as Talanor entered the room, closely followed by Sergeants Cameron and Graham. The three new arrivals took up posts leaning against the wall. Whiskey and mugs were passed silently to them.

"Leave the door open, Henry, or we'll suffocate in here," Alexander directed. He turned to the men of the patrol. "Tell us what you found."

Angus Mackay cleared his throat, drained his mug and leaned forward in his chair, forearms braced on his knees. Slowly he began to roll the empty cup between his large hands. When he spoke his voice was hoarse.

"We found Maelorn's army still in the canyon, Captain, still training with weapons and still waiting for something or someone." His eyes followed the movement of the cup, but Alexander knew he was seeing something entirely different.

"The army numbers about eight to ten thousand now, I'd say. Wouldn't you?" He looked to the other three members of the patrol for their confirmation of the number. "The canyon is filled with the hairy bastards. We tried to count the men in robes, too, and there are many more of them than there were a month ago. Probably a couple hundred at least."

"Can you tell me what they look like, the men. How do they move?" Talanor spoke from the shadows near the door.

Angus sat up and glanced over at the mage and then at his Captain. "We tried to get as close as possible to the floor of the canyon, closer than we were, Captain. The men in robes do not associate with the beasts, except when they try to train the things to fight with weapons. We found them camped away from the canyon on the other side of the ridge from where we," Angus gestured to his captain and his brother, "watched them. They appear to be men, large men, always dressed in black robes with hoods pulled well down over their faces. We were close enough to see that their eyes seem to glow, like a cat's, in the dark, but we couldn't make out any other features. They always move quickly, and it was hard to follow them. We did see their hands when they used a weapon, and they appear to be very bony, with little skin or muscle covering them." He looked to Talanor. "Does that make any sense to you?"

"Yes," the mage rumbled. "They're Spectres. Maelorn did not have them as part of his army in the War of the Brothers, but it seems he is powerful enough now to call them up from the depths of hell. They can fight like demons, moving so swiftly that they are almost impossible to kill. The only way they can be stopped is to sever their heads from their bodies."

One of the men swore and moved restlessly in his chair.

"You were right in describing their hands as bony. They have no flesh."

The room grew silent. Outside someone shouted, the words indistinguishable. Blacksmiths' ringing hammers and voices of many men were sounds of the night, just as they were sounds of the day.

"What else did you see?" Alexander asked at last.

Edward Mackay rose from his chair and moved to the open window. He leaned against the frame, looking out into the yard of the Fort. A vagrant breeze carried the scent of dust and men, and his own sweat.

"We saw hell, Captain." He spoke into the night, and his voice broke on the last word.

Hair on the back of Alexander's neck prickled. He wanted to stop Edward from telling what else they had seen, wanted to be some place cool and quiet, wanted to hear the soft voice of a woman. Instead he sat silently, waiting for the rough soldier who slumped against the wall to gain his composure and explain.

"The miners and their families, we know what happened to them, Captain." Edward continued his part of the tale. "They were brought into the army's camp in wagons, all of them—men, women, children—and thrown to the beasts like so much fodder." The stark, bleak words fell into the silence. "There was nothing we could do to help, nothing. We had to sit there, in our hiding places among the rocks, and watch them all die. I shall never be able to forget the sounds of their screams and the howls of the beasts." He turned haunted eyes to his captain, tears rolling unashamedly down his lined cheeks. "What in the name of all the gods can we do to stop this?"

Alexander rose from his chair and walked around the desk to the anguished man. He placed a comforting hand on the trembling shoulder. "We'll do all that we possibly can. But know this, we will not allow any more

145

Kaenolirians to be slaughtered in such a horrible way. I promise." He shook the stalwart shoulder gently, and Edward nodded and wiped the tears from his cheeks.

Turning away from the distraught Guardian, Alexander faced the other men of the patrol. "Get some rest now, and we'll talk more in the morning. But I must order you not to tell anyone what you just told us. Is that understood?"

"Yes, sir," Angus agreed for all of them.

Quietly the men rose and filed out of the office.

"Talanor, may I see you for a moment longer?" Alexander asked. "Ian and Henry, return to your posts for now. I'll want to talk with you in the morning as well."

The two men nodded and without another word followed the exhausted Guardians out the door.

Alexander moved to stand before the map of Kaenolir behind his desk, his back to Talanor. He stood for some time before finally turning to face the mage.

"We've got to find some way to stop them before they reach the Wall, at least to slow them down."

Talanor nodded in agreement. "Yes. I may have something that will help us do just that, but it will be very dangerous for the men who must carry out what I have in mind."

"Talanor," Alexander said wearily, "If it will slow Maelorn's army, we must try it. We have no choice. No choice at all."

Guardian and mage looked into each other's eyes. The knowledge of what lay ahead for Kaenolir was heavy on their hearts, their minds filled with thoughts of what they must do.

The mage was the first to turn away. There was much he had to prepare. He prayed the Ancient Ones for the time he needed.

"Have someone get my supplies and bring them to the lean-to you've provided for me. I also need Kailie now. Would you awaken her and ask her to join me?"

Alexander nodded. He watched Talanor turn and rapidly leave the room. With silent tread he walked to the window. Crossing his arms across his bare chest, he drew in his breath and with savage intensity he first cursed whatever gods might hear him for what they had so foolishly and arbitrarily done long ago, and then begged them to help him save his people.

Chapter Twelve

"Bring the Singer to me," Maelorn commanded a dark robed figure. He smiled in anticipation as he watched the Spectre hasten away.

It was time to break the spirit of the Golden One. He had defied his new master long enough. Yes, it was time to convince the Singer to follow the path Maelorn trod, time to pervert and twist the ancient magic the Goldenhorn possessed and use it as a tool to bring Kaenolir to heel.

The Singer must be taught to sing a new song, a song that spoke of Maelorn's might, a song that commanded obedience to his rule, a song that promised death to those who challenged him.

The Darkling threw back his head and roared with laughter. The irony of the situation pleased and amused him. A Warrior Singer sent from an ancient world as a gift would become an instrument of the very one he had been sent to control.

"'Tis fitting, most fitting."

~

The prisoner bound to the stone of Maelorn's tomb was unaware of the passage of time. The sun did not reach this black hole. Day and night did not exist for him; only the unending hours of inexorable pain and boredom had meaning.

Andrew Goldenhorn was a shell of the man who had been brought to this dungeon. He was gaunt, his ribs visible under the once-golden skin. His hair was matted and filthy, his body covered with grime and open sores. But for him the most degrading part of his imprisonment was the fact that he was forced to stand in his own filth.

His loss of weight loosened somewhat the fetters that chained him. Even the strap about his neck was not as tight as it had been when he was first imprisoned, but he did not attempt to use his voice. Singing the Warrior Song would be a meaningless gesture of defiance, and Maelorn or his dark thralls would surely find some new method to punish his insolence. Goldenhorn did not know how much more physical pain or mental anguish he could tolerate. Hope of leaving Sinnarock alive dwindled, and he longed for a release from the evil in which he was forced to wallow. He prayed frequently now for the final release of death.

A black-robed figure entered the chamber and came to stand before him. "The master wishes to see you."

Bony hands freed him from the chains and loosened the strap about his throat. Unsteady and weak, he fought to focus his attention on the man in the robe. It was difficult to think coherently. Did Maelorn have some new torture for him? His arms dropped to his sides as they were freed, and he stared stupidly at his hands, turning his head to view first the left, then the right.

Where was he being taken?

He sagged against the stone without the support of the chains. Hands reached out to grip him, and he haltingly took a step or two before collapsing in a heap. The hands pulled him upright and held him firmly in a grip that was just short of painful.

"Walk, Singer," the hollow voice commanded. "Walk, or you will taste my whip."

A low hum vibrated down Goldenhorn's spine, and he pulled himself away from the fleshless hands. It was a sound he was well acquainted with, and the comfort it had given him in the terrible days when he was first chained to the stone reached out to surround him again. The repetitive murmur offered courage and strength where the Goldenhorn thought not to find them. He steadied, and the fog of pain and torment began to clear from his mind. He straightened his shoulders and drew himself up to his full height.

The dark man, startled by the sound and made uneasy by it, turned his head from side to side to seek out the source of the humming. Unable to pinpoint it, he felt an urgent need to return to his master. He gave Goldenhorn a shove that sent the weakened man sprawling.

"Get up," the dark one barked. He brought up his whip and lashed Goldenhorn across his shoulders hard enough to leave a thin red welt in the dirt smeared on his back.

The strong and vital spirit that had been forced to dormancy somewhere deep within the Goldenhorn struggled upward as he pushed himself to his feet. The whip whistled again, but with a surge of energy Goldenhorn caught the lash and jerked the whip from the robed man's grasp.

"Enough," he rasped. The whip sailed through the air and landed in one of the burning pools near Alpean's tomb. His efforts were rewarded by the sound of faint laughter.

The dark man shrieked with anger and surprise, but when he raised his fists to beat the Goldenhorn, the Singer proudly faced the Spectre and defiantly dared him to strike. The fists dropped; angry red points glowed inside his hood.

A smile briefly touched Goldenhorn's cracked lips while he silently thanked his entombed cellmate for reminding him of who he was.

~

Maelorn sat naked upon a throne of burnished gold in a large chamber, an immense and monstrous creature engorged with hatred, suffused with power. Cauldrons of fire burned with orange/red flames around the perimeter of the cavern, creating tremendous heat, and Maelorn basked in it. Several robed figures stood in deep shadows behind the throne, arms folded, hoods pulled far down over their faces.

With an imperious gesture, the Darkling sent away the Spectre who escorted Goldenhorn. Licking his drooling lips with pleasure, he leered at the once beautiful Singer.

The bedraggled creature who stared back at him was not broken, nor did he grovel before Maelorn. In fact, he had the audacity to stand proud and unbowed. Fury rose like bile in Maelorn's throat, and he bellowed in rage.

"Kneel to your master, Singer. Now!"

"I kneel to no one," the Goldenhorn whispered, "except my king."

"King? What king? You have no king. Your king is dead. I am your master now, and it is I you will obey."

Goldenhorn smiled and lifted his head a notch higher. "No."

Maelorn leaped from his throne, a huge fist raised to club the insolent Singer. He could easily kill the man with one blow, but the Singer's death was not what he wanted, at least not yet.

The Darkling dropped his fist to his side and returned to his throne, his mocking hollow laughter ringing out.

"Ah, Singer, I shall let you live a while longer, for I have need of your talents. I brought you here to sing for me."

"I cannot sing; I have no voice. You have seen to that. And even if I could sing, the music given to me by my ancestors cannot be used in any other way than to protect the people of Kaenolir."

Again Maelorn laughed. "But you see, Singer, you will sing to protect the Kaenolirians. If you sing as I command, they will live as my subjects. If you do not sing, they will die." He shrugged. "'Tis simple, no?"

Goldenhorn gasped at the implication of Maelorn's demented strategy. He intended to forge the gift of the ancient Faerie into an evil device that would subjugate those whom Goldenhorn and his brother Singers had been sent to defend.

"Think about what I demand of you, Singer, think about it carefully. When I bring you before me again, you will sing as I command, or my Spriggans and Ghillies will feast on the sweet flesh of Kaenolir. Think very, very carefully about refusing me again, for the price of your defiance is high." Maelorn gestured to a Spectre waiting in the shadows. "Take him back to his cell. Chain him but do not strap his neck."

The Spectre bowed low, then turned to Goldenhorn and pointed to the entrance of the chamber. With a stumbling gait he moved to leave the aberrant presence. He turned back at the chamber's arched entrance to see several Spectres clustered about Maelorn's throne. Shifting shadows created by flickering flames were cast upon the chamber walls. With a sudden flare of a fire burning near the throne, Goldenhorn had a clear view of the Spectres and their master.

Each Spectre lovingly anointed Maelorn's massive body with oil, its cloyingly sweet scent filled the Singer's nostrils. Bony hands stroked bulging muscles and left them gleaming while Maelorn rolled his head against the back of the throne and growled deep in his throat. A Spectre stepped between Maelorn's huge thighs and continued the ministrations for several minutes. A guttural sound of satisfaction issued from the ugly, drooling maw, and Goldenhorn turned away in disgust, the sight of Maelorn's perversion too much to endure.

~

Back in his cell, Goldenhorn was given palatable food, as much as he could eat, and fresh water. He was chained, but only loosely, and the strap was not placed about his neck again. It seemed Maelorn was prepared to treat him more humanely, but only for the purpose of bringing the Singer into his fold.

"Alpean," Goldenhorn whispered into the silence. "How can I stop him? I will not help Maelorn become king of Kaenolir; I cannot. If I do not sing as he commands, the price in human life will be immeasurable, and I will have been responsible. But if I sing, the people will be forced to live under his evil dominion." There was no way out of the coil in which he was caught. He moaned softly and rested his head against the stone.

A thought niggled at the back of his mind. If he were free, perhaps he could somehow kill Maelorn or at least slow his plans enough so the Kaenolirians would have time to prepare for war. If he were free to sing the Warrior Song...

His thoughts were interrupted by an insistent hiss, and he turned to look at Alpean's tomb. A network of fine cracks spread across the surface of the stone, and in some places flakes were chipped away, giving the tomb a pitted appearance where only a short time ago it had been smooth.

"Alpean?" he called softly.

Freedom. Freedom but not only for himself. Freedom for the other prisoner in this chamber of horror as well. Freedom for Alpean.

The Warrior Song had been sung for centuries to keep an evil force forever imprisoned. But it had also been sung as a promise to Alpean that he would one day be free.

Of course! Why hadn't he thought of it before? His magic was not strong enough alone to defeat Maelorn, but combined with other equally powerful forces—

"Alpean," he croaked.

Another hiss, this time louder, stronger, came from the tomb.

Goldenhorn smiled. There must be a way to free both himself and Alpean. If only his mind weren't so sluggish.

"Think," he admonished himself. "Think." There had to be a way. The old legends. Perhaps the answer was there. What had Rhianna Lanee taught him all those years ago about the ancient history of Kaenolir?

He rattled his chains in frustration. There was something that he had forgotten, something he had been taught. It was there, just beyond his reach.

Alpean's gentle crooning came softly. *Calm yourself,* it seemed to say.

Goldenhorn listened and taking a deep breath, forced himself to rest against the stone. He would remember in time, but it did no good to strain his weakened mind and body now. He must give himself time to grow strong. He would eat Maelorn's food and drink his water and regain his strength. He must rest, truly rest, for the first time since being chained in Mt. Sinnarock.

He would find a way out. He had to.

Death no longer seemed a desired end. Life was important now, life and freedom.

He closed his eyes. He murmured Katrine's name and slept, a deep, healing sleep.

~

"My lord, the army will soon be ready to move. It awaits your command." A Spectre bowed low before Maelorn.

Maelorn grunted. He opened his mouth in a wide grimace of pleasure, showing his rapier-sharp teeth.

"Good. We will wait a bit longer until the Singer regains his strength." He ran his long fingernails lightly over his massive chest. "When was the last time the army was fed?"

"Six days ago, my lord."

A cruel, mocking smile curved Maelorn's mouth. "They should be very hungry when we leave the mountains. Very hungry and ready to kill."

"Yes, my lord. They will be ready to kill whatever puny forces the Kaenolirians can send against us."

"How large an army have the Guardians gathered to defend the Wall of Rhade?"

"I'm not sure, my lord, but men come every day to the Fort."

"In large numbers?"

"No, my lord. Only a few at a time. We are not able to get very close to observe the Fort and the Wall, but we know that some of the Guardian forces are still located in outlying towns in southern Kaenolir."

Maelorn rose from his throne and strode about the chamber. "Will their repairs to the Wall hold against our forces?"

"For a time, perhaps, but your army will prevail, my lord."

Maelorn paused and looked at the Spectre. "And the river gate? What of the fort gate?"

"At my last report, neither the river gate nor the Wall gate had been closed."

With a grunt of satisfaction, Maelorn again took his throne. "When the sun rises and sets seven times, we move."

"Yes, my lord." The Spectre bowed so low to the chamber floor his hood brushed the heated stone. Slowly, he backed from his master's presence. Once outside the chamber he straightened and moved swiftly along the corridor. Twin points glowed hotly within his dark hood. He could feel the surge of energy that always occurred when he was with his master.

"Soon," he whispered.

Soon the army would destroy Kaenolir, and he would be able to spend all his time with his lord and master.

Soon.

Chapter Thirteen

A shout from the Wall brought Alexander on the run. The lumber wagons from Shiptown were seen coming out of the Kiltan Hills. The wagons and their escort of Guardians were at the Skara Bridge when Alexander sent men to meet them and bring them into the Fort.

With a sigh of relief for the safe arrival of men and supplies, Alexander turned his attention to the immediate chore—closing the river gate—and climbed the interior ladder leading to a small machine shed were several men had been working for days on the gate mechanism.

"We're ready to try closing it, Captain." Walter, the chief mechanic, was a large, heavily muscled man. His ham-sized hands were permanently darkened with the grease he used in his work. He lifted one now to wipe sweat from his brow.

"Good. Give it a try."

Alexander stood back out of the way as the mechanic motioned for one of his helpers to assist him in moving the large lever that, upon release, would set the intricate assortment of pulleys, gears and weights in motion and, if the gods were at all sympathetic, would close the gate across the river. The two men positioned themselves, one on either side of the lever. The mechanic spit into his cupped palms, for luck, and took hold of the ancient iron. His companion did the same and with muscles bulging, stances wide and firm, teeth clenched against the strain, the two men slowly, steadily moved the lever from the left to the right.

Gears clashed and meshed together; pulleys lifted counterbalanced weights; chains clanked. And the massive gate began to close. The din inside the machine shed was deafening, metal striking against metal, chains clattering, and under all the noise was the sound of men cursing.

If Alexander and the men around him could have closed the gate on willpower alone, it would have been done.

"Move, you bastard whelp of the gods, move," Alexander breathed.

With ponderous majesty the gates slowly, slowly cut through the waters of the Skara toward each other. With a reverberating crash the two sections met in the middle of the river and locked into position with a violent shudder.

Utter silence greeted the feat and lasted for several heartbeats while the men in the cramped, stifling shed forgot to breathe. With a collective gasp for air, they began to grin at each other, and then their laughter and cheers and whoops of success rang out to be answered in kind by men on the Wall and in the Fort.

"We did it, Captain. By the gods, we did it." The red-faced mechanic grinned at Alexander, who grinned in response and extended his hand to the other. It was grasped in greasy strength and the two men laughed, a little drunk with their accomplishment.

"A job well done, Walter."

"Thank you, Captain Lamond. We can be thankful that the old-timers built things to last."

With a nod Alexander released the grimy hand. "Finish up whatever you need to do here to keep that gate locked in place, and then bring your men down to help with the Wall gate. The lumber from Shiptown has arrived, and I want you and your men to work with the carpenters."

"We'll do that. Shouldn't take too long to finish up in here. Then we'll be down."

"Good."

Alexander looked around at the circle of work-stained, tired men. "You all did well. I wish I could say that you were done, but we've much to do before we're prepared to fight the Darkling or withstand a siege."

Their solemn expressions greeted his last words, but his next words brought grins back to their faces.

"I also wish I had a keg of whiskey to offer you." Alexander smiled ruefully and turned away to descend the ladder. Still so much to be done, but closing the river gate eased one of his many worries. On level ground again he sought out Talanor and Kailie.

~

155

With the arrival of the lumber, men quickly set to work on the second gate. The weakest points in the line of defense the Wall provided were the two great gates. One of those weak points was now definitely strengthened, and Alexander and Talanor discussed ways to make the second less vulnerable.

Like its counterpart, the Wall gate had rarely been closed during the years following the Brothers' War. Many of the timbers of the massive structure had weathered and rotted; the chains and pulleys used to close and open it, while less complicated and fewer in number than those of the river gate, needed replacement or repair. It seemed wisest to rebuild the gate as best they could in the time they had and bar it to intruders. With spirits still high from the successful closing of the river gate, the men began to rebuild the Wall gate.

"I have an idea that might give us a little more time if the beasts get this far." Talanor stood watching the men fitting new timbers for the gate. He pulled thoughtfully on an ear lobe and watched a few seconds longer before turning to Alexander.

"I think we would be telling ourselves stories if we said the dark forces wouldn't get this far," Alexander said morosely as he wiped sweat and dirt from his brow. "What's your idea?"

"A deep pit in front of the gate, deep enough and wide enough so the Spriggans and Ghillies couldn't get to the gate without a great deal of difficulty."

Alexander chewed on his bottom lip, trying to visualize the effect of a pit on advancing forces. It just might work; at least, it might offer enough of an obstacle to discourage ramming the gate. Anything that would give them more time—

"We could drive some sharpened stakes into the ground at the bottom of the pit and cover the pit, or camouflage it, in some way so the creatures didn't recognize the danger until it was too late."

"Yes, yes. Good, good, Alexander. Let's see to it."

It meant moving the work force and the lumber to the south side of the Wall. When that was accomplished, a crew began digging the pit on the north side. However, the digging proved to be excruciatingly difficult; the soil, packed down by the feet of men and animals for centuries, and the suffocating heat allowed only short periods of time to dig before men were exhausted.

Talanor watched the slow progress and knew that at the rate the work was going, the pit would take much too long to dig and take too high a toll on the strength and stamina of the men who dug. He just might have something to speed the process. Long robe flapping against his legs, he strode hurriedly across the yard to the lean-to he'd been working in. He and Kailie had spent part of the morning filling small bottles with a black substance that had the consistency of fine sand.

A shadow fell across the entry to the narrow lean-to and Kailie looked up from filling yet another bottle.

"I'll need about four of the small ones, Kailie. Put them in this basket." Talanor rummaged in one of the packs piled against the wall and handed her a basket.

"What are you going to do?" she asked as she set three bottles in the basket, handling them as gently as she would have handled thin-shelled eggs.

"Make a hole easier to dig," he replied. "Do you want to see what this sand will do?"

Kailie put a cork stopper in the top of the bottle she had just filled, making sure that a long length of cord hung down the side of the bottle. She laid it carefully with the other three in the bottom of the woven basket.

She turned to Talanor. "Let's go."

~

"Get everyone away from the Wall and behind something substantial, a wall, a building, whatever," Talanor instructed a dubious Alexander. "Hurry, man, we haven't got all day."

Alexander swore and then shouted for everyone's attention.

"Get away from the Wall gate. Those of you up on the Wall, crouch down behind the parapet. Everybody in the yard move back and get behind something that will offer you some protection."

The looks of puzzlement were plain to see. No one but the mage seemed to know what was about to occur. He waited until all were safely out of range before calmly removing the stopper from the bottle he held. He lit the piece of wick extending from it, and when it was burning properly, tossed it into the hole that was the start of a pit. With undignified speed Talanor turned and ran for the corner of the stable behind which Kailie and Alexander stood.

An explosion rent the air, scattering dirt and gravel everywhere. Dust and smoke rose up in a choking cloud, and pebbles rained down like hail.

Alexander reacted instantly and pushed Kailie against the stone wall to shield her from the stinging pebbles with his body.

When the stones finally stopped rattling and the dust began to settle, Kailie coughed and shoved against Alexander's solid chest.

"Captain," she choked, "you're crushing me."

Alexander stepped back. "Are you all right?" he asked after a moment.

"Yes, I think so. No broken bones," she smiled.

"Sorry. I didn't mean to be so rough."

"It worked, Alexander, it worked!" Talanor's shout of triumph was heard all over the Fort. Alexander took Kailie's hand and together they ran to see the effects of the blast.

The group around the hole stared in disbelief. The hole was much deeper and wider than it had been.

"Baskers, what is that stuff?" Alexander demanded.

Talanor laughed. "For want of a better term, I call it firesand. I found it by accident in a cave on Cathorn many years ago. Nearly killed myself in doing so. Never thought I'd be using it like this, though. I found that if I put a bit of cording in it and set the cording afire, the firesand would explode. I also found that by simply dropping a bottle of it or throwing a bottleful at something, the firesand explodes and destroys whatever I threw it at. Lovely stuff. Just right for what we need." He looked into the hole and laughed again. "Now, Alexander, put your men to work. The digging should be easier. And when the soil gets too hard to dig, I'll throw in another couple of fireshells."

"You heard him." Alexander motioned to the stunned group of diggers. "Let's get back to work."

The digging was, indeed, much less laborious, and the pit rapidly expanded and deepened. Talanor used two more of his fireshells, as he called them, and within a few hours the task of digging was complete. Three men remained in the pit, driving stakes into the ground. The meaty thunk of sledgehammer against wood punctuated the accompanying sounds of rasping saws and cursing men as work progressed on the Wall gate at a steady pace.

Alexander and Ian Cameron stood on the edge of the deep pit, discussing the best way to camouflage it. Brief twilight that marked the end of another day settled over the land, but it offered no respite from heat or hot winds. Ian wiped his face with a blue bandana. Both men agreed that it would be the most expedient to leave piles of dirt on the outer edge of the pit. Most of the debris had been hauled away, but enough remained to conceal what lay behind the uneven mounds. A phalanx of creatures running with a battering ram or with ladders to storm the gate would be unable to stop their forward momentum until too late, and those coming behind them would force them into the pit and onto the deadly stakes.

"You know, Alex, we might be able to put hidden stakes to use in another way, too." Ian watched the last of the stakes being driven into the bottom of the pit.

"How so?" Alexander asked absently, his mind already on another task that would have to be done soon.

"Well, it seems logical that Maelorn will split his forces in two after he gets out of The Dlarmids."

"Probably. Crossing the Skara will slow him down somewhat, but if he sends part of his army down the river and the other part across the High Ghilana Plain, he could hit us in several places at once. We'd be stretched mighty thin along the Wall."

"Yes. If he comes down the Plain, that's where the stakes might be used. What if we drove stakes into the ground, shorter stakes then we've used in the pit, and wove ropes in among them? The ropes would entangle anyone or anything that runs through and send the unwary bastards into the stakes. What do you think?"

Alexander nodded his head slowly, deep in thought. "It just might work, especially if there was something to draw them into the area where the stakes and ropes were hidden." His mind was working rapidly to expand on Ian's suggestion.

It would be dangerous, perhaps even costly in the toll of men and horses, but if the highlanders could lead the dark army into the trap, they might be able to cause enough confusion to halt the advance. The grass of the Plain was very dry. A fire would spread quickly...

"Organize a work force to start making more stakes, Ian," Alexander abruptly ordered. "When that's done take a detachment of Guardians to set up your trap." He paused and looked intently into Ian's eyes. "You'll be completely out in the open."

Ian nodded in agreement. "You know, I think I'll ask Talanor if we might have some of those fireshells. They might give us just enough time to get back to the Wall.

Alexander laid his hand on his friend's shoulder. "Take care."

Ian grinned, almost recklessly, and gave Alexander a casual salute. "We'll get the stakes ready yet tonight so we can leave at first light." He turned and walked quickly away.

Alexander stood at the edge of the pit a moment longer. The river gate was closed and locked, a pit dug to protect the Wall gate, all in a relatively short time. Much had been accomplished, and although there was still much to do, Alexander allowed a small, brief glimmer of hope to flicker before he turned his back on the deadly pit.

Tomorrow, when the Wall gate was fully repaired, he must move men and horses out of the Fort and begin tearing it down. The advancing enemy could use the low wall and roof of the storage shed to mount ladders for easier access to the Wall. And he must call the highlanders together and discuss the plan that he and Ian had formulated.

"Alexander."

Talanor's low rumble broke into his churning thoughts. He turned to find the mage by his side.

"I must speak with you."

"Let's go up on the Wall. It will be quieter there."

Even as he spoke torches were being lit on the other side of the gate so work might continue through the hours of darkness.

A tall sturdy ladder leaned against the Wall near the pit, and the two men climbed it, stepped down over the parapet, and walked away from the gate toward a tower. They continued on past the tower until the clamor of hammers, saws, and voices was a muted background noise.

"Kailie and I have completed our preparations, and we'll leave for the mountains in the morning. I would like to ask you to allow the Mackay brothers to guide us."

Alexander walked to the parapet. He leaned on his forearms against it and looked to the north. Somehow he had known Talanor would be the one who would go into the mountains.

"Of course. You could have none better guiding you."

Talanor, too, leaned against the warm stone and gazed toward the north, toward the power festering and growing there.

"It is my plan to use the firesand to block the entrance to the canyon where the army is gathered."

The fact that Talanor offered the information of what he intended to do was not lost on Alexander. He turned to look at the mage. It was too dark to see him clearly, but his chiseled profile suggested strength and sureness.

"It won't stop them, but it should slow them down enough to give you a little more time to prepare."

Talanor turned to find Alexander's sharp-eyed gaze upon him. "It may also be enough to bring Maelorn out of Sinnarock."

"Bring him out?" Alexander asked in complete surprise.

"He must be destroyed, Alexander, if this insanity is ever to cease. Surely you must have realized that."

"Yes, I suppose I did, but I've never consciously thought about killing Maelorn. My immediate thoughts and concerns have been in stopping the Spriggan and Ghillie army he's gathered." Alexander sighed and turned back to face the north. "How will you kill him? You'll have to go through a whole army to get to him."

Talanor spoke so softly that Alexander barely heard his whispered words. "I will not be the one to kill him."

Puzzled, Alexander again turned to the mage. "But who then?"

"I'm not completely sure," Talanor paused. "The answer lies with Kailie, Alexander. That much I know."

"Kailie," Alexander murmured. The full implication of Talanor's quiet words hit him like a blow to the heart. He closed his eyes and drew in a deep breath. He swore quietly and succinctly. "Are the gods mad? How can she possibly carry out such an impossible task?"

"Because she must." Talanor reached out to grasp Alexander's shoulder. His hand was angrily shrugged away.

"No, not Kailie." Alexander walked several steps away before he turned and came back. "There must be another way, Talanor."

"She was chosen for this task, Alexander. Chosen by the Faerie."

"She may die. Maelorn may be too strong and she may be killed instead of him. Then what? It will all have been in vain. Baskers, Talanor, there must be another way. Take me with you. At least I—"

Talanor shook his head, his weariness and age suddenly apparent to the distraught Guardian.

"No, Alexander. It would do no good. The way is set. She has been chosen. You cannot alter that fact."

Alexander swore so violently Talanor took him by the shoulders and gave him a rough shake.

"Enough, man. Get hold of yourself. There is nothing you can do except defend this Wall. There is nothing either of us can do except to try to help her in any way we can. Accept that."

With teeth bared savagely and chest heaving with emotion, Alexander pulled himself away from Talanor's grasp.

"I'll do whatever I can to keep you from taking her with you, Talanor, I swear I will."

"No," Talanor stated firmly, "you will not. You are needed here. I am needed in the mountains. Kailie is needed on Sinnich. That is the way." Each of his last words was spoken sharply, distinctly, and their impact could not be ignored.

Alexander stared into the piercing blue eyes for a long, long time. Finally his shoulders slumped in weariness and resignation. Talanor was right, of course. He did not understand Kailie's part in the struggle to stop Maelorn; he only knew he did not want her to go with Talanor. So much danger. So many lives already lost. So many.

Leaning back against the parapet, he absently rubbed his nose with thumb and forefinger. Slowly he sank down to a sitting position. Drawing his knees up he rested his forearms across them and clasped his right wrist loosely with his left hand.

"Talanor, there have been times since I sought you out on Cathorn that I wished I'd never found you." His voice was flat with anguish. "I think, old man, that I could come to hate you."

"I'm sorry, Alexander. I am truly sorry," the mage whispered. "I do what I must as will Kailie. As you will." He ran his hand slowly down his beard, and turned away to retrace his footsteps along the top of the Wall. He couldn't remember ever feeling so old.

~

"Captain Lamond." The low, melodic voice brought Alexander's head around. "Talanor said I would find you here."

He saw Kailie standing a step or two away from where he sat.

"No," she laid a hand on his shoulder as he moved to rise, and crouched beside him. "Don't get up." Her eyes searched his features. "You are in pain. Is your shoulder troubling you?"

Alexander sighed and sank back against the unyielding parapet, stretching his long legs out in front of him. "There is much besides my shoulder to give me pain," he said with reluctance.

He looked into her golden-flecked eyes and saw mirrored there the beauty of her soul. She smiled at him, and he smelled wildflowers again. And ached to hold her.

"Kailie," he whispered.

She changed her position to sit cross-legged near his legs. "I must go Alexander," she said quietly, the smile fading from her lips. She used his name for the first time.

Without thinking he reached out with tanned fingers to touch the skin of her golden cheek, and without hesitation, she turned her face into the rough palm of his hand and smiled again, artlessly, naturally. If she had but known, it was a smile much like the one her mother had given her father that first day in the Seton store so many years before. And, like Goldenhorn, Alexander was completely enthralled by the woman who sat smiling at him.

Kailie reached up to take his hand in her own. "Will you let me tend your shoulder? I can relieve the pain."

He did not protest, only watched her. She came to her knees on his right side. "Will you remove your tunic, please?"

After a moment's hesitation he did as she requested, pulling his shirt over his head. Gently she placed her hands over the livid scars that marred his skin. Her touch was cool, but the effect was electric. The blood pounded through his body and rushed to his right shoulder. He sucked in his breath as he felt heat and then coolness where her hands touched.

Softly she began to sing. Music reached out to surround Alexander with comfort and a deep sense of peace. He felt her strength flow into him, and he had to close his eyes against the intensity of emotion that engulfed him. A soft moan escaped his lips.

After several minutes the Song of Healing stopped; her hands remained on his shoulder a moment more while his throbbing, pounding blood slowed to its natural rhythm. He opened his eyes to gaze into hers, and what he saw there sent his blood pounding again but for a much different reason.

Kailie removed her hands, the livid scars but faint tracks now across his broad shoulder. She smiled at him and handed him his tunic. He slipped it over his head and pulled it down. He gingerly touched his shoulder with his left hand but felt none of the pain that had nagged him since his wounds healed. A look of puzzled amazement crossed his face.

She again sat cross-legged beside him. "Is there still pain?"

"Not in my shoulder," he replied quietly.

She smiled sadly in understanding. "I must go, Alexander. If I am to help Kaenolir, I must go." She sensed that she was the cause of some of his pain, and it troubled her to know she could do nothing to alleviate it.

"Yes," he sighed. "I know. You are needed on Sinnich; I am needed here. For Kaenolir."

He took one of her hands in his, entwining their long fingers, his brown and strong, hers golden and delicate. They sat silently for some time, content with the moment. There might never be another time like this for them, he realized, and cursed their fate.

She reacted to his agitation by laying gentle fingers against his cheek. He reached out to touch her hair, meant only to touch her in that way, but with a strangled oath, he drew her to him, taking her parted lips in anguished frustration. Kailie came willingly, eagerly to his embrace, wanting to comfort him and needing in turn to be comforted.

But there was more to his emotion than pain, so much more than her need to comfort. So much more. Love welled up, strong and powerful.

When all else is done, this will remain. Love. . .it will never end.

The words of the Golden One flashed through her mind. His gift, he had said.

It was a gift beyond price.

Slowly she drew away from Alexander's embrace. Love was there, between them. In the midst of death and horror, it had come gently and swiftly to them both. Alexander rose reluctantly and helped Kailie to her feet.

When all else is done. . .

So much yet to do.

She smiled, dazzling him anew with her beauty. "I must go," she whispered.

He nodded. "There is no time for us now."

"But there will be, Alexander."

He gazed into her eyes, and touched each feature of her face as if to store in his memory not only the sight of her but also the feel of her.

He reached inside his tunic and extracted the silver knife from the band of his trousers. "Talanor gave this to me. It warned me when I was in danger. Take it with you when you go with Talanor tomorrow. It is the only protection I can offer you."

Kailie took the knife and felt it pulse against her palm. She recognized an ancient power and smiled. "Thank you," she whispered. She lifted her head to look into his eyes. "I shall keep it with me and find comfort in knowing the one who gave it to me waits for my return."

He took the hand that held the knife and wrapped his fingers around hers. The pulse of the blade beat strongly enough for him to feel it.

"Come," he finally sighed. "I'll take you back to the Fort."

As they walked along the top of the Wall, he glanced to the north, toward the mountains where Kailie and Talanor would go, and once more he prayed in silent supplication to the ancient gods.

~

"The canyon is just beyond this ridge, my lord." Angus Mackay breathed deeply and rapidly. The cold air of The Dlarmids cut like a knife, and he found it hard to remember that only a short time ago he'd been sweltering in the heat of a burning sun.

"Can we see the entrance to the canyon from atop the ridge?" Talanor asked.

"Yes. But if you want to get in close to the entrance, I suggest we wait a bit. By the looks of the sky, it will be snowing soon. We've only an hour or two of daylight left, and I don't want to get caught down here at nightfall. We need to climb the ridge as soon as we've rested. There's more protection up there than down here."

"Hmm. Yes. You're right, Angus. Let's go now. We'll rest when we get to the top."

Angus nodded and turned to lead the way up the steep and rocky ridge, the same ridge he'd led Captain Lamond to. He adjusted his pack more comfortably on his back and began climbing. All his senses were alert to any danger that might threaten them. When they were nearly to the top, he paused and silently motioned Edward ahead to check the top of the ridge. A few minutes later, Edward came back through the descending gloom, gesturing for them to come the rest of the way.

While Edward and Kailie found some protection from the frigid wind, Angus took Talanor to the hidden observation point among the boulders where they could observe the army of beasts and dark men. They heard and smelled the encampment before they saw it.

Talanor carefully eased himself around a huge boulder and hunkered down to look into the canyon below him. What he saw both amazed and appalled him. Countless bonfires lit the crowded canyon floor. Thousands and thousands of Spriggans and Ghillies milled about, their grunts and howls a monstrous clamor. He saw no dark-robed figures among the creatures and wondered about their absence until he recalled that they were encamped in another canyon nearby. That might pose a problem unless the Spectres were still training the army.

It grew dark rapidly, making it difficult to see the true configuration of the entrance of the canyon. From where he stood, it appeared the sheer, vertical walls narrowed quickly, leaving an opening no more than ten to twenty paces across. He would have to look more closely tomorrow, of course, and decide how to set his charges; but from this distance, it appeared the entrance to the canyon could be effectively sealed.

Talanor moved back from the edge of the ridge, motioning for Angus to come with him.

"Has the army grown in numbers since you were here on patrol?"

"It's hard to tell in this light, but I would say yes. The floor of the canyon seems even more closely packed with the beasts." Angus shook his grizzled head. "Where in all the gods' names are they coming from, my lord?"

Talanor sighed. "From hell, Angus, straight from hell." He rubbed cold hands together. "Come, let's find Edward and Kailie and get settled for the night." He hunched his shoulders against the wind. "I don't know which is worse," he muttered, "the heat of the plains or the cold of the mountains."

~

Dawn's bleak, gray light found the group of four in position along the top of the ridge, observing the encampment below. Snow had fallen heavily during the night and continued to do so as it grew light. Fires still burned in the canyon, and the milling beasts tried to warm themselves, often shoving one another out of the way to take a position of advantage close to a fire. Fights broke out often and usually ended when one or the other of the protagonists shuffled off to find another fire. Occasionally the scuffling matches turned deadly, and claws and fangs were used to kill. The fallen beast was quickly torn apart and summarily eaten with relish. The victor gained its momentary spot of warmth by the fire and quite often a choice piece of its hapless comrade.

"Nasty buggers, eh?" Edward whispered to Talanor.

"Have you seen this happen before? Eating each other, I mean?"

"Yes, the circumstances were different, but we've seen 'em feasting on the dead of their own kind. Either they're awfully hungry or just plain don't give a damn what they eat."

Talanor grunted in response. "Probably some of both."

"Look," Kailie pointed to the entrance of the canyon. "The Spectres are coming in."

"Good," Talanor murmured. "Get us down closer, Angus. We'll want to block the canyon with as many of the Spectres inside as possible."

Quickly and quietly they moved away, stopping to gather their packs before carefully climbing down the steep side of the ridge. Hair on the back of Angus' neck prickled as they picked their way down. This was about the spot where Captain Lamond had warned them of danger. He motioned for the other three to stop and get out of sight, and then he slipped down behind a boulder. In a few minutes a group of at least ten Spriggans passed a short distance away, led by two Spectres.

Kailie held her breath and watched the patrol come to a halt, the noses of the Spriggans lifted to sniff the air, the Spectres turning from side to side to determine what the beasts sensed. The little knife beat a wild pulse against her side. She dared not sing the Warrior Song but another Song came to mind, and she hummed softly.

The patrol shuffled about in confusion, refusing to obey the Spectres' commands. After several attempts to regroup them, the Spectres resorted to whipping the beasts back into line. At last the whips and curses prevailed, and the patrol moved past the hidden intruders.

Kailie breathed a sigh of relief, pressed a hand against her side, and turned to see Talanor watching her. She smiled and shrugged her shoulders. "The Song of the Flowers," she whispered in explanation. "The scent of wildflowers mixed with our scents and confused the creatures."

Talanor nodded. "Good thinking."

The four waited several minutes more until Angus was certain it was safe to move on. It was snowing harder, and the icy wind blew the white powder wildly about until they were unable to see more than a few steps ahead. They pushed on through deepening drifts until Angus brought them to a halt behind an outcropping of weathered rock.

"The entrance to the canyon is just around the bend," he whispered hoarsely. "What do you want us to do now, my lord?"

Talanor thought a moment before replying. "I think it would be more efficient if you and I first scouted ahead. If we can get in close to the entrance, I'll have a better idea of what we need to do. Then Kailie and Edward can join us and help set off the firesand."

Angus turned to his brother. "You and Kailie wait for us here. Keep alert."

Edward nodded once and turned to Kailie. "Let's find a place out of the wind, my lady." They moved deeper into the jumble or rocks and snowdrifts to try to find a protected spot. After they were safely out of sight, Talanor and Angus slipped into the whirling whiteness, moving cautiously and carefully until the entrance to the army's encampment was before them.

The two men huddled in the snow behind ice-encrusted boulders, quietly observing the narrow opening between two high walls of upthrust stone. There appeared to be no one guarding the entrance, but they watched for a long time just to be sure.

Finally, unable to stand the bitter cold any longer, Angus whispered to his companion. "Have you seen enough, my lord?"

"Yes, I think I have. No guards. The left wall extends past the right. Charges at its base and near the top of the right, along that crack, should send portions of both walls down into the entrance and block it." He nodded briskly and turned to Angus. "Let's get back to Kailie and Edward."

The two figures slipped silently through the snow and joined their companions. All were shaking with the cold from the long period of inactivity.

"There are no guards at the entrance of the canyon, so that makes our task a little easier." Talanor crouched near Kailie and removed a large bundle from his pack. He unwrapped it to expose a tightly woven basket, long and narrow in shape with a small opening tightly stoppered with a cork. He handed it to Angus along with a coiled length of cording. Another similarly shaped basket and more cording were produced from Kailie's pack.

"One of these will be placed near the base of the jutting entrance wall, the other in that crack along the top of the second wall. Angus, I'll ask that you place that one in position. Be careful as you climb down to the crack from the top. The going will be icy, I'm sure, and perhaps the rock is unstable. I'll place the bottom one. Edward, I want you to act as our signalman. When we have our firesand baskets in position, we'll signal you. When we've both signaled you that we're ready, we'll look to you for your signal, and then we'll light our fuses at the same time," Talanor instructed.

"And then run like the beasties are after us," Angus said.

"Yes," Talanor replied. "Precisely. And let's hope the charges are powerful enough to bring the stone down."

"What if the snow melts and puts out the fuse?" Kailie asked.

"Good point. The cord should be placed out of the wind on an area cleared of snow. Leave it coiled just as it is, but make sure you stick one of the ends of the cord down into the basket as far as you can. The cord is waxed and will burn one coil at a time. Whatever you do, don't put the cork back into the top once you've placed the cord in the firesand. The cord will burn slowly enough to allow us time to get away to safety. Meet back here after the fuses are lit." Talanor looked first at Angus and then at Edward. He murmured a phrase that the wind snatched away and then nodded to each man. "Are you both ready?"

At their nods of agreement the three men rose to leave the shelter of the rocks. Talanor turned to Kailie as the Mackay brothers moved away.

"You know what you must do?" he asked.

She gave him a brief smile, her lips nearly blue with cold. "Yes, Talanor, I know what to do."

He raised his hand in blessing and in farewell and turned to follow the Mackays.

Kailie waited only a few minutes after Talanor had gone; then she, too, slipped from the shelter of the rocks and turned her face into the frigid north wind. Shifting per pack, now noticeably lighter, she bent against the wind and hummed silently to herself as she headed away from the canyon. She had been hiking for perhaps an hour when an explosion ripped the air, followed a few seconds later by another. The absolute silence that followed made Kailie think that the cold, dark world of The Dlarmids held its breath.

She stood facing the direction from which she'd come and breathed deeply, sensing that the three men lived and were unharmed. But when she turned back to the north once more, she shivered, although not with the cold.

When a hideous, unearthly shriek rent the air around her, Kailie was prepared for it. It was like the howl she had heard the day that Sinnarock erupted, suffused with frustration and fury. The Darkling had been momentarily thwarted, but Kailie knew he would soon free his army and send it thundering out of the mountains and down upon the Wall of Rhade. Alexander's face appeared in her mind's eye, and she felt his touch.

When all else is done.

~

The way was hard, and an early darkness soon forced Kailie to stop. Wind whipped savagely against her, and snow lifted and swirled around her. She could seldom see farther than an arm's length ahead. And she was cold, so cold.

She struggled to the top of a ridge and sank down to rest for a moment. It was then that the little knife Alexander had given her began to beat and vibrate against her side. She saw a shadow emerge from the whirling snow off to her right. Another joined it, and then another and another came out of the gloom. Their stench reached her nostrils, and her stomach lurched with fear.

Spriggans.

And they smelled her. They came closer, forming a circle around her, keeping her in the center as they closed in. They snuffled and growled, and the sounds sent fear clawing its way up the back of her throat until she nearly screamed. She couldn't use the Warrior Song, not yet, but there was something else. She opened her mouth and began to sing, softly but with power. The stalking shapes came to a shuffling halt not far from her, puzzled by the strange sound.

Kailie continued to sing, the notes scattering with the snow on the fierce wind. Now there were other shapes moving just beyond the circle of Spriggans, large shapes that moved on four legs. The Spriggans tested the wind, uneasy, wary.

The Song changed. The music still came softly, but now there was an edge to it, a command.

The Spriggans broke from their circle, no longer the stalkers but the stalked, and drew together in a pack.

When Kailie shifted the tones of the music yet again, the four-legged shadows attacked, their growls mingling with the howls and grunts of the Spriggans. A Spriggan went down, dying grotesquely, its throat ripped away, in much the same manner as it killed. A howling shriek was cut short by a savage growl, and another creature sank into the snow, its black gore staining the pristine whiteness. Still another and then another fell before the onslaught of the shadows Kailie had called.

When the last Spriggan fell, its eyes open wide in the glassiness of death, Kailie ceased her Song and called softly. A dozen shapes came out of the whirling snow, and she waited for them to come to her, the great silver wolves of Kaenolir legend, enormous, beautiful, and deadly.

"I am Kailie." Her thoughts reached out to the wolf leader.

"Yes, we know you, lady. I am Torar, the leader of this pack. We came when you called."

"I have need of you, and Kaenolir has need of you once more, Torar."

"We will do as you ask."

"I must find a way to get to Sinnich Isle."

"You have a long way to go, lady."

"Yes. Will you come with me?"

"We will come."

"Evil walks this land. The Guardians will need you and your brothers after Sinnich."

"We know. We have waited for your call."

Kailie reached out to touch the soft fur of Torar's neck. *"I am very tired and very cold. I must rest before continuing on my journey."*

"Come, lady, we will find a place out of the wind. You will be safe while we are near."

With her hand in Torar's ruff, Kailie followed the wolf leader to a stunted stand of trees. Some of the wolves formed a circle of warm furred bodies around her, and nudged her down amongst them, while the rest burrowed into the snow, except for Torar. The pack leader stood watch, ears twitching, eyes searching the darkness, all senses alert to any danger, through the long, cold night.

Chapter Fourteen

The mountain shook and rumbled. Steam and smoke poured from the volcano's caldera while flames shot high and roared through the labyrinth of chambers and corridors. Maelorn's howls and screams of rage echoed and reverberated from the heated stone. He thrust two fawning Spectres away to leave them groveling at his feet. Some source of power moved within The Dlarmids. When he felt the explosions that sealed his army within the high-walled canyon, he shrieked again.

Whoever, or whatever, the power source was must be sought out and destroyed. No one, nothing, was allowed to stand in his way. For a moment he thought he sensed a second surge of energy coming from an ancient magic, but it was too fleeting to pinpoint. In his fury he dismissed it and sent a dozen Spectres scurrying to prepare his barge to carry him across the Strait of Tears.

His timetable had been disrupted; he'd not yet perverted the Singer to his cause. But the Singer was of little importance to him now. Goldenhorn would die a slow, lingering death in his chains. His bones would lie moldering beside Alpean's tomb.

"A fitting tribute," he mused.

There would soon be many bones whitening in the burning sun of Kaenolir. He smiled grotesquely, preening himself with his fingernails. He could taste the sweet flesh of Kaenolir, smell the sweet scents of blood and death. His power knew no limits now, and it would continue to grow as the Kaenolirians died or submitted to his rule. He could not be stopped. Sealing the canyon where his army waited was no more than an irritant. Whoever dared to seek him out would soon be dead.

His barge moved with great speed through the choppy waters of the Strait. When he pulled his black cape about his body and stepped onto the beach at the base of the Cliffs of Sorrows, he threw back his head and roared. The sound echoed and reechoed over water and land.

Maelorn had come to claim his due.

He raised his hand and with a guttural command he whirled away to free his army, his cape billowing like some gigantic vulture's wings.

~

"Danger comes, lady. Follow me."

Torar turned and loped across the snow. Kailie and his pack followed him into a nearby copse, where the trees lifted withered branches into the winter sky.

The silver wolves blended with the white landscape and seemed to disappear as they gathered around Kailie. They pushed her down into the snow and covered her.

"Clear your mind of thought, lady. 'Tis Maelorn who comes."

Kailie did as Torar commanded, clearing her mind of all thought and fear. Her heartbeat slowed; her eyes closed. She sank beneath the weight of the wolves and seemed to float somewhere between consciousness and unconsciousness. In this state, Maelorn would not sense her power. Nor would she know to fear his.

An immense black form flashed by, above and to the right of the copse. The wolves lay immobile, watching the Darkling pass. He was followed by a trail of Spectres, who moved effortlessly in his wake.

In only a moment the dark entourage was gone.

Torar turned his head and his pack moved away from Kailie. He bent to her, gently licking her white cheeks and forehead.

"Awake, lady. We must move while Maelorn is gone from Sinnarock."

She awakened instantly and rose to follow his lead. The pack loped tirelessly across the snow and soon passed out of the mountains into the Dark Land. When she stumbled in exhaustion, one of the wolves picked her up and placed her on the back of a comrade.

And so they traveled throughout the cold winter's day. When the wolf that carried her slowed and tired, another took her on his back. When she protested to Torar that she did not need to be carried, he only shook his head, the silver fur glinting in the gray light.

"This way is faster. We shall reach the cliffs by nightfall."

She did not protest again. The day wore on and as the last dim light faded into darkness, the wolves brought Kailie to the Cliffs of Sorrows.

Icy spray coated the cliffs that plunged treacherous and sheer to the roiling waves below. Kailie stared down. Her heart sank. She could see no way to descend the precipitous cliffs. Even if she were somehow able to do so, there was no boat to carry her to Sinnich.

Her shoulders slumped in dejection. Torar prodded her with his head.

"Rest now, lady. With first light we will climb down the cliff."

"But how, Torar?"

"There will be a way."

Again the wolves gathered around her, to keep her warm and to protect her. She slept, but fitfully. Her mind was obfuscated with dream-like images. She heard her father call her name, and then the golden king from the Horn of Kalora came to her. She drifted in fear and utter darkness and cried for her father. But it was the other Golden One who came to her.

Father. King. She could not distinguish one from the other.

Alexander's face swam before her, and she reached out to him, only to have his form slip like vapor through her fingers. She moaned with sorrow.

"Help me," she whispered to his shadow. "Oh, please, Alexander, help me."

Alexander's visage shifted and became her father's. Again he called to her, his voice raspy and faint.

"I'm coming, father. Wait for me. I'm coming," she sobbed.

Kailie woke to the dim light of another frigid dawn, her cheeks wet and cold with tears. She brushed them away and looked for Torar. Snow and sky melded into a gray-white tableau that had little definition out of which the wolf rose from his position of watchful sentry and came to her. The wolves that had warmed her throughout the restless night shook themselves and moved away.

"You cried out in your sleep."

"I dreamed of my father."

The intelligent eyes of the wolf looked into her distressed blue ones.

"Do not be afraid. We go to him now."

Torar turned and led the way to the top of the cliff. He looked at her once, and then without another glance he stepped over the edge.

Kailie pressed her hand against the back of her mouth to stifle a scream. She felt something brush her side and looked to see another of the wolves beside her. He, too, looked at her and then stepped to the edge of the cliff and over. Three more of the pack followed Torar and the second wolf.

At last, Kailie moved to the spot where the wolves had stepped from the cliff. She looked down the dizzying drop, and with a deep sigh to still her pounding heart she placed her foot in the print of the huge paws and took a step.

A narrow ledge, no wider than her spread fingers, snaked its way down the stone's icy face. With stiff fingers she clung to whatever handholds she could find and slowly made her way along the ledge. She heard the click of a wolf's claws behind her and felt the wind tug at her heavy tunic. The little knife beat a steady pulse against her side.

Time was no more as she prayed her way down the precipitous ledge. She slipped and was afraid to go on until Torar's command moved her, inch by painful, frightened inch, down the face of the cliff.

Waves crashed and clawed against the narrow strip of rocky beach. To Kailie they were like ravening beasts, snapping and growling at prey just out of reach.

She had climbed nearly halfway down when she felt the wind shift and grow stronger. The spray sent flying into the air with each wave soaked her through to the skin. She shivered, so violently she feared she would lose her grip and go tumbling into the watery churn below her.

A storm roared through the Strait, darkening the already leaden skies and hurling water into gigantic waves. The narrow, wet ledge became even more treacherous, and Kailie sobbed with each sliding step she took. On and on, down and still down, faltering again and again while Torar's voice called encouragement.

Her fingers were scraped raw from the rock, and she left bloody prints with every change of handhold. Tears froze to her face, and spray clung to her eyelashes and hair and dripped off the tip of her nose.

She pressed herself flat against the stone to keep the wind from tearing her from her precarious perch and slid her foot along the ledge. Panic choked her when her foot encountered nothing but space. She carefully turned her head to look. The ledge had come to an end.

A whimpering sob escaped her lips.

"Lady, look down. You are nearly to the bottom. Just a few more steps."

Weeping uncontrollably, she moved her foot until she found a point of rock large enough to get a toehold. Another step down. Another and then another until Torar's voice came to her again.

"Jump, lady."

She did so without question and landed in a sobbing heap on the smooth rocks at the bottom of the cliff.

"There is a cave just above the water line. We will wait there until the storm passes. This way."

Kailie pushed herself upright and leaning against the neck of a wolf, she half walked, half dragged herself into the narrow cave that Torar had found. It was dark inside but somehow warmer because she was no longer buffeted by the wind, nor did the icy spray reach them here.

The wolves stopped at the entrance; each shook the droplets of water from his fur and came to lie down beside the nearly frozen woman. Her teeth chattered loudly in the confined space, and tears she could not stop slipped down her cheeks to drip off her chin. She raised a trembling hand to wipe them away.

Gradually the wolves' shared body heat seeped into Kailie's cold and exhausted limbs, and she began to relax. Her sobs quieted to only an occasional hiccough. Feeling came back to her toes and fingers, and the painful scrapes on her hands stung and throbbed; but she grew warm and dry within the circle of silver bodies.

Exhaustion, the cold, and lack of nourishment had taken a great toll on Kailie's strength; and although she tried not to close her eyes, she felt herself slip deeper and deeper into the drowsy warmth provided by the wolves and the little cave. Just before she slept she roused at the cry of an eagle, faint and far away. It was a comforting sound, a sound from her childhood. She thought of her father and prayed for him and for herself.

~

The dreams came again, not so confused as before. Her father was there. She saw him distinctly now, still chained in a chamber deep inside Sinnarock. He looked into her eyes and smiled in encouragement.

"You've done well, my daughter. Soon, soon," he whispered.

The Golden One with the crown was there, too. It was difficult to see him clearly, and for a moment Kailie thought he was chained to the stone and her father was free.

The images of the two men drifted together and slipped away to be replaced by Talanor. He held out his hand to her, and when she reached to take it, he moved away, beckoning for her to follow. The trees of the Horn opened in an arched path before them. Talanor led her to a tranquil pool. Birds sang strange and beautiful songs; flowers grew in a riot of color. The warm air smelled of exotic fragrances that filled her head with their essence.

She turned to Talanor, but he was gone. Again the Golden One who was and was not her father stood near her.

"Come, my child." His voice touched a chord deep within her, and she followed him. He stepped into a boat moored at the edge of the pool, but when she did likewise, he vanished behind a misty veil.

"Don't go." She reached out to touch the place where he had been. Alexander was there instead. He took her hands and drew her with him down into the bottom of the boat.

When all else is done.

~

Slowly the grip of sleep and dream loosened, and Kailie surfaced to the reality of the cave and the wolves lying close around her. The cave was very dark, with only a faint glimmer outlining the opening.

The wolves slept except for Torar. He lay near the entrance, his head on his paws, ears twitching for the slightest sound of danger. When Kailie stirred, he raised his head and looked at her.

"Did you sleep well, lady?"

"Yes, Torar. I dreamed again of my father. And of a boat."

"It will soon be time to leave this place."

"How will we get to Sinnich Isle?"

"There will be a way. When it grows light, we will go. The storm is not so strong now."

The rest of the pack began to stir and stretch. One by one they silently left the cave, the only sound of their passing the faint clicking of their claws against the floor of the cave. Kailie shivered a little without their warmth, but her clothes were dry. Her hands were stiff and sore, but the scratches and cuts she had incurred on her climb down the cliff no longer bled.

Torar rose and turned his head to the entrance of the cave. It was lighter now, and the sound of the waves not so thunderous as when they'd entered. Kailie had no way of knowing how long they'd rested there. As it had been on the Horn of Kalora when she'd been with Rhianna Lanee, time was an enigma

177

here. She did feel a deep sense of urgency, however, and she knew that her task still lay before her.

"Is it time to go?"

"Yes, lady. It is time to go to Sinnich."

Kailie stood. She ached in nearly every part of her body. Without looking she knew her knees and arms were covered with bruises. Her hair was stiff with salt, her clothes caked with it.

Torar stepped from the cave into the bite of the wind, and following the base of the cliff, moved down the strip of beach until a pillar of rock, cut free from the cliff during eons of time, barred their way. He stopped. He lifted his head and sent a ululating cry into the air. The pack gathered silently around him. Torar looked at Kailie, and then he stepped through the narrow opening between pillar and cliff and disappeared from her sight. His pack followed him. Uneasy, but not afraid, Kailie stepped through the opening and onto fine, clean sand. For a moment so brief that it might not have been, she thought she saw the Golden One and wondered if somehow she had been transported back to the mystical Horn. From high above, the cry of an eagle floated down, and she looked up to follow its flight. Turning in wonder to Torar, she found him standing at the edge of gently lapping water. Beyond him bobbed a sturdy little sloop. It seemed appropriate to her that, surrounded by gray skies and grayer waters, the boat was painted a brilliant white.

~

The boat bucked and plowed its way through the Strait of Tears. Fog obscured the way, and Kailie had no way of knowing how close they were to Sinnich. Only Torar and two of the wolves sailed with her; the rest of the pack had been sent to join Talanor.

She set the sail and steered in what she thought to be a northerly direction. For a fleeting moment she saw the golden king beckon to her through the mist, and then he was gone. Shaking her head to clear her vision, she briefly feared for her sanity; but the immediacy of dealing with the boat, its sail and tiller, and the violent seas pressed the fear aside. Soon after, she heard once again the call of a sea eagle, and some inner sense bade her follow the sound.

The fog lifted just enough for her to see the distant outline of the western shore of Lorn Isle. Tears clogged her throat, and she mourned for what had been. The sight of her home faded from view, but she resolutely sailed past the isle, her hands stiff with cold, her arms aching with the strain of controlling first the tiller, then the sail.

Again, an eagle's cry alerted her to change course. She sailed on, knowing that Sinnich Isle was but a short distance away.

"I'm coming, father," she murmured through blue-tinged lips.

A particularly violent wave slammed into the boat and she cried out as it heeled far to port. Somehow the craft righted itself and continued to struggle through the heavy seas. Around her wind howled in frenzy and tore at the sail like a living beast. She tried to sing the Song of the Winds, but the music died on her lips, smothered by powers let loose by Maelorn.

Kailie fought on, no longer able to hear the cry of the guiding eagle.

"Father," she moaned, the word wrenched from her lips by the wild wind.

Rocks loomed out of the fog, directly in the boat's path, but she saw the danger too late to avoid it. She screamed and the wolves came to her. The boat ground savagely against the unyielding stone; and the winds ripped and slashed until the boat, its keel smashed, its sail torn away, broke apart, spilling Kailie and the three wolves into icy water.

She felt Torar grasp her arm with his teeth, his grip firm but gentle; another wolf came up under her, and she clung to its back. The third wolf swam strongly against the surf, and the last she remembered was watching the silver head bobbing in the waves and thinking that this was what it felt like to die.

~

Someone called her name, but the sound was so faint she could not identify the voice she heard. It came again, closer this time. She coughed and rolled to her side. As she did so, she felt her stomach muscles cramp, and she retched. Again and again her body regurgitated the salty water she had swallowed until, gasping and spent, her stomach was empty.

She lay quietly, sobbing softly.

"Lady."

She pushed herself up on an elbow and reached out to touch the fur of Torar's neck. *"You are all right? Your companions?"*

"We are all here with you."

"Are we on Sinnich?"

"Yes, we are on Sinnich."

Kailie sagged wearily against the cold, wet sand, her fingers digging spasmodically in Torar's thick fur.

"Come, lady, lean on us. We must go to the mountain."

The wolves gently nudged her, and she struggled to her feet to stand swaying on trembling legs. Torar began to walk slowly across the sand, and with a wolf on either side Kailie followed him with dragging steps.

Fog whirled damply about them as they made their way inland. The rough, uneven landscape, marked here and there with burned and stunted trees, appeared to be ancient lava runs that had crusted and solidified into porous rock.

She stumbled often and leaned heavily on the shoulders of the two wolves. Torar turned his head and looked back to check her progress.

"Not much further, lady. We are nearly there."

They trudged on, the way becoming steeper as they climbed the lower reaches of the volcano.

Just as Kailie felt the silver knife throb hotly against her side, Torar halted. With a warning growl, he herded Kailie and her two companions behind a large, irregularly shaped boulder. Two ugly creatures, similar to what Talanor had killed at the inn only larger, came down the path they had just left. One stopped, so quickly the other nearly collided with him, and sniffed the air. Out of the corner of her eye Kailie saw a flash, and the three wolves launched themselves at the Ghillies.

A shriek rent the air to be suddenly and effectively stilled as the wolves tore the throats of the ugly beasts and left them lying dead before they could recognize their attackers. Torar lifted his head and checked the air for other beasts that might be nearby. He turned to Kailie, his muzzle stained with gore.

"Come quickly. There are others not far off."

Kailie stepped from her hiding place and with a steadying hand on a silver ruff followed Torar off the trail and deeper into the jumble of rocks. They moved silently, the only sound an occasional click of claw on rock. The sulfurous stench of the volcano burned her nose, and she gagged against the retching spasms of her stomach. A constant rumble filled the air and the ground shook beneath their feet.

"Wait here."

At Torar's command she sank onto the rough ground, resting her back against a large rock. The three wolves were gone but a short time before they returned to her side.

180

"There is an entrance into the mountain just ahead, but it is heavily guarded. They are not expecting an attack. We should be able to surprise them, but, lady, we will need your Song."

Quickly, stealthily the three great wolves led Kailie to the entrance into the volcano. Alexander's knife throbbed rhythmically against her side, and the same sense of urgency that had driven her this far made her press on.

At least half a dozen Ghillies shuffled aimlessly about the cavernous entrance to Sinnarock. Torar and his companions flattened themselves against the ground and waited. The tension increased and one of the beasts, made uneasy by a sense of impending doom, growled low, and the others gathered nearby. It lifted its head to test the air, but the hot sulfurous gases obliterated any scent it might have detected. Unable to find the cause of its uneasiness it moved away from the entrance, growling a command for its companions to follow.

It was the moment Torar had been waiting for. He turned his head to Kailie.

"Sing your Song now, lady."

Exhaustion and fear forgotten, Kailie threw back her head, and the Warrior Song rang out. The beasts stopped in stunned surprise, bunching together. The intensity of the music increased, and they began to scream with pain, clawing at their ears to block out the sound.

A moment more, while the Song continued its devastating blow, Torar waited. Then with a growl he and his companions launched themselves into the midst of the thoroughly confused Ghillies.

Savage growls and barks, screams and shrieks mingled with the music, and within minutes the hideous creatures lay dead. Torar did not hesitate but turned and led the way into the mountain. The Song ended, and Kailie hurried after the wolves.

The attack outside the entrance was sure to bring more creatures who had been left to guard Maelorn's stronghold, and the wolves and Kailie had not gone far when several more Ghillies came racing toward them, fangs bared, claws lifted to attack.

Again Kailie lifted her voice to set the music echoing off cavern walls, its ancient magic warring with the evil that permeated Sinnarock. With howls of rage and pain, the Ghillies attacked; but the Song and the wolves were too much for them, and like their companions, they, too, sprawled in death while their gore darkened the floor of the cavern.

Deeper and deeper into the volcano Kailie and her protectors ran. The echo of the Song filled the corridors and chambers. Once Kailie thought she head an answering phrase, but she could not be sure. She ran on, gasping for breath, her throat raw from the gases, over the uneven floor of a tunnel.

"Torar," she called and stumbled to a halt. *"I must rest for a moment."*

"Only for a moment, lady. We must hurry."

Kailie leaned against the tunnel wall. She sucked the hot air painfully into her lungs, closed her eyes against the agony and tried to block out her exhaustion. The wolves surrounded her. Their tongues lolled and their sides heaved from exertion. They rested for only a short time before Torar urged them on.

They continued the torturous descent into the volcano. All the while the mountain rumbled and trembled around them, until they came to a place where three tunnels led away from a small chamber.

Torar hesitated and in that split second howls filled the air, and a troop of Ghillies raced into the chamber. Too startled by the sudden attack to sing, Kailie felt the fear she'd been pressing aside rise up inside her, and she screamed.

The wolves met the swarming creatures head on. A fierce and vicious attack was more than the creatures expected, and they retreated only to regroup and charge again, heedless of the fallen bodies of their comrades.

"Lady! The Song!"

But the evil that surrounded them stopped her throat in panic, and terror clogged her mind and weakened her body. She pressed against the hot wall, able to do nothing more than cringe there and watch the outnumbered wolves struggle against Maelorn's creatures. Torar's voice came to her again, more desperate now, but she was too frightened to respond. One of the wolves went down under the onslaught, and Torar howled.

His cry of fury edged with sorrow reverberated off the stone, and his haunting call shook Kailie to the core. She thrust away from the wall and moved closer to the melee, her eyes following the flashing, silver forms. Fearfully, she clutched the little knife and at last lifted her voice.

The Ghillies pulled back in stunned confusion, shrieking and howling. Music beat against them, and three of them sank to the floor in submission to a power they could not ignore or kill.

The two remaining wolves converged on the cringing Ghillies and dispatched them with cold precision. A last shriek echoed in the chamber, and then all was still except for the music. It rang over the bodies of the beasts and ended on a note of triumph.

Torar limped to his fallen comrade and whined. Kailie rushed to the stricken wolf and fell to her knees beside him. His intelligent eyes turned to her, and she saw pain and sorrow in them. She took the beautiful head against her breast, rocking back and forth, and began to sing again, but this time the music was low and comforting. It was the Song she had sung to heal Alexander's shoulder; she sang it now to heal her defender's many wounds.

The gentle crooning continued for several minutes until she felt a rough tongue lick her cheek; and when she looked down into the wolf's eyes, there was no more pain. Her arms fell away, and the wolf gathered himself to stand. He shook himself, gave Torar an open-mouthed grin and whined. The huge plum of his tail wagged, and for the first time in many, many long hours Kailie smiled. She wrapped her arms around the powerful neck and buried her face in the thick fur.

"Thank you, lady."

"No, my friend, thank you." Kailie smiled again and stood with her hand on his head. She turned to Torar.

"Which way do we go?"

"This way. I'm sure I heard the Warrior Song coming from this way."

"So, Torar, you heard it, too."

"Yes, I'm sure I did, even with all the echoes."

The mountain quaked violently and belched another flume of gases that flowed rapidly through its tunnels and caverns. Torar turned his head from side to side and then quickly took the left tunnel.

"Hurry. We will find the Goldenhorn down this way."

Sinnarock continued to rumble, and the stone undulated beneath their feet, causing them to stumble frequently as they ran on, ever deeper into the writhing mountain. They encountered no more Ghillies, but Kailie was sure they had not seen the last of the hideous creatures. Getting into the mountain and finding her father was only half her mission; they still had to get off the island. The Ghillies would try to stop them at every step of the way, for their master had ordered them to guard and kill.

She dare not think of that now. If she did, her fear would overcome her again, and there wasn't time for such an indulgence. Her jaw set firmly, Kailie followed Torar as he led them down the winding tunnel. At last, when she thought she could go no further, Torar slowed. A tremor jolted the mountain, and on the wall just ahead, red light flickered.

With silent stealth the wolf leader advanced along the curving corridor. For a moment he was out of sight, and Kailie quickened her pace. She came around the bend, half running, into a small, fire-lit chamber and came face to face with an image from her dreams.

Her father stood chained to the stone next to a long, high bier. He was dirty and thin, his golden hair dull, his eyes shadowed with weariness and pain.

"Kailie," he rasped. "Kailie."

"Father," she cried and rushed forward to clasp him tightly about the neck. At her touch he moaned with pain.

She pulled away to look at his beloved face through a haze of tears. "What has he done to you?" she whispered.

Andrew Goldenhorn smiled crookedly. "He tried to make me a singer of his songs. But he was not successful," he shook his chains, "as you can see."

"We must get out of here, father. Torar says there isn't much time."

"I heard your Song and knew you were coming. I tried to sing, but I haven't much of a voice."

"I thought I heard you once. Torar said he heard the Song, too."

Kailie looked about the chamber distractedly. "Is there a key for your chains?"

"Not here. The beasts always brought it with them when they came to bring me food and water. Sing the Song, Kailie, with as much power as you can. And pray it will be enough to break the chains."

Kailie grasped the chain imprisoning Goldenhorn's right arm and began to sing with all the power her waning strength allowed. It was enough. She heard the chains snap, and with the next phrase they fell from her father's wrists and ankles, and he stood free. Torar came to stand near him, and understanding the gesture, Goldenhorn used the great wolf to steady himself and walk away from the imprisoning stone.

He came to his daughter, and tears filled his eyes as he reached out to enfold her in his embrace. She sobbed against his neck in weariness, but fear and panic warred with the joy of knowing he was alive and free. His hand reached up to touch the salt-matted hair.

"We have one more task, Kailie, before we leave this hellish place." Goldenhorn stepped away to stand at the foot of the stone bier. When she looked questioningly at him, he reached out to touch the warm stone. There was a responding hum, loud and strong. Goldenhorn smiled. "We must sing together, Kailie, to fulfill the promise."

184

Kailie stepped to the other end of the bier and, like her father, placed her hands on the stone.

The Goldenhorn began to sing, and for a moment only his hoarse, hard-edged voice was heard. Then Kailie added her voice to his, and together they sang the Warrior Song, much as they had done that day so long ago when the mountain erupted and Maelorn burst free. How could they have known then that time would find them deep inside the mountain singing the Song again, this time to keep the promise.

The tomb trembled as earthquakes rocked Mt. Sinnarock with a steady rhythm. Cracks widened and lengthened in the stone as the dynamic music rose and fell, building in force and power until the sound of their voices filled the chamber and beat against the stone surrounding Alpean.

Torar whined as if in pain. The stone shattered and fell away under the hands of Goldenhorn and Kailie. Dust stung their eyes and when it began to settle they stopped singing. They had kept the promise.

He stood among the rubble of his tomb, immense in size to rival Maelorn, but dazzling in his glory. He was a king from another time, restored to his kingship.

Alpean was free.

Chapter Fifteen

Maelorn stood atop the ridge, his red eyes glowed with fury as he surveyed first his milling army and then the jumble of rocks and debris clogging the entrance to the canyon. He still sensed the ancient power that had brought the walls down, and he swelled with anger. He raised his arms in the air, threw back his head and gave a roar of defiance. The sound echoed off the mountainsides, reverberating among snow-covered peaks until it returned tenfold, like resounding claps of thunder.

The Darkling roared until the mountains themselves shook. Finally, when the sound had built to an intolerable level, he brought his hands down and pointed long nailed fingers at the jumble of rock and earth below him. Fire shot from his extended fingers and the obstruction exploded. Fiery pieces of stone flew through the air and struck the ground near where he stood.

He continued to roar and once more fire sprang from his stiffened fingers. In almost orgasmic ecstasy he thrust his body at the entrance of the canyon, and with one mighty heave he sent a last surge of fire. Stones blasted into the creatures that were amassed near the end of canyon, killing many of them.

The dead mattered little. At Maelorn's command the creatures surged forward through the opening, and their passage trampled the bodies of the fallen into a gory, black mess. Spectres gathered about their prince, and those closest to him fawned and groveled in obeisance. He panted with exertion and exhilaration; his eyes glowed red with satisfaction, and he slavered in jubilation.

The time had come at last.

He reached out and grasped two of the nearest Spectres and pulled them against his sides.

"We march, my darlings," he growled. "We march on Kaenolir."

The Spectres' bony fingers caressed Maelorn's heaving chest. He threw back his head and laughed in triumph. "No one can withstand me now. Kaenolir is mine," he shouted. He pushed the Spectres aside and leaped away to lead his army.

~

In the glow of many torches, Alexander watched as the last timbers were fitted into place. Just a few more hours and the Wall gate could be closed and barred. With tired steps he climbed the ladder to the top of the Wall. It was quieter here, above the noise made by the men knocking down the low walls of the Guardians' Fort and pulling down the storage building that butted up against the northern face of the Wall. The day's heat lingered, and he brushed sweat from his forehead with impatient fingers.

He stepped to the parapet and leaned against it to watch the scene twenty feet below him. Men wielded sledgehammers and pickaxes by the light of smoky fires and guttering torches. They moved in a bizarre red and black dance of substance and shadow and reminded Alexander of the underworld pictured in the old legends. The dust rose as the low wall was knocked down by the determined efforts of sweating, cursing men.

Alexander turned away and walked toward a crumbling watchtower. He had taken over the old tower to serve as his office and sleeping quarters. It allowed him some privacy while he was still close to the activity in the Fort and on the Wall. He saw Simon Stewart come toward him, his usually immaculate uniform dirty and rumpled from living and working in the same clothes for days. He gave his captain a weary imitation of a salute.

"The demolition is progressing rapidly, Captain. We should have everything knocked down and the debris cleared away by dawn."

"Good." Alexander instinctively looked to the north, a growing sense of uneasiness filling his mind. "I don't think we have much time left. Get the job done as soon as possible. Don't worry about clearing away the debris. Just scatter it about as best you can."

Simon nodded. He, too, looked toward the north and rubbed the back of his neck with a grimy hand. "How soon do you think the attack will come?"

Alexander sighed, breathing in the smells of dust, hot stone and acrid smoke from the torches. "It won't be long now." He turned to look at the younger man. "Let me know the minute Talanor and the Mackays return."

"Yes, sir."

"And, Simon, get some rest. I'm going to need you." The statement drifted off into silence.

"I'll strike a bargain with you, Captain. If you promise to get some sleep, so will I."

Alexander smiled and clasped Simon's shoulder. "All right, Simon. It's a bargain. Off with you now." With a gentle shove Alexander sent him on his way.

When Simon's footsteps had died away, Alexander turned once more to the north and allowed his thoughts to settle on a subject he had purposely pushed from his mind.

"Where are you, Kailie Fairchild?" he whispered into the darkness. "Kailie. Kailie."

Distress fraught with fear and uncertainty threatened to overcome his resolve, and he leaned against the rough stone parapet. He crossed his arms atop it, lowered his head to rest on them and closed his eyes.

Images of Kailie whirled behind his eyelids. The fragrance that was part of her filled his mind, and he yearned to touch her.

"Go with care. Come back to me."

He lifted his head and breathed in deeply. Turning away he walked the few steps to his tower. There was still a door, of sorts, and he pulled it shut behind him as he stepped into the stuffy little room. Half the roof was gone, and he looked up into the sky as he unbuckled his belt and felt the weight of his sword slide away. He pulled his sweaty, dirty tunic up over his head and grunted.

"I smell like a goat," he muttered. "Baskers, what I wouldn't give for a bath."

He eased himself down onto the lumpy pallet and pulled off his boots. With a deep sigh of weariness, he lay back. Stars sparkled coldly overhead, and he wondered if the gods were watching his puny efforts.

"I doubt it," he murmured. "The bastards."

He closed his eyes and immediately fell asleep.

~

"Alexander. Alexander, wake up."

Someone shook him roughly by the shoulder. "Wake up, man. We've work to do."

Alexander groaned and pushed himself upright. He groggily scrubbed the sleep from his eyes and tried to focus his attention. A candle flickered on the floor nearby, giving just enough light to see the features of the man who squatted on his haunches beside him.

"Welcome back, Talanor," he mumbled in greeting. He took in the large man's haggard features and sensed his fatigue.

"Did everything go as planned?"

"Yes. We blocked the canyon, but I don't think it will stop Maelorn for long. I could feel him close behind us all the way back. We've not much time, Alexander."

"So." Alexander pulled on his boots and reached for the dirty tunic. He thrust his arms through the sleeves and slipped it over his head. He rose and retrieved his sword. As he buckled it around his waist, he looked into Talanor's brooding eyes. "It begins."

"Yes. It begins."

The two men looked at each other in the wavering candlelight, each taking the measure of the other, gauging the strength that lay within. An unspoken question haunted Alexander's eyes, and Talanor saw it and understood.

"I don't know," he said quietly. "She lives, I know that much. Her life force is still very strong. And another has joined her force, equally as strong. Actually, two others, I think."

Alexander nodded and bent to pinch out the candle. He paused a moment in the darkness, letting his eyes adjust, before he turned to leave the room.

"Two?" he asked the big man striding beside him along the top of the Wall toward the gate.

"Two." Talanor clipped off the word, and Alexander knew it would be futile to question him further.

"Two," Alexander muttered again. He stopped midstride. Kailie must have been able to free her father from Sinnarock. But, who else?

The Warrior Song, he remembered at last, was meant to keep a source of evil entombed, yes, but it was also a promise, a promise to free Alpean the Steward. Why hadn't he remembered that before?

The answer hit him like a blow to the gut. "Alpean," he whispered breathlessly. Somehow she had freed Alpean, freed him with the power of her music.

And now what would happen? He turned to question Talanor, but the mage was nowhere to be seen.

"Baskers," Alexander hissed. "Why will you never answer my questions?"

He watched dawn streak the sky with subtle shades of gold. Once it had been his favorite time of day. Now he dreaded it, knowing that the burning light brought only more heat and discomfort.

And Kaenolir closer to death.

~

Exhausted crews worked to finish the last of the demolition of the Fort while Alexander exhorted every available carpenter and ironworker to complete the repairs to the Wall gate. Tired men doubled their efforts, a sense of urgency overcoming aching muscles and flagging energies.

The gate was pushed shut with a mighty crash, and although still unbarred it seemed an impregnable bulwark. There was no shout of triumph or elation at their success in closing the gate; there was still the massive bar to lift and place in the iron supports mounted on the timbers. Horses and men, pulleys and ropes were hastily put into position to lift the timber hewn from one tall, aged fir tree. Slowly, almost painfully, the bar was lowered, guided by more ropes held in the calloused hands of men who struggled to keep it from swinging away. It fell into the supports with a resounding, meaty thunk, and effectively barred the gate.

The men stood silently for several minutes, breathing deeply, taking in the sight of the barred gate, before dropping the ropes and moving to unhitch the horses. Quietly they congratulated one another on their accomplishment.

Alexander dropped the rope he held and stepped back to view the gate. He breathed in the raw, pungent wood scent emanating from the logs. The muscles in his arms and legs quivered in delayed reaction to the tremendous strain he had placed on them. Sweat trickled down his forehead into his eyes, and his hand shook as he wiped it away. He raised his head to look up at the gate that now barred the Wall of Rhade to intruders from the north. It rose starkly between huge pillars that served as support, a monument to the skill and labor of desperate men.

How long, he wondered, *would Maelorn allow it to stand?*

Alexander turned away to seek out Ian. Before the gate was closed, Ian had placed heavy planks over a corner of the pit and moved his men and horses out into what was left of the Fort. They would soon be on their way to the High Ghilana Plain to await Maelorn's army.

Alexander doubted the feasibility of the plan to send fifty mounted highlanders into the jaws of the advancing dark forces, but it seemed a risk worth taking. Perhaps, after all, he was merely prolonging the agony.

Damn you, Maelorn. Damn you to hell.

He climbed the ladder to the top of the Wall, crossed it and found a ladder to let himself down the other side into the Fort. Simon hurried toward him.

"Get these men out of here, Simon. We haven't—"

His command was interrupted by the screams of frightened men and the howls of attacking beasts.

An hour. We only needed another hour. The incongruous thought slipped through Alexander's mind as he reached for his sword. Hot blood pounded through him as he ran to the aid of the men still in the Fort.

"Ian," he shouted but did not wait for his friend to join him. A Ghillie, its mouth red with blood, reared up over its kill and raised a battleaxe as Alexander ran toward it.

"You misbegotten bastard," Alexander roared. "It's time for you to die."

He knocked the axe aside as if it were nothing more than a stick and plunged his sword into the beast's belly, ripping downward as he struck. The Ghillie opened its mouth, grunted in pain and topped over, its limbs twitching in death.

Alexander did not watch it fall, but turned to meet another of his enemies. The yard was full of shaggy creatures, and their attack had caught the men still working by surprise. One man wielded a hammer like a club, and Alexander heard the sharp crack of bone as the blow of the hammer's heavy head crushed a skull.

There was no time to think, only time to react. The Guardians fought with measured precision. Gore from the beasts they slaughtered dripped from their swords and spattered their arms and clothing. More Guardians from the other side of the Wall rushed down the ladders to aid their comrades. Talanor took up his sword, found Alexander in the wild crush, and standing back to back the two men fought with concentrated deadliness.

It was over as quickly as it had begun.

The surviving creatures slunk rapidly away into the brightening day. The man-things had proven too much for them. They would wait for their comrades to join them, and then they would kill the things as their master had ordered them to do. But for now they would wait for the rest of the army.

Three Spectres who had watched the attack from a slight rise called to the remaining beasts. They had learned what they had been sent to determine: There were gates to block the Wall and the river, and the men were prepared to fight.

It made little difference. Lord Maelorn would easily subdue the men. Their pathetic efforts to protect themselves would serve only as a momentary irritation.

The Spectres turned from the hill, and with a sharp command the beasts fell into step behind the dark forms.

~

Ian swore the same harsh, profane words over and over again. His chest heaved to draw air into his aching lungs.

"Somebody get this stinking bastard off me," he screamed.

Alexander heard his friend's cry and began searching for him. "Ian, where are you?" he shouted.

"Over here. By the barracks. Baskers, Alexander, hurry up."

Alexander found his friend half buried beneath the huge body of a dead Ghillie. He looked around for some men to help pull the carcass away and found Talanor at his side. Each man grabbed a heavy leg and after a couple of tries managed to pull the beast off Ian's lower body.

"Next time, Ian," Alexander panted, "get out of the way."

Ian continued to swear, a reaction to the fighting blood still coursing through him.

Alexander looked at Talanor, and the two grinned at each other. "Are you all right?" Alexander offered Ian a hand and pulled him to his feet.

"Yes, I'm all right," Ian growled. He looked around the yard of the Fort at the scattered bodies of beasts. There were men's bodies, too, several of them. Ian swore again.

Alexander followed Ian's gaze. The silence that had followed the attack was punctuated now by moans. He moved away to help with the wounded and to see to the dead. Talanor stopped his hand as he reached to strip away the tunic of a seriously wounded man.

"Let me take care of the wounded. You see to the work that remains to be done on the demolition."

Alexander nodded and rose. He looked once more at the wounded man, touched his forehead in salute and turned away, calling for Simon. He ordered several men who had been working on the gate to join the crew pulling down the walls of the Fort. He took a half-dozen Guardians from demolition duty and sent them to the Wall to stand watch. He castigated himself for not having done so earlier, but the need for as many hands as he could muster had outweighed the need for sentries.

"Scatter the stones. Don't worry about hauling them away. We haven't time." He gave final instructions and sent the men to their tasks.

Simon organized men to help Talanor move the wounded to the top of the Wall and others to carry the dead to the south side for burial. A common grave was hurriedly dug for the six men killed in the attack, hasty words were spoken, and the grave filled in. Alexander knew there wasn't time for an appropriate burial, yet his heart ached for the men who had died and for their families. A deep-seated fear that these were but the first of many to die in battle left a sick taste in his mouth.

~

The last stone was pushed away, and the few planks over the corner of the pit that had been used to move horses and men to the north side of the Wall were carried away. Nothing remained standing that might aid the beasts in an attempt to gain the top of the Wall.

"Get the men up the ladders," Alexander commanded to Simon. "We've done all we can here."

Ian came across the littered yard, leading his horse. Alexander watched him and his men come and once again felt despair.

"It's time to go, Alex."

"Yes." Alexander gripped the other man's shoulder in a hard clasp of friendship. "Go with the gods," he said quietly.

Ian clasped Alexander's free hand and then turned to mount his horse. He looked down into the green eyes clouded with worry. "Watch your back, my friend," he said.

"You, too."

Ian nodded and turned his horse's head, and the company of highlanders fell in behind him. None of them looked back.

Alexander watched them until they were out of sight. What was he sending them to? His shoulders sagged under the weight of responsibility, and he swore. He turned away and stepping quickly he toured the ground of the half-demolished Fort. He had lived within its confines or close by all his life. He knew every timber, every stone that comprised its structure, and every man who proudly wore the uniform of the Guardians, and every man's family. His father had been captain of the Guardians and his father's father. A Lamond had commanded this Fort since it was built. He cursed again the fate that dictated he tear it down.

He turned his back on the scene of destruction and climbed the ladder left standing for him. When he reached the top of the Wall and stepped over the parapet, the ladder was pulled up. It thumped against the stone with a hollow thud of finality and foreboding. Alexander could not help but wonder if any of them would ever climb down again.

~

Maelorn led his army out of The Dlarmids at great speed. His Spectres were quick to whip any stragglers back into line, and, like a great black herd, the dark forces spread out and moved closer to the heart of Kaenolir. After a time, Maelorn called a halt and prepared to divide his forces. Part of the army would advance down the Skara in boats that had been prepared for them and the other part would advance across the High Ghilana Plain to spread out along the Wall, drawing the Kaenolirians along its length.

It mattered little to Maelorn that the Guardians had decimated a small advance force. It mattered little to him that the Kaenolirians had closed the Skara and Wall gates against him. It mattered little because he had grown too powerful for mere mortals to oppose him. He threw back his head and roared with triumph and pleasure.

Maelorn's euphoria was shared by his Spectres. Their master was happy; they had done their work well. Soon, very soon, they would lay Kaenolir at his feet, and whatever else he desired.

The roar was suddenly strangled in Maelorn's throat. He screamed, and his fingers clawed the air around him.

"No," he shrieked. "It's not possible." He stumbled and nearly fell, and several of his Spectres clustered around him

His ugly, black head turned toward the north. He felt a surge of intense power from that direction, and he seethed with frustration and fury. Someone was inside his stronghold, someone who possessed the Faerie magic. Unable to support himself he sank to the ground. He screamed, his body wrenched by convulsions. The Spectres moaned and pressed against him, begging him to rise. When his writhing ceased, they wiped spittle and blood from his lips and sweat from his body.

"Alpean is free," he gasped.

Maelorn turned again to the north as he stumbled to his feet. "You are too late, brother. I will have Kaenolir in my grasp before you can do anything to stop me," he vowed. Hatred for his brother rivaled his desire for power, and for a moment he considered returning to Sinnich and destroying Alpean. But, no, there would be ample time to dispose of him. He was but one and Maelorn had an army at his command. Alpean's freedom would do the Kaenolirians little good. What could one man do against so many?

His strength returning, Maelorn threw back his head and laughed. "Brother, by the time I am through with you, you will wish you had never left your tomb of stone." The malevolent laughter rang again as Maelorn whirled away, his minions following in his wake, to lead his forces against Kaenolir.

~

Ian Cameron brought his company of mounted highlanders to a halt. They were not far from the place where they had placed a network of ropes and sharpened stakes to entangle unsuspecting foes. Ian has chosen the spot for the trap carefully. The rolling plain, burned to brown stubble by the sun, spread out in all directions around them. Just beyond a low rise, in a depression that had once been lush with belly-high grass, Ian had laid his trap.

Deadly stakes were hidden in tall stalks of grasses and weeds. Ropes had been woven around the stakes to trip anyone or anything that blundered into them. Such a device could not halt an oncoming force, but it could decrease its numbers and slow and confuse the advance.

Leather creaked behind him as men shifted in their saddles. Someone coughed and a horse stamped as pesky flies irritated it. At last Ian glanced at the men gathered near him.

"Let's go," he said quietly and lifted the reins of his horse.

The Guardians skirted the staked area and moving in a northwesterly direction rode for several minutes before Ian again called a halt. A gully, once the bed of a meandering stream, extended for some distance and offered a hiding place for the men and their mounts.

"We'll stop here. We have a while to wait." Ian glanced toward the north, looking for any sign of dust that would indicate Maelorn's forces. In the distance, The Dlarmids' snow-capped peaks rose grimly against a high, colorless sky. A crow, disturbed by the men, flapped slowly away, its raucous call echoing over the desolate plain. A keening wind, hot and dry, raised a dust devil nearby. He called for six of his men to position themselves as sentries and ordered a two-hour rotation. When night fell, he would set the guard in pairs and range them farther afield to listen and watch. If Talanor was correct, they shouldn't have long to wait.

"Get some sleep," he ordered the remaining highlanders; then he, too, found a place where he could rest his back against the gully's bank and still be in the shade it provided. With a gusty sigh, he tipped his hat over his eyes and tried to sleep.

Nightmarish forms moved in and out of the shadows of his dreams as he dozed. He felt the cold breath of death and shivered, though the sun baked the earth of the Ghilana Plain and all that moved on it. In unfocused slow motion, he saw and smelled again the terrible, stinking scene on the fishing boat, relived the attack of the Spriggan that had killed young Robert Campbell as he patrolled the docks at Shiptown. Ian knew when he opened his eyes the shaggy, brutish creatures of his nightmares would be all too real, and he moaned as he dragged himself out of the half-sleep in which he floated. Better to be awake and face the enemy than try to fight it in dreams.

Ian pushed himself upright and spat the dust from his mouth. He coughed and took a swig of tepid water from his canteen. What he wouldn't give for a taste of the highland whiskey he'd grown up with. He took another swig of tasteless water and grimaced. No highlander should have to resort to water to quench his thirst. For a long moment he silently cursed the fates that had brought him to this place. And wondered why it was that Kaenolir must suffer so.

~

The highlanders viewed the billowing clouds of dust through shimmering heat waves. Not a word was spoken as Ian and his men watched the oncoming menace. They had been observing the clouds since dawn. Maelorn's army, at least part of it, came rapidly toward them. It was not long before they were able to make out a dark line moving below the dust.

Someone swore quietly while another soft voice exhorted the gods to guide their efforts this day. At this distance it was not possible to make out distinct forms, but Ian knew well that the creatures of his nightmares composed the advancing horde.

The sun beat down on the waiting men, and Ian wiped sweat from his eyes with an absent swipe of his hand. The dark forces were close enough now to make out individual creatures and a contingent of Spectres.

"Get ready," Ian spoke aloud for the first time since they spotted the column. "You all know what to do." His gaze ranged over the handpicked men who waited with him. He knew each of them well and had chosen them specifically. A feeling of remorse drew down the corners of his mouth as he thought again about what lay ahead. It was very possible that he'd chosen today for them to die. He lifted his hand in salute and mounted his horse.

His men did the same. For a tense moment they waited; then with a highlander battle cry they burst from the gully and raced straight for the approaching creatures. Those at the front of the column stumbled and paused briefly before the surprised Spectres and a large number of Spriggans reacted to the Guardians' charge. With howls and shrieks of anticipation, the column's frontrunners increased their speed and made directly for the man-things and their horses. They could smell blood and meat and their desire to kill and eat made them even more dangerous.

Ian and his mounted company charged in a double column over the dry plain until it appeared they intended to hit the hellish army head-on. At the last moment, Ian pulled to the right and his column peeled away. The other column veered sharply to the left until they were but a long, thin line racing toward the maddened creatures. Instinctively the Spriggans fanned out, brandishing their axes.

"Now," Ian roared and the Guardians abruptly wheeled, again splitting into two groups. Each group began to curve back in the direction from which they had come, drawing Spriggans with them. The Spectres thought they saw a chance to cut the Guardians off before they could regroup and sent some of the Spriggans straight ahead while keeping the rest of the column in reserve. It took the dark men several moments to realize that the dust stirred up by the racing horses was mixed with smoke; but they were unable to see that, as the Guardians raced back toward each other, they set the stubble aflame with torches. Flames greedily licked at the dead grass, and the wind rapidly whipped the line of fire into a blazing inferno.

Spriggans still charged wildly toward the horsemen, intent only on killing them, and were oblivious to the shouted commands of the Spectres. Too late, the creatures saw their danger. In confusion and fear they began to run to and fro seeking a way out of the encroaching flames. Some of them saw that the flames had not yet come together at the point where the horsemen now waited for them, on the other side of a narrow depression. They made a frenzied dash for the opening, and others soon followed suit when they saw the highlanders.

"Steady, steady," Ian warned as the slavering beasts raced toward the waiting Guardians. "Hold your positions." He felt his mount quivering beneath his knees and laid a comforting hand on the sweaty neck.

A dozen or so Spriggans outran those closely bunched behind them and launched themselves into the depression. The beasts screamed as they became entangled in the cleverly concealed trap and fell on the deadly stakes. Unable to stop their forward rush and eager to get their share of meat, other Spriggans ran pell-mell onto their mates, becoming tangled as well in the trap. All around them, flames leaped high as the wind gusted, and those Spriggans who had stopped themselves from hurtling into the trap were surrounded by fire. Their cries mingled with the roar of the flames for only a brief time.

"Now," Ian again commanded. "Ride for the Wall. We'll have company soon enough."

Even as he spoke Spectres began moving the rest of the Spriggan army away from the fire toward the Wall of Rhade. It would not be long before they overtook the Guardians' racing horses.

Ian still had one trick left, thanks to Talanor, and he prayed it would be enough to get most of his men to safety on top of the Wall. They would not use the firesand until the Spriggans were very close.

The horses tired quickly now. Ian glanced over his shoulder to see a lathered animal go down and its rider kick free at the last minute to roll away from the falling animal. A comrade swerved without a break in stride and leaned low in the saddle to pull the fallen rider up behind him. The horse slowed perceptively with its double burden and fell behind.

They pounded on toward the Wall. Just a little farther. Ian could hear the labored breathing of the horses, and above their whistling gasps he began to hear another sound. Directly to the east of them and closing fast were the Spriggans. Their howls as they drew near their quarry sent chills down Ian's spine, and if he lived through this day, he knew it would be a sound he would never forget.

The Wall was not far now, but the creatures were gaining fast.

"Ready your firebombs," Ian shouted into the wind.

He heard a scream from close behind him as a fast-paced Spriggan pulled down a lagging horse and rider. He forced himself not to look back but kept his eyes on the Wall. Their timing would have to be perfect.

The Wall of Rhade, its height an imposing barrier as well as a source of protection, loomed before the Guardians. Ian looked to his left; the Spriggans were gaining rapidly on the exhausted horses. Behind him his men urged their mounts on, extracting the last strength and spirit from them. Another comrade fell, and then another to the ravening jaws of the Spriggans.

Ian pulled his mount to a sliding halt as he neared the base of the Wall. Ten Guardians immediately joined him while the remaining soldiers rapidly dismounted, pulled grappling hooks from the bags they carried behind their saddles, and set their horses loose.

"Pikes," Ian shouted and a line of twenty Guardians ran to position themselves, long pikes at the ready, some distance from the men swinging the hooks to lodge at the top of the Wall. As soon as the hooks were set, soldiers began climbing the ropes.

The ten men with Ian ranged in front of the pikemen, firebombs in their hands. They planned to stop the progress of the rushing Spriggans with the bombs, fall back behind the pikemen while they killed as many of the creatures as they could, throw another barrage of firebombs while the pikemen retreated until they reached the Wall and the dangling ropes. As soon as a man reached the top of the Wall he positioned himself to throw firebombs in an effort to give the men still on the ground or on the ropes time to reach safety.

The plan worked well for several minutes. Firebombs effectively eliminated several Spriggans at a time, but there were always more to fill the gaps left by the dying and maimed. Screams and howls filled the air, and dust and smoke from the burning plain combined to choke the struggling men.

"Back," Ian roared, and the pikemen again set their pikes.

Several of the highlanders had reached the top of the Wall, and Ian heard explosions off to his right. Those Spriggans trying to come around to get behind Ian and his small band were stopped for a short time. Pikemen cleared the way in front and then fell back. More explosions and more dead Spriggans gave them time to reach the ropes.

"Wait, wait," Ian commanded his ten men as the Spriggans began to close in from the left. More explosions sounded as more men reached safety. The Spriggans were thickly clustered as they came toward the men still on the ground. Ian waited another ten heartbeats.

"Now," he shouted and five firebombs burst in the midst of the oncoming creatures. The severed leg of a Spriggan flew through the air to land with a plop three paces in front of Ian. It jerked grotesquely and then was still.

"Hah," he grunted as his face contorted in a grimace of relish.

Elsewhere, bombs thrown by the Guardians on the Wall also fell into other tightly massed Spriggans and took a terrible toll. But still the creatures came at them.

"To the ropes," Ian commanded when another volley of firebombs cleared the area. They turned and ran the few paces to the Wall.

Out of the smoke and dust, a Spectre loomed. Ian raised his sword to meet the dark-robed threat. It, too, brandished a sword and as the two blades crossed, Ian knew he was in a fight for his life. He remembered Talanor's words of warning: The only way to kill a Spectre was to cut off its head. Out of the corner of his eye he saw the last of his men grasp the ropes and begin pulling themselves to safety. He thought he heard the Spectre laugh, a hollow, mocking sound. Too late he realized that several Spriggans had gathered around him. Frantic shouts from atop the Wall and more explosions sounded around him. With great calm, Ian struck and parried; but as he closed with the Spectre, their swords locked, he knew that when he broke free the beasts would have him. He reached for the dagger he always carried at his side; and as the Spectre gave a final shove to free itself and send Ian into the waiting Spriggans, he swung the dagger in a powerful arc and severed the Spectre's head from its shoulders.

As the figure slowly crumpled to lie in a dark heap, its hood fell back. For a moment Ian stared into the sightless eyes of a skull before it tipped forward. It hit the ground with a soft thump and rolled to the feet of one of the creatures. It stooped to pick up the skull, and then tossed it away when it discovered the thing it held was only dry bone. It turned with its mates to the man-thing that stood poised, waiting for them.

Six of them shuffled toward Ian, so intent on killing him that they were unaware of the three men who stood on the Wall directly above them with firebombs poised. They waited until the Spriggans were grouped closely together but still several feet from Ian. With a shout of warning to Ian, the first man threw his firebomb, and the air exploded with fur and gore. The blast peppered Ian with pieces of flesh and earth and left his ears ringing. Before the dust had settled he was sprinting the last few feet to the Wall. He hurriedly stuck the dagger in his belt and sheathed his sword before grasping a rope left dangling for him and began to climb.

Firebombs exploded on the ground below him as the beasts converged to pull him from the rope. He could hear his men shouting encouragement above him and beasts bellowing in anger below him. Once or twice he felt a tug on the rope as he scrambled upward. A rock pried from the crumbling parapet sailed by him to land with a meaty thunk on the head of a Spriggan who had managed to reach Ian's rope. Ian heard the beast grunt and felt the rope sway as its grasp relaxed. He didn't pause in his frantic climb, not even when two of the Guardians began pulling him up. He reached the top of the parapet, and eager hands pulled him up and over.

Gasping great gulps of air into his lungs, he grasped the shoulder of one of the Guardians who had pulled him to safety. They gave each other a raffish grin before turning back to the parapet.

"How many firebombs do we have left?" Ian called out. "Bring them to me."

Four highlanders moved away from their positions to being him all that remained of Talanor's firebombs.

"Baskers," Ian muttered at the meager number. "Where's Talanor when you need him?" he grumbled.

He peered over the parapet at the Spriggans milling about down below him. Spectres moved among them trying to force them away from the Wall, but they had little success in controlling the aroused beasts. The man-things were so close that hunger overcame fear of the Spectres' whips and clubs.

"There's a nice batch of the bloody buggers below me, Sergeant, complete with a couple of Spectres," one of the Guardians a few feet from Ian called out. Ian joined him and handed him one of the four firebombs he held.

"Drop it where it will do the most damage," he instructed.

The man beside him grinned. "Watch," he said softly as he fingered the small bottle. He waited for just the right moment and tossed the bottle into the milling Spriggans. He grunted with satisfaction when the smoke and dust cleared.

"Well done," Ian said as he viewed the carnage. He moved on along the parapet, stopping now and then to check on the condition of a wounded

Guardian or to see if he should drop the few remaining firebombs. But it appeared that the Spectres were at last beginning to exert control over the creatures once more.

"Sergeant, look there," an excited Guardian cried. "The fire, look at the fire!"

In their concentrated efforts to reach the Wall and to destroy as many Spriggans and Spectres as they could, they forgot about the fire. It raged now, out of control, an impenetrable line of flames and smoke. The fire cut off any avenue of retreat for this portion of Maelorn's army. They could not pull back any distance from the Wall, and they could not move westward along it. The only way left open to them was to the east, and if they didn't move quickly, that path would also be blocked.

The Guardians heard the Spectres' screams of warning and commands sounding above the grunts and growls of the creatures. They lashed out with their whips and clubs in an effort to get the Spriggans massed together and moving eastward along the base of the Wall. At last some of the beasts reluctantly began to move, but others attempted to get to the men by prying exposed stones loose and using the resulting holes as handholds and toeholds. Intent on satisfying their hunger, they were oblivious to the danger moving up behind them.

Ian and his highlanders watched the scene unfold below them with a mixture of horror and relief. Flames raced across the plains, and the smoke stung the eyes and noses of the soldiers. The fire's ominous roar muffled the cries of the Spectres and the Spriggans' shrieks.

"We've got to get out of here," Ian said. "Come on," he shouted to the men strung out along the parapet. "Move!"

He turned to look once more at the wall of fire, or he would not have caught the movement out of the corner of his eye. Somehow one of the Spriggans had made it up the Wall and over the parapet and came now in its shuffling gait toward the unsuspecting Guardians.

Ian shouted a warning and raced toward the approaching beast. Men turned as he ran by. When they saw the new danger, they drew their swords and followed him. They met the beast with the highland battle cry, and even the speed and savageness of its attack could not save it. The Spriggan went down under the onslaught of six Guardians and died without having tasted one morsel of man-flesh.

"Baskers," Ian swore. He was breathing heavily as were all the Guardians who had joined him in dispatching the Spriggan.

"Come on," he commanded. "We've got to get moving now, or the fire will catch us, too. Hurry," he urged. "Let the ropes down on the other side."

With one last look at the body of the Spriggan, Ian spat contemptuously in the dust and turned to lead the way down off the Wall. What was left of the brutish horde moved eastward, and Ian feared that it would not stop until it had reached the Balagorn Sea and a way around the crumbling terminus of the Wall. He feared it would not stop until it reached Riversend and the nearly defenseless people who waited there.

Chapter Sixteen

The exhausted Guardians, several of their number wounded, pressed onward toward the Skara River. If they reached the river by dawn, they could be in Riversend soon after nightfall. Ian hoped they would arrive in time to warn the garrison and make a few preparations before the Spriggans attacked.

A man stumbled and fell in the dark. The going was rough along this stretch. The river cut through land that until two years had been a swamp. Campeon Marsh had extended all the way from the Balagorn coast and along the northern bank of the Skara, but now the marsh had nearly dried up. Instead of pools of stagnant water and thick marsh grasses teeming with life, much of the land lay pocked with sun-baked mud holes and drying vegetation that served to trip and entangle anything that passed by. There was no sign of the rich variety of birds, no small foxes or rabbits, no river otters.

"Sergeant, there's a man down."

Reluctantly, Ian called a halt. "All right," he mumbled. We'll stop here for awhile."

The highlanders sank to the ground where they were. With heads hanging and chests heaving they welcomed the brief respite even though they knew they must press on in a short time.

Ian moved among them until he came to the man who had fallen. He shook the soldier roughly by the shoulder.

"Get up, man," he exhorted. "We've a ways to go yet, and I need every one of you." He helped the exhausted, wounded man into a sitting position. "We've come too far to give it up now."

"Yes, sir," the man muttered. "How much farther to Riversend?" he whispered.

Ian shook his head. "Don't be thinking about Riversend yet." He slumped down beside the younger man, too tired to do much more than just sit in the stinking mud. "Got to get to the river first. A few more hours," he muttered. "Got to keep going. Just got to keep going."

"Yes, sir."

Ian absently patted the soldier's arm. "You'll make it. We'll all make it. Haven't come this far for nothing."

He fell silent and listened to the sounds around him.

No, he decided. He'd not come this far to lie down and die in this muck. Baskers, he'd not thought to live to see the end of the day when he saw those Spriggans trying to circle him and get him from behind. He'd not thought to get forty of the fifty highlanders who'd set out with him this far either.

A man nearby coughed and spat. Another man groaned as he stretched aching muscles.

The sky seemed blacker than the inside of a hole, covered, in part, by dense clouds of smoke. No stars, no moon, but plenty of stinging, biting insects.

Funny, Ian thought, *when everything else is dying, the damn bugs are still here to torment us.*

He swore pungently and staggered to his feet. "Let's go," he croaked. He didn't wait to see if the men followed him. He assumed they would.

~

A few scattered lights gleaming in the darkness was the only indication they had reached Riversend. Like other towns and villages it had worn a mantle of prosperity and thriving industry for decades. Now, the mantle was tattered and torn. Vagaries of weather, lack of products, the death of industry had all but destroyed the town. Houses stood empty, businesses boarded up, riverboats idle and rotting at the pier, people afraid of their own shadows. Perhaps not all of the townspeople understood the threat from the north, but they all understood that their town and their livelihood were dying or already dead. They all sensed that they were in danger; and from the time Captain Lamond called for every able-bodied man to go to the Guardian's Fort, they had lived in constant fear. Reports of shaggy-haired creatures multiplied, and every death that occurred, natural or otherwise, was attributed to the shadowy "beasts" that came out of the night. The contingency of Guardians left to protect the townspeople was a small comfort against so monstrous a threat.

Ian and his men stumbled down the main street toward the large timbered building that housed the Guardians left stationed at Riversend. Light glimmered from two or three windows on the first floor, but there was nothing else to indicate activity.

"Baskers, where is everybody?" Ian grumbled.

The large double door with the Guardian crest mounted above it was tightly closed to the night and whatever creatures moved in it. Ian grasped the heavy brass knocker and banged it solidly against the panel. When no one answered, he banged it again and yet again, accompanying his efforts with choice profanity.

"Who's there?" someone barked from the other side of the closed door. "What do you want?"

"By the gods, open this damn door and let us in before we knock it down," Ian shouted. "We're Guardians!"

"Guardians?" A heavy bar moved and the door opened a crack to allow a gleam of light to touch the haggard, mud-streaked faces of Ian and the men clustered around him.

The door swung wide and they pushed past a flabbergasted soldier to enter a large lobby.

"What are you doing here?" The Guardian stared in disbelief as the weary men straggled inside.

"Where's MacAllister?" Ian asked the young soldier. "We've come to warn you. Go get him. Now."

He stared at Ian a second longer, turned on his heel, and hurried down a hall to the right. Behind him, Ian's troop collapsed onto the available furniture and the floor, content for the moment to rest.

"Ian? Ian Cameron?"

Ian turned slowly to face a tall, sleepy-eyed Guardian who pulled on a shirt as he came into the room. His bare feet made no sound as he crossed the worn planking to stare intently into Ian's weary face.

"MacAllister," Ian nodded.

"What are you doing here?" Robert MacAllister looked about the room at the filthy, exhausted men. "Where did you come from?"

"There's too little time to be wasting it in the tale of our coming here, Robert. We've come from the Wall, and there's a Spriggan army, or what's left of it, on the other side. As soon as they find a way around, they'll head for Riversend."

Robert McAllister swore. "We can't begin to hold off an army. Half my garrison and most of the men of the town are gone to join Captain Lamond. There are only women and children and a few old men still here."

"I know that, but we've got to make some decisions very quickly on how we can defend the few people still here." Ian rubbed the back of his neck and looked around the room at the lounging men. "I've wounded that need attending to, and we could all do with some food and water. Do you have any to spare? And maybe something clean to wear? We stink of marsh mud and smoke."

"Of course, I'll see to your wounded and have food prepared. I'm sure we can find clothing as well; the uniforms may not fit but they'll be clean. Then you and I can get down to the business of dealing with the Spriggans." He turned away to roust some of his men and motioned for Ian to follow him.

He pointed to a door that stood open about half way down a long corridor. "See what you can find in there to clean yourself up a bit. I'll join you as soon as I've seen to your men."

Ian nodded and stepped into the room MacAllister indicated. A stub of candle burned fitfully, casting his shadow in grotesque proportions against the wall. He found a pitcher of clean water, poured a generous amount into one of the mugs he found on the table, and drank thirstily. After satisfying his thirst, he poured the rest of the water into the porcelain bowl that sat beside the pitcher on a bench. After scrubbing away much of the grime caked on his arms and face, he felt refreshed. As he toweled himself, he wandered about the sparsely furnished room. It looked much like the quarters of any other Guardian in Kaenolir. He tossed the towel down near the bowl of dirty water and dropped into a wooden chair positioned next to the table on which the candle burned. He slumped forward to rest his elbows on his knees and his chin on his clasped hands.

Baskers, but he was tired, tired of the heat, the dirt. But most of all he was tired of living in fear. At times during the battle, he had been so fearful that the coppery-tasting gorge rising in his throat had nearly choked him. When he closed his eyes, he could see the Spectre rise up in front of him and hear its hollow laughter as it lifted its sword to kill him.

He could not comprehend what was tearing Kaenolir apart, why evil walked his homeland, destroying land and lives. He'd asked the gods a thousand times why these things were happening, but the gods gave him no answers. Perhaps they did not hear him.

He swore a particularly sour expletive and cursed the fates that had given him enough of the stuff of nightmares to last the rest of his life.

His thoughts took another turn, a path he rarely allowed himself to take. A pretty, freckle-faced wife and two little boys, who had their mother's infectious laugh, had fled Shiptown along with the rest of the townspeople. He couldn't think of them without his heart breaking. They shadowed his nightmares, too. Tears came to his eyes and he dashed them away.

"Ian?"

He turned to watch Robert MacAllister enter the room with a tray of food and a steaming mug of tea.

"You can eat while we talk." He placed the tray next to Ian on the table and drew up another chair to sit across from him.

"Thanks, Robert," Ian said as he began to eat. The food was plain and simple, not much of it but what there was, was hot. He could not remember when he had last eaten.

"Alexander and I came up with a plan to try to slow down the advancing army," Ian began. "It worked much better than we hoped."

While he ate, Ian filled in the details of the dash across the grasslands, of the rope and stake trap, and of the struggle to reach the top of the Wall. Robert listened silently, and when the tale was finished, he sighed and rose from his chair to pace. A tall, lean man, still with bare feet, he moved silently about the room.

"How many Spriggans and Spectres do you think survived?"

"Hard to tell. With all the smoke from the fire, I never really saw what was left of the army. When we first saw them coming across the plain, I would guess there were several thousand."

MacAllister swore softly. "How are we going to stop them if they attack Riversend with an army? Even if only a few hundred make it around the Wall, I've only fifty Guardians. Some of the people might be able to help, and there are the men you brought in. You've got, at the most, thirty-five able-bodied troops, but they're all exhausted."

He rubbed his brow in frustration and ran a hand through close-cropped brown hair. "By the gods, man, we're completely vulnerable. The garrison sits in the middle of the town with no fortification whatsoever." He stopped pacing to return to his chair.

Ian drained the last of the tea from his mug. "I suggest you start spreading the word to the townspeople to leave Riversend."

"Leave?"

"Yes, they'd have a better chance if they scatter over the countryside. Those who are able or who want to stay behind to help the Guardians should come here."

"I suppose you're right."

Ian shrugged. "Perhaps we're merely prolonging the inevitable, but it seems a better idea than remaining in Riversend and waiting to die like so many cornered rats."

Both men rose to leave the room, but before Ian reached the door, MacAllister laid a hand on his shoulder.

"There's one suggestion I would like to make before we get down to work, Ian."

"What's that?"

"I would like you go through my chest over there and find some clean clothes. There should be something in there that will fit."

"That's very generous of you, Robert."

"Actually, not generous at all, Ian. You stink to high heaven, and if I'm going to have to be cooped up with you for any period of time, I'd like to be able to breathe without having my sense of smell insulted by your stench."

Ian grunted and then grinned ruefully. He picked at his dirty tunic and sniffed loudly. "Not exactly the sweet smell of heather," he said as he stepped to the chest Robert had indicated.

Robert gave him a mock salute and left the room.

~

Dawn colored the sky when four Guardians rode north out of Riversend. They were to scout the rocky coastline in an effort to find the remnants of the Spriggan army and report its size and how soon it would reach the town. Another scouting party of three Guardians crossed the river and moved south to learn if it would be safe for the women and children to travel in that direction.

The townspeople had been advised to pack what food they could carry and be ready to leave at a moment's notice. But many of the older women, whose children were grown and whose husbands had gone to the Fort, and many of the old men elected to stay and give what assistance they could to the Guardians.

Two hours past dawn, the south scouting patrol returned and on their advice, people began leaving their homes and crossed the bridge over the Skara. Some traveled in groups of ten or twelve, others with three or four friends or family members, but none went alone. Young mothers herded silent children off the roads and pathways into the countryside toward what they hoped would be safety. Some of the travelers were lucky enough to have the use of horse-drawn carts and wagons. All moved as rapidly as possible away from the threatened town.

By noon the scouting party sent north returned. The news they brought was not good. A portion of the Spriggan army was coming down the coast at a fast pace and would be within sight of Riversend by late afternoon. There were about five hundred creatures, probably more, with at least twenty-five Spectres in command. The rest of the army had apparently waited out the fire and moved back across the High Ghilana Plain toward the Fort where they would join up with the rest of Maelorn's horde.

"Damn," Ian swore. "Will the bloody bastards never stop coming?"

Robert MacAllister looked up from the map he was studying with the Guardian who had led the scouting party.

"Ian, take a look at this map." He pointed a finger to a detailed section of coastline about two miles east and a bit north of Riversend. "Look, just here, where the river begins to broaden as it meets the sea. The Skara carries a lot of debris—rocks, logs, whatever—that is eventually pushed out to sea, especially with the spring floods. However, because of the drought during the last several years, the river flow has been greatly reduced, and the debris has been piling up at this point. The creatures can't go through it so they'll have to go around it. And in doing so, they'll have to go through here." Robert drew his finger down the map.

"So?" Ian questioned him.

"Well, this is a strip of the marsh that the drought has not dried up. And along this edge of it," he drew his thumbnail back and forth along a short section, "along here the way is filled with stretches of bog, mud holes, and some quicksand."

Ian stared at the map for several seconds before looking up into Robert's eyes. A thin smile curved the other Guardian's lips.

210

"My men know this area very well. Every one of us played in the marsh and hunted there as we were growing up. It would not take much to lead the Spriggans into the marsh."

"Bait the beasts."

"Yes," Robert said.

"Get them mired down in the mud and quicksand and kill as many as we can without having to meet them head on."

Ian stood, deep in thought. Not much of a plan, but there was little they could do in the short time they had before the creatures reached Riversend.

"Let's hope it works. And for those that do get through, we can position the rest of the Guardians and townspeople in the logs and rocks and pick the bastards off as they come through." Ian tapped the map with a broad fingertip. "What have you got besides swords and spears for weapons?"

Robert shrugged. "Not much. Pitchforks, slingshots."

"Slingshots?" Ian asked incredulously.

"Some of the old men are pretty good with them. Some of the women, too."

"I'll be damned," Ian muttered. "What a way to fight a war."

MacAllister rolled up the map and walked outside to the people gathered in the dusty yard. He shouted for their attention, and when they quieted, he began giving orders.

~

Ian wiped sweat from his brow with the rolled up cuff of his sleeve. The sun beat down from above; insects swarmed around the people hidden in the flood detritus and bit and stung exposed skin. And over all hung the oppressive stench of mud and the dying river.

Ian, the able-bodied of his highlanders, and thirty or so townspeople whom Robert MacAllister had allowed to remain behind found hiding places among the logs and piles of sand and gravel left by the Skara as it met the Balagorn Sea. If he stood up from where he crouched behind a jumble of weathered logs and other driftwood, he would be able to make out the marshy ground where Robert and his Guardians lay in wait for the Spriggans. So few against so many.

Ian swore and spat in the dust at his feet. For a moment he looked back over his shoulder toward the west, toward the Wall and the men who

211

defended it. He had not ventured to think of Alexander and Talanor or the lovely Kailie. He smiled to himself as he recalled how Alexander looked at her. The smile faded slowly as his thoughts turned to his own family, his wife and red-haired sons, his aging mother, his two Guardian brothers billeted in Fairtown. He had not seen his family in months, didn't even know where they were now. He prayed they were all safe. He knew his brothers were probably on their way to the Wall, if not already there.

"Baskers," he grunted. "When will it all be over?"

The hot air suddenly vibrated with the howls of Spriggans as they spied the men on the edge of the marsh. Ian knew that although the sun stood low in the afternoon sky, the day was far from over.

~

Spriggans and Spectres poured into the marsh, the scent of flesh and a lust for blood spurring them on, and the beasts snuffled in excitement. With a headlong rush the Spriggan vanguard turned away from the path the Spectres had instructed them to follow. They ran through puddles of slimy mud and stumbled and tripped on the coarse swamp grass that grew in rough patches among the mud holes. Behind them, Spectres screamed for them to return to the road that wound around piles of driftwood, but the commands were not heeded. Spriggans who had remained on the rutted track stopped and lifted their noses to test the air. The smell of man-flesh was extremely strong and too close to ignore. One by one, they broke ranks and ran into the marsh.

Spriggans fanned out over the rough ground in an uneven line, as the waiting Riversend Guardians had hoped they would do. It would be much easier for the smaller force to pick off individual Spriggans as they struggled through the marsh than to try to attack the hundreds marching down the coast road.

As the Spriggans ran deeper into the marsh, they encountered waiting Guardians. Robert MacAllister and his men lay hidden among reeds, in bunches of tall marsh grasses, and among twisted, dead trunks of rotting trees until their quarry was close enough to take down. The men waited for just the right moment, leaping out of their hiding places to dispatch Spriggans who became mired in mud holes and quicksand or waiting until the creatures ran by their hiding places to attack them from behind. MacAllister had instructed his men to kill as quickly and as efficiently as they could and then move to another spot. They were also instructed to take on only one Spriggan at a time. If a group came near, they were to let it pass and wait for other Guardians to help them or wait for the beasts to spread out.

Ian Cameron and his troop of Guardians and townspeople waited in the hot afternoon sun for Spriggans to come out of the marsh and down the road. They could hear the cries of Spriggans and an occasional shout from one of the soldiers as the afternoon wore on. Ian was so intent on listening to the sounds of the fighting in the marsh he nearly missed the Spectre who came up behind him. A fleeting whisper of sound warned him of danger, and he rolled to his side and bounded to his feet in one swift movement. A sword whistled by his head, and the blade whacked into the log in the spot where he had been hiding. Before the Spectre could free his weapon, Ian was on him.

"You stinking bastard," Ian gritted through clenched teeth. He held the Spectre in a powerful neck hold until he could draw his short sword. "Time to die," he whispered.

The Spectre screamed and tried to pull away, but the highlander's hold could not be broken. Ian used the point of his blade to find the bony throat of the Spectre; then with a thrusting motion he pushed the blade up and out. Ian heard a hiss of air and a strangled gurgle before the skull slipped out of the dark hood. Ian stumbled to retain his balance as the Spectre's form crumpled at his feet. The skull lay a short distance away, the jaws opened wide on a silent scream.

Ian walked over to it and stood staring at the grisly thing. With a savage motion, he brought his booted foot down and stomped shattered bones into the dust. He stood, breathing heavily, and stared at all that remained of one of Maelorn's minions. "Back to hell with you," he said and then spat contemptuously toward the broken white fragments.

A shout from one of his men brought his attention back to the task at hand, and with a last look of disgust he turned away. Several Spriggans had found their way out of the swamp and were coming down the road.

~

"Father, Lord Alpean, look there, along the shore. Spriggans." Kailie Fairchild shielded her eyes against the lowering sun and gripped her father's arm.

"They've come this far already?" The Goldenhorn shook his head and turned to Alpean. "This is as good a place as any to go ashore. We must try to help the people of Riversend."

Alpean nodded. "Look, there, in the pile of flood leavings. Men are fighting." Softly, he cursed his brother.

Goldenhorn brought the tiller sharply to the right and steered toward the rocky shore. "Get ready to lower the sail, Kailie," he called.

The craft bobbed as it made its way through the choppy surf. Just as Kailie had been led to the white boat that carried her to Sinnich, so too had the three of them been led to this boat where it bumped against the rocky beach below the mountain. It had taken them swiftly down the Balagorn coast to Riversend.

"Now, Kailie."

She lowered the sail and as the boat floated into the shallow water, Kailie moved to the bow. The boat ground into the sand and all three jumped out and splashed the few steps to the shore. Alpean drew his sword as he ran and Goldenhorn followed his example. He threw Kailie a look over his shoulder to make sure she followed close behind as they raced across the shore up to the road."

"This way," Alpean cried as he sprinted toward the rocks and logs where beleaguered Guardians and townspeople fought.

Sword raised, Alpean launched himself at a group of Spriggans that had cornered two Guardians. The unexpected attack from the rear turned the creatures around; and while Alpean fought them from the front, the Guardians moved in from behind. After several moments of furious fighting, five dead Spriggans littered the ground. Two others, badly wounded but still able to move, scurried away.

Alpean grinned at the two surprised Guardians, turned on his heel and ran toward more Spriggans. "Follow me," he shouted without looking back, and the two men did so without question. Kailie soon lost sight of him as he fought his way through the creatures.

"Kailie," Goldenhorn called. "Stay close to me. There are Spriggans all around, even over there in the marsh." He stopped and waited for her to catch up. "We must use the Song. There are just too many, even with Alpean's sword."

They found a place where they could climb up onto a large pile of driftwood. Goldenhorn reached back to give Kailie a hand, and together they looked down on the battle going on all around them.

Spriggans scrabbled over flood detritus, trying to find the hiding places of the entrenched defenders. It was clear that they had been successful. The body of an old woman lay curled in a fetal position among the logs where she had tried to protect herself from attack. The scarf covering her head was bloody as were her hands that even in death were lifted to fend off an attacker. Kailie prayed she had died swiftly.

Guardians were positioned in two different places, some in the marsh and others among the rocks and driftwood. Kailie watched in horror as a big man with bright red hair tried valiantly to keep three Spriggans at bay. Everywhere she looked there were creatures and men, but so many more creatures than men.

"Oh, Father," Kailie breathed. "There are so many."

The Goldenhorn raised his head and the Warrior Song poured out of his scarred throat. After a moment, Kailie's voice joined his and the combined power of the two voices spread over the unlikely battlefield. At first their Song was met by silence, but as the volume and intensity of the music grew, the beasts began to squeal in pain. They clawed their ears and tried to run away from the maddening sound, but there was no escape. Spectres went rigid and were held prisoner by the Song as surely as if they were chained.

The force of the music pushed creatures and dark-robed Spectres to their knees as they whimpered in fear and pain. Men and women, who had been fighting for their lives only moments before, watched the cringing enemy in amazement. Alpean shouted a command and the Guardians moved swiftly, killing the Spriggans within reach of their swords.

Kailie suddenly changed key and in a counter melody to what her father sang, she directed her music at the group of Spectres who groveled in the dust of the road. The ten who had survived the fighting and the Song were suddenly pulled upright off their knees. Their hoods were jerked back by some invisible hand to expose hideous skulls. A sound similar to the swish of a falling blade came with the words she sang, and the death heads toppled from bony shoulders and rolled in the dust. Slowly the dark robes buckled to lie like black stains spreading across the road. A powerful, commanding phrase came from Kailie's lips, and skulls and robes disappeared as if they had never been.

Again, Kailie shifted pitch to blend with the Warrior Song her father sang, and the music increased in volume until the last of the Spriggans lay dead. Only then did the two Singers let the music slowly fade. In the ensuing quiet, all that was heard was the moan of the sea.

215

~

Goldenhorn and Kailie moved from one still form to another. Here and there exhausted Guardians sat with heads hanging or walked about in a daze. Kailie's eyes filled with tears when she came to the body of the old woman. She knelt beside her and crooned softly. There was no response and Kailie wept. She felt a gentle hand on her shoulder and lifted her gaze to her father.

"Come, child, there are many who need you. There is nothing you can do for her."

"I know," she sighed, wiped her cheeks and stood. For a moment she looked to the southwest, towards Fairtown. Goldenhorn followed her gaze and understood her anguish. Neither of them spoke of the woman who filled their thoughts at this moment, but both prayed silently for her safety.

"Come." Goldenhorn took her hand and led her to the first of many wounded. Darkness was falling and there was still much to do.

~

"My lady, there is one more Guardian who needs your healing. He lies down there," the soldier pointed toward the road. "But he is too badly hurt to be moved."

Kailie motioned for the man to lead the way, and she followed him on leaden feet. When he came to the fallen Guardian, he knelt in the dust and held a flickering torch so that Kailie could see.

She gasped as the light illuminated the form on the ground. It was the red-haired man she had seen fighting off three Spriggans, and she recognized Sergeant Cameron, Alexander's friend. He was covered, it seemed, from head to foot with blood and gore. One arm lay bent at an unnatural angle; shards of bone stuck out of the torn flesh. His tunic was saturated with blood from wounds on his shoulder and arm where skin and muscle had been torn away. A long gash ran across his face from hairline to jaw, and Kailie feared he had lost an eye. He lay so still she thought she might be too late, but she caught a flutter at his throat. She knelt beside him, listening intently to his shallow, labored breathing. Kailie placed her hands gently on Ian's chest and began to sing.

Music, bonny, sweet music, surrounded him and wrapped him in its gentle phrases. Ah, how wonderful to simply float on its waves. The music brought images of a highland lake, the sound of a woman's laughter, and a squeal of delight from a small boy. There were no creatures here, no nightmares, no death, only a feeling of peacefulness. The woman came into view and he smiled in greeting. She saw him and with a cry ran toward him and flung herself into his arms. She murmured his name over and over, and he held her crushed to his chest. He held her for a long time before he looked away, over her head toward the Wall of Rhade. Alexander stood there, beckoning to him, a look of pain and anguish on his face. He lifted the woman's face and brushed her tears away and bent his head to kiss her lips. Little hands tugged at his legs, and he bent to pick up two small boys, each with bright red hair and a smattering of freckles across their noses. He gave each of them a fierce hug and loving kiss and set them once again on their feet. The woman's quiet sobs broke his heart.

"I must help Alexander," he told her softly. "But I will come for you. Take care of the little ones, dear heart."

The image drifted away to be replaced by intense, excruciating pain. He cried out and felt the blood rush through his body. His right arm burned and his left shoulder quivered. Music beat against his battered body until it seemed to enter it, and he could feel each note as it coursed through him. He tried to pull away from the weight on his chest, tried to block out the all-powerful music that commanded him, but he could not. Ian screamed in agony; the music would not let him be. It lifted him, and the pain wracking his body slowly began to drain away. He settled gently back to earth when the last of the pain was gone and his blood no longer pounded.

A soft moan escaped from between Ian's parched lips, and he opened his good eye to stare up into the face of the most beautiful woman he had ever seen.

"Kailie," he whispered.

She smiled at him and touched a cup of water to his lips. Her hand lifted his head so he could drink.

"So, Ian Cameron," she murmured softly. "You decided to remain with us after all."

Chapter Seventeen

The dark mass halted. Dust stirred up by the creature army floated on heavy, still air. Off to the east smoke from the burning plain rose in thick, gray-white clouds. At dawn Alexander had sent men to range the Wall, but they were too few to patrol its length. He could have sent messengers to Riversend and Fairtown for the rest of the garrisons quartered there, but he did not want to pull all the Guardians out of those two towns and leave the people completely unprotected. As it was, most of the men of Kaenolir now walked the Wall of Rhade.

Talanor came to stand by Alexander's side as he watched Maelorn's army prepare to attack.

"Men all positioned above the gates and along the Wall?" Talanor asked quietly.

"Yes," Alexander responded in the same quiet tone. He continued his observation of the inhuman forces. Silence lengthened between the two men. There were no more words to be spoken, nothing more to do but wait to see how Maelorn came at them.

The morning wore on. Heat from a burning sun soon made the stone parapet hot to the touch. The wind died down completely. There was little conversation along the Wall. Even pesky flies that tormented man and animal alike ceased to be an irritation. It was as if, Alexander mused, the earth held its breath, waiting.

Waiting.

That was all they could do now, just wait. Some of the men prayed, but Alexander found he could pray no more. Who, he wondered, would hear his entreaties. He allowed himself one fleeting thought of Kailie and whispered her name to himself in a litany of love. He sighed and looked up at the sky and longed for rain. If he could only feel the rain, hear the sound of birdsong once more, he might die happy.

How much longer?

The attack came at noon.

Wave after wave of Spriggans and Ghillies raced over the plain, some carrying heavy battering rams, others brandishing battleaxes or short stabbing spears. Boatloads of creatures came down the Skara, intent upon ramming the river gate closed against them. Spectres moved at the front of the lines to urge the dark horde forward and to direct the attack against the Wall.

Talanor took up his position with the men directly above the river gate. Firebombs were stacked in neat piles every four feet.

The same arrangement was in readiness above the Wall gate where Alexander would direct the defense. Guardians and civilians ranged along the Wall, some with firesand bombs, some with oil that could be lit and poured down upon the attackers, still others near piles of heavy stones that could be thrown down on the beasts as they converged at the base of the Wall. Many had other weapons close at hand—pikes, short spears, swords, and knives—should the attack be carried to the top of the Wall.

Maelorn's spawn charged over the plain. The advancing beasts were but a short distance from the demolished Fort when huge silver forms launched themselves at the attackers. Savage growls and screams of agony punctured the air when the wolves attacked.

"Jagar," Talanor whispered with a grim smile.

From his position Alexander saw the wolves and remembered the intelligence he had seen in the eyes of the wolf Talanor called Jagar. How he and his pack had known to come to help them now, he did not know, but he was grateful for their coming.

The turmoil caused by the great wolves' attack forced the Spectres to pull back, and the ensuing confusion brought a roar of rage from the creatures in the rear. The ground in front of the Fort became littered with shaggy bodies, and it was only with great difficulty that the Spectres were at last able to get some of the creatures to move around the wolves and jump the low walls that stood in the way of their objective. Battering rams were retrieved from the clawed hands of the dead and dying, and creatures charged forward once more toward the Wall gate.

"All right, now, get ready," Alexander called. "Let them hit the pit first before you throw your bombs."

Off to his left Alexander heard Talanor's roar of command and the sound of explosions. He felt the Wall shudder when the force of heavy boats rammed the river gate. Explosions came rapidly, one after the other, as firebombs were dropped on the struggling creatures below.

And the ancient gate held. One by one the advancing boats smashed into the boats ahead, propelled into each other and held against the iron gate by the force of the river's current. Firebombs rained down relentlessly, extracting a lethal toll, before the Spectres were able to get some of the boats turned against the current. Some creatures made it ashore where their commanders tried to keep them from scattering long enough to send them to join the assault on the Wall.

With savage howls the creatures, Ghillies for the most part, Alexander noted, bearing stout battering rams ran awkwardly onward. There were four groups running abreast, and with a final surge they mounted the piles of debris and plunged into the yawning pit that awaited them. The close-packed beasts, charging behind the rammers, hit the pit a second later and fell to their deaths, as had their comrades, on the sharp stakes rising obscenely upwards in the bottom of the pit.

The screams of the dying were terrible to hear, and Alexander and his men watched in fascinated horror as the pit began to fill with shaggy bodies. The bodies falling on top of the ones below suffocated those creatures not speared by the stakes.

Alexander held off the firebombs for a few seconds more. He dared not allow the pit to fill completely, or the carcasses of the dead would serve as a platform for the rammers to attack the gate.

"Wait for my command," he shouted. "Watch out for the wolves."

Three heartbeats.

"Now," he cried and threw a firebomb into the beasts bunched behind the pit. Many explosions sounded as his men followed his lead, aiming carefully to avoid hitting the wolves.

Further along the Wall defenders kept creatures carrying ladders at bay with burning oil. The wolves left the area in front of the Fort, filled now with the bodies of the slaughtered, and rushed to attack those creatures coming from the aborted river assault. The beasts struggling up the riverbanks had little chance against the wolves, and soon the river was filled from bank to bank with dead and dying.

The beleaguered forces attacking the Wall gate withdrew.

"Hold your firebombs," Alexander commanded. "We've none to waste." He breathed in gulps of hot, heavy air, and leaned his shaking arms against the parapets. Wiping sweat from his brow, he looked down into the Fort. The carnage that came into view as the smoke cleared was almost unbelievable.

Bodies, sometimes piles of them, littered the yard of the Fort. The pit directly below was nearly full. When he turned to view the Skara, he saw waters black with floating carcasses. His breath gusted out of lungs that were on fire with the smell of smoke and the stench of death.

Talanor came striding toward him, his face begrimed but creased with a grin of triumph.

"We've turned them back," he roared.

Alexander found breath enough to wheeze, "At least for now."

Shouts from down the Wall drew Alexander's attention, and he ordered half of his men to guard their positions while taking the rest with him as he rushed to the aid of the men trying to keep ladders away from the Wall. Out of the corner of his eye he saw Talanor reach for his sword as they ran. Several Spriggans had managed to reach the top of the Wall, and with a wild yell, Alexander launched himself into the melee.

His burst of speed drove him into the center of the fighting, and the blood lust rose up in him, hot and compelling. He yelled again, the wild highland cry that had not sounded in battle in nearly five hundred years, and gloried in the killing instinct that drove his sword arm. Unaware that Talanor fought at his back, he lunged and skewered a hairy beast in the chest. Before the thing could fall Alexander had pulled his sword free and attacked another. A Ghillie raised its battleaxe to protect itself; but Alexander's sword sliced through its raised arm, and arm and axe went flying with the force of the blow. The creature looked in perplexed bemusement at the gory stump and then at Alexander. Its beady eyes filled with hatred, and it roared in pain. Alexander laughed and met the creature's rush with ease. The thing screamed once and slumped to the ground, its life's blood pouring out between clawed fingers that clutched at the gash in its neck.

"Alexander," Talanor's shout penetrated the blood-crazed haze in which Alexander fought. "Watch your back."

Whirling to meet the new threat, Alexander came face to face with one of the Spectres. Talanor stepped up beside him, and the man-like thing raised its sword.

"Prepare to die," it mocked in a hollow voice.

"Not today," Alexander retorted, and before the Spectre could move to protect itself, two swords whistled. For a moment the shape of the robed creature remained upright; then as its head tipped forward and off its shoulders, it shuddered and disappeared in a wisp of ash. Alexander stared at the spot where the creature of hell had just stood. He lifted his eyes in amazement to Talanor and found the mage looking back at him, surprise written in the lines of the mage's features as well.

"Baskers," Alexander breathed. He turned to face whatever foe still threatened but lowered his sword, its point resting against the stone. Only dead Spriggans and Ghillies met his glance.

He wiped sweat from his face with a filthy left hand. Slowly his blood cooled, and he realized that battle sounds had faded away to an ominous silence. He looked to the west into a setting sun and turned to Talanor.

"We live to fight another day, Talanor," he murmured.

"So we do," the big man said softly.

~

Alexander and Talanor sat with their backs against the parapet, silently chewing on stale brown bread. There was a little cheese to go with the bread and a lukewarm, tasteless broth. Alexander paused in eating to consider that if Maelorn were not so intent on a war, he need only sit back and wait for the defenders to starve to death.

"Why does he send an army against us, Talanor? If he is powerful enough to call the beasts and Spectres to join him, why doesn't he just kill us all and be done with it?"

Talanor sighed and set his cup aside, wishing for a mug of the cold, dark ale he brewed on Cathorn.

"Why?" he murmured. "Because I think he finds pleasure in watching us suffer, in prolonging our deaths. He must have suffered immeasurably while sealed in Sinnarock. I think he's making the people of Kaenolir pay for that now."

"Do you think he will stop with Kaenolir?" Alexander voiced the worry that had been niggling at the back of his mind for some time. "Will he be content with just this country when he could—" Alexander broke off his question and swore.

Talanor grunted, leaned his head against the Wall and closed his eyes. All around the two men, Guardians and the men of Kaenolir either ate or tried to rest. Alexander had already sent the squads to patrol the Wall. Although he doubted that Maelorn would attack again so soon after the day's defeat, he could not be sure. He followed Talanor's example and closed his eyes as he leaned against the warm stone of the parapet in exhaustion. His thoughts strayed at last to the highlanders he had sent out to meet Maelorn's army on the Ghilana Plain. Smoke from the burning grasslands, seen earlier in the day, seemed to indicate that they had been able to execute some of their strategy to stop the advance of part of Maelorn's army.

But what of the highlanders, he wondered. *What had happened to them? To Ian? How many more would die before this tragedy played out?*

The darkness closed around them, and with it came guttural grunts and smacking sounds that were indefinable. Out of curiosity both Alexander and Talanor came stiffly to their feet and peered over the edge of the parapet.

"What is that noise?" Alexander asked.

A torch burned near Talanor, and he tossed it to the ground below. It flared briefly but gave just enough light for the two men to see several shaggy forms bent over the bodies of their dead comrades. The beasts turned in surprise, muzzles dripping with gore, at the sudden blaze of light.

Alexander swore softly and turned away, swallowing heavily to force down the hot, sour bile that welled in his throat.

"Well," Talanor shrugged. "I don't think they'll attack anymore tonight."

"I suppose that's one consolation," Alexander snorted.

"Noisy eaters, aren't they?" Talanor said as he resumed his seat. He settled back with a tired sigh.

Alexander choked on the laughter that inexplicably threatened to escape. "I think I'm going mad," he said and dropped down beside the reclining mage.

"I think we should get some sleep," Talanor murmured. "Tomorrow will be today all too soon, I fear."

Alexander grunted and closed his eyes. He found it difficult to block out the sound of the feasting on the ground below, but at last exhaustion took its toll. His head rolled toward his shoulder and he slept.

~

Maelorn sent his forces at dawn. This time the attack was spread out in a long line, several ranks deep, along the Wall. The beasts came with battering rams to breach the crumbling structure in as many places as they could. The Kaenolirians were hard pressed to fend off rammers and those with ladders. Many of the creatures reached the top of the Wall along with their Spectre commanders, but time after time they were driven back, slaughtered where they stood, their bodies set afire and heaved over the parapet to fall on those clustered below.

Each firebomb was dropped where it could do the most damage. Talanor carefully monitored the use of the limited supply. There were fewer wolves on the second day of fighting. Although imbued with Faerie magic and power they could be killed. Those remaining fought viciously, killing whatever they stalked; silver coats begrimed with gore gave testimony to their efficiency.

There were many more wounded to be cared for than had been the case yesterday, and the number of dead climbed quickly. Talanor's skills in healing and his supplies of medicines and salves were in great demand throughout the long day. Hurrying from one fallen man to another, he glanced up and gasped in alarm as he saw Alexander go down under a Spriggan's attack, but Simon rushed to his Captain's aid and dispatched the creature from behind. All along the Wall, Kaenolirians fought with determined effort, but no matter how many creatures they killed, it seemed there were dozens more to take the places of the fallen.

Talanor rose from tending a wounded civilian to look to the north.

"How much longer will you play with us, Darkling?" he muttered. "You could destroy the gates, this Wall, and the Kaenolirians with one blow if you wanted."

Someone called his name, and he directed a bitter curse toward the north before he turned away.

~

"My lord, we are ready to send the reserves against the Wall." A Spectre bowed low before his reclining master. "Do you wish to lead the attack?"

Maelorn laughed in malicious glee and stretched his massive limbs. His naked body gleamed with scented oil as he lay among the plush cushions of his couch. The sumptuous furnishings of his black tent gleamed with gold inlays and precious stones in the light of innumerable candles. "Soon, my pretty, soon. Do not be so impatient. We will let them struggle for a while longer before we destroy them. It gives me pleasure to watch their pathetic efforts to save themselves. I enjoy listening to the sounds of battle, the music of dying." He laughed again and reached out to beckon the Spectre closer. "I have waited for this day for five hundred years, and I would savor my triumph. Soon enough I will be king of Kaenolir. And then we move on."

"But, my lord, you felt your brother escape the mountain. You felt the ancient magic."

"Do not fret, my precious one." He stroked the hooded head and smiled. "My brother can do nothing to stop me now. I am more powerful than he. I am more powerful than the magic of the Faerie," he boasted. "I will kill Alpean at my leisure, after I have destroyed the Kaenolirian army and demolished their puny wall." He reached for a tall goblet on a table beside his couch and drank its contents in one gulp. Purple wine dribbled from the corner of his mouth and onto his gleaming chest. With a caressing touch the Spectre stroked away the wetness and listened with delight to the growl of contentment from deep within his master's throat.

"I love you, my lord," he murmured.

"I know, my pretty. And soon we will celebrate my destruction of the Guardians and my victory over the Kaenolirians. We will drink their blood together." He touched the Spectre kneeling beside him. "When it is time to send in the reserves, make sure your brothers keep the old mage and the Guardian captain you told me about alive." He leered at the Spectre. "Then we will tend to Alpean and to whoever is offending me with the Faerie magic. I know the Goldenhorn still lives to sing his Song, but I sense someone else sings as well, and that someone freed the Singer and my brother." He pulled the Spectre up beside him on the couch. "Ah, my little one, there will be much to please us before this day is over. You will see."

~

A Spriggan reared up from a fallen Guardian and clutched its battleaxe with both hands. A man-thing screamed and came toward it, holding a sword in one hand and a short spear in the other.

"You shaggy bastard," the man shouted. "I've killed a hundred of your brothers today. How many more must I kill before the stench of you is gone?"

225

The man came with a rush and the Spriggan howled. It parried the first sword thrust as it had been taught, but it was too clumsy with its weapon, too slow in its response, to escape the upward thrust of the stabbing spear. It screamed in pain, gore spilling from the gaping wound to run down its side and leg. It pulled back, but the man came after it. With a cry of rage and pain it swung its axe. Suddenly it stiffened and dropped the weapon, scrabbled at its ears and whimpered, then screamed in obvious distress. The man stopped, staring at the creature in amazement. The beast cried out again and sank to its knees, but the man gave no quarter. His sword slashed through the air, and the creature slumped to the ground.

All around Alexander, Spriggans and Ghillies that had reached the top of the Wall screamed in pain, caught up suddenly in the throes of agony. The defenders did not understand what was happening, but they quickly moved to take advantage of the situation, and slaughtered every creature within reach.

Talanor reached Alexander's side just as he withdrew his sword from a dead Ghillie.

"Do you hear it, man?" He laughed with almost hysterical glee. "Listen, Alexander, listen!" he cried and shook the Guardian until the madness died from his eyes.

"What?"

"Listen!"

Alexander's chest heaved as he drew in hot, malodorous air. His sword lowered as he focused on what the mage was saying

Again Talanor shook him, hard, and when Alexander lifted a hand to brush away the mage, he heard what Talanor heard.

Music.

Incredibly beautiful, powerful music sung by two voices, one deep and rich, one high and sweet.

Men sank to their knees while some rested against the parapet for support and watched as the beasts cried out, broke ranks and ran back across the plain while some of those still alive jumped from the Wall, trying to escape the punishing Song. Many died as they tried to run from the force that poured over them like a crashing wave, but not even the Spectres' whips could make the survivors turn back.

They came from the east, walking rapidly along the top of the Wall toward the exhausted defenders. A man and a woman sang the Warrior Song of the Golden Ones and sent the Faerie magic out over the retreating dark horde to the one who commanded it.

Behind the Singers marched a troop of Guardians, led by two sergeants. Several men and women, most of them elderly, followed proudly in the footsteps of the soldiers.

Across the plain, the message of the Song came clearly to Maelorn, and he screamed as he bounded up from his couch, pushing the favored Spectre away.

He shrieked and raged; his fury at having his will thwarted knew no bounds. "You shall not see the setting of tomorrow's sun," he vowed, shaking his fists, kicking furniture, shoving away the Spectres who came running. He came to a halt and shook his fist in the direction of the Wall. He suddenly whirled away to take command of his forces. There would be no Kaenolirian alive at the end of tomorrow's fighting. Nothing would save them. Nothing. Not even the Faerie magic of the damnable Warrior Song.

Chapter Eighteen

The Song continued for some time, its command too forceful for the creatures to withstand. The shaggy bodies of Maelorn's horde littered the plain, and the hot sun and thick dust settled like a shroud over the silent Ghilana Plain where the only sounds were the moans of the wounded and dying. The last note drifted away and the Singers, who stood in the midst of the defenders of Kaenolir, looked at the tired and dirty men. Talanor stepped forward to grasp first the woman, then the man, in a hard embrace.

"Kailie, Andrew," he said, his eyes brimming. "The gods have been kind after all." He smiled at each in turn. His glance took in the faint scars on Goldenhorn's neck and the ones on his wrists. "But not the Darkling, I see," he murmured.

"No, Talanor, he was not kind." Golden eyes bore into Talanor's and the mage understood what the Golden One had endured. "I would be dead were it not for my daughter. She found me in Maelorn's mountain and freed me."

Both Talanor and Goldenhorn turned to the woman who stood quietly at her father's side. The ravages of her journey were written in her features, and Talanor saw within her eyes the price the Faerie magic demanded.

"You are weary," the mage said. "We have little to offer you in terms of refreshment, but you must both rest. Maelorn will give us little time before he strikes us with all his power."

"No, Talanor," Kailie murmured quietly. "Time to rest will come later. There are many wounded who need my Healing Song. We will need their strength on the morrow, so let me work before Maelorn comes." Her eyes searched the faces of the men nearby, and Talanor knew she searched for one face in particular. When she found it, her lips parted in a soft smile, and she moved to meet the man who came toward her.

Alexander pushed his way through the men toward Kailie. She held out both hands to him as he came up to her, and he took them in a painful grip. His eyes searched the features of her face and saw, as Talanor had, the effects of her journey into Sinnarock. Fine lines of weariness and pain etched her mouth and furrowed her forehead. Her eyes were completely golden, he noted almost absently, the sparkling blue faded from their depths. Her clothes hung loosely on her too slender frame. He wanted to crush her to him, draw her deep within himself, and protect her from Maelorn's vengeance and the Faerie obligation.

She smiled, her eyes filling with tears as she took in his haggard face. Deep grooves of fatigue and worry lined his features. He was filthy from smoke and dust and from the gore of the Darkling's creatures, but she saw none of that. His image had kept her going when she would have faltered; his presence here on the Wall gave her a sense of reality that combated the insanity in which Kaenolir floundered.

Alexander loosened his grip and brought her fingers to his mouth.

"My lady," he whispered. "Kailie."

"Captain," she whispered in return.

"Alex?"

"Ian," he breathed. His heart ached for the pain and suffering he saw etched in his friend's face. A dirty scarf hid the empty eye socket and part of the jagged scar that would always mark him, but he was alive. He took Ian's outstretched hand and drew him against his chest in a hard embrace.

Both men stepped back after a moment.

"Did you forget to duck?" Alexander asked to cover the emotion he felt.

Ian grinned ruefully. "If it weren't for your lady, I wouldn't be here."

Both men turned to Kailie, and she smiled up at them as Alexander drew her against his side.

"I'm glad to have you back, you and your men. I see you brought the Riversend garrison with you, too."

Ian sighed. "What's left of it. I'm sorry there are so few of us."

"I'm sorry, too," Alexander said quietly.

Talanor joined them, and placing his hand on Kailie's shoulder, he smiled. "Forgive me," he said, "but the Goldenhorn would like to meet you, Alexander. And Kailie and I have much to do."

"Of course." Alexander relinquished Kailie and smiled as he stepped away. "I'll see you later," he said quietly.

"Yes," Kailie murmured and returned his smile before turning to Talanor. "I'm ready," she said simply.

Alexander watched the two as they made their way back toward the Wall gate where the wounded had been taken. He had feared he would never see her again; now he feared he might have to watch her die. He turned to Ian. "Take your men and position them along the Wall wherever you think they are needed. Have MacAllister do the same. Then all of you try to get some rest."

Ian nodded and stepped away.

"Ian," Alexander called softly.

The other man stopped and looked back. Both men stood silently and looked deeply into each other's eyes. At last, Ian smiled wearily and walked away.

Alexander followed his friend's progress along the Wall and relief combined with sorrow. Had Kailie saved Ian's life only to have Maelorn take it tomorrow or the next day? When he felt someone beside him, he pulled his gaze away and looked into golden eyes so like Kailie's.

"My lord," he said respectfully. "I am Alexander Lamond, captain of the Guardians of Kaenolir."

"Yes, I know. Kailie spoke often of you during our journey from Sinnich. And I am Andrew Goldenhorn." He gave Alexander a slight smile. "While Kailie helps Talanor with the wounded, I would like to tell you how Kailie freed me and what I know of Maelorn's powers. Is there a place where we might have some privacy?"

"Yes. I'm using one of the towers as my office. It isn't much, but it's all I can offer. Come with me."

Simon Stewart approached them from the direction of the Wall gate. Alexander stopped to give him orders on posting the watch and feeding the men.

"Except for those on watch, the rest should get whatever sleep they can. Would you also bring food and drink to my tower when you have time?"

Simon saluted and hurried away. Alexander and the Goldenhorn continued along the top of the Wall until they came to Alexander's tower. He paused at the door to listen to the music of Kailie's Healing Song. As he listened, he felt his weariness slip away, and he straightened his shoulders and stood a little taller.

The music intrigued him. It was so beautiful with its intricate melodies sung in words he could not understand; but to the creatures and, to a lesser degree, to Maelorn the notes of the Warrior Song caused pain, even death, as he had witnessed today. He shook his head, not comprehending the ancient power that had created and still infused the music, but he was thankful that the Faerie had given Kaenolir such a rare gift.

Alexander turned to Goldenhorn. "I do not understand," he told the Singer, "but I am grateful."

Goldenhorn smiled. "The Faerie have not forgotten Kaenolir, Captain."

"I pray you are right." With a nod Alexander opened the rickety door and ushered Goldenhorn inside.

~

Darkness came quickly, the twilight between sunset and night but a brief period of half-light. Alexander stood alone near his tower quarters and listened to the sounds emanating from Maelorn's encampment.

A deep but muffled rumbling like the rhythmic stamping of thousands of feet hummed through the Wall's stones and vibrated on the air. Soon the creatures' voices lifted in an unearthly cacophony of howls and shrieks, punctuated by a single voice whose roar carried to the men on the Wall and made the hair prickle on the back of Alexander's neck.

Maelorn.

The bellowing grew in volume and intensity as the night wore on, and the creatures' answering cries increased with it. The constant uproar made it impossible for the Kaenolirians to sleep, and each man dealt with his private thoughts in a different way. Some men gathered in groups and talked quietly while others kept lonely vigils as they prowled the top of the Wall. Some wrote letters by the light of flickering torches, although the writers doubted the letters would ever reach their loved one. Still others stood along the parapet, their backs to the north and stared out into the darkness, as if they might put from their minds for even the briefest time, the horror that would surely come with the dawn.

"What do you suppose the bastard's doing?" Ian asked from out of the darkness. He came to stand beside Alexander.

"I don't know. Calling more of the creatures from hell, perhaps. Stirring them up to such a pitch that not even the Warrior Song can stop them." Alexander shook his head. "I don't know."

"Well, tomorrow will be the end of it, and maybe we'll die not knowing what any of this," Ian gestured to include the expanse of plain, "means. Hardly seems fair that we can't really understand what we're fighting."

Alexander rubbed his nose and closed his eyes. "We fight to destroy something that would destroy us. Why Maelorn wishes Kaenolir in ashes is something I don't understand."

Ian shrugged. "'Twould seem he prefers the stench of hell wherever he is."

"Yes. And after tomorrow Kaenolir will be in hell."

Ian grunted. The two continued to look to the north until Ian directed a particularly vile epithet toward Maelorn and walked away.

Alexander snorted in agreement and silently heaped his own curses on Maelorn's head. It was some time before he felt a light touch on his arm and turned to find Kailie beside him. He smiled and covered the fingers that rested lightly on his skin. They both turned to look northward, as the bellowing became a constant roar. Both sensed the rage and hatred that permeated the sound, and Alexander felt the fingers beneath his tremble. He freed himself from her touch by turning to face her. Gently he placed his hands on her slender shoulders and drew her into his arms.

She came eagerly into his embrace, and they stood for long minutes with their arms around each other. She rested her ear against his chest and listened to the strong beat of his heart and smiled as it drowned out Maelorn's evil voice. He lifted a hand to caress the soft braid that hung down her back.

"Your father told me of the many Kaenolirians Maelorn had imprisoned in Sinnarock, loggers and sailors for the most part, he thought. Maelorn had them killed before he left the island. I had feared that they were all dead, all those who simply disappeared. Now I know for sure." He sighed and her embrace tightened about him. "Your father told me, too, of Alpean," he said at last, "and that he waits for Maelorn on the plain." He rested his cheek against the top of her head and sighed again. "There will be a terrible battle tomorrow."

"Yes," she whispered. "Maelorn is very powerful now. Alpean knows that this time the two brothers will fight to the death. Whoever wins will be king of Kaenolir."

"Tomorrow," he said quietly. "You must promise me that tomorrow when the Wall is overrun you will not let yourself be taken." He held her away from him and looked steadily into her eyes. "If I cannot get to you, use the little knife. Promise me, Kailie," he demanded and gave her a little shake.

"Shh," she hushed and laid cool fingertips against his lips. "I will not be taken, I promise."

He looked at her for another long moment, and then drew her back into a fierce embrace. She wrapped her arms around his waist and hugged him tightly.

"And you must promise me that you will take care."

"Yes. I will be careful. And if the gods allow, tomorrow we will stand in this spot together and Kaenolir will be free."

"Kaenolir will be free," she said quietly.

"And will we be together?" he asked.

She drew back to look into his eyes. Her dazzling smile suddenly flashed out. "We will be together," she promised, but she did not tell him where or how.

He took her mouth then with passion and hunger. After a time he lifted her in his arms and carried her to the hot, stuffy confines of his quarters and laid her gently upon the lumpy pallet. With only the stars shining through the hole in the roof to witness the lovers, they gave and took of the golden king's last gift.

~

Maelorn strode before his army as it marched across the plain toward the Wall of Rhade. His huge body glistened in the rays of the rising sun, and the golden crown on his head caught and held the blinding light. A coven of Spectres moved behind him, faceless and forbidding. More of the dark creatures marched in a line in front of the army. Behind them came the Spriggans and Ghillies, innumerable and demoralizing, rank upon rank as far as the eye could see, howling in excitement and brandishing their weapons. It was as if the slaughtered had been replaced thrice over.

The quiet defenders on the Wall looked out upon the faces from hell and recognized death. The smell of fear was thick in the air, and Alexander knew the fear was not only for themselves but also for their families and friends left behind in Fairtown and the southern lowlands. The horror that faced them across the plain would soon be stalking their defenseless loved ones if they did not stop Maelorn here at the Wall.

Talanor stood beside Andrew Goldenhorn and watched the advancing horde.

"Look at the bastard, would you?" someone said.

The man standing next to the speaker spat in contempt over the edge of the parapet. "Struts like he thinks he's king already."

His companion grunted in agreement.

"Andrew," Talanor said quietly to the Golden One. "If we do not live to see another sunrise, I would have you know that I feel honored to have called you my friend. We have seen our beautiful Kaenolir in the best of times and now in the worst. In the end, if the Song cannot keep the enemy at bay, I would have your sword beside me."

"My sword will fight beside yours, Talanor." Goldenhorn squeezed the mage's shoulder in friendship and turned to watch Maelorn. His mind shifted and for a moment Katrine's face swam before his eyes to block out the Darkling. He whispered her name and asked the Ancient Ones to protect her when he no longer could. At a light touch on his hand he shook himself and found his daughter beside him. Alexander stood with her, and a smile curved Goldenhorn's lips as he reached out to take Kailie's slender fingers and held them tightly for a moment. He lifted his gaze to Alexander, and the two men looked at each other for a long moment. Goldenhorn nodded as if in approval, and the Guardian captain returned the nod in silent understanding.

A bellow split the air, and Maelorn stopped the forward progress of his army. He continued to roar until the ground shook with the sound. Finally, with utter disdain in every line of his body, he extended his arms and aimed his hands at the Wall gate. Flame shot through the air, and the timbers burst apart, disintegrating like so much kindling under the force Maelorn hurled. Spriggans and Ghillies clamored in excitement, and the Spectres were hard pressed to keep them from charging toward the opening.

Maelorn raised his hand above his head, and the noise behind him abruptly stopped.

"Kaenolirians," his voice rolled across the distance. "I can kill you all with one stroke of fire."

Again his hands flung fire toward the Wall, and a whole section of it exploded, dust and stone flying through the air. The fiery bolt instantly killed the men who had been standing there.

"You see, little ones, how easily you die?" Maelorn laughed.

Alexander swore helplessly.

The Darkling raised his hand yet again and sent a fiery blast that destroyed another section of the Wall and killed several more men.

"What do you intend to prove with your display, Maelorn?" Talanor's voice dripped with scorn. "Do you think to frighten us to death? Your powers are great, but there are others just as great." He began to chant, the strange singsong incantation that Alexander had heard when Talanor sang to the waves. Flames flew toward Maelorn, but he reached up and sent them flying upward to sizzle harmlessly and disappear.

The Darkling threw back his head and laughed again. "You send too little, old man," he roared.

He jabbed the air above his head with his hands and lightning flashed, striking the earth near the Wall. Men cringed and moved back from the violent spectacle. Maelorn let the lightning hiss and snap for several minutes before he brought his hands down with a chopping motion, and with a mocking command, he sent his army against the Wall of Rhade.

Alexander watched them come, thousands of creatures eager for the blood of the few Kaenolirians who guarded the Wall. They loped across the dried plain in a solid mass and screamed in frenzy. None of them carried weapons now; and as Alexander prepared himself to meet the onslaught, that seemed an ominous sign. The beasts would attack with claws and teeth and brute strength without the cumbersome weapons to impede them. They would kill in the way of all flesh-eating predators, not as soldiers.

Today I die, he thought, almost with relief. *Today the nightmare finally ends.*

The great silver wolves attacked, and many of the beasts were killed before they reached the Wall. Talanor commanded the soldiers to drop the last of the firebombs. He watched many more creatures die. But the number of dead was not enough to halt the assault. Spectres leaped up onto the Wall and engaged the desperate Guardians. Over it all rang the Warrior Song, but there were too many Spriggans and Ghillies. Creatures scaled the Wall with ease, and hundreds of them poured into Kaenolir through the breaches.

Nothing could stop them.

Maelorn's maniacal laughter rang out as he sent fiery bolts into the midst of the struggling defenders. He screamed as pleasure rippled through his body, screamed with triumph and satisfaction. He speared a Guardian with a single bolt, held him aloft and listened with relish to the man's cries of agony. He released the bolt and laughed as the body plummeted from the Wall to the milling beasts below.

Time after time he aimed his hands at the ancient barrier and watched whole sections crumble under his powerful blasts of fire. His army charged, unfazed by the Warrior Song, infused with the power Maelorn commanded.

The Kaenolirians fought a battle they knew could not be won. Men stranded on isolated sections of the Wall died as the beasts overwhelmed them, and no one could offer them any assistance. The creatures attacked from all sides, and Spectres came at them from above, no longer tied to the earth but lifted and buoyed up by Maelorn's strength.

Alexander and Talanor fought side by side, trying to keep the creatures from Alexander and Kailie, but as many beasts as they slaughtered, more came to take their places. The Wall grew slippery with gore and the defenders spattered by the filth.

Talanor cried out a sharp warning as three Spectres whirled past them, headed for the Singers.

"Alexander! Look to Kailie!"

The Spectres screamed as they swooped low between the fighting men and the Singers.

"They're going to try to take them," Alexander shouted to Talanor. "Kailie, Goldenhorn, look out!"

Goldenhorn's sword whistled and the Spectres veered and swung away to be joined by at least a dozen other dark forms. They paused momentarily before coming on again, intent on taking the Singers captive as their master had ordered.

Alexander swore as he watched the Spectres gather. He looked wildly about for Ian but could not find him.

"Talanor, they're coming again. We can't stop them," he cried. He shouted to Kailie, "The knife, Kailie, use the knife!"

She shook her head and touched her father's arm. "Stop your Song, Father."

Goldenhorn looked at her in amazement, but he did as she asked. She smiled at him, that smile that reminded him so of her mother, and then she turned to the north. She took a deep breath and closed her eyes. For a moment she hesitated, but the golden king seemed very near; and his image in her mind gave her strength and the courage to do what she had been chosen to do. With her heart beating hard against her ribs she opened her mouth, and the music of the Last Song rang out over the bloody plain.

As the first notes sounded, men locked in deadly combat with shaggy beasts dropped their weapons and sank to their knees. Spriggans and Ghillies froze as if turned to stone. Alexander turned in the direction of the music to look at Kailie and gasped at what he saw.

A golden, shimmering light so bright, so beautiful it hurt to look at her, surrounded her. The music she sang was unlike any earthly song, and it rang with an ancient magic that had existed before the dawn of man. Notes rose and fell in melody and counter melody, in crescendo and decrescendo. Man and beast alike felt the power of the Song, but the beasts heard it and died. Spectres screamed in agony, cried out for their master, and burst into flames that burned them rapidly to ash.

Spriggans and Ghillies, spread out over the plain awaiting the command to rush the Wall, shrank away from the Song and tried to run from its power, but to no avail. Their hearts burst as they ran and death came in mid-stride. Those who had charged into the breaches and reached the south side of the Wall screamed and died where they stood.

And as the terrible, relentless music killed it also consumed. Fire began to spring suddenly to life wherever the body of a creature lay, and men scrambled to their feet and moved hastily away to escape being scorched by the flames. Everywhere the defenders looked they saw fire. Flames burned white-hot but smokeless and turned to ash all they touched.

Talanor struggled to Alexander's side, and even the unflappable mage found it difficult to comprehend what his eyes saw. "There's no sound," he said in a half-croak, "no sound of fire."

Alexander listened but heard only a faint hissing. He wasn't completely sure he heard even that over the sound of Kailie's singing.

Ian came to stand beside the two, his tunic filthy, his red hair matted with sweat. He bled from several wounds and would have collapsed if Alexander had not reached out to clasp him tight.

"What is happening?"

"I don't know," Alexander whispered.

"What is she singing, Goldenhorn?" Talanor asked the Golden One as he joined them.

Goldenhorn shook his head. "You took her to Rhianna Lanee. What did Rhianna teach her?"

Talanor shrugged and looked again to Kailie. "Rhianna would tell me nothing nor would Kailie." He sucked in his breath. "Look at her."

Kailie stood now on top of the parapet with her head thrown back and her neck arched while the music poured from her. The golden aura in which she was wrapped grew even brighter, and it was as if she had become the Song she sang. Every fiber of her being vibrated. Her features grew indistinct; the lines of her body blurred and shimmered.

"Kailie," Alexander cried out and would have rushed to her had not Talanor and the Goldenhorn restrained him. As strong as the two were, it took their combined strength to hold him back.

"No, Alexander," Talanor shouted in his ear. "You cannot help her now."

"Kailie!" Alexander lunged against the arms that held him and drug his captors a step or two before they were able to stop him. "It's killing her," he cried. "The music, it's killing her." He screamed in anguish but could not reach her. "No," he sobbed. "Oh, Kailie, no."

The music rose in a deafening crescendo, and as its power intensified, white flames leaped higher and higher until no Spriggan or Ghillie remained. There had been thousands of creatures, created to serve an evil purpose, but not one was spared by the music or the flames. The plain was a sea of fire; it burned in pools atop sections of the Wall that still stood. It flashed in the air to destroy the last Spectres.

Alexander quieted and Talanor and Goldenhorn eased their grips on him. He stood staring at the glowing form, but as the Song built to its final phrase, he was forced to turn away. He could not endure the sight that met his eyes. She, too, was all white flame, consumed by and made one with the Song she sang. The men around them cried out in agony and covered their ears. Alexander stumbled against Talanor, and both men stepped back.

"Kailie," Alexander whispered. "Kailie." He cried out in pain as the music continued to build, and unable to bear the sound, he sank to the ground while the Song beat on them all.

~

The last notes drifted away. With ears ringing, men came slowly to their feet, too numb to speak. Alexander pushed himself upright and stared at the spot where Kailie had been. She lay crumpled in a heap near the base of the parapet. With a cry he rushed to her side with Talanor, Ian and the Goldenhorn only a step behind him. He fell to his knees beside her and gently gathered her into his arms. She seemed weightless and nearly transparent. It was as if the music had taken everything and left only a husk. He did not know if he held flesh or spirit.

"My love," he whispered and shook her ever so slightly. "Don't leave us. Stay. Stay." He rocked her gently back and forth, crooning the same phrases over and over again while Talanor and Goldenhorn knelt near the lovers. Goldenhorn reached out to touch Alexander's shoulder.

"She will come back, Captain. She went far away and stood among the Faerie for the time she sang the Song. But she will come back."

Alexander looked down into Kailie's face. He could see tiny veins just beneath her pale skin, and deep blue shadowed her eyes like bruises. A faint pulse beat at her temple. Her breathing was light and shallow, barely raising the bones of her ribcage. When he touched her cheek with his fingertips, she felt cold.

"A guard tower still stands on this section, Alexander," Ian said quietly. "Why don't you take her there? I'll see if I can find some blankets." He took only a step when he stopped in his tracks.

"Maelorn!"

The light wind that scoured the plain of the ashes of the dead carried the sound of the Darkling's name to the men on the Wall.

"Maelorn, 'tis time for you to die, little brother."

"No!"

The men on the Wall of Rhade looked on as two giants came across the plain. One was beautiful, the other ugly. Once, long ago, they had been brothers. Now they were adversaries. One had been king; the other coveted the crown. Here on the Ghilana Plain they met after five hundred years, and they would fight to the death to see who would wear the golden circlet.

The stunned men watched as the two came together on a field of battle. The combatants fought with broadswords, and their blades flashed and rang as each tried to gain the advantage.

They charged and locked together. Maelorn grunted with strain, his mouth pulled into a hideous grimace, as he tried to free himself from Alpean's grasp. He pushed Alpean back and thrust out his long-nailed fingers, but no lightning leaped from their tips. He screamed in rage and thrust again.

"Your power is gone, Maelorn," Alpean laughed. "All you have left is the strength of your arm. How well can you wield a sword, little brother? As well as when we were young men in training?" Alpean laughed again. "I doubt it. You never were very good with a sword. It was your way to let someone else fight for you." He hefted his sword with both hands. "There is no one left who will fight for you, Darkling, no one but yourself. So fight. Fight and die, brother, for I intend to kill you."

At Alpean's mocking laughter Maelorn cursed in frustration and fury. To those on the Wall, it was a malevolent, vicious sound, and more than one man shivered as he heard it.

Maelorn moved with great speed, and his sword clashed against Alpean's with a ringing clatter. Again and again Alpean parried his brother's assault. Alpean flipped Maelorn's sword aside with disdain, and Maelorn stood panting from exertion and seething with hatred.

Back and forth across the dusty plain the antagonists moved, performing a dance of death. Alpean turned away Maelorn's every charge, but with all his skill he could not break through Maelorn's defenses. Both were covered with sweat and dust, and Maelorn was slashed and bleeding from several wounds. His left cheek dripped red from a long gash that went from temple to jaw.

Again they came together, chest to chest, as each tried to gain the upper hand. Maelorn's ragged breath whistled in his throat as he strained to push Alpean away.

"Time to die, Maelorn," Alpean whispered. With a mighty shove he freed his sword and sent Maelorn staggering backwards, off-balance, sword point down. Too late the Darkling realized his danger. Alpean's bloodied sword flashed once, and Maelorn looked down in surprise at the silver blade that cleaved his chest. He sank to his knees, and as he did Alpean pushed his sword deeper into Maelorn's heart. With a twisting motion he ripped it apart.

Maelorn's body jerked as he struggled to free himself. His heart destroyed, he whimpered softly as a dark void opened before him.

"You win, Alpean," he whispered. "This time." He fell back as the last of his strength flowed from him.

"Yes, Maelorn, I win." With a savage motion Alpean pulled his blade from Maelorn's chest, and lifting it high above his head, he brought it down and neatly severed Maelorn's head from his shoulders.

A wild keening came from the bloodied head, and in horror Alpean staggered back. White sparks leaped into flames that rapidly devoured the Darkling's body and then his head, and the wailing ended on a choked cry as the flames roared high into the air. For long minutes they burned with intense heat and blinding light.

As suddenly as the fire began, it dropped away. All that remained of Maelorn to stain the soil of Kaenolir was a bit of ash. That, too, was gone in a moment when the wind lifted it and scattered it to nothingness.

Far to the north the sky turned fiery red, then white, then red tinged with black. The rumble of an explosion crashed against the air and shook the ground.

"Sinnarock," Goldenhorn whispered. "It, too, dies."

The sound of the mountain blowing itself apart was heard throughout Kaenolir. Gray clouds of ash boiled into the sky, their underbellies tinged blood red.

Far to the north, across the Strait of Tears, Sinnich Isle sank slowly into the sea and was no more.

Chapter Nineteen

A cool breeze played over the empty battlefield. On its tail came gray, heavy-bellied clouds, and the smell of rain was like ambrosia to the people who had lived in a parched world for what seemed an eternity. When the first fat drops plopped against the cracked soil, they stirred the ashes scattered on the plain. The raindrops fell faster, and life-giving water washed away the remnants of Maelorn and his hellish army.

Tired men lifted their faces to the rain, and men who had neither laughed nor cried during Kaenolir's travail, now did both. They had not thought to live to see the end of the day. The day had not yet ended, but they had lived to see the end of a power that had nearly destroyed all who opposed it. Someone began to sing, and one by one other voices joined in, and the music was a soft accompaniment to the sound of rain.

Andrew Goldenhorn climbed down a ladder to seek out Alpean. He found the king of Kaenolir sitting by the river, watching the rain.

"My king," Goldenhorn said softly to warn Alpean of his presence.

Alpean turned his head to see who addressed him and smiled at the Golden One.

"Ah, my friend," he sighed heavily. "The rain feels good, doesn't it? I loved the fragrance of the rain when I walked this land, and I find I still do. Even after all this time." His voice trailed off, and he turned back to his contemplation of river and rain.

Goldenhorn took a seat on a flat rock beside the king. Both sat quietly for some time. Rain soaked them through, but neither seemed to notice. Close at hand a bird suddenly began to sing, and Goldenhorn smiled. The river rushed by, blending its music with the sound of the rain.

Alpean stirred at last and pushed wet hair away from his eyes. He rose and stretched his aching muscles. Somehow he did not seem the giant who had battled Maelorn, but simply a large man, taller than most.

The Goldenhorn rose, too. "What do you plan to do now, my lord?" he asked. "Will you pick up your crown once more?"

Alpean smiled sadly. "My time is past, Golden One. Once I was king here, but no more. It is best I leave Kaenolir to her people, I think."

"Where will you go?"

Alpean shrugged. "I'm not sure. Perhaps to one of the islands off the Trayonian coast. I always liked the western coast."

"I'll not be returning to Lorn. You are welcome to the house and whatever else the island has to offer. It is a beautiful place. My family and I were happy there."

"Thank you, my friend. And you, what will you do now that there is no need for your Song? Will you return to the Faerie?"

"No, my lord. I have too much to keep me here. My wife waits for me in Fairtown. I could not leave her behind, and she could not come with me if I left." Goldenhorn looked over the plain through the veil of rain. "I love her very much, you see. And, of course, there is Kailie." He smiled thinking of his daughter and Captain Lamond. "I will enjoy being a grandfather, I think."

Alpean laughed and took the Singer by the arm as they walked back toward the Wall. "I would like to say goodbye to Talanor and Kailie, if she is awake. Captain Lamond, too. Then I will go."

As they walked, large silver shapes came to them out of the rain and Alpean paused. One of the majestic beasts came to Alpean and touched his hand.

"I am Torar, my king. It was I who brought Kailie Fairchild to Sinnich."

"I am grateful. You and your pack have been faithful to my cause and me. I am grateful for that, too." He stroked the silver head. *"Do you return to the Faerie?"*

"My mates return, but I wish to go with you just as Jagar goes with Talanor. I heard you speak of Lorn Isle. It will be lonely on Lorn, my king, and I would be with you."

Alpean smiled and took Torar's head in both his hands and looked into the bright, knowing eyes. *"Come with me then, Torar. I welcome your company."*

He freed the wolf and turned to Goldenhorn. "Let's find Talanor. It is time for me to be on my way."

As the two men made their way toward the Wall, silver shapes slipped away into the rain and mist.

~

She was dreaming, not the nightmares of the past, but a lovely, peaceful dream. Once again she walked beside the golden king through the forests of Kalora. Birds sang and blended their songs with the music floating on air made fragrant by the myriad flowers growing underfoot. The golden king smiled at her and took her hand. He led her to a bower shaded by stately oak trees and sat with her upon lush green grass.

"This may be the last time we are together, my child," he said quietly. "You have been the instrument of the Faerie because Kaenolir needed you. And though the blood of your father still flows within your body, the Songs you sang are silent now, their purpose done." He touched her hair with his fingertips and then her eyes, her cheeks, and finally her lips.

"Do you remember the last gift I gave to you?"

"Yes, father, I do," Kailie whispered. "You gave me the gift of love." She smiled. "You gave me Alexander."

"Yes. And now I set you free. Free to return to your Alexander and be happy. Even though I would prefer to keep you here with me." He smiled somewhat sadly into her sparkling blue eyes, eyes that again held a piece of the sky in their depths. "Go to your captain, Kailie Fairchild. He waits for you."

~

Alexander couldn't remember the last time it felt so good to be clean. He scrubbed his skin until it was nearly raw to free himself of the gore and stench of Maelorn's creatures. He burned his clothes and polished and ground his sword until no trace of hell remained. He kept a silent watch beside Kailie until he could no longer stay awake.

And then he slept, for a day and a night, as did most everyone else who'd been on the Wall. Sleep was the first step to help all of them heal.

This morning he'd sent the civilians back to their families. Tomorrow the Guardians, except for a small contingent who would remain to rebuild the Fort, would mount their horses and ride throughout the width and breadth of

Kaenolir, spreading the news that Maelorn and his horde had been destroyed. Kaenolir was safe and would soon blossom and flourish as it had in the past. The Guardians were to find their own families and to give aid to people returning to their homes.

He'd sent Ian on his way this morning, too. One of the loggers from Shiptown remembered that Ian's family had gone to stay with some relatives in Fairtown. Alexander had ordered him to find his family and stay with them until he was fully rested and recovered from his wounds.

"I'll be back whenever you need me, Alex." Ian extended his hand. Alexander took it in a strong grip. "Take care of your lady."

Alexander smiled and nodded. Ian mounted, gave Alexander a crisp salute and rode away.

~

"There you are, Alexander. I've been looking all over for you." Talanor huffed as he half-ran, half-walked toward the Guardian captain. "She's awake and asking for you."

Alexander looked toward the tent he'd set up on a knoll near the river on the south side of the Wall and sighed heavily. He grasped Talanor by the shoulder and looked intently into the old mage's tired eyes.

"Is she all right?" he asked quietly.

Talanor grinned broadly. "She's very weak and still tired, but she'll be fine." His laughter rumbled up from deep within his chest. "Go, she needs you."

Alexander smiled and lifted his head to the sky. The sun shone warm and serene from a brilliant blue dome. Breezes whispered around him and lifted curls grown long on his neck. It was a glorious day to be alive. With a last grin at Talanor he hurried away.

~

The flap of the small tent was tied back to catch an occasional breeze and allow the soft light from the lowering sun to enter. Alexander sat with his back against a pile of cushions, and Kailie curled against his side with her head on his shoulder. He gently caressed her golden curls.

"When Talanor took me to Rhianna Lanee on the Horn of Kalora," she began quietly, "I met the king of the Golden Ones who taught me to sing the Last Song. He also gave me three gifts. Somehow he knew I would need strength and courage to reach Sinnarock and free my father and Alpean. He knew, too, that it would take courage to sing the Song, and he gave me the strength and courage I needed." Her gentle voice stilled.

Alexander drew her away to look down into her face. "And what was the third gift?" he asked.

She smiled the smile meant for him alone and it dazzled him. "The third gift he said would be given when all else was done. The last gift was the gift of love." She touched his face with cool fingertips and traced the new lines that had been added to his features. "And surely it is the most precious gift by far."

"Your golden king is very generous, my love," Alexander whispered as he drew her back against him.

~

The Goldenhorn walked with a steady, mile-eating pace on the road through the Lake Country. All around him the ravages of the long drought were visible, but already there was evidence that the land had begun to live again. Green grass peeped through the dry stubble of fallow fields. Trees had begun to leaf out, and everywhere the songs of birds filled the air. He even noticed wildflowers pushing up among tall, dead weed stalks. Pure, sweet water flowed in the streambeds that had been sucked dried by a merciless sun. He smiled to see his beloved Kaenolir come to life; but he felt very much alone as he walked, though all along his way he encountered people who waved or called a friendly greeting.

He longed for the sight of only one face, and if he kept up this pace he should reach Fairtown, and Katrine, by nightfall. At the thought of having her close again, he quickened his step.

He saw her long before she noticed him. The setting sun softened the lines of her slender shape and gleamed in strands of her hair. She moved with the grace he remembered, and he knew that a little frown of concentration creased her brow.

She was so occupied with weeding her flowers that she did not look up until she heard footsteps. She clasped her hands against her mouth to keep from crying out, for surely the tall, golden-haired man who came toward her was not her Andrew. Yet this man walked with the same proud step and carried his broad shoulders in the same easy manner.

The man stopped at the gate of her small garden and stood staring at her. She returned the look a long moment. Then he smiled and held out his arms to her.

"Katrine, my love," he said simply.

Her tears nearly choked her as she called his name and ran to him. When she was crushed in his embrace and could feel the sinew and bone of his too-thin body, she finally believed that he was real and not just a cruel apparition.

"Don't cry so, my Katrine. Hush, my sweet. It's over."

She pulled away to look up at him, her heart in her eyes. "Kailie?" she whispered.

"Kailie is well and in the strong, capable hands of a fine man named Alexander Lamond. They will come to us soon."

Katrine sank against his chest and sobbed. He let her cry and held her firmly in his embrace. The tears, he knew, were her catharsis, the cleansing of her fears.

At last her sobs eased and Katrine stood quietly. She raised her tear-streaked face to look into the amber eyes that smiled down at her and read in them the pain and sorrow of the struggle to rid Kaenolir of Maelorn's malevolence.

"And the Song, Andrew, what of your Song?"

His mouth curved in a wistful, sad smile. "The Song is no more, my love, and I hope there will never be a need for it again." He brushed the last of her tears away before they turned and arm-in-arm walked down the narrow path to the cottage.

The sun slipped beneath the horizon, and for a time the crescent of a new moon was visible. It seemed a good omen to Goldenhorn. Kaenolir would start anew, would live again, but this time without his Song. He had been faithful to the Faerie promise and had lived to see the ancient magic come to fruition in his daughter.

The Song was done, the power it had given him gone.

Close by a night bird began its plaintive trill, and for a moment he imagined he heard a familiar phrase. The evening breeze, fresh, cool, and clean smelling, shifted and came from the east. Another night bird began to sing, and this time, as he listened more carefully, Goldenhorn was sure he heard a phrase from his Song. Softly, he hummed the notes and was answered

247

by yet another trill. He paused with Katrine to listen, and his heart soared. He felt the spirit of his brother Singers all around him. He was not alone after all.

The Golden One smiled. He realized now that the Song was not dead as long as he lived, as long Kailie lived, and her offspring.

He looked into Katrine's eyes and laughed. At her questioning look, he took her hand and led her inside.

And all through the night, whenever he awakened in the unfamiliar surroundings of the cottage, the song of the night birds lulled him to sleep again.

Epilogue

He walked for a long time along a path that wound its way into the heart of misty shadows and veiled trees that comprised the Horn of Kalora. As he walked he leaned heavily on the stout staff he had cut and shaped so many years before. The weariness that plagued him was apparent in every step he took. And not for the first time Talanor cursed his foolishness in returning to Rhianna Lanee's domain.

"I hoped you would return to Kalora."

The melodious voice came from behind him and brought him to an abrupt halt. He had just decided she was not going to come to him after all and he might just as well leave this accursed place and head for Cathorn. But he was tired, so very tired. The sound of her voice pleased him immeasurably, yet he'd be damned before he would let her know that.

When Talanor turned, Rhianna Lanee stood on the path he had just walked.

"Yes," he sighed. "I have returned."

"You look weary, Talanor. Was your journey so difficult?"

"Not the journey, Rhianna. No, not this journey." He looked at the beautiful woman of Faerie and smiled.

"Then why are you so weary, old friend? Kaenolir is safe, is it not?"

"Yes, Kaenolir is safe at last. Maelorn is dead, destroyed by his lust for power and killed by his brother. The fires of the Last Song consumed his evil army. Yes, Kaenolir is safe."

"Ah," she whispered. "Do you think that there is nothing more to do for Kaenolir?"

Talanor gave her a keen glance before turning to look up the path he had taken to find Rhianna.

"I suppose. The people have little need of my counsel now. They are well equipped to govern themselves. Captain Lamond is a very competent soldier who will see to it that the country is secure." He shrugged his shoulders and leaned against his staff in a manner that spoke of his fatigue.

"Besides," he said somewhat petulantly. "I'm an old man and I'm tired. I think that after my admirable work to help Kaenolir I deserve a rest."

Rhianna laughed and Talanor heard the merry tinkle of bells. She did not care for the Talanor who sagged against his staff, and it pleased her to hear the irritation in his voice. "Yes, old man," she chuckled, "you are deserving of a rest. However," she stepped to him and slipped an arm through his, "you may not find the rest you think you need here."

"No?" he asked.

"No," she said firmly. "I want to hear all about Kailie and the Last Song, about Maelorn and your Captain Lamond, and the Goldenhorn. And about Alpean. You've much to tell me." She hugged his arm as they began walking slowly down the path. "I want to know all that happened. Then you may rest."

"How long will you let me stay with you this time, Rhianna?"

So, he had come to stay with her, had he? It was about time. No more running back to Cathorn or off to Kaenolir whenever he felt like it. This time she would keep him where he belonged. Here on Kalora. With her.

"For as long as you wish, old friend. Until the time comes when we are needed again." She reached up and gave a playful tug to his beard. "Is that long enough?"

"Hmm. Perhaps," he said.

Printed in the United States
52471LVS00004B/277-327

9 781424 103775